To Nancy Thank you!

Jonathan Stars (Mitch)

N-hanced

Jonathan Stars

D1571047

ACKNOWLEDGMENTS

The following people are responsible for making this book so much better than it would have been had I been left on my own. Some of them went through endless rounds of listening to me blab on and on while I worked through the details. I owe them a great debt, and so do you.

Dan Beard
Matt Bliton
Ivan Boivin
Sandy Callis
Thom Cannell
Christine Mikrut
    Campbell
Janice Child
Zack Constan
John Couretas
Valerie Clark Cranfill
Tom Deits
Bill Diedrich
Brandon Forbes
Robyn Ford
Doug Kelshaw

Cheryl Knox
Eddie Lahti
Richard Lassin
Tom Lott
Sharon Oatman
Linda Peckham
Steve Purdy
Dan Redder
Dave Riedle
David Rumohr
Clyde Stretch
Ray Walsh
Thora Wease
Sue Winkelstern
Mark Wolfgang

And all the other writers from Skaaldic Society and Delta Township Public Library's Writers' Roundtable who shared their opinions and expertise over the past two years.

PREFACE

I like reading Science Fiction, but I hate being confused by the lingo. So I'm including a glossary on the last few pages. Some people may think that makes this more like a textbook. In that case, don't use the glossary and just have fun. If you're reading this with a Kindle, iPad, etc., it will not be convenient to jump back and forth to the glossary. To avoid that, go to the book website and print out a copy of the glossary. The next few paragraphs will help place you in the world of the book. There are online appendices explaining many details about the concepts and products introduced in the book. Find them online at this website:

http://www.n-hanced.com/appendix.php.

While you're there fill out the guestbook form so I can notify you about future works from the N world.

First of all Virtual Reality and N-hanced are not the same thing. A 3-D movie with Surround Sound is a primitive form of VR using two of your senses to make you feel as if you're somewhere other than a theatre. With full VR, all your senses can be engaged. VR can be as simple as augmented reality, where you see objects not physically in your environment, like a digital clock in your field of vision. Or it can be so complex you're convinced you're actually somewhere else, in a place where you can reach out and touch objects and people not physically there.

The advancement of nano technology will allow people to have computers inside them, providing the VR experience unobtrusively—no glasses, contact lenses, gloves or apparent sound systems of any kind. Since these devices are computers, they're completely programmable, allowing them to run any application the user chooses, from devices to control digestion, to eliminating cancer, repairing damaged DNA and otherwise amplifying the human experience.

N-hanced is an application that runs on the nano computers in the brain. Its main feature is Effortless Instant Knowledge, but it also ramps up VR to the Nth degree and provides emotion control.

This story is fairly faithful to the timetable of technological advances Ray Kurzweil predicts in his books *The Age of Spiritual Machines* and *The Singularity is Near*. When other prognosticators disagree with him, it's rarely over *whether* these changes will take place, rather *when* they will happen. And of course all that depends on if we survive. During speaking engagements in 2011 and 2012, Ray would hold up a cell phone and say, "In twenty years the technology in a cell phone will be available in a package the size of a blood cell." If that is indeed the case, I'd like to have a teaspoon full of them in my body, networked together to make a supercomputer that will respond to my every request.

We are headed into a time of unprecedented acceleration of technology that will allow for wondrous living. But those same tools allow for horribly disastrous outcomes, many of which someone with a set of instructions found on the Internet and a thousand dollars worth of lab equipment can accomplish. For the dark side of the story see Bill Joy's article *Why the Future Doesn't Need Us* in the April 2000 Issue of *Wired* magazine. I tend to side with Kurzweil's optimism, but I don't doubt there will be some frightening moments along the way and many bodies piled up in the process. Here's hoping I'm wrong about that.

Because of the dangers some would say, "Let's put the brakes on here." But this tech wagon doesn't have any brakes. And you can't slow it down enough to install any. So all we can do is focus on steering. As Ray himself said on the June 17, 2011 interview with Bill Maher, "People talk philosophically, 'Oh, I don't want to live past 100.' You know, I'd like to hear them say that when they're 99. And when they get cancer and there's a new treatment, there's no philosophical debate, 'Well, do I really want to extend my life?'" This is why the technology is racing forward. We want the fruit from the tech tree—the real tree of knowledge, and we're willing to pay the price, whether it's physical or spiritual.

Ray says that by 2045 we will reach a technological singularity—a time when advancements are moving so quickly that a person who is not enhanced by merging with machines (and these machines can be as soft and pliable as flesh and blood) will not be able to keep up with the pace of change—thus the name of this book, *N-hanced*.

PART ONE

CHAPTER 1

Charlie Noble muttered as he hustled down the hall to the nano lab, his eyebrows weighed down with worry. The CEO of Corridor CyberDynamics had just scorched him—at least that's how it felt—and his face was glowed to prove it. Funds for Charlie's N-hanced project were nearly gone.

As he burst into the white room, Milo and Linda looked up from the workbench.

Milo caught the expression on Charlie's face. "Sheesh! What'd he say to you, Boss?"

Charlie gave him a grim look and waved away the question. "Make it work, and none of that matters." He joined them at the pristine table as they leaned over a pair of glistening cylinders of meat at right angles to each other. "So what are we doing this time?"

Milo TwoDogs swung his head, and his braided black ponytail rippled down his back. "I'm positioning the T exactly in the center of the synapse."

Charlie's team had developed N-hanced, an app for tiny proTein computers in the brain. It would act as traffic cop for electrical signals in the synapses. Problem was, it didn't work.

Charlie frowned. "I thought our Virtual tests showed precision isn't important."

Milo blinked hard. "Well… yeah. But if the sims were right, we'd already have a finished product."

"All right," Charlie sighed. "Give it a try."

Linda stared down at the magnified nerve cells. "C'mon, baby," her words muffled by a mouthful of pretzels. "You can do it."

Milo reached for the button. A blue flash shot along one of the nerves making the meat twitch and split open with a pop. The three of them jumped back and watched as steam hissed from the rent flesh.

Charlie closed his eyes and raked his fingernails through his sandy, choppy hair. "Shit." The word seemed out of place coming out of a face genetically modified to look like Superman. "It's getting *worse*, not better."

Milo put his hand on Charlie's arm. "Hey, relax, Buddy. We're almost there."

"Almost isn't good enough. Our money's gone." Charlie didn't mention he'd augmented investor funds by wiping out his personal savings and taking on loans against future earnings from his patents. Everything was on the line.

Linda froze, a fistful of peanuts halfway to her mouth. "No money? What exactly *did* Santa Claus tell you in there?" Linda Sullivan had pixyish features, a turned-up nose and a bobbed, blonde haircut with a few untamable strands. Before her genetic rebuild, she was nearing three hundred pounds. She now sported the popular petite model.

"He said we're out of time, and the money's almost gone."

"Anything we don't already know?" Milo rolled his eyes. "I swear, if it weren't for Herr-CEO's cheery demeanor—"

"Don't forget he pays us well," Charlie said.

Milo shrugged.

Linda's eyelids fell to a cynical half-mast. "You're only defending him because he's family."

"*And* he lets us keep the patents. Work for Orchard, and they own everything you invent." Charlie drew a deep breath and blew a resigned stream of air out his nose. "All right, I guess you guys need to know about this." He replayed his conversation with Rob.

"I don't know what to tell you, Charlie." Rob's eyebrows climbed up his freckled forehead. "Our provisional on the patent runs out tomorrow. After that, Orchard gets their shot at it."

Charlie's jaw tightened. He knew to the minute how much time they had. Every bit of work he'd done over the past twenty years targeted N-hanced as the final prize. As far as he was concerned N would be the great democratizer, bringing hope and prosperity to the downtrodden by making users instant experts, helping them solve their own problems.

It wasn't just N's knowledge feature compelling him. He couldn't wait for the emotional stability. And those benefits wouldn't be his alone. He was *not* about to let Orchard beat him to it!

"Yes, sir. We're almost there. Just a little stush in the system." Charlie tried not to sound desperate.

"That's what you said last week—and the week before that."

Charlie lowered his head and nodded.

"And don't call me sir. I was your father-in-law, for chrissake."

"Of course." Charlie's mind veered away from the despair of Barbara's pointless death—just one more reason he craved N's emotion control. "But the Virtual tests say we should be there. All we have to do is make it happen in Real."

"Well, it's gotta happen soon. The investors made it clear there won't be a third round of funding without proof of concept. Not that it'll matter once the patent goes away." Rob's face softened. "I don't mean to be hard on you, son. I'm under a lot of pressure here myself. Did I tell you if we don't get this, it could bankrupt us?"

"Yeah." It came out a whisper.

Rob got up, stepped from behind his desk and squeezed out one of his cherubic smiles. "I shouldn't have pulled you away from your work. Go back in there. I'm sure everything'll be fine." He gave Charlie a comforting pat on the shoulder, but his eyes made a distracted roundtrip to the digital clock in the upper corner of his vision.

Charlie waved away the vid playback.

"No pressure, huh?" Milo made a disgusted "tsk," and shook his head.

Charlie rolled his hands out. "So, what the heck is screwing us up?"

Milo adjusted his ponytail. "I'm fresh out of ideas."

Linda reached into a bag of chips. "What if they just don't like each other?"

Milo smirked. "Very funny."

"I'm just saying—"

"Yeah, I know. Why don't you stuff your face and stop talking?"

"Hey, that's not very—"

Charlie slapped the table. "No, wait a minute!"

Milo and Linda jumped. "What?"

"Say that again, about how they don't like each other."

"Uh... like they're incompatible. You know, like in a relationship where the chemistry is wrong." Linda shot Milo a cold glance. "Maybe the nerve cell just thinks the T is ugly."

Milo shook his head. "Don't be crazy."

Charlie's gaze swept the floor. "We assumed since the Ts work everywhere else in the body, they'll also work in the brain. What if we got that wrong?"

Milo's eyes opened wide. "Holy shit, man! I think that's it! All this time I thought the problem was our programming."

Within a half hour Milo found an incompatible ion in the T and rebuilt it. They held their breath as he hit the test button. This time the tiny computer passed the signal through as if it were invisible.

"Yes!" they screamed in unison, jumping and slapping each other on the back.

Then Charlie stopped and waved them down. "Wait! Wait!"

"What?"

"That's only part of what we need. Test it the other way. Intercept the signal from the transmitter and substitute one of our own."

Milo flicked dismissively. "You worry too much, old man. It'll work."

"Show me."

Switching out the command line, Milo hit the button. Sure enough, the nerve receptor picked up the altered data.

Charlie held up a hand. "OK, now repeat it a hundred times."

Milo raised an eyebrow and pursed his lips. With a wave of his hand, all the tests repeated flawlessly in a matter of seconds. "Told ya."

Charlie's face relaxed and a huge smile took it over. "I'll be damned. We did it!" He grabbed hold of Linda's head and gave her a big wet kiss on the cheek. "I love you, you crazy wench!"

Linda threw him a look of mock arrogance. "Well, of course. Why else did you hire me? For my brains?" Then she got serious. "I get to be first!"

"Oh, no." Charlie put up a palm. "I've been waiting twenty years for this."

"No, no. I mean I want to be the first to upload my expertise."

A sly smile crept onto Milo's face. "Careful what you ask for, sister. We get your smarts in the machine, and we won't need you any more."

"I gotta tell Rob." Charlie started out of the lab and shouted over his shoulder, "Thank Jesus. We can finally get this thing off the ground. Ye-haw!" When he got to the door, he spun around and shook his index finger in the air. "We're gonna be number one! Yes!" and he was gone.

* * *

A few weeks later Charlie was N-hanced full time. At first it only gave him instant access to information—nothing from any of their experts. Even then he was amazed by how he knew anything on the Net without tedious reading. The answer to whatever he wondered was in his head almost before he'd compose the question. More important to Charlie, though, it gave him the emotional control he'd been praying for his whole life. His nervous habits melted away, and he worked with an inexhaustible fury completely free of fear. Now it was time to move it to the next level.

Charlie's goal wasn't to simply have book knowledge the way the Net presented it. He wanted to *feel* what someone else knew, the way they felt about it, intimately, with all their passion. But he was also hesitant. He'd spent most of his life trying to avoid emotion—so much of it having been negative. Then came the day Linda finally uploaded her knowledge into the N-hanced servers.

She lay back in the reclining oChair, playful as a puppy. "C'mon, guys, let's go!" It only took a moment for the server to lock onto her profile.

An Artificial Intelligence (AI) program asked her a series of questions in her areas of expertise and mapped the locations in her brain. Then it asked personal questions in order to wall off sections for privacy. Linda had nothing to hide. In fact she insisted on having the guys in the room and laughed as they blushed and squirmed while she revealed intimate details of her life.

Finally the program initiated a Brainstorm, and the server converted the results into meaningful data. A lifetime of experience transferred in less than a minute! The whole operation took no more than an hour. Charlie couldn't wait to get inside her head.

"OK, guys, this is it." Charlie flicked a finger, opening the gate to the section of the server, which gave him access to Linda's thinking. Linda and Milo fastened their gaze onto him. Charlie's face went slack, and his eyes glazed over. He opened his mouth and slurred, "Duh... I feel shtupid."

Linda looked shocked. Then, when a wicked smile snuck onto Charlie's lips, she slapped his arm. "You fucker!" She giggled. "What an asshole."

Milo laughed, "Oh, that was precious."

Linda said, "So what is it *really* like, shithead?"

Charlie held up a hand. "OK. Honestly? It is *completely* awesome." He blinked his eyes and shook his head. "Let me find a way to describe it. When I normally think about numbers using basic N, I have something like a calculator in my head. I can perform operations in a snap. But *you* think about numbers with something bordering on reverence. To you, they're organized by colors and grouped in shifting patterns, making them a joy to work with. It's like going from the black and white of Dorothy's Kansas to the brilliant kaleidoscopic land of Oz. Through your eyes I see the relationships between numbers, and how they... hold the secrets of the universe. I feel—What?—almost in love with them. It's beautiful."

Linda squealed, "That's *exactly* how I see them. *Exactly!*"

"I knew you were crazy about math, but I had no *idea* it could be like this. Not only that, but I feel more calm and relaxed—more trusting. It's as if absorbing your way of thinking makes life easier. But," Charlie's face got serious, "I also feel an uncontrollable urge to eat. Where are the chips?"

Linda turned to Milo, eyes heavy with mock contempt. "He's fucking with us again."

Milo shook Charlie's arm. "What else? What else?"

They spent part of the afternoon comparing how N's data is organized versus how Linda's mind works. Then they set up a schedule for uploading from the experts they already had contracts with and detailed what characteristics they wanted in their alpha testers.

So finally... finally N was ready for the next round of funding. Charlie was ecstatic. *Twenty years and it's all falling into place.* Then...

"C'mon, dammit!" Charlie was in a panic as he raced across town in one of Orchard's ubiquitous oCars. He rocked in his seat, pointlessly trying to make the vehicle go faster. oCars drove themselves, so rocking and shouting were all he had left.

"Moooove!"

It was less than a week since Charlie first tried N-hanced, and he was now on it full time. When he'd come into work that morning, Linda wasn't in the building. From his office he opened a VR line to Milo, which dropped him into the white lab. "Where's Linda?"

Milo looked up. "Oh, hi, Boss. Uh, don't know."

"She's always here before anybody else. You try to comm her?"

Milo paused. "Nnnno?"

"Weren't you curious?"

"I guess I was thinking about my work. You OK?"

Charlie followed Milo's gaze down to see his hands shaking, Linda's intuition inside him now frantic, demanding. "Something's wrong." He had already opened a line to her, but even her digital Personal Assistant didn't pick up.

He hired a public Skeet cam and had it circle her house. Most of the windows were still opaque. That was inconceivable. Linda always let the light in everywhere she went. Then, through the only transparent window, Charlie spied a broken cup of coffee on the kitchen counter, brown drops slowly puddling onto the floor. It could only mean one thing. In order to avoid destroying evidence at a crime scene, the ubiquitous oClean shut down when someone in the vicinity was injured. Linda lived alone.

Charlie sprinted down the hall and threw a final VR burst at Milo. "I'm going over there!" That's when he ordered the oCar he was now riding in.

When the car finally arrived at Linda's place, he leapt out of the portal, bolted to the front door and pounded on it. Running around the outside of the house, he knocked on all the still opaque windows, calling her name. Circling back to the front door, he felt drawn to a rock next to the porch. Picking it up, he removed a plastic plug on the bottom, uncovering an old-fashioned key. *How did I know...?* Then. *Of course. Linda!* The key opened the door, and he rushed in.

He flicked and the lights came on. Directly ahead of him, Linda lay naked on the wooden floor; sets of evenly-spaced bloody gashes across her arms and torso, as if some wild animal had gone at her. "Jesus!" Charlie dashed forward, slipped on a pool of blood and fell next to her, wrenching his shoulder. "Shit!"

Righting himself, he kneeled and reached for her neck to check for a pulse. As soon as he touched her skin he jerked his hand away. She was cold. *Too late.* Then *Ohmigod! This is a crime scene, and I just contaminated everything.*

Backing out of the room, he cursed the bloody footprints he left behind with every step. Outside he commed 911. "This is an emergency! One of my employees has been murdered!" The AI dispatcher locked onto his location and logged off. Charlie sat down on the porch to wait, his head in his hands. When he noticed a mark on the side of one of his shoes, he ripped it off and fought back a wave of nausea. The whole bottom was stained red with Linda's blood. He tore off the other shoe and flung them both into the street. *I'll never wear those again.*

His heart thudded with a burst of panic when he thought about how losing Linda would affect the project. Then he realized with her expertise in the servers, it wouldn't make any difference at all. Feeling ashamed for thinking it, a ball of guilt welled up in his stomach. After a few minutes he remembered he had N-hanced control over his emotions. He gave the virtual knob a twist and the knot in his belly unwound. That lasted until the police arrived—and Charlie became a suspect.

CHAPTER 2

It was a madhouse. Every foot of the slope swarmed with spectators crushed shoulder to shoulder behind the snow fences, trying to find the best view. High ski season in Park City, Utah meant it wasn't too difficult to make an announcement and lasso a crowd of ten thousand split between Real and Virtual Reality attendees. And a cheering crowd would subtly influence the investors. It didn't matter that most of the cheers would come from people who either wanted Charlie to succeed or fail because of bets they'd made. Most of them were waiting to see if he would die. To them, Charlie Noble against the mountain was no more than a to-the-death boxing match. They would scream their bloody heads off. Just what Charlie and his team wanted.

A guy with a shock of electric red hair sailing over his left eyebrow and sparking against his cheek said, "He'll kill himself."

"I hope so."

"It's all a fake. He's done it before," said another.

"I'll bet five-hundred oCredits he does it. I've heard about this N-hanced thing. Read about it on Wired. It's Real."

"Bullshit. Nothing's Real any more. It's all VR. I'll bet he's not even here."

"Bet me?"

"Five hundred?"

"Yeah."

"OK, you're on."

It was hard to believe it was only four months since Linda's still-unsolved murder. So much had happened. The original investors came through with another round of funding, and today was a major demonstration for a new group of money people. His company had uploaded the expertise of nearly a hundred contractors, and Charlie was having a ball trying them on for size. With each new skill he acquired, he felt more like the Superman his face was modeled after. CCD now had ten alpha testers using N-hanced, with approval ratings ranging from fantastic to galactic. The word 'thrilled' couldn't begin to describe how Charlie felt. That word hadn't been invented yet.

He closed his eyes and inhaled deeply. A cold rush froze the hairs in his nostrils and filled his head with the fragrance of pine trees. Opening his eyes he looked out over the snaking rows of observers winding down the mountainside. He raised his hand to his eyebrow and made a gesture like clicking the button on an old-fashioned camera. It switched off his VR, showing that only about a quarter of the spectators were there in Real. The rest attended using their oMe2 Virtual Reality double. Thousands more would choose views interpolated from hundreds of tiny flying mosquito-sized Skeet cams hovering up and down the mountain. Still others—billions, as it turned out—would watch a summary of the event later. He made the camera click gesture again, turning his VR back on.

A crew of six surrounded Charlie as he prepared for the official recording of his first Olympic snowboard run. Actually, it was his first time on a snowboard—ever. Two of the crew were Really there, and the other four were VR-ing in from various locations.

From her place in Lansing, Michigan fifteen hundred miles away, Terra Fromma made some wardrobe adjustments and selected the final colors of Charlie's ski outfit. It had a series of backward-sweeping, elongated triangles that would shimmer up and down his sides and change colors as he changed speed. She pretended she needed to adjust his collar as an excuse to breathe in his scent. Leaning against his six-foot-three-inch body, she rolled the collar with her oTouch-activated fingertips. oTouch, oCloth, oEyes, oCredits, oMe2; Orchard International practically owned the lower-case letter "o," putting it in front of everything they manufactured or wrote software for.

Terra pretended to brush some lint off the back of Charlie's pants and gave his behind a squeeze.

Charlie squeezed the muscle in his butt back at her.

Pushing herself at arm's length, she grinned, one eyebrow cocked. "All set, boss."

Charlie gave her his famous N-smile, filled with the innocent enthusiasm of Jimmy Stewart, and he switched to a Private Channel (PC). It projected a static copy of himself to everyone else so they couldn't overhear their conversation or read his lips. "I'll be back in Lansing before noon. I have lunch with Jeff and a couple meetings after that."

"Oh… Lunch with Jeff. Will you be all right?"

"Sure, sure," he lied.

"I mean, having to shut off N… I know what that does to you."

He shrugged it off. "Yeah, I'll be fine. So, are we still on for tonight?"

"8:00. It's already on my schedule."

"You read my mind, sweetie."

"Of course I did."

Charlie got a comm from Rob. "Oops. Boss calling. I'd probably better not leave it to my oMe2. See you tonight."

"OK. Bye."

He watched her wave away the comm, and her face disappeared.

Charlie flicked open the line and found Rob standing in front of him, foggy breath pluming from his mouth. "Hey, boss. What's the haps?"

"I just wanted you to know we picked up four more investors who will be taking a look today, giving us a total of nine new ones." Rob flicked their information to Charlie. In a nano second he knew everything publicly available about them, along with some private data. "Depending on your show, we could go over five big ones. But no pressure, of course, son."

Rob Reynolds' gapped-toothed grin pulled his round cheeks so high Charlie could hardly see anything but the sparkle in his eyes. Charlie had a special affection for him. Even though Rob was younger than Charlie by thirty years, Rob called him son because he was the father of Charlie's third wife, Barbara, who had died in a car accident six years earlier. The self-driving oCars hadn't become mandatory yet. Seems you could repair broken DNA, but you still couldn't put Humpty Dumpty back together again. Charlie had a hard time getting over her loss and dealt with it by throwing himself even harder into his work. That was not a problem today.

"Things are going great here, boss." Then his lips tightened. "But I keep wishing Linda could see us. She would be so proud of how far we've come."

"I know. But having her expertise scanned into the N-hanced servers is the next best thing to having her here."

"Not even close."

Charlie pictured Linda at her desk littered with empty food containers, and how she chewed with her mouth open, unable to stop the wild flow of ideas long enough to swallow. He flashed back on her funeral thinking how odd it had been when only five people showed up in Real. The others couldn't be bothered with anything more than a comfy, long-distance VR appearance.

Remembering that cold day and how much he hated snow, the irony of his doing this demo here in February was not lost on him. He sighed and glanced at Rob. "You know sometimes I get the feeling Linda's looking over my shoulder."

Rob nodded thoughtfully. "You still feeling guilty about her death?"

Charlie shook his head. "That's not it. I felt guilty for thinking we could do without her. It even feels slimy saying it now."

"Yeah. I see what you mean."

Charlie shot him a pained smile. "Thanks for the support, Rob."

"It wasn't your fault, you know."

"You don't know that."

"Is there something you haven't told me?"

"No. Just that I still think it may be corporate espionage. If what happened is because of N, it *would* be my fault."

"Wrong. And besides, there's still no evidence."

"It's a feeling I have."

"You mean Linda's intuition? Can't go to the police with that."

"After the way they treated me last time, I won't go to them for anything."

Rob nodded and looked down at his shoes.

"You know, I'm gonna find out what happened to her." Charlie's tone was jagged. "Once we get some expert investigators into the system, I'll be able to do a better job of finding her killer than Sherlock Holmes. I don't believe in that 'no evidence' crap the police came up with."

"Now don't go sticking your nose in where it doesn't belong." Rob's forehead furrowed with concern.

Charlie reared back. "Are you saying I should forget about it?"

"No, son. But there are laws about interfering with an ongoing investigation."

"Ongoing? Ha! They're not doing anything."

Rob nodded slowly. "Maybe." He paused, then looked directly into Charlie's eyes. "Just so you know, I miss her too."

"I know."

Rob's eyes regained their spark. "Well, I'm glad I had a chance to come up here and give you this little pep talk."

Charlie laughed "Yeah, you have been kind of a downer."

Rob patted his shoulder.

Charlie raised his face skyward. "OK, Linda. This one's for you." He kissed his hand and flicked a pair of bright red lips into the clouds. As they faded he turned back to Rob. "Anything else?"

"Nope. Just want to wish you good luck. And give me a ring later."

"How about a nice bracelet instead?" It was one of their running jokes. "Now go have a VR cigar, and relax until your part."

"Oh, now you're making fun of me."

"I am not. But you know, you would give *brilliant* speeches if you strapped on N. As CEO you have a responsibility—"

"Yeah, yeah. Not just yet. OK?"

Charlie gave him a resigned shrug. "All right. Anyway, you can count the money after the show."

Rob chuckled. "I'll do just that. Have a good time. And be safe. We *need* you 'round here, son." Rob waved off the PC to release Charlie, but he stayed online invisibly to watch the rest of the setup and nervously await his little spot in the show.

CHAPTER 3

The Bostwick family came out of the Tusayan, Arizona oService convenience store and headed back to their oCar. It was fast-charging on the hot pad at the battery island. Eight-year-old Billy broke into a run yelling, "I got dibs on the good seat!"

Jeanie started forward, then shifted to nonchalance, looking around to see if anyone had noticed her momentary lapse. "Oh, who cares? Dibs are for babies."

They had stopped here because their mother, Dory, wanted to be sure they had the full charge for their trip around the canyon, even though there were plenty of stations along the way. Wilford had long ago realized a few painless accommodations like this kept peace in the family. Besides, he wanted a Dove Bar. In his opinion, the fab machines didn't do justice to that particular flavor just yet. His eyes went glassy with the first bite and he chuckled when his salivary glands shot a stream out of his mouth.

The oCar sensed their arrival, the walls dissolved and the seats reached sideways, caressing each of them as they sat. Once everyone was safely inside, the walls reformed and the oCar headed north on 180, the kids involved in their own VR activities while Wilford and Dory watched the forest.

As they crested a hill, Dory straightened up and looked over the horizon. She didn't see a hint of the canyon, just more trees. She smiled as she got ready to ask Wilford a question. It was going to sound an awful lot like, "How long until we're there?"

"Um, the Net tells me we're only a couple miles from the canyon, but I don't see a thing."

Wilford shot an N-hanced Virtual Viewer straight up out of the car, stopping it at a quarter mile. Then he flicked the scene over to her Interface Space. "There ya go."

"Wow!"

"You know, Honey, you can do almost the same thing with Net11."

"Yeah. Sorry. Sometimes I think we're still living back in the days when there was... oh, I don't know... paper. And I keep forgetting you're testing that N thing, 'cause you look so normal."

"Normal? What'd you expect?"

"Oh, I guess a weird robot head or something."

"C'mon, we've been past that since VR. Hey, do you remember that *Star Trek* movie, *The Future Begins*; that little screen they stuck next to Scotty's eye? I told you by the time the twenty-second century rolls around, there's *no way* they'd be wearing something like that. The way the Enterprise shook whenever they were under attack, that little gadget was just an accident waiting to happen. I kept wanting to yell at the screen, 'Take that thing off. You'll put your eye out!'"

"I remember. Always the practical one. Anyway, you seem mostly like... well... you."

"Only N-hanced."

She gave him a sly smile and put her hand on his leg. "Oo, yeah, enhanced! You Amelican man so hot. Me make love to you long time."

His face fell dead serious. "Honey, the kids."

"They can't hear anything. They're off in their own little VR worlds."

"But they could switch to Real at any time and we wouldn't know."

"They don't look shocked to me, so I think we're fine."

He gave the kids a final glance and squeezed Dory's hand. "You so hot, too."

They watched out the windows in silence for a few minutes. Then she asked, "How much longer?"

Wilford was just about to tease her when all the trees fell away from the road on the left and they both gasped. Dory reached out and tapped the kids to bring them back to Real.

They began with a grouchy, "Whaaat?" followed by, "Oooo! Look at that!"

Wilford ordered the oCar to slow. In a half-mile they came to a parking area and pulled in. The oCar's seats delivered them to the pavement.

As they closed the distance to the canyon, Wilford found himself overcome by the height. He crouched lower with each step until he was nearly crawling. "Oh, my God! I never expected it to feel like this."

Dory hung back, also affected, but the kids ran to the edge, fearless. "OK, kids. Turn your VR completely off. I want you paying attention in Real." The kids flicked their oEyes transparent.

Wilford turned back toward Dory. "I've seen pictures, but in person it's awesome." Then he remembered he could dial down the fear with N. He hesitated for a second, wondering if being a little afraid might be a good idea. He turned the knob just enough until he could stand up again. "Wow! It's just amazing. And the colors. Beautiful!"

As Dory got over the initial wonder, she tuned her attention to other visitors. "Jeez, Willie! Look at those kids running along the edge. Their parents aren't even paying attention. And look over there!"

To their left, a teenage couple stood on a rust-colored rock jutting into the abyss. The boy bent his girlfriend over the edge backwards while one of their friends vidded them. Wilford said, "Whoa! What the hell are they doing?"

Dory pulled her kids close. Then she saw a female park ranger and motioned her over. By the time she got there, the teens had climbed off the rock. Dory told the ranger what they'd seen. "Have you ever lost anybody?"

"We average seven deaths every year. But about half of them are folks who hike down into the canyon without enough water. I'm afraid you can't keep 'em from being stupid."

Dory said, "Unbelievable."

The four of them walked down a path onto an outcropping with another breathtaking view.

Wilford said, "You know, seeing this reminds me of when I was a kid. I used to have these dreams where I could fly. They weren't nightmares, either, because it gave me a feeling of power. I could just lean forward and the air would buoy me up like I was lying on water." With that, he leaned over the edge and did a swan dive into the canyon.

Jeanie screamed, "Daddy!"

Dory shouted, "What the fuck?"

Billy who had been looking elsewhere swung around. "Mommy, you said the F word." Then his eyes followed her gaze over the edge, and his mouth fell open. "Huh?"

They watched in frozen horror as Wilford hurtled downward in slow motion, arms straight out from his sides. When he finally hit, he was just a dot, so far away there was nothing to see but a tiny curl of dust, and nothing to hear but silence. A black California Condor soared far overhead and screeched. A gust of wind came up and a dry brown leaf skittered over the edge. It zigzagged lazily along the arc Wilford had taken. Dory thought about following it. Following it down to the little dot that was her husband. She leaned forward. Then she thought of the kids and shifted her weight back. They would need her. She began to sob. Jeanie and Billy each took hold of one of her hands and cried with her.

The continuous feed from Wilford's N-hanced program was terminated. A timer began at the N-hanced server as it attempted to reestablish the connection. In a few hours Rob Reynolds would be notified N was experiencing a communication "issue" with one of its testers. Despite the excitement at the ski slope in Utah, this was not going to be a good day for Rob—or for Lester Charles Noble.

CHAPTER 4

Charlie watched the Utah sky. Just as predicted, the clouds dissipated, the sun came out and the air was crisp and still. The snow underfoot was perfect. He dropped the snowboard and expertly spun it under his oShoe covered feet. Then he stomped on its edge, flipping it in the air over his head and caught it casually without looking.

The Skeet wrangler stood, splayed his fingers and a hundred of the tiny cams arranged themselves in a dome shape exactly twenty feet in all directions from Charlie.

Charlie stared at the vid streaming into his oEyes and grinned. "Now that's what I'm talking about."

The wrangler swung his arms in a semi-circle to view what the combined cams saw from all angles.

The director, said, "Looks great from here. Check it out." She used her software to extrapolate Charlie's image from half a mile away, zoomed it overhead like a helicopter, and finally got right up in Charlie's face, all without moving one of the Skeets. "During the run I'll choose what I think is the optimum point of view. Anybody else can override it and decide what they want to see. Time for your test, Bert. I'll hold steady and see if you can grab your own view independent of mine."

The wrangler rolled his hands away from his chest—palms curved down—to check the view from above. Then he flicked the image clockwise and chuckled as the landscape spun like a merry-go-round with Charlie at the center. "Yes, ma'am. It's a beautiful thing. I'm ready whenever you are."

The director said, "Not a minute too soon. Everybody else good to go?" They all gave her a thumbs up. She opened the VR lines to the investors. Once they all had arrived, she gave a nod to Charlie. "We're live!"

A bass synthesizer thrummed a low and ominous pulsing note. All attendees' VR space displayed the spinning N logo, but Charlie watched the investors. He knew seven of the nine new investors were already sold. He only needed to keep them warm while he convinced the other two. Calm and focused, Charlie took these last few seconds to study them. These were the movers, the shakers, the money takers, the decision makers. If they were on board, any project was assured of success. The music crescendoed to a thrilling, sustained chord and the announcer shouted, "Ladieees... aaaand Gentlemeeeen... Charlieeeee... Nooooble." Charlie's beaming face appeared in front of the masses, arms raised high and wide, and a VR supernova showered down on him. A giddy cheer rolled up the mountain. His Persuasion expert program went to work.

"Welcome... everybody! Today... you will see a demonstration... like nothing you have eeeever seen before." Charlie turned and raised his hands again, drawing out the cheers.

The esteemed Dr. Ray Kurzweil, inventor, futurist and founder of Singularity University acted as commentator. Charlie was thrilled to have Ray participating since his predictions had led Charlie into nano technology. Ray began. "We're here on the top of Ninety-Nine Ninety, the highest peak in Park City, Utah, nearly ten-thousand feet above sea level. It's no accident Mr. Noble chose this date, time and location for his demonstration. Exactly one year ago to the minute Bobby 'Snowball' Bouchene took home the 2034 gold for the oUSA in the downhill snowboard event." The 3-D of Bobby accepting the gold medal appeared in everyone's oEyes, and the cheer climbed still higher. "In just a few minutes Charlie will snowboard down the challenging Ninety-Four Turns slope."

Charlie took over. "I would like to introduce you to the founder and CEO of Corridor CyberDynamics, Mr. Rob Reynolds." Charlie swept his arm majestically and stepped back as the rapt spectators responded passionately.

Rob seemed to emerge from a tunnel in the snow a few feet to the right of Charlie. As soon as Charlie noticed the sweat on Rob's forehead, he erased it in VR.

Rob's eyes darted nervously. "I am very proud to be here today to help introduce CCD's exciting new product, N-hanced. Um, N is the next generation in human evolution, which many experts are calling a *revolution*."

There was only so much Charlie could do in VR to improve Rob's anemic presentation. As a precaution he scanned the crowd for potential hecklers. Just as an angular-faced kid opened his mouth, Charlie muted him from the video feed—and Rob's oEars. Charlie read the twerp's lips as the kid mimed a now innocuous, "Get on with it, asshole." Charlie thought, *Rob, you're going to have to let me N-hance you—assuming I live through this.*

Rob finished up with, "I think you'll be blown away by what you see here today. But you're not here to listen to me. So let me give you back to Charlie." He made a lame attempt at a flourish.

Charlie applauded vigorously and stepped to the front. "Thank you, Rob!" Rob's exit drew polite applause, but Charlie boosted the VR knob until the response was enthusiastic.

Rob turned and waved back over his shoulder as he disappeared into the VR tunnel.

Charlie's gaze swept the faces, reestablishing contact, drawing them back in from the lost momentum. "For all intents and purposes, I will be able to perform as if I were Snowball himself. And it won't be long before you can, too. That's why we're up here today. With N-hanced, no one will have to start at the bottom ever again. From now on, we start at the top!" He threw out his arms and another cheer showered over him. Charlie turned from side to side, stirring the crowd higher, but he could also feel the bloodlust from those who were betting on his broken neck. He saw the bookmaking ghouls now only gave him a twenty-five percent chance of success, with fifty-percent predicting a major injury and the final twenty-five percent hoping for his death. The entertainer in him loved it.

Charlie studied the investor's reactions. He needed to be careful about how much confidence he showed. These were the most powerful moguls on earth. Since he was not required to be Real until the run, he could present a different face to each of them. So he split up and performed nine private speeches, each like a separate romantic dance. Each investor a partner. Each a lover. Seducing one. Submitting to another. The same speech delivered with different body language and eye contact. The most energy devoted to the two who still needed convincing.

Little cracks of excitement began to appear in Dr. Kurzweil's typical stoicism. "Today mankind is poised on the threshold of a technological singularity, an explosion in superintelligence. We have gone as far as we can physically and mentally, reworking our genes with Orchard's oGER. The world is loaded with geniuses and people with photographic memory. But it's not enough. We need to slash the time..."

"Slash." The word triggered Charlie's memory of finding Linda's slashed and naked body in her living room. Detectives said it looked like murder, but there was absolutely no physical evidence of the killing itself at the scene—something impossible these days. That had proven good for Charlie, since he was no longer a suspect. But there were still some detectives who believed he was responsible. Picturing her lying there again, he shivered and flicked the image away in time to hear Dr. Kurzweil say, "N-hanced will use the T computers in our brains to let us master whole bodies of knowledge, effortlessly."

Charlie heard a murmur cascade down the mountainside, gathering in volume across both Real and VR attendees. He focused, smiled broadly and took control. "The main problem today is the rate of change is *accelerating.*

By the time we figure out how to turn on a new device, two new generations are available. That is no longer acceptable."

There were shouts of support from all directions. "You're right about that!" and "Damn straight!" Some people applauded and others laughed. Charlie nodded his approval—his fraternity—his camaraderie. "Before long, anyone who isn't using N-hanced will be left behind." One of the two holdout investors came over to him. Charlie made direct eye contact with the last one and led with a smooth dance step and gentle caress. The guy backed off, so Charlie smiled, lowering his eyes. *Your lead.*

"People, this will be the end of the days of slow, tedious classroom and computer learning. There will be no more study. No more research. You will simply..." Charlie pointed to his head, "...*know*. I couldn't *be* more excited! Can you tell?" Charlie could feel he'd gone a little over the top, so he dialed it down a notch and tried to lighten the mood. Turning to his Skeet wrangler, he said, "Hey, Bert. Did I forget to take my pill today?" The man's face lit up with a smile, and he blushed from the attention. The rest of the team laughed, as did many of the spectators. The holdout investor frowned. Charlie caught his eye privately and shrugged to say, 'That's for the plebeians.' He could feel many of the others leaning in, drawn to the seductive side of N-hanced. They wanted to be his friend, his lover.

"I believe N will lead us into to an unprecedented age of understanding between all people, and usher in an era of peace the world has never known." The crowd spun another long cheer. Charlie waited as it built into a chant, "Char-lie! Char-lie! Char-lie!" His performing side rode it out until it couldn't get much higher. Finally, he raised his hand to speak.

While the noise settled, Dr. Kurzweil whispered as if it were a golf tournament, "Charlie is taking an unprecedented risk for any product introduction ever. He has never been on a snowboard before. In fact, he hasn't been on a snow sled in over seventy-five years." Then Ray lost all restraint and improvised away from Charlie's script. "This is one dangerous mountain. I can't imagine how this will turn out."

Charlie said, "Let me finish by saying, once you experience N, you will *not* want to go back. Ladies and gentlemen, from this day forward, mankind will no longer crawl. Starting now, we fly!" With that, Charlie threw his board high into the air. Then he just stood there and grinned. As the board reached its apex and began falling straight toward his head, a gasp from the crowd quickly turned into a rumble, then a roar.

CHAPTER 5

At the last second Charlie crouched and sprang upward, doing a back flip, smacking the snowboard with his feet the moment he was completely upside down. The board sent snakes of carbon nanotubes up around his lower legs and ankles, locking itself to his feet. He continued the flip until he was fully upright and rocketed down the mountain, building up speed to the first jump. The booming, slamming music Snowball was known for roared into the spectators' oEars. Charlie turned it off for himself so he could concentrate.

Then it happened. It started as a trickle, like a leak in a dam. Charlie felt the pressure and tried to hold it back. He heard a crack, and an all-out explosion as Bobby Buchene's wild personality took over. Charlie's eyes flew wide open. It was so out of control, the feeling terrified him. He wanted to pull over. To stop. But Bobby knocked the control freak in Charlie aside. *Outta the way, old man!* He hit the edge of the first jump going ninety miles an hour and launched into oblivion, the hiss of board against snow fell to silence, leaving nothing but the wind and the pounding of his heart in his ears. Charlie's mouth fell open. He found himself flying ass over teakettle and back to ass again, overwhelmed with a passion he didn't know existed. Bobby pushed against him, demanding more looseness, more control. Charlie tightened up. He could feel he wouldn't complete the third flip in time. He would land on his head. He saw the future, his own broken neck—and a funeral.

Then a calming, warm hand reached inside and untied the knot in his stomach. A voice said "Breathe." It was Linda. "Give yourself to Bobby."

"How?"

"Breathe." She pushed his chest outward and Charlie felt his shoulders relax. Bobby tucked Charlie's head forward, rolling him—just in time to land on his feet. The board skittered sideways, but the Bobby in Charlie pulled it back. He picked up speed.

Charlie swallowed. Then he giggled. *Yeah! I can do this!* He laughed and shouted, "Yeah!" and threw his hands in the air. The crowd roared.

A spectator shouted, "Look, he was just messin' with us."

Swerving back and forth, Charlie let himself go with complete abandon. A series of a dozen flags appeared in front of him. He moved in tight Ss as close to each of them as possible, reversing the board and going down backwards past half of them, ice spraying his face. In a highly un-Olympic-like move, he reached out and slapped the last two flags sideways. They whipped back and forth, waving him on.

As he thundered down the straightaway, he spotted a row of moguls. Arching toward them, he used each one to leap and perform a series of classic grabs; a Bloody Dracula, Roast Beef, Rusty Trombone, Steak Tartare and a Cross-rocket. Then he swung back onto the course to build up speed for the next jump.

Charlie scrutinized the course and used every swirl and divot to accelerate. He hit the edge of the ramp, and the world went silent again, this time overcome with bravado, not fear. He reached down and commanded the board to release from his feet. Taking it in his right hand, he twirled it like a drum major's baton, up along his right side, over his head and passing it to his left hand. He stretched his chest outward, challenging the aerodynamics. It held him in the air longer than gravity would allow, an icy Mikhail Baryshnikov. *Wait... wait... Now!* Twirling the board down his other side, he reattached it to his feet just before landing. He shifted his weight back, digging the board into the snow. The board growled and a powdery, virgin rooster-tail sprayed out behind him, floating down in slow motion. People cheered, but all he could think was *Boring.* The Bobby in him wanted more.

Charlie felt a burst of barbaric glee wash over him. *This isn't the Olympics. I can do anything I want.* And what he wanted now was something crazy. Something memorable. Veering off the course again, he aimed for the orange spectator fence to his left. He could see people tense up. Charlie watched for the right spot where the snow met the fence, then he crouched. In a quick leap, he threw the board sideways and slid along the face of the fence, pushing it to a forty-five degree angle. The board clattered like a machine gun as people scurried back in panic, shouting and screaming. *Eat that, you betting fools!* Bobby's competitive defiance was exhilarating.

Charlie headed back onto the track and began building up speed for a special treat. For years both skate- and snowboarders had performed tricks while riding down steel handrails. This run had a twisted threat called the Killer Corkscrew. Many boarders had ended their careers on the KC. Charlie took a deep breath, crouched and jumped, pulling the board up onto the railing. Lifting his left shoulder, he shifted his weight and rolled clockwise along the pig's tail of steel, upside down and right side up again. Halfway through the third curl, he had a crazy idea. He changed his angle, tucked his head and yanked his knees up to his chin. Threading the eye of the needle, he shot out of the last spirals like a spinning cannonball. At first the spectators gasped, afraid something had gone wrong. But when he unfolded and landed upright, they began shouting. It built to a roar. Charlie grinned ear to chilly ear. *Loose. Easy.*

Pummeling toward the last jump, Charlie spied the tops of a stand of pines peeking over the edge of the mountainside near the end of the jump. Not a second's hesitation. Not even the question "Can I do it?" He smacked the ramp and angled off the edge toward the pines. As he went airborne, he leaned and hit the top of the first tree. Snow exploded as the limbs whipped away from the board. Floating through the air, he tapped three more treetops, each sending down a shower of snow, which burst into a brilliant sun-drenched rainbow, angling multi-colored beams across the crowd. *THIS is the art of flight.* His fists high, he shouted, "Woo-Hoo!" Then he spun backward into a tight tuck to perform his trademark Triple Wildcat known as the Snowball.

Back on the ground again, he swerved, and swooped and soared the remaining few hundred yards of the run, the Skeet dome zigged and zagged, fighting to keep its position above him.

Near the end of the run he began to slow, everyone expecting the standard sideways-slide stop. Instead Charlie fell forward, board flying away behind him. Another gasp escaped the throng. He tucked and did a triple summersault, landing on his hands with his feet straight up in the air. Suspended in that position for a couple seconds, he bent backwards slowly until his feet came down past his ears, touching onto the snow next to his hands. In a final burst, he snapped upright. Then he threw his arms wide repeatedly, turning and bowing. It took more than two minutes for the deafening laughter, cheers and applause to subside. The last investor came over. And by now half the others wanted to sleep with him—and they were straight. Charlie thought, *Gotcha!*

Except for the whacky stunts, it would have been an Olympic medal-winning descent, but of course Charlie wouldn't exactly have been a "natural" participant. Still slightly breathless, he said, "Thank you for coming to our little demonstration. I hope it convinces you to be a part of our new world—our N-hanced world."

For everyone but his crew, the close-up of Charlie's face was replaced with the N-hanced logo, a 3-D spinning N in a split circle terminating in an upward-pointing arrow. The announcer said, "N-hanced, for an infinite you. With N, you'll be able to say, '*Now* I Know.'"

The investors were directed away to other information links. A holler flew from his team as they assembled in VR all slapping him on the back. Charlie faced each of them in turn and shook their virtual hands. "Great job, everybody! We'll be doing lots more advertising pieces together real soon. Thanks for your hard work. I'll be in touch. But right now, I gotta ride the oL." The team continued to shout their goodbyes while he picked up his board and started the short walk to his oCar. He had a virtual meeting to attend. Taking a deep breath, he stretched his neck. It was not going to be an easy one.

CHAPTER 6

The side of the vehicle dissolved and Charlie tossed his board into the back. *And thank you Linda. Are you still there?* No answer. He sat down and the seat conformed to his body and rotated him into a forward position. He settled back as the vehicle found its way down the mountain.

The oCar said, "Welcome, Charlie. Did you have a nice time?"

"It couldn't have gone better, KITT! Thanks for asking." Charlie called the oCars KITT. It was the name of the talking car in *Knight Rider*, a crime-fighter TV series from the mid-'80s.

oCars drove themselves. They were rental only and customized themselves for each passenger using VR. The same car looked different to every rider simultaneously. They were covered with a paint that picked up available light, day or night, which they used to replenish the battery. Some had run for thousands of miles before stopping at a charging station.

The car said, "I'm taking you back to Lansing, is that right?"

"You are correct, sir."

"Anything special I can do for you today?"

"No, thank you."

"I could tell you a joke."

Charlie smiled. "No. No jokes today."

"Would you like to hear the limerick about the young man from Nantucket?"

Now Charlie laughed. "Apparently I underestimated your sense of humor. By the way, don't ever tell anyone I taught that to you."

"It's too late. I already did."

"What?"

"Just kidding."

"Good."

Charlie stared out the window and thought about how things had changed in the past twenty years. People seemed happier. Most of their needs were met, and they could choose how they looked. Orchard's Genetic Engineering and Reconstruction—acronymed oGER, which people pronounced the same as 'ogre,' partly because of unfounded rumors about monsters created during early trials—made people smarter and cleared up most psychological problems. But as always, some people you liked and some you loved and some pissed you off. There just seemed to be fewer of the type who pissed you off.

People didn't travel as much any more. About a quarter of the population were Sitters, who opted to stay in their houses, living in the ever-changing splendor of VR. They never felt any different from the Movers. But even the Movers didn't go places as often, since so many of them worked from home via VR.

There had been some changes, just not the ones many of the Science Fiction writers had predicted. There had *not* been a massive Armageddon— at least nothing with bombs or robot rebellions or the unnamed something that devastated the world in *Mad Max* or Cormack McCarthy's *The Road*.

Not that there hadn't been some tense moments. Some people were simply assholes, even today. It seemed as if a disproportionate number of assholes aspired to power, where they could do the most damage. There were little assholes who could hack a computer or a virus or the software in a T and then bless the rest of the world with their assholiness. But nothing extraordinarily disastrous had happened, if you didn't count the Green Plague.

And the air wasn't filled with dirigibles, or flying cars, or people wearing jet packs. Rockets were not leaving for Mars every five minutes. You could, however, order nearly any physical object or cooked meal from a fab. The fabs really kicked the stuffing out of the stock and commodities markets, making things like gold and diamonds about as valuable as—well, a toothbrush.

So, he thought, *the world is pretty much the same—only different. And I'm going to be a part of one of the biggest changes ever.*

Charlie had an alert set for a VR meeting in the University of Southern California office of theoretical mathematician Erik Kozlovski at 9:00 AM, so he had thirty minutes to spend composing. He decided to write in the recording studio he dreamed up. Between the composing and the meeting, he wouldn't know he was in the car for most of the trip. Just as he was about to VR into the studio, he got a priority comm from Rob. Charlie took it immediately and found himself sitting across the desk from his boss. "Howdy, Rob."

"Ah, Charlie. I just wanted you to know that before you were offline, Corridor CyberDynamics received bank transfers to the tune of five billion oCs. I think it might have been the handstand at the end that sealed the deal."

"Sheesh! If I'd known that's all they wanted, I could have saved us a lot of trouble. Anyway, your appreciation is duly noted."

"OK, Buddy. I'll leave you to your ride. But if you'll allow me just one second of excitement, I'd like to add, *We're in business now, Mama!*"

"That we are. And don't call me Mama. See you soon."

"You, too. Over."

Rob's office faded and Charlie found himself back in the oCar, which was now on a main road and building up speed. Soon it would enter an acceleration tunnel that would bring it up to the speed of the enclosed cross-country oL, Orchard's Elevated superhighway that powered oCars at a thousand miles an hour inside a vacuum tube. He would be back in Lansing in less than two hours.

Music played in Charlie's head all the time, even before N. But back then it was sometimes an odd, bluesy eight counts, which got stuck in an irritating loop. These days he could compose symphonies in his head and see the full score as well as play all of the instruments simultaneously while doing any number of other jobs. N allowed him multi-tasking the way everybody else only dreamed of. Or he could focus on one activity and work at an incredible pace.

He loaded up a song he'd been working on called *Mama Said*, <http://www.n-hanced.com/mamasaid.php> which was influenced by some of his favorite bands from the '60s; Free, Led Zeppelin and the Rolling Stones. He kick-started the process by swallowing all their music in a gulp. Then he gave the song his full attention, reworking the rhymes in order to make the story work.

Momma tried to teach-a me right
She said, "Lookin' at girls that way
Ain't polite"
I always tried to do what she said
So when I start to think that way
I just turn my head.

But look at that girl over there.
She's dancin' with a smile that says,
"Git on over here."
Now come on boys, uh, is it jus' me?
She wants me to look
Hey, she wants me to see

All the instruments kicked in for the chorus.

My mama said, "Now, don't you look."

My mama said, "Now, don't you look."
Mama said, "Now, don't you look."
But I just had to.

The harmonica came in with a long mournful bend as the guitar played a jagged, halting rhythm, leaving room for interesting and energetic drum fills.

It sounds good, but I'm not sure if I like the false rhyme between "that girl over there" and "git on over here." I still might send it out and see if anyone complains. It sure kicks though.

The lyrics made him think of Terra. His relationship with her had a strong influence on the song. She was very sexy, and by the way she acted and dressed, he was pretty sure she didn't think there was anything degrading about showing it. Charlie looked forward to tonight.

CHAPTER 7

At five minutes to nine, Charlie was still in his studio, with his body in the oCar barreling across the country on the oL. He felt a rising awareness reminding him about his meeting and wound down the session.

The CCD sales team signed contracts with most of the people who licensed their expertise to N-hanced. It was these experts' experiences that would make the difference to the N-hanced user. Since nobody on the sales team used N, an important but distracting part of Charlie's job was to woo the most reluctant experts.

He selected a preset of business casual clothes—his usual white, cotton-like Jordeen work suit and Borzun walkers. Then he sent a comm to Erik Kozlovski. Erik returned the invitation signal, and Charlie found himself standing in front of the client.

"Velcome, Meester Noble." Erik spoke with a thick Russian accent and held out a hand equally thick.

Charlie shook it, struggling to return the solid grip. "Please, call me Charlie. And what would you like me to call you?"

"Erik is fine." He pointed toward a chair and Charlie sat. He guessed the man was about two hundred fifty pounds and six feet four. Very stocky, he gave the impression of being much larger. Eric lowered himself into the chair across from Charlie.

Charlie wanted badly to have Erik sign with CCD. Erik had invented Very Good Privacy (VGP), a high-level encryption algorithm, which replaced Philip Zimmerman's Pretty Good Privacy (PGP) in 2020. Having Erik on board would influence the scientific community's acceptance of N-hanced. But he had given the sales team a hard time.

"Well, Erik, I understand you have some reservations about working with our company."

"Dah. Dat is right." Erik held his chin in his hand with a scowl on his brow.

"Do you understand how N-hanced works?"

"I saw vid. I understand good enough. People from your company try to explain how dees license work. My English not too good if somebody talk fast, and doze selling people talk much fast. I get angry and terminate comm."

Why doesn't he using translation software? "I see. You know, we can converse in Russian if you'd be more comfortable."

"No. My Russian not so good any more, either. I kind of stuck between. I make you stop if I no understand." Erik sat back in his chair and grinned, but his eyes were empty. Charlie felt danger.

"OK, then. Let me explain how N-hanced might be good for you. Contracting with us is a way for you to share your knowledge with the world. You already do that with your eBooks and lectures. All we're suggesting is you do the same using this new technology."

"I not so fast to like new technology."

"I understand. Let's see if an analogy will help. May I ask how old you are?"

"I am seventy-five years Real."

Charlie thought the man looked about thirty. "Then you're old enough to know what research was like before the Net. Remember the old library card catalogues?"

"Of course." He nodded his head wearily at the memory.

"The next change brought us the search engine, which often produced thousands of hits. Today's aggregators combine those hits into a single concise summary of all knowledge available, weeding out the garbage."

Erik said, "Yes, I like dees very much."

Loosening up a little? "N-hanced takes that one giant step further. Once people get a taste of Effortless Instant Knowledge, it's the way they'll want all information—all the time. Most people won't take the time to research things the old way. It's a matter of knowing something in seconds versus studying for months or years."

"I don't know. It smell fishy. So how I make money?

"We'll charge a very low fee for the amount of time they use. We're looking for quantity on a global basis. We think most people will want the knowledge continuously, and we'll offer them even lower rates."

"What about people who make money from my brain?"

"Ah. I think I see where you're going. We work it like music downloads. Music providers charge the same amount for a casual listener to play a song as they do for a professional musician who uses the same song to inspire their own music. Same way with us. Anything else is too complicated to track."

Charlie waited for an uncomfortable minute, then continued. "Now here's something I usually don't like to bring up; using the combined knowledge of others in your field, including what your colleagues already know about your expertise, they will likely recreate your work, effectively eliminating the need for what you know. In other words, it may be a matter of allowing us to license your work and get paid, or having others synthesize your work and you make nothing. It probably sounds unfair, but I wouldn't be advising you properly if I didn't mention it."

"So you say. But I pretty special or you not be here. Besides, you try to sell someting. You have reason to lie."

"I guess it does look like a conflict of interest. But that doesn't mean what's good for our company won't be good for you. A deal between us is what they call a Win-Win. You've heard of that, haven't you?"

Erik stared at him with dead eyes. Charlie waited again, but he still couldn't get a read on Erik. The man was a brick wall. *Time to play the ego card.*

"You know, we've already signed Terry Slattery and Boz Wharfman."

Erik scoffed. "Doz hacks? Ha! " He waved his hands dismissively. "Together dey couldn't do addition on calculator to get out of paper bag."

Charlie smiled inside as he pictured the twisted metaphor. "So work with us then. I'm only here because I want the best for N-hanced. You're it." Seeing Erik's resistance, Charlie changed directions. "I hate to say it, but this revolution is going to happen with or without you."

As soon as it came out of his mouth, Charlie realized he could have phrased it more delicately. And indeed, it seemed to hit a sore spot.

Erik's face folded into something Charlie had never seen before; a double frown. The man surged out of his chair and gestured emphatically. "In Russia I hear enough about revolution for lifetime. You know what I tink about revolution? It like great big turning wheel. When it stop, you right back where you started. Same bullshit, different day! Come, meet dee new boss, same as dee old boss, uh? A revolving wheel—it run over people. I seen dat. Up close. So don't talk to me 'bout no revolution! Dat jus' piss—me—off!" He threw himself back into his chair, which thudded against the wall. Then he crossed his arms and stared out the window, jaw muscles twitching.

Again Charlie waited. Waited until he thought Erik was ready to listen again. Finally, slowly and more quietly he said, "You know, I think I understand a little about what your work is like. I used to write a database book. Every time I'd write the next edition, it took me four hundred hours. If I were to do that now using N-hanced, it would take no time at all, and my PAs would do most of it. The world of information transmission is changing. We want you to profit from that change and not be left behind."

Erik straightened up. "How you mean I be left behind?" He lurched forward, his eyes two angry slits. "Do you blackmail me?"

Uh, oh. Charlie raised his eyebrows and a palm to show concern and slowly shook his head. "I see how it could look that way. But— no, no. It's just what our computer models tell us is going to happen." Charlie had seen a similar reaction before—

"Good, because I have friends from old country who can make little people like you disappear."

—but not followed by a threat like that. "I understand." This was part of the difficulty of being the messenger of bad news. Fortunately, he knew how to convey the right attitude with his body language and eye contact— but he didn't get it quite right.

Erik leapt out of his chair, eyes blazing. "You understand nothing!" He threw his huge left fist into Charlie's cheek. Charlie felt pressure and heard a "Whump," but no pain. He found himself in the oCar. The buffer of VR protected him, but not from shock and fright. A second later, and with a "Whoosh," he was sucked back to the California office with Erik standing over him, fists at chest height, jaw jutting forward from his red face.

Charlie replayed the last minute on fast forward to figure out how to best act and tone things down. Palms out in front of his chest and head tilted down slightly, he presented an attitude of submission. "I'm sorry. I'm not sure what I said, but— let's leave all this alone for a while. Why don't you take some time—"

"Why don't you shut up, asshole!" Erik threw another punch.

Again the pressure threw Charlie back into the oCar, then back into Erik's office.

"OK—"

With a backhand to Charlie's face, Erik shouted, "I terminate you!"

Flung back into the car, Charlie put his hand on his chest. His heart pounded. *Terminate me? Did he mean the comm? Or was he talking about my life?* This was a total surprise—and a first since he'd been using N. He could negotiate almost anything. And he always knew when a situation was getting out of hand. Even though Erik made Charlie nervous, the final eruption came out of nowhere. Whatever happened with Erik was more than his difficulty with the language. A *lot* more.

What the hell just happened? And why didn't my PA stop me? Then it occurred to Charlie maybe Erik had a mental imbalance he'd chosen not to repair. There were stories of people who didn't like being "normal." It was like when bipolar people tried mood-leveling drugs. Some of them would rather face the devastating lows than give up the creative highs. More recently, some people reversed oGER's optimum mental balance. Whatever the reason, Charlie was not getting the contract today. He sent a comm to legal and sat back to watch the winter landscape fly past the window.

It took Charlie a few minutes to recover from the meeting with Erik. In the old days he would have been upset for days by a confrontation like that. *Thank God for N.* He clapped his hands and leaned forward. "Time for a little cheering up!" He swept his VR desk clean and transported himself back into the studio to play with the song.

By the time he shot out of the I-80 oL near Chicago to the slower 94 artery up through Kalamazoo, he had the second verse to *Mama Said*.

<http://www.n-hanced.com/mamasaid.php>

Back when I took Biology
The best looking girl in school sat right in front of me.
I smelled her perfume, felt her heat
Nothin' poor Mr. Norton said could ever compete

One day she wore a peek-a-boo top
I tried not to look but I just couldn't stop
Mr. Norton told me, "Go to the board."
I couldn't stand, I took an F that I just couldn't afford.

And then the chorus played again,

My mama said, "Now, don't you look."
My mama said, "Now, don't you look."
Mama said, "Now, don't you look."
But I just had to.

Charlie added a searing slide guitar lead. It had some fire inspired by his run-in with Erik. *Oh, yeah!* He played it back a couple more times. Just one more verse to go.

That's enough for today.

The oCar joined highway I-69 north, transferred to I-496 across Lansing and dropped onto the old city streets at the US-127 interchange by Bake N' Cakes, finally making its way to downtown East Lansing and Beggar's Banquet on Abbot. As his ride deposited him curbside, it turned red and drove off to its next customer. Charlie watched after it and shook his head, overcome with how much life had changed because of the invention.

oCar tech was amazing, and more than a little sad for Charlie. If it had been around a little earlier, Barbara would probably still be alive. He wondered how many other people had similar experiences with lost loved ones. Within three years of its introduction the number of highway deaths plummeted from forty-thousand annually to a few hundred, most of them caused by drivers of manual vehicles or animals leaping onto the old roadways. Since all oCars were on the same computer system, when a leading vehicle experienced an obstruction—a child, rock or deer in the road—the speed of all cars on the route adjusted together. There was never a traffic jam. Is was beautiful—and sad.

A gentle beep brought Charlie back to the present. He had to meet Jeff inside Beggar's in ten minutes. He took a deep breath. Contrary to what he told Terra, meeting Jeff was harder every time. In fact, it was getting darn near impossible.

CHAPTER 8

Charlie and Jeff had met at East Lansing's Beggar's Banquet for lunch at 12:30 almost every Thursday since 1993. That Thursday lunch had started with Jeff and various friends of his while he was still a student at MSU back in the early 70s.

Jeff and Charlie belonged to the Lansing Orange Computer User Group, acronymed LOCUG and pronounced like 'low cut.' After a meeting at Impression 5 museum, Jeff invited Charlie to lunch. They found they shared an interest in technology and gadgets in particular. Jeff was an automotive writer, and after a few years, when Charlie mentioned he'd like to write articles on technology, Jeff encouraged him until Charlie ended up with hundreds of articles and seven books. They met, married and divorced their second wives about the same time, hung out and played cards. Then they met and married their third wives. Things started to go sour between them when Jeff lost Susan, but they soldiered on, acting more like brothers, like blood.

As Charlie pulled open the hundred-year-old barn wood door and stepped into the main room at Beggar's, he was hit by a blast of loud music and the funky smell of spilled beer. Management pumped the fragrance in since oClean made the Real thing obsolete.

Beggar's Banquet Restaurant and Saloon was founded in 1973 and named after The Rolling Stones' 1968 album of the same name. Right now the relentless drive of Led Zeppelin's *Immigrant Song* played directly in Charlie's head from the public program. Even though it was one of his favorite songs, he curled his fingers to lower the volume.

The bar ran along the right wall and featured numerous unique concoctions on tap from area microbreweries as well as the standard fare of liquors, generic national brand beers and popular mood-altering nanoceuticals. All the walls were done up in the same hundred-year-old barn wood. Paintings, photographs and VR works by local artists hung on the walls, and kinetic and static sculptures dangled from the ceiling and perched in various corners. But the patrons were the real works of art.

Most people used oGER to make themselves more beautiful, but many students added something unique. The more conservative among them simply displayed oTats. A guy passed Charlie with a vid of Abbott and Costello performing *Who's On First* playing across his cheek. oTats were T apps that traveled anywhere on the body and formed full-color images. They worked the way octopuses manipulate chromatophores beneath their skin to change color and either blend in with their environment, ward off predators or attract a mate. oTats were exactly like that, and for all the same reasons.

Gaebril Jones was the most popular bartender in East Lansing, in part because of his willingness to do anything to entertain the clientele. Charlie elbowed his way up to the bar. "Gaeb, what the heck is that around your neck, you whack job?"

Gaeb juggled a dozen glowing VR drinks in slow motion. They continued to twirl and tumble with the clickety-clack of a teppanyaki chef, as he ran his fingers through the six-inch long wiry hair. "Lion's mane. I don't think I'll keep it for very long, though." He pinched his nose and made a face. "Stinks."

"Well, just sic some NanoClean on it."

"I'll be doing something different next week, anyway. Get you anything?"

"Naw. I'll wait until I get to my table."

"Saw you on the Net this morning. Delicious run down the slope." He turned to a waving customer.

A man with an ear splayed like a Bloomin' Onion pointed at Charlie. "Hey, you're that guy. Charlie, right?" The VR tag above his shoulder said <Private>.

Charlie shrugged. "That's my brother. So, Private, how come you don't have any oTats?" Mutilants were usually heavily tattooed.

The guy scoffed. "What's the point? They're temporary. Where's the commitment? People should make their decisions and live with 'em."

Charlie nodded. "I see." Then his expression shifted to a bemused frown. "Wait a minute. If oGER can change anything, even that ear of yours is temporary. I'm not buying it."

Private tilted his head and raised one eyebrow. "Kinda makes my argument bogus, don't it?" He chuckled.

"Why not just use VR?"

"Where's the commit—?" He stopped and smiled. Raising a hand next to his eyes, he made the gesture to switch VR off and back on. " You changed your face with oGER. What's your excuse?"

"Hey," Charlie shrugged, "I'm not the one preaching commitment. But as long as we're coming clean, I'll admit I'm the guy on the mountain."

"Yeah, I know. I can read your tag, dipshit." He laughed good-naturedly and held out his hand. "Mark Mehaffey."

Charlie's jaw dropped. "Mark? The Mark who grew up across the street from me?"

"The same."

Charlie recovered and shook his hand. "Sorry for not recognizing you, but you look— different."

"Don't we all."

"I guess." Charlie nodded. "So what you doing here?"

"I just installed a piece." Mark pointed toward the ceiling at a moving sculpture with brightly-colored Koi splashing in and out of a blue-green ball of water.

"Niiiice. But why here? You've got work in some of the best galleries in the world."

"Favor for a friend." He pointed toward the corner at the bronze bust of Bob, the original owner and patron of the arts from way back.

"Of course."

"And speaking of art, Virtual Baby was your invention?"

Charlie shrugged and smiled.

"Brilliant!"

"Thanks, but I was just in the right place at the right time. Hey, I have a meeting in a few minutes. We should get together and talk about old, old, old times."

"Sure, and I can kick your ass at chess."

"Not any more you can't."

"We'll see."

They laughed and shook hands again.

As Charlie continued on down the bar he saw people using nano structures to change the shape of their skin. A woman made up in Goth black stood at the bar. She smelled musty like a forest and had one-inch long fleshy spikes sticking out of her neck. They rotated first one way, then the other. It looked to Charlie as if they might hurt, and maybe for her, pain was the attraction.

Near the end of the bar, he saw an attractive redhead with a whirling rainbow bobbing a few inches above her head. Her eyes lit up when she saw him and she flicked him an invitation to join her. Charlie guessed her PA read his pupil dilation, because her facial features shifted until she became his VR ideal of a heartbreaking beauty.

Charlie chuckled to himself about how easily he was being had. He used N to craft a gentle rejection and opened a PC. "I'd love to get together with you, but right now I have a lunch date with a guy. Uh— a straight guy."

She laughed. "Maybe another time."

The smell from the coffee machines engulfed him as he passed the half-wall at the end of the bar. On the other side lay a small dance floor. A blonde woman with a border collie mod undulated to the music, arms above her head, gaze on the floor. Her partner, a slim guy with angular features and snake-like appendages slithering out of his nose and ears, rubbed up against her. They both looked stoned.

Charlie called out, "Hey, Gaeb."

Gaeb was switching out a pot at the coffee machine and looked up.

Charlie tipped his head in the couple's direction with a questioning look.

Gaeb pointed at a VR sign behind the bar listing today's nanoceutical specials. "Mexican Donkey Fuck. Brand new this week."

Charlie turned off his advertising filter and read the sign. "NEW! - Mexiphoctin – MDF 3°C – 1 hour." All nanoceuticals ran an hour unless the user stepped out of the bar, where they deactivated, eliminating the liability insurance. Charlie nodded and flipped the filter back on.

As he passed the couple, Charlie had to restrain an impulse to pet the dog-faced lady. Right now he needed the privacy of the restroom so he could change from Superman into Clark Kent.

The restroom sparkled thanks to oClean. It was empty, so Charlie locked the door. He went into one of the stalls, dropped the lid down and sat. With the first two fingers of his right hand he summoned his IS, the two-foot VR Interface Space block used to control all non-verbal computer functions. People called it the IS—pronouncing it ice—or ice cube.

Jeff was a purged Luddite and insisted Charlie meet with him as an equal. That meant Charlie had to turn off N and VR. It was like when he was a kid with a loose tooth. He tied a string around it and attached the other end to a doorknob, but he could never slam the door. Right now time was running out. He took a deep breath, let it out and with gritted teeth, double-tapped the VR icon. It shut off everything; N and VR and all other levels of T. Instantly he felt dull, confused. The nausea boiled up. The IS vanished as he jumped up and lifted the seat. He threw up. Hard. His head pounded. *Fuck!* He wiped his mouth and tossed the paper into the water. Then he dropped the lid and sat, head in hands.

For some reason shutting off N got harder every time. He thought the nausea and headache were caused by switching off N's balance system. But after a year of use, he wondered if there were something addictive about N. What he did know for sure was he hated giving it up, even for one hour a week. The symptoms would pass in a minute. But now he was Normal, which compared to being N-hanced, was frankly—stupid. He went from having nearly all accumulated human knowledge on the tip of his brain, down to what amounted to a pamphlet. He could barely figure out where he was.

Aside from intelligence, N also helped him keep his demons at bay. When he was N-hanced, he put them in their place and dialed emotions up and down at will. As a normal person he had self-esteem issues and a stack of obsessions. He felt a tide of anxiety rising up underneath everything and picked at the edges of his fingernails. He felt like a fear stone lay in his stomach. Since he was used to relying on N, he wasn't in practice using the defensive parts of his brain. You could become *very* dependent on N.

If there were ever a test of friendship, this is it. If only Jeff couldn't tell when N is on or off— For the first time Charlie realized he could use N's acting module to act normal. *Why didn't I think of that before?* He stood up and the room reeled. *Jesus! All right. That's it. That's what I'm doing next time. Honesty is overrated.* He got out of the stall, went to the sink, cupped his hand under the faucet and rinsed his mouth. Looking into the mirror, he watched the color come back into his cheeks. He noticed he was slouching, and shook his head in disgust. Looking through his oEyes for the last time, he saw it was 12:27. *Time to get a move on.* With a blink, he turned his remaining VR assistants off. *A complete cripple.*

Just as Charlie unlocked the door, the handle jerked out of his hand. A guy with a perfect Ken Doll face and blond crew cut came in. "Hey."

Charlie nodded. "Hey." He looked for the man's ID tag, but with his own T off, saw nothing.

Ken's face lit up with recognition. "You're the guy I saw on TV this morning. The one with the snowboard."

Charlie smiled. "Yeah, that's me." *So this is what it's going to be like from now on.*

The guy drew back and punched Charlie in the stomach. Charlie squeaked out a tortured, "Awwwk," doubled over and stumbled back against the wall. He couldn't catch his breath, and a ball of fire radiated outward from his stomach. It felt like the man's fist was still in his middle.

"I got a message for you. Luddites say lay off. People aren't meant to be machines. Understand?"

Charlie hadn't seen the punch coming and had no protection from the pain. He was terrified. *Jesus. I can't run. I can't even move.*

"I said, you understand?"

Charlie looked up and nodded, his face frozen in fear.

Ken pushed the door open with his butt and pointed his finger. "You been warned." He turned and the door slammed behind him.

Charlie coughed and found he could breathe in short gasps. *What the hell was that?* His mind raced with a few possibilities, but nothing made sense. Finally he was able to stand. He adjusted his clothes and pushed the door open a crack to see if the guy was nearby or if anyone else looked threatening. Pushing it open the rest of the way, he shuffled out.

Snake and dog were still humping on the dance floor. Their feet rustled, and they snapped their fingers to music Charlie could no longer hear. The Ken Doll was nowhere to be seen in the main room, but his defenses remained on high alert.

Beggar's looked dull and sounded quieter without VR. The barn wood walls were the same, but he couldn't see most of the artwork. He heard noises from some of the other patrons and the clatter of dishes. Sun coming through the front window made him squint and sneeze, hurting his gut and head.

Charlie's anxiety notched up as he passed through the wide opening opposite the greeting station into the first of two dining areas, again scanning for the Ken Doll. Peeking around the corner, he made his way into the quieter third room, to his and Jeff's favorite reserved six-top table by the front stained-glass window. Jeff hadn't arrived yet, and they didn't expect any of their other occasional Beggulars today. Charlie sat with his back to the window so he could see Jeff when he came in—and watch for trouble. His hands were cold, but sweat dripped from his armpits. He held one hand out and watched it shake. *Damn!* Then, with all his high tech tools turned off, he did something he rarely did any more—he just sat there. He stared at the door and picked at the side of his fingernails.

CHAPTER 9

Charlie jumped when Jeff's silhouette appeared in the archway. For a second he thought it was the Ken Doll.

"Been here long?"

Charlie took a breath. "Just sat down a minute ago." He watched Jeff for signs of aggression. *Let's find some common ground today.*

Jeff took off his coat and hung it on the back of his chair. "And it's turned off?"

"Yep." Charlie felt like a guilty junior-high-schooler being asked if he'd been smoking.

"So, what you been—"

"Can I get you gentlemen something to drink?" Larry was an attentive and clever waiter and student who had waited on them every week over the past two months. Charlie thought he was just enthusiastic enough to be amusing. The dancing oTat Donald Duck on his neck froze whenever he took orders.

Jeff said, "What's on tap?" Beggar's hadn't printed menus for more than fifteen years. As a Realie, Jeff needed someone to read the items to him. Larry read from his IS, and Jeff picked a locally brewed Black and Tan.

Larry turned to Charlie.

"The usual." Trying to grease the coming conversation with Jeff, Charlie told Larry, "Did you know Jeff is a certified beer taster and famous author on home brewing?"

"Really? Who do you agg for?" Larry was referring to aggregating, where humans sometimes compiled and edited computer-generated information and stories and added their own comments.

"No, no. He *really* writes—well, *used* to write—for magazines back when they were printed on paper."

"Paper? Damn. I wanted to major in writing, but they told me I wouldn't be able to make a living at it."

Charlie said, "Nobody'll be able to make a living at much of anything in about ten years—" He saw Jeff start to react, so he stopped. Fear rising, he picked at the edge of his fingernail.

Jeff eyes chided. "Larry, there will always be a place for creativity, no matter where these damn computers take us. Study writing if you want. Don't let anybody tell you differently."

"So, what magazine you write for? "

"The most popular one was *Brew Your Own*."

Charlie watched as Larry flicked, likely searching for 'Jeff Martin' and *Brew Your Own*.

"Got it." Larry reached into his IS with both hands, making the motions of picking up and opening a magazine. A couple more flicks and he said, "There ya are! Got a picture and everything." He pulled his hands up near his face. "Jeez. These old things smell so great. Why did they ever die out?"

Jeff scowled. "Exactly. *why*? You want the long story?"

Hoping to avoid the tirade, Charlie said, "Are we taking too much of your time, Larry?"

"Naw. Traffic's always updated right here." He pointed to his eyes. "It's never too busy this time on Thursday." Turning to Jeff, he said, "So you actually wrote all this stuff on your own. Didn't you have a PA or anything?"

"We had spelling and grammar checking software, but most of the time I turned them off."

"Man, I admire you guys. It was probably like being one of the Pilgrims settling the country without power tools."

"Yeah, something like that," Jeff laughed like he was out of practice. "Charlie used to write too."

"Oh, no. My junk wasn't even in the same galaxy. Jeff wrote automotive, too, and took a lot of his own photos. He took the picture of that wine barrel right there." Charlie pointed at the wall. "Trust me, Larry, he was the best."

"I can see that. I'll check out the automotive later. But right now I'm going after your drinks." He turned and dashed off in the direction of the bar.

When Jeff was seventy-five, he had taken oGERs age reversal until his body was age thirty-two. Since giving up high-tech three years ago, he'd been aging normally again.

For someone who didn't any T at all, Jeff was in excellent shape. He worked out regularly, which took a special kind of discipline, since health clubs were extinct. And he only ate what he needed to maintain his weight.

Jeff tapped his forehead. "Hmm, where was I? Oh, yeah, what you been up to this week?"

Charlie realized he'd been holding his body tense and rolled his head and shoulders to loosen up. "Mostly programming, but I did the snowboard thing for the investors this morning, and I started writing a new song on the way back here." *Skip Kozlovski. Keep it upbeat.*

"I'd ask how the snowboarding went, but I see you're still in one piece."

Doesn't sound like he had anything to do with the Ken Doll. "It was a blast using Snowball's skills. He's a wizard. Haven't you done some snowboarding?"

"Nooo. Not since I was diagnosed with Raynaud's disease back in the 90s." He held out his hands with their yellow-white waxen fingers. "Shuts down the blood vessels and it's worse when it's cold. "

Charlie knew a couple months of oGER would fix it, but he tried not to let annoyance show on his face. "Sure, sure. I forgot." *God. I can't remember shit without N. I've known that for forty years.*" And what's happening over at the school?"

"Fewer live students all the time. And if N-hanced takes off, the university will disappear." Jeff's face clouded. "You know, I'd stop you and that fucking thing if I could."

Here it comes. Charlie's eyes darted anxiously. He imagined *Bad Moon Rising* by Creedence Clearwater Revival playing. The two of them were sailing into the stormy seas where they'd spent so much time during the past months. Most of Jeff's work dried up in the late '00s when print went into decline. He finally stumbled into a job as a writing professor at the university. Each change in his life hacked off another piece of his self-respect, but lately he blamed most everything on N-hanced.

"Now that computers do most the writing, I'm hanging on by the skin of my teeth. I have to write for other professors—most of 'em kids who wouldn't know a noun if it bit 'em on the ass. How do they get those jobs? There's this one guy—when I'm done writing for the idiot, he's winning fucking awards. And *I'm* the one on the verge of losing *my* job. Where's the justice?"

Seems like his normal grouchy self. If I had N going, I'd make him laugh. But this— Charlie almost shook his head.

Larry came back with their drinks. Jeff closed his eyes and sipped the Black and Tan, drawing in some air to pull the fragrances back into his olfactory system.

Charlie loaded his coffee with sugar and cream. He noticed Larry's astonishment. "Tastes like hot chocolate."

"Why not order hot chocolate then?"

"Free refills." Charlie's eyes twinkled.

Larry chuckled.

Jeff opened his eyes. " Tell Gaeb it's perfect."

"Got it. You guys want the usual?"

Jeff nodded. "*Huevos Rancheros*. Hot beans, runny eggs, with salsa, sour cream and extra guacamole on the side."

"Just like in the computer."

"If you can trust a computer."

"Got it." Larry gave a little salute and headed off to the kitchen.

Jeff picked up where he left off. "I don't know what I'm gonna do if I lose that job. I saved quite a bit. But it doesn't make up for all those years earning next to nothing. And we live so much longer now, I doubt I'll have enough to make it till I'm a hundred-twenty. Probably have to take an early dieout."

"It won't get that bad. Cost of living is supposed to plummet again. They're saying food, clothing and shelter'll cost so little in the next ten years, your money'll last till you're physically eighty. That's a hundred-thirty Real."

"Yeah, and then I suppose you think I'm going to have my brain scanned and live in an android body after that. I don't trust that shit any more than I do having T-bots running around inside my balls."

Charlie knew this was the place to keep quiet, but he doubted he'd be able to. Jeff was so angry about tech, he'd rather die than change.

The irony was that Jeff had always been an early adopter. It was part of the glue of their friendship. Charlie liked tech, but he waited for the second generation of anything new. But Jeff would camp out on store sidewalks in order to own Serial Number One of every new gadget. The way Charlie saw it, what happened was Jeff's own fault. Now he was a card-carrying Luddite, with a boatload of animosity toward anything remotely high tech. And if Charlie represented anything these days, it was high tech.

Charlie could feel the blood rising in his face. *T-bots inside your balls, indeed!* He leaned forward to tell Jeff off when Larry returned with their lunch.

Fightus interruptus.

But Charlie knew it wouldn't last. Lately it never did.

CHAPTER 10

Jeff turned his head as Larry came into the room. "Ah, here we go."

Larry set the plates in front of Jeff and Charlie and stepped back to wait for their reactions.

Charlie leaned in and let out a quiet sigh. He closed his eyes and let the pungent fragrance of the hot food wash away the conflict.

They both scooped some of the beans onto their forks and blew on them. Taking a bite, Charlie rolled the food around in his mouth savoring the flavor arc from the balance of spices, enjoying the grainy texture. He nodded to Larry, but Jeff held up his index finger. Poking one of the eggs with his fork, the yoke ran over the whites. "That's what we're looking for. Thanks, Larry."

"Great. I'll check back."

Jeff scooped the salsa out of the steel cup and arranged it around the edge of his beans. Charlie dipped a thick taco chip into the Guacamole and shoved the whole thing into his mouth, hoping they hadn't overdone the spices. *Cumin, subtle. Onion, sweet. Perfect!*

Jeff said, "You know, this artificial food is pretty good. It's one thing about tech I can't complaint about."

Charlie almost choked.

"It reduces pollution from trucking and the chemical runoff from chicken farms, not to mention the cruelty of slaughter. Stuff's more consistent, too. And the artificial grains and hops make a damn fine brew, which I never thought I'd hear myself say.

Me either. Thank God. Maybe we're not so far apart after all. "And prices have gone down since I started coming here."

"Yeah, but it'll probably turn out to be some kind of government conspiracy that ends up killing us all."

Charlie smiled and nodded. *Yep. Too good to be true.* "So, doing any dancing lately?"

"Yeah, taking a Lindy Hop class." Jeff sneered. "But I suppose that'll all go the way of the Dodo bird once N means nobody will have to go to classes any more."

Charlie set his fork down. "Aw, c'mon. I'm trying to talk about other things here. Do you always have to turn it around and pick a fight?" *Well, now you started it.*

"OK, Tech-man, tell me this; where's the feeling of accomplishment gonna come from when nobody has to work at anything? You want everybody to live like a bunch of stoned-out beach bums."

"No, no. N-hanced people will be totally absorbed in inventing and creating."

"It sounds like a high tech drug to me."

Charlie leaned in. "It's not like that at all. You don't want to do drugs when you use N."

"Because N *is* the drug."

Ouch. "Noooo. People use drugs to dull the pain of life. With N, you can dial that down. It lets you concentrate better than ever. Productivity, inventiveness, creativity, real communication—that's what's exhilarating. Not some artificial exuberance. If *you* were using N, you'd write like the wind."

"It wouldn't be *me* writing."

"But it would feel like it was you."

"See. It's an illusion. A lie. N is a stoned—out—fucking—lie!" He slapped his palm on the table.

Charlie sighed and lowered his voice. "N is technology. That's what you're against." He changed directions. "Let's face it, it's not really technology you're against. Tell me, when are you gonna get over what happened to Susan?"

Jeff clouded over and looked away.

Charlie knew he'd opened the wound. "Hey, I'm sorry. But you've got me at a disadvantage. I never was very good at debating, because I can't remember facts when I'm riled up. Hell, I can't remember facts when I'm not riled up. If you'd just let me stay N-hanced when we get together, I know I could explain things to you so they'd make sense."

"Bullshit!" Jeff's finger was in Charlie's face and fire burned in his squinted eyes. "When you first started using that N shit, you manipulated me. I could practically feel my body temperature dropping from the snow job."

"That's not true."

Jeff rolled his eyes.

But Charlie knew it was true. With N-hanced, he oozed liquid charm, and he had all the answers. He could feel people lean in, drawn to his magnetism. But right now, he wasn't N-hanced. He felt stupid—and embarrassed.

"Look, I used to be where you are." Charlie brought his palms up. "Well, not *exactly* where you are. And not for the same reasons. But you remember how I used to be about tech. When I'd go off on one of my tirades, you'd say, 'Don't take it out on me.' Well, that's what I'm saying to you now. Don't take it out on me."

Jeff shook his head. "It's not you. Well... it's not *just* you. But you have to admit, you're right in the middle of the next big change. Who the hell else *am* I supposed to talk to?"

"But what happened to Susan can't happen any more. Companies have to use computer models to test everybody before they're allowed to use any new device, whether it's medical, oGER or N-hanced. You just got caught in the last phase of the old school."

"You think *that's* gonna convince me? That's the same crap they sold us back then. They said age reversal was completely safe, that it'd been tested over and over. They lied to us. Hell, you were there. You know what happened. I was young again, and Susan was dead. She was my chance to be happy. It took me seventy-five years to find somebody like her. She was perfect."

Charlie had to fight not to move his lips. He'd heard the speech before. *They had to put me—*

"They had to put me in the psycho ward in Owosso, all because of fucking technology! And those liars and their goddamned COMPUTERS!" He slammed his fist on the table and jumped up, knocking his chair over.

Charlie made a calming motion with his hands and spoke quietly. "Come on, Jeff. Tone it down a little."

"Fuck that! Everybody needs to know!" He turned to the few other diners in the room and continued shouting. "People, listen up! This technology is dangerous! It's stealing your lives and sucking your souls dry! Turn off your VR and purge your T! Do—it—NOW!"

But nobody heard a word. They had their VR filters on and Jeff knew it. He pushed his fists into the side of his head. "Uhhhh!" Turning back to the table, he picked up his chair and threw himself down into it, defeated. "It's fucking useless. It's gonna happen anyway, isn't it?"

Charlie didn't say anything. He found himself feeling sorry for Jeff. He lived in a different, more primitive world from everyone else. A world that fell further behind every day. Jeff and the those like him were becoming the real Left Behind.

*　*　*

Rob Reynolds leapt out of the chair in his office at Corridor CyberDynamics. He had seen enough of the playback from Wilford Bostwick's data feed. The man's swan dive into the Grand Canyon hours earlier threw Rob into panic mode. He needed Charlie in the office right now. This was a potential a big time crisis. *For cryin' out loud. Why now, when Charlie's comm is down for that damned Thursday lunch of his?* Rob composed the encoded message and sent it by o6Degrees, the product based on six degrees of separation theory. It flew across multiple comm channels, bouncing from person to person, searching for the shortest route to anyone close enough to Charlie whose PA recognized him. *Sorry to disturb you, my boy.*

The receiver of the message was a slim eighteen-year-old girl in very short blue shorts, a horizontally striped long-sleeved shirt with bare midriff, sporting a 3-D oTat of a spiky-haired guy with an outrageously long tongue that disappeared down into her shorts. She balanced on high platform shoes with her blonde pigtails swinging as she walked up to their table.

Charlie tensed, wondering if she were bringing more Ken Doll trouble. Instead, she said, "Boss needs you to comm him."

Charlie blinked. "OK. Thanks."

She eyed him. "Who the hell *are* you?"

"Uh, nobody really."

"Whatever." She gave him dismissive shrug, swiveled outrageously and stalked off. Their eyes followed her until she disappeared through the doorway.

Charlie cleared his throat and gave Jeff an apologetic shrug.

"Oh, just take the damn comm." Jeff turned away in disgust.

Hustling to the restroom, Charlie locked the door and fired up the first level of T. He turned on VR, flicked his Interface Space into view and double-tapped the N icon. It felt like the ceiling opening up and the sun pouring in after a moonless night spent in a graveyard. He stood straight and tall, and his brain came back online. "Thank Jesus." He took a deep breath and swallowed. All the tension melted away in a relaxing warm shower, the anxiety ball in his stomach loosened and fizzled. With his eyes closed, he let the feeling wash over him. Finally he opened his eyes. With a nod he found himself sitting across the table from Rob in his office.

"Yeah, boss."

"Wilford Bostwick died two hours and forty-two minutes ago."

"Oh, man… I liked him. We going to the funeral?"

"Maybe. But that's not what I called about. He took a swan dive into the Grand Canyon—in front of his family." Rob flicked the vid to Charlie.

"Whoa! But why would he do that? He was stable. A perfect candidate. Gotta be an accident."

"No, it was clearly suicide. I checked the data streams before calling you. Could have anything to do with N?"

"Naw. Well… w-what do you mean?" A blast of doubt bored into Charlie's chest. He pushed it away.

"You're with Jeff now, right? You don't seem your usual bright self."

"Yeah, well—"

"You'd better turn your brain back on and get down here. We may have a situation on our hands."

"Be there soon as I can. Bye."

"'K. Bye." Rob waved, and Charlie found himself back in the restroom.

Hurrying back to the table, he pulled up Bostwick's data from the servers.

"Sorry, Jeff. Gotta go. Same time next week?"

"Yeah, sure," Jeff said flatly, turning his eyes away.

Jeez, Jeff. Will we ever be real friends again?

As he left the table, Charlie summoned an oCar. In less than thirty seconds it was curbside, gaping mouth in the side, the seat was a Mick Jagger tongue sticking out, ready to swallow him whole.

CHAPTER 11

Corridor CyberDynamics was built in 2023 at the tail end of a project aimed at turning Michigan's failed automobile economy into a "high tech corridor." It took up three blocks on the west side of South Washington Avenue across from the now abandoned Consumer's Power plant next to the old train station.

The CCD offices were far too expansive for the number of people who showed up for work in Real. It was originally built to house 500 employees, but it quickly became clear most employees preferred to work via VR on a flexible time schedule. It also meant nobody wanted to buy the CCD real estate, so the company stayed put and Real workers had huge offices. In 2030 the place got a VR facelift. The architects made it look physically impossible; stretching the façade into a shape Charlie said looked like an upside-down brick-and-steel soft-serve ice cream cone.

The oCar dropped Charlie at the main entrance. A dozen other oCars sat at the curb with people sliding out. Deep in thought, he kept his head down and slipped into the lobby through the two-story-high invisible curtain.

For all the expanse of glass, nano-simulated-marble floors and solid flat walls with high ceilings, the lobby was remarkably quiet. During the facelift, Charlie invented software using Adaptive Audionics to remove echo from the space. He earned a patent for the process. His patents provided him with a good income, and he didn't have to work if he didn't want to—until the day he threw his entire savings into the N-hanced project. That was a year ago, and he was still all in, even though investors were once again in support of N. His financial position was one more reason N-hanced had to succeed. If it failed, he would essentially be broke, waiting for his next licensing check.

His innovative ideas were one of the reasons Rob hired him. Charlie was in the initial group of software engineers around whom the CEO built the company. They sold many of their products through Orchard's oCode Store.

In the center of the lobby, a solid-looking 3-D logo floated twenty feet in the air and changed periodically to feature CCD products. It currently displayed the N-hanced logo with its spinning N inside a circle. It usually made Charlie feel a swell of pride, but after the news about Bostwick, it cast a shadow of foreboding.

Charlie nodded politely to everyone he saw, but presented a preoccupied air to ward off talk—small or big. He needed to get to work. His first stop: Rob.

*   *   *

Rob paced and shook his head. "Man! We just got the new investors this morning. If there's something stushy with N, the liability could shut down the whole project. Maybe even the whole company. And just in case I sound too callous, are you feeling suicidal?"

"No, nothing that desperate. Besides, I'm sure it's just a coincidence. I studied the black box recording, and I can't see how Bostwick's jump has anything to do with N. And he was the opposite of depressed. He was exhilarated to be at the canyon."

Charlie called up the data blocks and spread them out in front of the two of them, pulling the pertinent ones forward. "See the big anxiety spike when he first looked down into the canyon? And here's where he dialed it down, but he didn't turn it off. That means he was still in touch with instinctive danger feedback."

"What about this?" Rob pointed to a zigzag chart with a rainbow peak.

"That's the emotion graph, which goes with the audio, when he's talking about his childhood dream." Charlie stacked the graphs vertically and expanded the graph so it lined up with the audio. "You can see he's excited when remembering it. But how that makes him jump a second later is not at all clear. During the fall, it's as if he's still reliving the dream. See? There's no change in the fear graph, even though his fear is fully functional. Maybe it's some kind of stush with his VR program. It's been a long time since one a VR accident, but it wouldn't be the first. But only Orchard has access to that code."

Rob nodded. "So what's next?"

"Let me go over the data and look for a security breach in N. I'll fire up my PAs to see if they can spot anything unusual going all the way back to when Wilford joined the program. See if there's any emotional problem we missed."

"All right. I've taken care of a few comms from worried investors. Now I'll try to keep us away from the NewsDogs. That's not gonna be easy. There were quite a few people in the canyon who recorded the whole thing—including his family's reaction." Rob shook his head. "It's all over the Net. People eat that shit up, sick sons o' bitches. I just don't want it to point back to us. Now, if it *is* our fault, we'll do the right thing. But there's no reason to fold if we don't need to."

"Right."

Rob frowned. "Should we comm the other alphas and warn them?"

"They already know. And they're smart enough to know it could be related to N-hanced. They're no more interested in going back to normal than I am."

"OK. I take it you saw the protesters out front?

"Protesters? No. But I did see some people getting out of cars as I was coming in. What are they protesting?"

"You."

"Me? What did I do?"

"When you were in Park City you talked about the Biblical 'end of days' and the 'left behind.'"

"No, I didn't."

"Yes, you did. Take a look." Rob clicked the vid link and flicked to the section where Charlie said, "People, this will be the end of the days of slow, tedious, rote classroom and computer learning." Then he to, "...anybody who doesn't eventually use N will be left behind."

"I did say that." Charlie scoffed. "But there was nothing Biblical about it. They're taking it all out of context."

"Yeah, that never happens, does it? But that's not all. You've got some fans, too."

"Fans?"

"A bunch who call themselves the New Disciples of the Apocalypse. They're calling your speech The New Sermon on the Mount."

"What? Bullshit."

Rob raised an eyebrow in mock disapproval. "Charlie! That language is totally unbecoming of the Prince of Peace."

Charlie sniffed. "So who are these people?"

"My PA show a seventy percent chance it's something made up by the NewsDogs."

"Good grief. Those people give dogs a bad name."

"If there isn't such a group, you can bet the Dogs have hired some actors by now."

"Don't we have enough to worry about?"

Rob chuckled. "Hey, I'm just the messenger. But I beefed up security just in case. Go by their office when you leave so they can escort you out of the building."

Charlie shook his head. "All right. I'd better jump on this Bostwick thing."

"Let me know what you find out, even if it's nothing."

"Gotcha."

"Hey, why'd it take so long for the server notify me?"

"It's on a timer so we don't get bothered every time we lose a network connection."

"Shorten the time, will you? Use a different setting for yourself, if you want. But I want to know as soon as there's a hint of a problem."

"Five minutes OK?"

"Make it three."

Charlie's hands moved in his IS cube. "All set."

"OK. Get going. Oh, and don't do anything impulsive."

"You mean like jumping into the Grand Canyon? No problem. But now that you mention it, I'm assigning a PA to watch over my shoulder— and one for each of our testers. Thanks for the suggestion."

"C'mon, son. I can't lose you. I mean it. Don't climb any ladders. Don't climb any stairs. In fact, see if you can't spend the rest of the day strapped to your oChair."

They both squeezed out smiles that didn't quite make it to their eyes.

CHAPTER 12

Charlie went directly to his office, but he hadn't stopped working since he'd turned N back on after lunch. N-hanced performed true multitasking. His External Brain did data retrieval and research. The EB processed, summarized, and reported anything important, like an executive secretary who knows what he needs even before he does—and when to interrupt.

That wasn't anything exclusive to N-hanced. PAs had been doing the same thing for more than ten years. The difference with N was, the user knew the results and what they meant without having to read, watch vid, or listen in real time. With N, a PA wasn't just an assistant, it was *you*. As of the current version, users could have up to eight copies, all coordinating with each other. There was no point for an un-N-hanced person to have more than one PA. They simply couldn't absorb the results fast enough.

Unfortunately, none of the PAs had reported anything out of the ordinary about the Bostwick incident. Charlie turned his full attention to his EB and absorbed the results a second time. *Nothing out of the ordinary? It's not as if people take a dive into the Grand Canyon every day.* Then something else occurred to him; *What if it was sabotage?*

*   *   *

Charlie had a huge corner office consisting of four smaller offices, that once belonged to employees who now worked remotely. Most of the time he substituted his favorite Tahitian vista rather than look out the windows at Real—which, during February in Michigan, was snow. The room was empty except for a lone oChair. Built from sky-blue carbon nanotubes, it fit like a glove. He did the majority of his programming in the chair, but if he wanted to walk around more freely, he could banish it to a corner with a wave of his hand.

He sat down and called together his PA team. They appeared around a circular, curly-maple VR table.

"OK, guys. let's go over every square inch of every module in the program. I want to make sure nothing penetrated the security shell and touched our code. Look for anything as small as one pixel. I'll grab some of the modules, and you divide up the rest amongst yourselves. Got it?"

Their young, eager faces answered as one, "Got it."

"OK, go." They scampered away.

He waved to open a garage door in one of the walls and signaled for a block of code to come to him. Positioning a beam of coherent light at an angle across the gleaming surface, he began running his fingertips along the upper face, feeling for irregularities. He worked his way down and back in rows, the way farmers used to plow their fields.

He continued along the other sides, then magnified the block further while tipping it on edge to inspect the corners. This one was perfect. He shrank it, moved it to the wall opposite the overhead and called for another.

The simple plastic cube made him think about the 1968 movie *The Graduate*, starring Dustin Hoffman. In the twenty-first century, nano became the new plastic.

But nano went far beyond plastic. It could be used to make anything— and make it out of trash. The alchemist's dream come true. Ironically, it made gold, platinum and diamonds worthless—or certainly worth less. The only thing of value now was information. With information, you could even make food. Without it, you could starve. Survival information was relatively inexpensive. Higher end stuff retained price.

Charlie finished with the module and called for another. It was going to be a long afternoon.

CHAPTER 13

Charlie thought back a few years about Robbie, Barbara's and his little boy.

"Daddy? Tell me a story."

"What do you want to hear?"

"Um... do the one about Green Plague."

Robbie was a VB, a Virtual Baby, a toy Charlie invented for CCD's 2028 Christmas season. VBs became an unexpected smash sensation, which sent ripples echoing throughout the culture.

Charlie and Barbara sat on opposite ends of the couch. Robbie kneeled on the floor looking up at his father, the boy's angelic face full of anticipation. Barbara smiled and flipped the pages of a VR magazine while she eavesdropped.

"OK. Let's see... A long, long time ago, waaaay back in 2021—"

"Before I was born, right, Daddy?"

"That's right, Robbie. The Green Plague swept across the entire earth."

"Where did the Green Plague come from, Daddy?"

"The scientists who looked at its DNA thought the Chinese probably released it. The plague was designed to kill only people with non-Chinese DNA."

"Are the Chinese people bad?"

"No, they're not bad, Robbie. But the population in China had grown so large, a lot of people were starving. Their leaders were desperate to save their people, and they made some bad decisions. "

As part of CCD's pre-release testing, Charlie and Barbara "adopted" Robbie as a five-year-old in January of 2027. With tongue firmly in cheek, they named him after Barbara's father. Once they fell in love with Robbie, the joke disappeared. Part of the concept was to have the VB read its owner's reactions and change its behavior until the owner was hooked. It worked so well they had to modify the algorithm to include negative interactions, because some testers became so attached they quit their jobs to be with the VBs all the time. Barbara suggested VBs would probably find a strong adult market. She was so right.

Soon couples who wanted children—but didn't want to be tied down—started buying the program. They set the preferences so they could enjoy the cuddling, the big eyes, giggles, and teaching it how to walk and talk, while avoiding things like temper tantrums and diaper changing. They'd turn the child off when they wanted to go out, no babysitter required. They could try their VB at different ages, and the teenage years were a breeze.

After Barbara died, Charlie went into a depression, and abandoned the boy—or "toy," he kept reminding himself. He felt guilty but he couldn't help it. Every time he looked at Robbie, the memory of Barbara stabbed him in the heart. *Besides,* he'd remind himself, *he's only a toy, right?*

Charlie signaled for the next module, this one of polished aluminum, and continued with his memory of Robbie. "So the Green Plague killed everyone who came into contact with it—"

"Daddy, you forgot the part about the Chinese who got the Green."

"Oh, that's right. The plague mutated into a strain which killed over 50 million people in China."

"Serves 'em right." Robbie scowled.

"Oh, no. That's not the way to talk, son. How would you feel if the plague killed your friends, Lee and Xiang?" Charlie could hardly believe he was giving morality lessons to a computer program. *Amazing.*

"Oh, yeah," Robbie looked hurt, obviously considering what losing his friends would mean.

Barbara said, "Popcorn anyone?"

Robbie jumped up and down, "Me, me, me!"

Charlie nodded, pointed at himself.

Barbara headed for the kitchen.

"So the plague traveled around the world killing everyone it touched, when—"

"Why did they call it Green, Daddy?"

"Well, the people who caught the bacteria got boils all over their skin, and their body fought the disease with a green protein. Then the boils would burst."

"It was gross, right?"

"Right."

"Cool!" Robbie jutted out his jaw and made little fists.

"And since we had overused antibiotics for so many years, none of them would work on the plague. When the boils broke, the people bled to death."

"Cool"

Advances in genetic engineering and nano tech meant people could live forever, creating a panic about overpopulation. VBs got so popular the population went into decline. Charlie and Rob went to Washington, D.C. for a ceremony and received a plaque for their invention. But some religious groups screamed that VB was the demon seed.

Barbara came back with the popcorn. "Still feel like eating after that delightful story?"

"Gimme," shouted Robbie as Barbara handed him the virtual bowl.

She and Charlie each took a bowl and she returned to the couch.

Robbie grabbed a fistful and stuffed his mouth. "How bib bey fop buh puag?"

Charlie frowned. "What?"

Barbara raised her eyebrows. "Don't talk with your mouth full, young man."

Robbie chewed furiously and dry-swallowed, making his eyes bug out. Barbara smiled.

"How did they stop the plague?"

"A very smart man at Orchard had invented a special nano that could run many different apps. He went to their medical engineers and they figured out a way to make it protect people who used it."

Robbie bounced with excitement, and popcorn flew from his bowl.

"Orchard told the United Nations about it. Even though there were a lot of people afraid of nano technology, the leaders of all countries were desperate, and they agreed to distribute it worldwide. The particles copied themselves so fast that all the water systems were treated in just one month."

"But...?"

"But, what?" Charlie noticed Robbie was rocking and his eyes were darting. *Too much fidgeting.* Charlie adjusted the program and the boy calmed down.

"You know—" Robbie flicked a piece of popcorn into the air and caught it in his mouth. "—they figured out how to use Ts for other things."

"Why don't *you* tell *me*?"

"They made the Ts beat up the bad bacteria." Robbie face pinched with distress. "I like it better when you tell." His voice grew whiney.

"OK." *Is that stage fright, or is the program stroking my ego?* He made a note to check with his team. "They figured out how to program Ts to fight other bad bacteria and viruses. They also made it take over the work of the good bacteria in our bodies, for example the ones that digest our food—and it did a better job."

"No more farts, right?" Robbie giggled.

Charlie smiled. "Right."

Robbie cupped his hand, jammed it into his armpit and pumped his elbow. He squealed with delight as the escaping air made a whooping sound. Charlie couldn't help himself and laughed, too. Barbara gave a sideways glance and a frown which melted into a smile she tried to hide.

When Robbie finally stopped, he smelled his fingertips and said, "And no more stinky armpits or butts or bad breath either."

"Right." Charlie laughed again, and Robbie joined in with a little boy's forced laugh.

Charlie summoned a cylindrical brass module and checked in with his PAs. Still nothing. He ran his fingers down the cool, smooth brass and slipped back into his memory.

"How do you know about stinky armpits, Robbie?"

"VR, Dad, VR. Sheesh. Me and my friends smelled lots of gross stuff. There's a really stinky cheese that smells just like a poop. Wanna smell it?"

Charlie raised a palm. "No thanks. I'm eating popcorn."

"OK. Hey, I know, tell about the fat people."

"Sure. Once T was all over the world, Orchard started to think about other things they could do with it. Somebody came up with oDiet for weight loss."

"And everybody wanted that one, right?"

"They sure did."

"Tell about the stinky people. The floods."

"Floods...? Oh! You mean the Luds. The Luddites."

"Yeah, them."

"There's a group of people suspicious of technology who call themselves Luddites. But some churches objected to using nano, too."

"They're whackos, right?"

Charlie started to smile, but when he saw Barbara's raised eyebrows, he stopped. "We'd just as soon you didn't talk that way. OK?"

"OK."

"Some of these people demanded oGov remove the Ts from their bodies."

"That was purge."

"Purge, right. The courts decided they would be purged for free. Some people called the purged 'Carriers.'"

"And those Kar... Kar-ee-ers were stinky. You could smell them a mile away."

"Well, they did have bacteria on them, and they smelled like old-fashioned people. Yes."

"Hmm... I know. Tell about the eyes and ears." Robbie reached into his bowl and came up empty-handed. He stood up. "Can I have some of yours, Daddy?"

"Sure."

Robbie climbed up into Charlie's lap. Charlie pretended to pour some of his popcorn into Robbie's bowl. As the boy began to eat again, Charlie looked down at the white skin in the part in Robbie's hair and kissed the top of his head, breathing in the fragrance of salt and oil. When he looked up, his eyes met Barbara's. Her face beamed with adoration.

"OK," Charlie's voice faltered. He looked back at Robbie. "Where was I?"

Robbie looked at Charlie and a tiny wrinkle appeared between his eyes. "Are you OK, Daddy?"

Charlie glanced at Barbara and back at Robbie. "Perfect."

"The Eyes and Ears," Robbie said, and tried to put his whole fist into his mouth. vPopcorn tumbled onto the couch.

"Right." Charlie cleared his throat. "Once people had Ts taking care of their health, somebody came up with the idea of oEyes. They use it to show the names of people they're looking at, or restaurant names on the street in front of them. But it can also be used to completely replace the world with an artificial vision."

"That's VR, right?"

"Right. Orchard did the same with sound, and called it oEars. And then they created oTouch."

"And that's where I came from, right?"

"Uh... yes." Charlie glanced sideways at Barbara. He wondered if he hurt Robbie's feelings with his answer—if Robbie had any feelings. It sure seemed as if he did. But when he looked, he just saw Robbie's drooping eyes. It made him smile.

"OK, young man. It's time for *you* to go to bed." He stuck his finger in Robbie's ribs and tickled him. Robbie screamed with delight. Barbara beamed as Charlie picked Robbie up high above his head, roared like an airplane, and zoomed him off to his room. He knew it wouldn't settle him down, but he couldn't help himself. It was too much fun. No wonder people bought VBs—and loved them.

Remembering that day made Charlie sad because he missed the boy. *C'mon, guy! It's only a computer program. Sheesh! You did too good a job building that one.* He could turn Robbie off in his eyes. But it wasn't so easy to do in his heart and mind. He flicked away a tear and dialed down the heartache, leaving an emptiness with no dial.

Charlie's work with the modules hadn't turned up anything. Each PA reported in as it finished. "Nothing, nothing, nothing..." talking so fast it became a purr. As he wound down his last piece, they finished, too.

"OK, let's run a simulation to see whose software is doing what. I want to take another look at the moment Wilford decided to fly. I want to make sure nothing from N overrode the VR program."

The team used the black box data to recreate the incident, but when they got to the jump, he didn't jump. "What the hell? OK. It's probably not in our software then. Maybe it's in VR, or it's something he decided to do on his own—which is just crazy." Charlie shook his head.

As an afterthought, Charlie checked the black box to make sure it hadn't been interrupted. It was fine. And there were no extra input lines. "Dammit! It's not a suicide if the guy wasn't despondent. He clearly thought he could fly."

Charlie motioned for his PAs to gather around the table. They reported a final nothing, with no suggestions. "Hell, guys, I'd hate to have someone else die in order to find the problem. Stay in the machine and start scanning every line of code, and tell me if you notice anything suspicious." He stood, stretched and flicked them out of view.

Walking down to Rob's office, he found the door open. He poked his head in and cleared his throat.

Rob looked up.

"OK, boss. We finished checking the security and didn't find a thing. I'm heading home now. I'll pick up with my team tomorrow. If nothing shows up there, I'll contact Orchard about a likely problem with their VR software. How'd you do with the NewsDogs?"

Rob shook his head. "They came and got some vids and quotes from the protesters, but there's nobody left now. It's too cold for marching. Keep your eyes open when you leave, though. Then check in first thing tomorrow. If any of them come back, work remotely. In the meantime, stay safe."

Charlie executed a loose salute and headed home. He didn't think he'd be able to relax.

CHAPTER 14

Charlie slipped from the vehicle in front of his condo building. A slim, mid-twenties-looking man got up from the steps and headed toward Charlie. "Mr. Noble? I've been waiting for you." His VR tag read "Matthew Levine."

Remembering the Ken Doll, fear whipped through Charlie "Who are you? What do you want?"

Instead of answering, the man ran at Charlie with his arms outstretched. Charlie stepped toward Matthew, grabbed his wrist and rolled him over his shoulder onto the ground.

"Ooofff!"

Charlie stepped to Matthew's side and twisted his arm, rolling him onto his stomach.

Matthew lay face down on the pavement. Charlie had his arm jacked up behind his shoulder with his foot on Matthew's back. "I said, 'Who *are* you?'"

Cheek against concrete, Matthew's speech was muffled and edged with pain. "I'm Matthew Levine. I needed to see if you're who I think you are."

"And who do you think I am?"

"Can you let me up?"

"I said 'Who do you think I am?'" Charlie pushed Matthew's arm a notch higher.

"Ow, ow! You're hurting me."

Charlie bent down so Matthew could see his eyes and pressed harder. "Who *am* I?"

"Ow! You're the second coming of Jesus Christ. The Messiah"

"Oh, shit. Who told you that?"

"I figured it out when I heard you give your *Sermon on the Mount* in Park City. Then you descended from the clouds, just like in the prophecy. Can you let me up now?"

Just what we need; more people worshiping junk on the Net. Charlie scanned him and decided he was harmless. He raised his foot and lowered Matthew's arm.

Matthew rolled over, sat up and rubbed his shoulder. "You have miraculous powers."

"It's judo."

"I mean your *other* miracles."

"Wait a minute. Are you one of the New Disciples of the Apocalypse?"

"Yes. It's my group. I'm the only one so far."

"Did the NewsDogs hire you?"

"No. I work for the oIRS. I'm a tax collector."

"Your name is Matthew, you're a tax collector, and you want to be my disciple." Charlie's voice dripped with cynicism.

"Yes." Matthew grinned.

"And nobody *paid* you to do this?"

"No."

"When's the last time you visited a psychiatrist?"

"There's nothing wrong with my mind."

"Says you." Charlie stuck out his hand. "Here, let me help you up."

"Thanks." Matthew stood and brushed himself off.

"Why did you run at me like that?"

"I wanted to hug you. Can I hug you now?"

"Hell, no!" Charlie stepped back, hand up. "So what's this crap about the Second Coming?"

"When I heard you talk, I realized they made a mistake in the Bible. These are the N-Times, with an N—" He traced his finger in the air. "—like N-hanced. Not end like rear end."

"Listen, I'm not the Messiah. I'm an eighty-five-year-old programmer/inventor. I don't walk on water or raise the dead."

"But you *do* perform miracles. You came down the mountain like an pro—without any training. It was a *miracle*. People went crazy."

"Look, I'm an inventor, like Ray Kurzweil or Dean Kamen."

"Who's to say what a modern-day messiah would look like? Just because you're not a carpenter doesn't mean you're not the The Chosen One."

"Well, choose one of those guys, not me."

"The prophecy says you will have many trials and tribulations in the coming days. Wherever you go, Lord, I will be there."

"Hey, there are laws against stalking."

"I would never harm you. I want to help you get your message out. For years I wondered what my purpose in life was. When I saw you on the mountain, I knew it was to protect you."

"Bullshit. The way I put you on the ground, you think I need any goddamn protection? And a messiah wouldn't talk the way I do."

"Modern time require a modern vocabulary. Besides, I've heard it all. I'm a tax collector."

"Yeah. Well listen, Matthew, I got a date in a little while. Do whatever it is you're gonna do, but leave me alone. Got it?"

Charlie started up the steps, then turned back. "You know what a Ken Doll looks like?"

"Yeah?"

"You see anybody looks like that come near me, you break his arms. How's that for the Prince of Peace." He continued up the steps and opened the door.

"It shall be done, Master."

"And stop with that *Master* shit, will you? " He let the door close and headed down the hall.

*   *   *

Charlie lived in the trendy area just north of downtown Lansing, called Old Town, a five-minute drive from CCD. After the real estate bust in the '10s, he bought a large condo built in the '00s. A couple years ago he stripped out everything and filled the place with an experimental form of programmable matter (PM) known as claytronics—nano particles which could be assembled into just about anything the user liked. Want to change where the walls are? Just wave your hand. Different table and chairs? Make it so. Rather have the place filled with beach sand and sit in a cabana chair? That, too. Even the pipes and electrical could be repositioned and functioning within minutes.

Charlie's condo door read his credentials and opened into his Tahitian over-the-water bungalow. He loved the setup, especially when it was twenty degrees in Lansing. A gentle salt breeze snuck under the thatched roof, paddled down by the ceiling fan. He squinted over the rough-wood railing and scanned the cat's-eye blue-green water until he saw the familiar fins of the resident pair of dolphins. Ordering a margarita from the bar, he instructed the PM system to build a table and chair by the railing. Sitting down, he licked the salt, and sipped the sweet and sour. Steel drum music playing in the background.

While eating a fabbed pizza, a new melody took shape in Charlie's head. He changed the room into his studio, summoned a VR guitar and tried some variations. Once he had the whole thing worked out, he thought, *Yeah, can't wait to see the look on Terra's face when she hears this.*

CHAPTER 15

As Charlie finished writing the song, he heard the gentle beeping signaling Terra's proximity. On time, as usual. He dismissed the guitar and checked himself out in the VR mirror. *Looking good, my man.* He winked and saluted to his reflection. Strolling to the door, he waited for the bell. With a flick of the wrist, the studio became apartment.

He gestured the door open. "Well, if it isn't Miss Terra Firma." It was his frequent joke on her last name, Fromma. If she didn't like it, she never let on.

She raised her eyebrows and gave him a sly smile. "What's *up*, sweetie?" Her dark brown eyes traveled down his body and settled just below his waist. She slowly scanned upward until her eyes locked onto his. He felt a thump in his chest. As she stepped inside, she put her hand on the back of his head and gave him a firm kiss. She smelled like caramel.

Releasing Charlie, Terra strutted into the room. His eyes followed.

She looked twenty-five years old and was leggy, with long, thick black hair which fell in an easy curve to her shoulders. He found her stunning, and he apparently wasn't alone. Whenever she entered a room, everyone watched. Yet she had a humble quality which seemed to befriend the green-eyed monster in other women.

Charlie remembered when he'd first met her. Milo introduced them at closing time one Friday night three years ago, knowing Charlie had been mourning far too long over Barbara. Milo said he knew if anyone could bring Charlie out of the funk, it would be Terra. He was right. Milo knew Terra from the game company over in Brighton where he'd worked before coming to CCD. The first time Charlie met her he seemed to come back to planet Earth—or "planet Charlie" as Milo said. Charlie had been grateful to him ever since.

Tonight she wore a short white skirt and a low-cut pink top with no bra. When the material of her top gapped he could see her nipples. He suspected it was intentional. She sat down on the couch and put her feet up on the ottoman. No underwear.

Charlie swallowed and felt a warm swelling in his groin. He liked when she went natural. But today he wanted to talk, so he looked away. "Uh, eaten yet?"

"Um,-hum."

"How about some wine then?"

"That would be niiiiicccce."

He went into the kitchen and she sent a virtual voice after him, "You know, this programmable matter thing you've got here is weird."

Charlie called back over his shoulder. "Leave your VR on and you won't notice it. I wan to virtualized everything and be free of any physical possessions." He chose some PM wine glasses from the menu and fabbed a Merlot.

Terra giggled. "God help you if we lose electricity. So what happened after your mountaintop triumph?"

"I had a *really* crappy afternoon. First some guy who looked like a Ken Doll punched me in the stomach." Charlie poured the wine.

"Mm."

"Then there was Jeff." Charlie sat the bottle down and turned toward her. "And then one of our testers died."

"Oohhh. You'd better tell me about *that*." As soon as she knew he was looking, Terra got off the couch, giving him another peek. Then she joined him in the kitchen and leaned back against the counter.

He handed her a glass and filled her in on the details of his day. Terra listened intently, asking intelligent questions, clearly following everything.

"And then Rob tells me I've got two religious groups chasing after me. One that wants to own me, one that wants to stone me."

"And one says she's a friend of mine," Terra added with a laugh, quoting *Take It Easy* by the Eagles.

"Right. One of my so-called disciples accosted me outside the condo." Charlie's eyes flew open. "Jeez! I forgot all about him. Was some guy hanging around the front door when you came in?"

"No. Just your usual groupies."

"What?"

"Just kidding." Terra waved dismissively. "Nobody was outside. So what did this guy do?"

"It's this tax collector named Matthew. He came running at me, and I laid him on the ground."

"You can lay me on the ground any—" She stopped when she saw the comic frown on his face.

"Ahem. If I may continue, Miss Firma?"

Terra giggled.

"After that thing with the Ken Doll, I thought it was a mugging. Turned out he was going to hug me. Anyway, he said these are the N-Times—" Charlie drew an N in the air. "—not 'end times,' and the N is from N-hanced. He said I'm the Second Coming and I perform miracles."

"I can attest to that," Terra flirted.

"He said he wanted to protect me. So I told him if he ever saw the Ken Doll, to kick his ass."

"I like this guy."

"You would." Charlie snickered. "But at lunch—" He sighed. "You know, this thing with Jeff has gotten so bad, I even considered he might have something to do with Bostwick. I mean, he stood up in Beggar's and shouted at the other customers, 'Turn off your VR and purge your T! Do—it—NOW!' Fortunately, nobody could hear him. I don't know what to do. I realized today I could fake acting normal around him, so I wouldn't have to go through the sickness when I turn N off. But I hate lying. Which reminds me, I want to apologize to you about saying I'd be all right turning off N at lunch.

Terra gave him an understanding smile. "That's not the kind of lie I worry about."

"Still—"

She shook her head and waved away his objection.

"You know, I'm starting to wonder if Jeff and I even have a friendship any more."

"Well, you know, friendships do end. People change, and a friend has a responsibility to act like one. I don't think there's any rule says you have to hold on till eternity. But then, I'm not I'm completely impartial. I may be hoping you'll have more time for me." She gave him another sly smile and put her hand on his thigh.

Charlie ignored her touch. "You know, it's as if I saw how he's changed for the first time today. It's like a marriage gone bad. It started when he lost Susan. The changes have been almost imperceptible, like how the seasons change from summer to fall to winter. Every time we meet it gets darker one minute earlier. I got this flash he might drag me down into that self-pitying black hole of his. And then he expects me to turn N off just to suit him. Hell, I got divorced for less than that."

"I *do* understand," Terra gave a an apologetic tip of the head. "But right now you sound a little like him; feeling sorry for yourself and not doing anything about it. I know you can—how do you say it, 'dial it down?' Or maybe you can use N's psychology module." She raised a hand. "But you can tell me to buzz off if you want."

Charlie nodded. He knew she was right. He just had to remember the help he needed was right inside his head. Performing what his N testers liked to call an attitude adjustment, he let out a sigh and smiled at Terra.

Then he leaned close to her and gave her a big wet lick up the side of her face.

"Oooo," she screamed, wiped it off and whacked him on the arm. They both laughed until tears came to their eyes and then laughed some more.

Charlie said, "That reminds me, I've got something I want to show you."

"Ooo, I can hardly wait."

"No, not that," Charlie laughed. She had a one-track mind and he liked it. "I wrote a song for you." He got up, went to the middle of the room and made three copies of himself. With a wave, he gave each one an instrument—drums, bass and keyboards—and strapped on his star-shaped guitar. They got settled into their places. "It's called Beautiful One." He counted off, "A-one, two, three." They played the intro and then he sang.

Beautiful One
<http://n-hanced.com/beautifulone.php>

Just like in the movies
Well I held your hand in mine
We took a walk down a country lane
And all the words just seemed to rhyme
I waltzed you through the garden gate
You asked me if I'd stay
I kissed you softly on the cheek
Cause you knew what I'd say

One of his copies joined in on the harmony.

CHORUS
You're my beautiful one, my beautiful one,
My beautiful wuh-hu-hun
You're the sun my beautiful one
My beautiful one
You're my beautiful one, my beautiful one,
My beautiful wuh-hu-hun
You're the sun my beautiful one
My beautiful one

Terra jumped up to dance. Every so often she lifted her arms above her head and her skirt flipped up to reveal her pubic hair. *Whew, she is hot!* He smiled wide and launched into the second verse.

I felt so warm when I saw you smile
That I fell right thru the floor
We talked so late that the sun came up
Then we laughed and talked some more

We held each other oh so tight
As the shadows disappeared
We made sweet love in the morning light
Then I whispered in your ear

CHORUS

The key modulated up a step, and he played a melody on guitar. Then he came back singing.

I brought you sixteen roses
You put them by the bed
You kissed me for the note I left
Cause this is what it said

CHORUS

When he finished, Terra was grinning. She bounced up to him, hugged him around the neck and gave him a big kiss. "I love it! Thank you so much, you big lug. But you know you don't have to write a song for me to get me into bed. It's not called seduction when you have a willing partner." She stripped off his guitar, and tossed it aside. Then she began undressing him. Charlie looked over his shoulder and dismissed his doubles. He undid the buttons of her blouse and she wriggled out of it and the skirt, letting them fall to the floor, revealing her tan with white patches in all the sensitive areas. He summoned a sultan's bed complete with a canopy which included overhead mirrors. They climbed in

*   *   *

After a few uninspired minutes, Terra sighed. "Um— Do we need to download some oMy?"

"No. I'm sorry. It's just this thing at work. Something's stushy and I can't see what it is."

"You mean with Mr. Bostwick?"

"Say, you are a little mind reader, aren't you?"

"Only the parts you let me read."

"I haven't walled off anything from you."

"Oh." Her voice dropped with disappointed.

"What?"

"Nothing."

"What?"

"Nothing. I mean literally nothing. There's nothing up there." She tapped his forehead.

"Why you little shit." Charlie jumped on top of her and tickled her ribs.

Terra screamed and laughed. "Stop you empty-headed fool!" She flailed weakly.

Charlie grabbed her wrists and held her down. Lowering his face to hers, he kissed her until she went limp. Finally he lifted his head. "Besides, you know I can focus if I want to."

"And you don't want to?" She pretended to look hurt. "What am I, chopped liver fab?"

Charlie rolled off and lay facing her, resting his head on his arm. "You know what I mean."

"Sure. But we can talk about Bostwick if you want. I'm all yours for the next— uh—" She glanced at the right corner of her eyes. "—thirty-seven minutes, no matter what you want me for. When that money's gone, I'm outta here, buster. But you can purchase more of my services now if you like. Cha-ching!"

Charlie pouted. "Hey, come on. Give an old guy a break. You know I'm eighty-five."

"Right. Eighty-five going on twenty-five."

"Now, just a minute. I'm not a day under twenty-seven."

"Ah, I see. So that's the age when a man gets too old to perform his amorous duties. Want me to comm one of my girlfriends?"

"Oh, God, no! I tried that once back when I was twenty-three—the first time I was twenty-three. Too complicated. A threesome that is, not twenty-three, although that *was* complicated. But now you mention it, it might be fun to watch you and your girlfriend going at it."

"Um-hum. You would." She pinched her face in mock disgust. "I'm not gay."

"Yeah, I know. I mean, I didn't think you were."

"So, you want me to get her?"

"Noooo. Like I said, too complicated. It would be too hard with two of you."

"Well, it's not hard enough with just one of me."

He laughed and raised his hands in submission. "OK. I'll tell you what. I'll give you one hundred percent of my attention."

"It's OK if you need to work. After all, the guy did die."

"No, no. My PAs are working on it right now. They're faster than I am anyway. If I relax tonight, maybe I'll be able to concentrate better tomorrow." He moved closer and sang a couple of lines of the chorus of Marvin Gaye's *Let's Get It On*. When he got to the "Ooo" high note, he touched her thigh. She sang an "Ooo" of her own.

As their hands and mouths explored and delighted each other, his oOdeToJoy kicked in. Terra gave him a helping hand, and he entered her. A warm quicksilver sensation flashed across Charlie's neck and scalp. She let out a hoarse moan. They each added VR fantasies, which fed off of and wove into each other. He imagined the bed expanding into infinity and melting into a clear, deep-blue body of water. They sank below the surface and breathed with gills. They spun and twirled, while Terra's hair extended and waved elegantly in slow motion, wrapping around them. The water lifted, becoming an amorphous blob that floated into the sky. As they pressed their hips toward each other, Terra merged their thighs and lower legs into a mermaid's tail. They undulated erotically as one, swimming through the water like a two-headed porpoise, leaping ecstatically out the sides and coming back into what was now a giant shimmering teardrop.

Charlie buried his face in her neck, and Terra gasped and arched her back. With eyes closed, they watched from within as their teardrop fell from the sky. It landed on a desert island, shattering into millions of tiny, brightly-colored foam beads which scattered and flew around them.

The mermaid tail transformed back into legs, and Charlie licked Terra's ear and blew on it, making her shiver. He blew past her at the beads, shaping them into a colorful whirlwind, which spun around them. Terra waved it into a tornado which picked them up into a huge cloud of flowers, the fragrance engulfing them.

Charlie called out, "Hold on to me," and drew a pair of snow-white angel wings on his back. They flew above the flowers and dove back through, turning them into sweet, colored marshmallow fluff. Growing multiple arms, Terra stroked Charlie in a dozen sensuous places. He dipped his head and sucked on her breasts, his hands squeezing her behind. Feeling her body tense, Charlie knew he'd caught her by surprise as a mass of goose bumps raced across her skin under his cheek. He could feel her stomach tighten and her insides grab at him. With a fierce pulse of his wings he pushed hard into her one last time. Golden sunlight exploded from the top of his head and silver moonbeams streamed from hers. "Ahhhh!" they sang together.

Charlie held onto the sensation as long as Terra did. As it subsided, Charlie laughed. For all its wonder and urgency, the complete loss of control of an orgasm seemed so ridiculous and sub-human. Terra stroked his face. Nudging her mind, he felt her move aside, letting him slip inside her head, where they huddled together for a moment and watched Charlie through her eyes, immersed in her feelings for him. He spread his wings and glided down in long lazy circles while Terra held to him tightly with all the arms. Kissing her softly, they alighted back in the room.

Her extra arms dissolved as he lay her down on the bed. Retracting the wings, he slid down beside her. She put her head and one hand on his chest and closed her eyes. He kissed the top of her head, then lay back on the pillow, watching her awesome beauty in the overhead mirror. Soon they both slept.

*   *   *

Charlie dreamed about his erotic adventure with Terra. That dream was replaced by one set in a shadowy alley. Anxious, he kept saying, "Where is it? Where is it?" He saw a movement out of the corner of his eyes, but when he turned to look, something black slithered out of sight with a scraping sound that turned his stomach.

He felt a hand on his shoulder. It was Linda. She pointed toward the wall and said, "Look away from it."

Understanding her meaning, he tried to define the thing's shape by looking around its edges, building a silhouette. But it wasn't working. When his eyes got close to the edge, the thing slithered away again. Then he found he could step a little closer as long as he looked away. But every step took him closer to the danger and raised his anxiety.

By now he knew a million things it could not be. He tried to narrow it down further until only one option remained. It was like looking for a piece of a jigsaw puzzle when he didn't have the box; he knew the size and shape of the piece, but not the picture. Finally it worked! Now he knew! His fear dissipated, he fixed his gaze on it. And it froze. "Ha! Gotcha!" He reached for it. And it turned to dust and blew away. Noooo!

CHAPTER 16

Charlie woke with a start. Sitting up, he pressed the heels of his hands against his eyebrows. *Why didn't they tell me?* Now he knew what had been bothering him about the Bostwick incident. *And why didn't I think of it?* With N-hanced, he didn't need to look at the time—he always knew. *2:07 AM? Shit!* He'd been asleep almost three hours. With N-hanced's Fas-Sleep, he rarely needed more than two hours. *Gimme that hour back.*

He made a half-hearted attempt to slide out of bed quietly.

Terra stirred. "Umm… What's up? Everything OK?"

"The bastards didn't tell me."

"Who?"

"My PAs."

She frowned and rubbed her eyes. "Huh?"

Already connected to his team, he stood impatiently as his clothes wrapped themselves around him. Then he called an oCar. "I can't talk now. I gotta go."

"Wait—"

"Let yourself out. I gotta go to the office." His heart pounded as he went through the the door.

Charlie raced down the hall of his condo building. Gesturing to assemble his PAs, he placed himself at the head of the table as he continued to run. *OK, listen up, fuckers!* Panicked and pissed, he was beyond polite. For the first time, talking to his virtual selves actually felt crazy.

Why did we waste all that time yesterday? You knew damn well we were going in circles. There are people's LIVES at stake here. WHAT'S THE FUCKING DEAL?! he thought—

—but they spoke. "Can you be more specific?"

Are you kidding? You know everything I think. Why weren't we testing security with one of the outside expert systems we licensed?

71

"Why didn't *you* think of it?"

Come on! Your jobs are to be my assistants. You warn me if I forget to comb my hair. I'm human. But you never forget anything.

Every programmer knows he needs outside eyes when testing his own security. Otherwise he only checks for tricks he already knows, not tricks other programmers know. That leaves holes big enough for hackers to drive a Trojan horse through. *Damn PAs. That's what happens when you start depending on computers; you forget how to think for yourself.*

He flew down the stairs two at a time, now talking out loud. "So, what's going on? Why didn't you speak up and have us test with the standard protocol?"

"You told us not to."

"What? What are you talking about?"

"Yesterday when you came back from Park City, you told us we would run a special test later in the day, and you wanted us to ignore normal external security testing."

"Why the hell would I do that? I didn't even know Bostwick was dead then."

"You said no other programmer is qualified to test a system as complex as ours. To test our system the way an outsider would, you needed to be unaware of the way you normally implement security. You wanted it erased from your memory. So we stored it in your External Brain and partitioned it off from your access."

"No way!" Charlie could hardly breathe. "All right then, retrieve the vid from my instructions and play it for me."

"We can't. It's been erased."

Of course. He felt as if he were losing his mind, like he was being gaslighted—by himself.

He slapped the building door open and threw himself into the cold, slipping on the new snow, then righting himself. *Fuck I hate snow! I should have taken that job in San Diego.* He stopped and put his hand out. It shook. *Come on. Slow down. You make bad decisions when you're upset. Take it easy, kemosabe.* He dialed down the stress knob until he was normally. Tromping toward the oCar parked at the curb, he realized it wasn't set up with his color—and it had two people in it. One was Matthew who looked asleep. The other, a pretty blonde girl, brightened when she saw Charlie, and shook Matthew. He blinked, turned and waved the window open.

Charlie's shoulders fell. *Shit. I do not need this right now.* His car arrived and pulled to a stop behind Matthew's. Charlie bolted.

Matthew stuck his head out the window. "Master, I got a second disciple. We're calling her Mary. Delicious, huh?"

Charlie kept moving. "Yeah, great. I can't talk to you now. The shit just hit the fan. No, it *smashed* it." He lowered himself onto the seat.

"That's OK. We're going fishing."

That stopped Charlie. "In February?"

"Fishing for men. We're going to find more disciples."

Charlie sprang from the seat and strode around to Matthew. "Listen, this has gone far enough. I don't need a bunch of whackos following me around. You got that?"

Matthew's face fell like he'd been slapped. "Yeah... sure."

Damn it. Can't you be nice? "S... sorry. Listen, I gotta go. But think about this for a while. 'For there shall arise false Christs, and false prophets, and shall show great signs and wonders; so as to lead astray, if possible, even the elect.' That's from the Bible. It's Matthew 24:24. You should know that one." Charlie ran back to his vehicle and jumped in. When the portal closed he said, "CCD and make it snappy!" It was pointless command. oCars always knew where their charges were going and got there fast.

*   *   *

All the way to his office, Charlie stewed. Standard protocol for final testing of a software security system is to have outsiders try to break in. Large companies offered hefty rewards to anyone who could hack their system, as long as the hacker told them how to fix it. A number of hackers made a good living doing just that.

Now his PAs were telling him he had them erase his memory in order to avoid having outsiders attack N. But they didn't need outsiders. All they had to do was use the N security expert systems they already had licenses for.

Erasing my memory to run a security test could be dangerous—even deadly! I've never done anything like that in my life—ever. Of course, if I had, I wouldn't remember, would I? The logic spun in circles and made him dizzy. He felt as dumb as he did during his weekly lunch with Jeff.

He arrived at CCD and ran to his office. "OK guys, early in the project we decided it was important to make decisions about what information to keep in the wet brain and what to shunt off to the EB, right?"

"Right."

"We decided to keep as much personal memory as possible in the user's wet brain or their onboard T, for when they're offline from the servers."

"Check."

There was no reason for down time. Most people took astronomical amounts of memory with them, feeding the T with glucose from bodies. Swallowing a teaspoonful of devices one sixth the size of a red blood cell gave the user a half-billion times more computing power than IBM's Watson computer—the one that beat the all-time winners on Jeopardy back in 2011. No one was ever out of touch with his or her most important memories. The system was full of fail-safes and foolproof—except for whatever was going on just now.

"Are you sure it was me who ordered this memory erasure?"

"We know you."

"You *are* me."

"Technically, we're not." Charlie's heart thumped in his throat. His vision narrowed and went white. A hot rush surged through his body. He tightened his stomach to push blood back into his head until he could see clearly again.

He spoke slowly and angrily. "Listen carefully, now. I want a test by one of the expert security systems we did *not* use to build N. In fact, use all of them. And before you run the test, tell me if I or anyone else told you not to do a thorough job, or said to erase or hide the memory of it from me—or *you*."

"No."

"No what?" *Jeez.* He felt like the father of a teenager.

"No, neither you nor anyone else have given us any instructions to hide anything further."

"And is there any code with instructions to mix up VR and Real?"

"No."

"All right then. I want to see the tests as they happen. This is gonna be like in an old-time math class; show me your work. Got it?"

A chorus of "Yes."

"All right. Do it—NOW!"

* * *

Charlie anguished about repeating the same work he'd done yesterday—especially with lives at stake. *Hell, my own life could be in danger. If I can't trust my PAs to watch out for my programming, how can I trust them to protect me from a skydiving fantasy?* Then he remembered his angel-wing flight with Terra the previous night. *I lived through that. But maybe I'm not really alive at all. Maybe I just think I am.* He shook his head to clear it. It was all getting a little too existential.

Today's work would be different from yesterday's. This destushing program worked quite differently from his own. It scanned the surfaces with a low-powered laser and high-frequency sonar. If there were stush in N, this should find it. But he still didn't think he could trust the results.

They worked until onsite employees began arriving at 7:40. Charlie closed the door for more quiet, even though he could have blocked them in VR. He didn't want any eyes on him. He listened to the steady purr of "Nothing" coming from the PAs. *Come on, guys. Find something. Anything.*

CHAPTER 17

At 8:00, VR staff walked the halls in conversation with the Real workers. Charlie left notice for Rob to comm him the moment he got in. At 8:05 Rob pinged him. Charlie opened the channel and Rob appeared in front of him.

"Did you have a good night, Charlie?"

"Well, sort of. But then I woke up to discover my PA team was withholding information from me."

"I didn't think that was possible."

"Me either," Charlie scoffed. "And I still don't know exactly what's going on. But I've got a bad feeling this Bostwick thing may not have been an accident. I'm not ready to say it's my fault yet, but I wanted you to know my report of 'nothing' yesterday may need a bit of a revision."

"Well, I trust if there's something there, you'll find it."

"Thanks for your vote of confidence, but to tell you the truth, my own confidence is shaken. There's something stushy going on, and I'm suspicious I may not be able to see it even if it came up and bit me on the ass."

"Anything I can do to help? Extra staff?"

"No. I'd have to set them up with N. Some people don't adjust to it right away. I can't take the time for that right now. I'd rather finish this scan and do a check of every line of code before I start bringing in other people."

"All right. I'm here if you need me. Keep me updated."

"We're not dating, are we?" Charlie delivered the joke flatly and felt like a horse's ass for saying it. Nothing was funny right now. Rob faded away and Charlie found himself back in his office with a module in his hands.

*   *   *

By 1:00 PM Charlie was numb from the constant din of "Nothings" from his PAs, but he was afraid to turn it down for fear he'd miss the one that mattered. He'd split the team into two groups. One worked with him to repeat yesterday's failed attempt to find the security opening, and the other searched the billions of lines of code to look for errors. Both used the expert destushing system.

And then it came. "Got something," yelled one of the PAs.

Charlie jumped and caught his breath. "Let me see it!"

The PA flicked it his way. And there, highlighted in pulsing red, was a line of code he recognized all too well. It said "User Abort ON."

"SHIT!"

Charlie knew the line intimately. It had caused him thirty-six hours of unpaid panic on a project he did for a client many years ago. He would never forget that code, and here it was back to haunt him. Accusing him. Telling him he was responsible for Wilford Bostwick's death.

"Wait a minute, guys. I haven't used that code for more than thirty years. It's outdated. Someone would have had to insert it manually. Even then it would have been eliminated during compiling. It's flat out impossible."

"Unless your memory was erased."

Right. "Or if someone else hacked the system. Any ideas about how to pursue this?"

"Let's look at the backups until we find the date it was inserted."

Charlie clapped his hands. "Perfect! We started two years ago. Open the backup from one year ago and show me if that line is in that code."

"Nope, not there."

"Keep splitting the difference. How about six months ago?"

"Nope."

"Three months ago?"

"Yes!"

"OK. Now go back four and a half months."

"Not there."

A few more tests and they found it first appeared on Friday, October 13, 2034—last year.

"Ha! Friday the thirteenth. My lucky day. Now let's look at the vid of all code added the day before that backup. Each of you check three hours until you find it."

Seconds later one answered. "Here it is!"

There stood Charlie surrounded by floating code modules. He waved at them like the director of an orchestra, clearly commanding the damning line into place.

"And why don't I remember that? Do any of you?"

"No."

"Did anyone tell you to erase if from your memory or mine?"

"Not that we can remember. But if they had, they could have just as easily erased the memory of the erasure. We don't verify vid in here since the facility is secure."

Charlie nodded. *Secure? Bad assumption.* "What happens if we remove that line from the code?"

"It's integrated now. It can't be removed without serious reprogramming."

"How about we leave it but switch it to User Abort OFF?"

"That will work."

Charlie sighed. "Good. Do it. But we need to keep looking for the opening in the security layer. If it can't get past security, it can't do any harm. Let's go."

As Charlie worked, his mind chattered back at him. *Could I actually have done this myself? Could I be responsible for Bostwick's death? Has N been infiltrated? This couldn't be Orchard. It's not their style. If they really wanted us, they'd do what they do with everybody else they want to buy; they'd take us out to dinner and shower us with candy and gifts until we wanted to be one of the trees in their happy little orchard. No. This thing cannot—be—Orchard.*

What about Jeff and his Luddite buddies? I know he couldn't do something like this, but I've never met any of them. What about the Ken Doll? Or Erik Kozlovski? He's certainly capable of violence. But that date... Friday, October 13. Wait a minute! That's ten days after Linda was murdered! Could it be related?

That code looks like my work. With my erased memory, maybe it is. If somebody else put this together, they could not have planned it better. Charlie felt the bottom dropping out from under him. He couldn't breathe, so he dialed it down. But it seemed as if there were no more notches left on the dial.

It can't get any worse—can it?

CHAPTER 18

Chad Rodriguez was a quarter Hispanic and a renegade programmer whom Charlie selected to be one of the N-hanced alpha testers from hundreds of applicants. This afternoon Chad rode his classic motorcycle, a 2011 FXDF Sedona Orange Fat Boy Harley-Davidson, down to Springport, forty miles southwest of Lansing. It cost a lot to own that bike in these days of the oCar, and the limited number of roads open to motorcycles made it a hassle. But Chad could afford it and was willing to put up with the limitations. He wasn't a typical biker. Small and thin, riding was only a hobby for him.

Chad used N in his work, but recently he'd used it to settle some old scores. Today he wanted to settle with a huge biker named Jonesy who lived in Springport, a town taken over by a gang of bikers back in 2031. Ten years ago Chad met Jonesy in a bar in Grand Ledge. Jonesy came up smiling with his hand out. When Chad shook it, the creep crushed it while pummeling the side of Chad's head with his other fist. When he was done, Chad was on the floor moaning, with a broken nose and cracked teeth, while Jonesy rode off on his bike, laughing all the way, ha, ha, ha.

Holding the side of his head, Chad had mumbled, "What was that?"

"Oh, that's just Jonesy," said the bartender. "He's an asshole. Sorry he picked you today."

Me? Today? He does this every day?

Chad had a lawyer check up on Jonesy, but the prick didn't have a pot to piss in, and Chad didn't want to spend the money to prosecute. But now, ten years later, he had a different weapon. He had N. And he had a plan.

Chad came into The Sportsman's Bar with a bullwhip on his hip, ignoring Jonesy, but absolutely aware of where he was every second. This town had its own laws, so the bar was filled with a blue haze of smoke—

most of it legal. Flicking some credits at the jukebox, it read from Chad's list of favorites and played *Mama Told Me Not To Come* by Three Dog Night.

He turned on the N-hanced charm, making fast friends, proposing sucker bets to win free drinks, and playing 3-D VR pool with the moon-gravity settings. The balls careened around a six-foot sphere positioned three feet off the floor. There were six exit holes, but since it was virtual, players could insert their cue anywhere in the side of the sphere. Once the balls stopped moving, players could rotate the sphere in order to shoot from any comfortable position.

Since the balls weren't on a flat surface, they traveled in an arc rather than a straight line. That, along with the rounded sides, complicated the game immensely. After hitting the cue ball, it took a while for the rest of the balls to come to a stop, suspended in space, rather than on the sides of the sphere.

With N-hanced working for him, Chad ran the sphere every time. But he finessed it, making it a spectacle instead of humiliating his opponents, winning over everyone in the place—except Jonesy. He gave special attention to Jonesy's girlfriend, Sara, and repeatedly brushed a little too close to Jonesy. He would hit the cue ball and tell a joke while engaging somebody in one of the sucker bets, then tell another joke and subtly invade Jonesy's personal space—often.

"Hey, how about this one? OK, now this takes place a few years ago, you know, before the oCar. This guy's in his 40s, and he's doing okay in his business. So he buys a brand new BMW, and he's out on the interstate for a nice evening drive. The top is down, the breeze is blowing through what's left of his hair, and he decides to open 'er up. The speedometer climbs over 100, and he sees flashing red lights behind him. He gets nervous, but then he starts thinking, 'Hey, there's no way they can catch a BMW,' so he jams his foot down on the accelerator. Now he's going 110, 120, 130. Yee-haw!"

His rapt audience shouted back, "Yee-haw!" Jonesy rolled his eyes, but Chad could tell he hung on every word.

"But the red lights stay close behind him. He thinks, 'Oh, man. What the hell am I doing?' and he pulls over.

"The state trooper comes up to his car and takes the guy's license without a word. Finally he says, 'You know, it's been a long day. This is the end of my shift, and it's Friday. I don't feel like doing a whole bunch of paperwork. So if you can give me a good excuse for the way you were driving—something I haven't heard before—I'll let you go.'

"The guy thinks for a second and says, 'Uh… last week my wife ran off with a state trooper, and I was afraid you were chasing me down to give her back.'

"The trooper peels off his sunglasses and says, 'Have a nice weekend.'"

The place erupted in roars of laugher and a few squeals of delight. A little curl crept onto the corners of Jonesy's mouth and disappeared. Chad gave a hidden wink to Sara. Today he was going to take her away from Jonesy. *Sara Smile* by Hall and Oates came on the jukebox. She went dreamy-eyed. It wouldn't be long now.

The balls still bounced around the sphere from the previous shot, so Chad strode up to Jonesy. "Hey, Buddy, I'll bet you I can cover up a drink with a hat, and I can drink it without picking up the hat."

"Fuck off."

"Aw, don't be like that. Everybody else is having a good time. Right, y'all?" Chad turned with a broad sweep of his arms, barely missing Jonesy's face.

"Yeah! Come on Jonesy. Do it."

Jonesy fixed Chad with a wilting stare. "OK, asshole. But we're using my hat."

"Sure." Chad snatched the hat from Jonesy's head, ramping up his irritation. "OK now, if I do it, you gotta pay for the drink. If I don't, I pay, and *you* get the drink. Deal?" Chad extended his hand.

Jonesy ignored the hand and signaled the bartender. The bartender looked at Chad and said, "What'll it be?"

Chad dropped his hand. "How about Glenlivet?"

Jonesy squinted, "Fuck you. That's expensive shit."

"I lose, it's yours. Pretty tasty stuff." Chad smacked his lips.

Jonesy licked his own lips and nodded. The bartender poured, and Chad started to put Jonesy's hat on it.

"Wait a minute, fucker. Let me see that hat." Jonesy gragged it and looked it over inside and out. Glaring at Chad he covered the shot glass.

"OK. Ready?" Chad stuck his head under the bar and made outrageous slurping noises. Emerging, he wiped his mouth and finished with a satisfied, "Ahhhh."

Jonesy picked up the hat. The golden scotch still in the glass, Chad picked it up and downed it.

"What the fuck?"

"Hey, I didn't touch the hat, you did."

Jonesy steamed, but his buddies slapped him on the back, congratulating him for being taken by their new friend. He worked his jaw and balled up his fists.

Chad said, "That's OK, Buddy. Let me buy you one for being such a good sport." He turned to the bartender. "Glenlivet for my friend." He slapped Jonesy on the arm. Jonesy shook off the touch.

Chad turned back to the pool sphere. "Two ball from the top hole, three from over here." He aimed and whacked the cue. Balls whirled madly. Twenty seconds later the two ball flew out the top and burst into a shower of sparks. Ten seconds later the three ball spun out the side with a pop and a puff of smoke. Everybody cheered except Jonesy, who glowered into his drink.

Projecting an oMe2 for the crowd, Chad reached into his pocket and handed Sara his bike key. He VR-ed the image of his bike to her along with a vid of how to start it. "Act like you're going to the restroom, then go out the side door. Take the chain from my saddlebag and lock Jonesy's bike wheel. Then fire up my bike and sit on the back. I'll be out in a minute."

She ambled down the hall.

Chad sauntered back to Jonesy and handed him the pool cue. Jonesy scowled at the cue. Realizing he was being made a servant, he threw it across the room.

"Say, Bud. Seeing's how we're such good friends and all, lemme make you another bet. Those are some pretty nice leather pants you got on there."

Jonesy's frown nearly split his face in two.

"Probably cost you, what, two- three-hundred cs? I'll bet you twenty I can stack a deck of cards on your leg and cut 'em in half with this bull whip and not even touch the pants." Chad slapped the bar, transferring twenty to the bartender.

Everybody hooted, "Do it, Jonesy. Do it."

Jonesy hissed. "My cards, asshole!"

"No problem."

Jonesy signaled and the bartender brought a new deck. Jonesy unwrapped them, took the cards out of the box, and set them on his leg. He struggled to keep them from sliding off each other.

Chad took the whip from his belt and waved everyone back. "Don't want to hurt anybody. Now I need complete silence." The jukebox went dead. Chad whirled the whip around his head, and everybody shuffled back outside a ten-foot circle, leaving just he and Jonesy inside. He made a few practice swings, squinting in an unnecessary display of concentration. With N, he could have been blindfolded and cut to any card in the deck.

"Whack, Whack," went the whip. Little bits of dust popped off the tip and sparkled in a beam from the overhead light. Then he paused, squinting, studying, measuring. Even the refrigerators fell silent.

Like a fly fisherman, he drew back slowly, once, twice. With a final powerful jerk, the whip snaked back over his shoulder. As he brought his arm forward, the leather hissed past his ear, straight for Jonesy. The tip came down one inch on the far side of the deck with a "Ka-Whack!" A fountain of half cards exploded in all directions.

Everyone cheered, their racket drowning out Jonesy's scream of pain. When the cards settled, his pants were split wide open with a big bloody welt down the center. The crowd gasped.

Chad said, "Wow, man. Sorry. I guess you win."

With the slow realization he'd been had, a look of homicidal fury emerged from the pain on Jonesy's face.

Chad was out the door in three seconds and on the road with Sara five seconds later. "Yee-haw!"

*   *   *

All the way back to Lansing, Sara held onto Chad, her head against his back in a loving clutch. Once she reached into his crotch. Chad gently repositioned the hand around his waist. "Not now, baby. Gotta watch the road."

As they crossed Bishop Highway, he noticed smoke rising from one of the houses off to the east. He rode closer, and as they passed a row of trees, he saw flames through the windows. Pulling to a stop, a tag showed five-year-old Andrew Bellows inside alone. Using N-hanced vision, Chad dialed infrared sensitivity and light frequencies until he saw the boy's location.

A small crowd gathered. A lady called out, "I commed the fire department." Chad checked their ETA. Five minutes. Too long. He had to move now.

He swung off the bike and turned to Sara. "Listen, there's a kid in there. I'm gonna see if I can get him out. You stay here. If it blows, you don't want to be any closer than this." She held onto his arm. A pleading look in her eyes begged him not to go. He nodded to say it would be OK and pulled away from her.

When Chad was a kid, he wanted to be a fireman. As a teenager he studied fires and wrote reports on firefighting for school. Today he had N. He knew everything about fires. He turned to the crowd. "Everybody get back! Back to the road! Do it! It's gonna blow in three minutes!" They did as they were told, scurrying wide-eyed.

Chad sprinted around the outside of the house, studying the doors, the windows, and the fire. He could hear Andrew crying, "Ow," and see his outline as he touched the hot doorknob over and over. And then, "Help me, Mommy," followed by coughing. He knew the living room outside the boy's room would explode into flashover if the kid got the door open. He'd be killed instantly.

Standing outside the bedroom window, Chad saw the glass was Safety/Safety; it would break without cutting. He shattered it with his elbow and popped the latch. He shouted, but the boy couldn't tell where the sound was coming from above the roar. "Mommy?" he called and coughed.

Chad chinned himself on the sill, climbing up until he came down into the room on his hands. The smoke wasn't as bad as he expected. The main fire in the living room sucked air out of the bedroom instead of pushing much smoke in. Chad dashed over to the boy and put his hand on the small shoulder. Andrew jumped and turned toward Chad. The boy's face was a mask of fear, like one of the kids in Chad's firefighter game. Chad was a high-scorer and dreamed about the rescue. Now he picked up the boy and went out the way he had in his dream—through the door into the living room. The exact wrong move.

A blast of air sucked Chad and the boy into the room. Now the hot gases had the oxygen they needed. They exploded in a fireball, blowing Chad and the boy backwards, knocking them flat. The blast took out the side of the house with a low-pitched *Ka-Whoomp!* Their clothes erupted in flames. When they inhaled to scream, fire poured down their throats. They were dead in seconds.

Outside, pieces of wood, glass and siding flew everywhere. Some of the smaller fragments rained down on Sara. She flinched, but she couldn't take her eyes off the house. Standing there in shock, she didn't hear the approaching sirens until a fireman tapped her on the shoulder. She startled, and then burst into a fit of uncontrollable sobbing.

CHAPTER 19

This time both Rob and Charlie got the alarm that Chad Rodriguez was dead. And so did the members of Corridor CyberDynamics' board of directors. One of the stipulations the investors made in yesterday's agreement was that they be notified immediately about any company news which might affect their investment. Within ten minutes, they called for an emergency meeting. All calendars placed it at 2:00—45 minutes away.

Charlie panicked for what seemed like the hundredth time today. *Two alphas dead. That can-not be a coincidence. And why did Chad's watchdog PA fail? And that means the rest of us are in danger.* As if on cue, he got a comm from Rob. Charlie flicked open the line and Rob stood in the room with him.

"Charlie, are you OK?" Rob put his hand on Charlie's shoulder, the concern on his face clearly personal.

Charlie patted Rob's hand. "Physically, yeah. But not happy at all."

"So what's going on? Two of our alphas dead in less than twenty-four hours?"

"Rob, we're working as fast as we possibly can. I just don't know."

"And what about your own safety?"

"Least of my concerns."

"Well, not mine! It sounds to me as if N-hanced has been compromised in some way. I think we'd better shut it down until you can figure out what's going on."

Of course he's right. But if I shut it down, I won't have the smarts to solve it. And the idea of getting sick again so soon made him... sick. "Look, just a few minutes ago I found a clue. It's a line of code which might let an outsider insert a command. We changed it back so the switch is now in the off position. I feel terrible we didn't find it a couple minutes earlier. I'm betting Chad would still be alive. We're working on our second pass at the security layer to see how the code could have been inserted in the first place. But I think we can add more safety if we shut off Net access to the other testers so no commands can come in from the outside—at least until we find the access point. The alphas will still be able to use the data stored on the servers, and they'll be able to use the Net on their own, the old-fashioned way. They just won't be able to integrate it through us."

"How do you know there isn't a death command floating around on the servers just waiting for some predetermined time?"

Yeah. How? "We have all kinds of safety measures to prevent that. I don't think—"

"But that's what the security layer is for, isn't it? And it failed."

"Right. But whoever did this won't have a way in without the Net, and since we fixed it, that line of code won't let them interrupt the process." Charlie left out the fact that an opening in the security layer might allow the culprit to reset the switch, but he was pretty sure it couldn't happen with the Net down. "Rob, let's contact the alphas, tell them we've made some changes and give them two options. They can disconnect from the servers or we can leave them connected and shut down the Net access."

"I don't know. I thought continuing was risky after we lost Bostwick yesterday. But now I think we need to stop. This whole thing's got me spooked."

"Me, too. But we'll let them decide. We'll remind them they're being recorded. We'll make it clear if they elect to stay connected, anything happens is their responsibility."

Rob reared back and frowned. "Charlie, is this you I'm talking to? You sound like one of our goddamned lawyers. What about doing what's right? I'd feel terrible if anybody else were hurt and we could have prevented it." He stopped talking and seemed to be thinking.

Charlie could feel the clock ticking. He wanted to get back and see what else he could find before the board meeting.

Finally Rob said, "I'll tell you what. We'll let them decide, but I want you to lay it out for them honestly. Be clear about the dangers, and be specific about the things we don't know—especially that there could be some stush on the servers."

"That's more than fair, Rob. Thank—"

"It's more like irresponsible. But I'm going to trust because you're N-hanced, you have a point of view I couldn't have. I'm also hoping it has an equal amount of wisdom attached."

Charlie thought, *He's right. It is irresponsible. What am I doing?* But he felt compelled to move forward. *Is N really that addictive?* He reached over and dialed down the doubts. As soon as he did it, he doubted he should have and had to give the knob another tweak.

Charlie immediately contacted the remaining testers and explained the situation, while Rob solemnly observed in full view of everyone. The chorus was thunderous. "Leave N on!" All of them were in the middle of critical projects they couldn't finish without N.

So there it was. But Charlie couldn't help but wonder, *Are they as addicted as I am?* He shuddered at the thought of having to go through what he was beginning to think of as N withdrawal. But he also felt queasy about what he had just done, and what he was afraid might be coming.

As soon as Charlie reconnected with his PAs he asked the obvious. "Did you find any opening in the security?"

"No."

Shit! How did this guy get in? "All right, then. Keep going. I need to look at Chad's data stream." The purr of their not-so-sweet nothings continued. The big question on his mind was, *How could Chad's extra PA have failed to stop him from the fire? Maybe the problem really is with Orchard's VR system. But if that's the case and PAs can't help... Well, the switch is off now, and with N disconnected from the Net, nobody can send any commands in—I hope.*

There were a couple other things eating away at Charlie about Chad's death. Charlie felt as if he had bonded with him, so it was a personal loss. As testers went, Chad was different. Once he was N-hanced, he went a little wild. Charlie decided to keep him on because he wasn't destructive, and it was interesting to see what less responsible people might do with N. With the explosion at the burning house, Charlie wasn't so sure he could say Chad wasn't destructive any more. And that didn't even take into account the little boy. The thought gave Charlie another stab of guilt.

Studying Chad's data stream yielded no more clues than Wilford Bostwick's had. Charlie wanted to compare the streams from both men, but his time ran out. He got the alarm reminding him it was almost 1:45 and time to meet Rob in the conference room. He blew out a frustrated "Fffff."

"OK, guys, keep at it." *So how am I going to tell the board some old code I used thirty years ago magically inserted itself into our preeminent app while my memory was erased? Yeah, that'll go over big.* He took another deep breath, let it out and started down the hall.

CHAPTER 20

Charlie and Rob dragged themselves into the boardroom fifteen minutes early and went over their strategy. Charlie sat, and Rob paced and talked. "OK, what I want to do is lay it out for the board the same way we did for the testers. I'll explain the testers themselves unanimously and enthusiastically chose to continue. There'll probably be a vote about whether the project should be put on hold. Since you can read people's intentions, I want you to let me know where the vote is heading as their attitudes change during the meeting."

"Got it."

"I'm going to give them the option to sell their shares back to us at a reduced price that will cover the cost of the project up to this point—which I'm afraid is substantial. It'll mean a considerable loss, but it'll prevent a total loss down the road. We can expect some complaint from yesterday's newcomers, but they're big boys. They'll know it's a good offer, under the circumstances."

Charlie shifted in his seat. He wanted to argue about buying back shares. Depending on how many investors pulled out, it could severely cripple or even end the project. But his PAs told him making it easy for the investors to back out would likely trigger their gambler's instinct. They would let their money ride hoping to recover their losses, so he gave in. "OK. I— I guess that makes sense."

Charlie appreciated Rob's business ethics. It seemed he often risked everything in order to stay honest. It had the effect of making people want to work with CCD all the more. The thought made Charlie uncomfortable with his own recent dishonesty, and that it might come back to hurt Rob's reputation. *Jeez, was it only yesterday I convinced myself I could lie to Jeff? Once you start, it doesn't take long to fool yourself into believing anything. Where is it all coming from? Is it really because I believe N will make the world a better place? Or because I've been on this quest for more than twenty years and can't let go now. How is that any different from the investors who can't cut their losses? Except if I'm wrong,* lives *are on the line. I thought N would make people more ethical, not less.* But there was no more time to dwell on that now. They had a meeting to run—*and more lies to tell?*

*   *   *

At exactly 2:00 PM the fifteen investors arrived, filling in their designated seats around the boardroom table—nine new shareholders from yesterday, and six who had joined over the previous two years. Every VR attendee was a Primary. Even though an oMe2 is a legal representative, this meeting was apparently too important for a Secondary.

Rob sat at the head of the table and Charlie to his right. Charlie PC-ed Rob that the odds of a shut down were only thirty percent. But he sensed a strange vibe he couldn't put his finger on—and when using N, that was unusual.

Rob began. "Ladies and gentlemen, I know you're all very busy, so I'll get right to it." He continued with a tight summary of the situation. Then he made the offer to buy back their shares. There was some grumbling, but Charlie's PAs had predicted correctly. They all turned it down, if not joyfully. Then Rob let Charlie take the floor.

Charlie filled them in on his discovery that at the time of their deaths, both alphas were reliving a dream. "At this point we think the problem may lie with Orchard's VR, not N-hanced."

Recent investor, Bertrand Wilson from Worldwide Properties based in London, England, raised a finger and growled like Churchill. "But no one has ever reported any such accidents with VR before. Why would your testers be the first cases ever?"

"There were many accidents early in VR history. But it's true there haven't been any in seven years. That being said, my team is trying to find out if there's a connection. We discovered an unexplained line in our code. I deactivated it even though there's no proof it had anything to do with the deaths. We're not done checking for weaknesses in our security layer." Charlie didn't mention the rogue code matched a mistake he used to make years ago. "At this point it doesn't look like our program."

Jim Higgins leaned in. "You think the system was hacked?" Jim was CEO of Walsh Industries International based in Chicago. WII signed on during the first round of private offerings two years ago.

"We were still working on that at the time this meeting was called."

Bertrand jumped in. "That does not answer Jim's bloody question. If it's not your code, then the system has been hacked. Right?"

That would be right if I knew for sure I didn't do it as part of some amnesiatic security test. "Not necessarily." As soon as he said it, he wished he hadn't. There was only one other option.

Bertrand bellowed. "Then, it might be an *inside* job?"

"I'm really not comfortable making either conclusion right now. We need more time to examine—"

Bertrand cut him off. "I move we put the project on hold pending a full investigation. Let's have a vote. All in favor—"

"Point of order, Mr. Wilson" Rob stepped in. "I am the chairman of the board. It is my job to call for votes, and only after discussion has been closed." Charlie relayed to Rob that the chance of a shut down was now near fifty-fifty. But something still felt askew. It was as if some of them were acting out a scene from a play.

Bertrand shifted in his chair. Eyes tightening, he was clearly not used to being outranked.

Jim held up a calming hand to Bertrand and looked at Rob. "If I could add something here, please?"

"The chair recognizes Mr. Higgins."

"I can see how Mr. Noble is trying to get to the bottom of this, and we all want the project to move forward as quickly as possible. As he said, there still isn't any proof this is more than a tragic coincidence. We've seen stranger things in our own companies. I say let the project continue with the safety measures he's taken." He paused. "That's all."

Bertrand snapped, "Do your job, Mr. Chairman."

Rob said, "Is there any other discussion?"

"Christ, man!" Bertrand slammed his palm on the table. Then he jerked his head along with everyone else, as if being called by an unseen voice.

Charlie looked to the right and flicked the urgent comm into view. Since this was a "Do not disturb" meeting, there was no way the news was going to be good.

CHAPTER 21

"Hey, boss. How was lunch?"

Gary Billings' eyes twinkled. "Great, Ginny. Have you ever been to that gourmet restaurant down the street where they have those amazing hamburgers?"

"I don't know. I really can't afford anything gourmet with what you pay me. What's it called?"

"Oh, I forget. But it's got these two yellow rainbows coming from the ground, up through the roof and back down again."

"Yellow rainbows...? Are you... are you talking about McDonald's?"

"Yeah, that's it."

She laughed. "Gourmet, huh? OK, you got me again." She raised her hands in surrender.

Gary spun around and shot her with his pointed fingers. "Pow, pow, pow." His fifteen-person company, Billings Laboratories, had been successful enough in the past, but once he began testing N-hanced, he made a patentable discovery nearly every week. He loved N.

Ginny said, "You seem in an unusually good mood today. What's up?"

"Oh, I'm back to using N-hanced fulltime."

"N-hanced. That's the program *supposed* to make you smarter?" There was a teasing sarcasm in her voice.

"Uh, yeah. Can't you tell?"

"No." She rolled her eyes. "Say, when's it coming out for the general public?"

"They don't know yet. We're only in the alpha phase. Might not go public for a year."

"You said you're back using it full time?"

"Yeah, since I stopped going out with Tina."

"Awww. What happened?"

"She said I was too smug when I used N. Do you think I'm smug?" He stuck out his tongue.

"Goofy, yeah. But I've never seen smug."

"How about now?" He raised his chin arrogantly.

"Oh, yeah, now *that's* smug."

Gary reared back. "Hey, I'm your boss. I could fire you."

"No you can't. You need me."

"Oh, yeah? I could replace you tomorrow with an android."

Ginny pretended boredom. "What are you talking about? I am an android."

"Really? I thought you were a robot. Anyway, Tina couldn't stand me when I was using N, and I couldn't stand her when I wasn't. What's a guy to do?"

"You might try going out with an android." She winked.

"Nothing personal, but I'm not quite there yet."

"Oh, don't worry about my feelings. Nothing you say can affect me, affect me, affect me, affect me—" She hit the side of her head and crossed her eyes. "Urrrhhhh! Ah. That's better."

"OK, enough play. I've got work to do. Check on me in about an hour in case I get too wrapped up."

"Gotcha."

*　　*　　*

Gary began work on a nano-chemical app inspired by a sideshow act. He wanted to use Ts to protect people—especially children—from poisonings, both accidental and intentional. Even now there were more than a million cases a year in the oUS alone.

When he was a kid Gary's family went to the Ionia Free Fair every year. The sideshow always fascinated him, with its large, brightly colored illustrations of the Human Skeleton, the Fat Lady, Rubber-Skinned Boy, the Sword Swallower, the Fire-Eater, the Tattooed Man, Seal Boy, Magico The Magician and Whip Boy. Gary went to the show every year, even though he thought some of it was a gyp; some of the performers played two characters, and you had to pay extra to see a few of them. But he liked it better than the rides—*and* because it lasted forty minutes and cost the same as a ride. Frugal and fascinating.

The act which changed his life was The Fire-Eater, who also happened to be The Tattooed Man. This was back in the days when only veterans had tattoos. His head was shaved clean, and he had scary pictures all across his face and scalp. After blasting flames out of his mouth for a couple minutes, he moved on to a grand finale where he drank acid. Making a big demonstration of putting on rubber gloves and showing a beaker of sulphuric acid, he explained how powerful it was, and how it could eat people's faces right off, "Just like Freddie Krueger in *Nightmare on Elm Street*." The girls squealed, and the boys said, "cool!" But Gary knew Freddie was burned in a fire.

The guy put a few drops of acid on a big piece of white paper turning it black. Smoke billowed up. "Burned clean through," he'd say holding it high in the air, turning left, then right, making sure everyone could see the holes.

"Can I get a volunteer?" Nobody wanted to go near the stage. He walked down from the stage saying, "Please, it can be anybody. Anybody at all." But he already had his eyes on some innocent boy. As he got up to his victim, he would say, "Oh, thank you, sir. How nice of you to help out." He would lead his patsy up the stairs while the boy eyeballed his friends for help. "Let's have a big round of applause for this brave young man."

Being careful his ward didn't dash off, he continued, "So, young man, what's your name?" and before the boy could answer he'd say, "Good! And where do you live?" And again he'd cut the boy off. "Wonderful! Not much of a talker, are you?" He'd roll his eyes, the audience laughing the whole time.

"Now I want you to watch closely to prove to everyone this is not a trick." He walked back to a fringe-covered stand, poured some of the liquid into a white dish, pick up the dish and carry it to the front of the stage. Then he tripped, bowl first, toward the boy. Everyone gasped, only to have a bowl full of confetti rain down over the boy and into the audience. Everyone erupted with laughter and applause.

Next, he held out a thin beaker full of white crystals. "In this container we have common household sugar. Would you like to taste some to prove it?" He'd held it out to the boy who shook his head. The man rolled his eyes again. "Anyone else? … No? All right, you'll just have to take my word for it. Now watch as my assistant and I induce an amazing chemical reaction." He poured acid into the beaker and mixed it up with a glass stick. He gave the boy a huge plastic baseball bat. "Wave the magic wand over the beaker, and say the magic word." The audience laughed again.

The boy always looked confused.

"What, you don't know the magic word?" He'd snatched the bat and scanned the audience. "Can I get another volunteer?" In a few seconds the beaker made an evil hiss, and a black, snake-like column of carbon would squeeze out the top. After the steam dissipated, he presented the snake to the boy. "Ladies and Gentlemen, let's have a big round of applause for…" he would turn to the boy and ask his name and turn back to the audience and finally say, "Billy!" And of course everyone clapped wildly as the dazed and embarrassed boy descended the stairs to rejoin his friends, who slapped him on the shoulder and shook his hand and examined the snake.

Finally The Fire-Eater poured acid into a clear wine glass, swirled it dramatically and drink. He smacked his lips and closed his eyes as if it were the most delicious wine imaginable. Then expressions of pain filled his face.

He held his stomach, and his eyes grew big around. He rolled his head back, opened his mouth and belched a huge blast of smoke and fire. He looked back at the crowd, threw out his arms and yelled, "Tah-dah!"

The audience shouted and applauded. "Hurray!"

"Thank you. Thank you very much." He bowed deeply. "Don't any of you try this at home. I'm what you call a professional. OK? All right, then. Please move along to the next stage where you will meet the Amazing Alligator-Skinned Boy!"

*   *   *

Afterward Gary asked his mother how the man could drink acid. She said he probably coated his mouth and stomach with a chemical that protected him. It was the drama of the act that got Gary interested in chemistry. He was nine when his parents gave him a Mr. Wizard chemistry set for Christmas.

It stuck with Gary, that idea of using a coating with a chemical for protection. Now his plan was to write an app for T which would sense dangerous chemicals entering the mouth, encapsulate the molecules and neutralize them before they could cause harm.

Gary worked in his Interface Space with a T chemistry template. Once it worked in the model, he placed a batch in a Petri dish. He selected a super-energized solution of sulfuric acid mixed with hydrogen peroxide known as Piranha solution, named for its ability to devour flesh. Smiling as he remembered his childhood dream of being able to drink acid, he imagined himself in front of the crowd at the fair. He removed the stopper. In his mind he poured the solution into a wine glass and swirled it, looking at its "legs." Then in Real he drank sixteen ounces straight out of the beaker.

Feeling the burn, he dialed it down inside N-hanced. He smiled and closed his eyes to show the audience how delicious it was. As the solution reached his stomach, it bubbled, releasing oxygen, expanding his stomach violently. He dialed down the pain again, lay on the floor and belched. By now his esophagus had collapsed and no more gas could escape. His stomach grew large as a basketball. Although he felt no pain, he pretended it hurt and opened his eyes wide for the audience. His stomach exploded. The Piranha had eaten a small hole in his aorta, and a thin stream of blood shot across the lab in a beautiful, red pulsing arc. The solution reached his spine, paralyzing him. As the hole in the aorta enlarged, the blood oozed. He imagined blowing the fireball out of his mouth and bowing as the audience applauded wildly. *Thank you. Thank you very much*, he thought he said, but he made no sound at all. *Now don't any of you try this at home. I'm what you call a professional. OK? All right, then. Please move on to the next stage where you will meet the Amazing Alligator-Skinned Boy!*

Ten minutes later Ginny came in to remind Gary about his appointment. She found herself staring into the room below through a smoking, ten-inch hole, which had burned through his body—and the wooden floor.

CHAPTER 22

Charlie, Rob and most of the board members sat at the boardroom table, faces slack, stunned by the news of Gary Billings' death. There was no longer any question N-hanced was somehow responsible for killing its users. It only took a minute for the board to vote. It was unanimous. N-hanced was now on hold pending a full investigation.

Again Rob offered to buy back their shares, and again all investors declined.

Jim Higgins spoke sympathetically. "Mr. Noble, I want you to know I believe in your product and its potential to become a profit-maker." Heads nodded. "From the response I see in this room, I think I can speak for all of us when I say we want you to find out what's wrong and fix it. Bring in outsiders if you have to. Run it down like your life depended on it—because, professionally, it just may."

"I understand." Charlie held his face steady. *Threatened twice in twenty-four hours. How did things get so stushy?* "I can't thank you enough for your vote of support. I can assure you this is of utmost importance to me." He said it all with proper deference—body language and eye contact individualized for each attendee. Most of them seemed to relax. Charlie wished he could say the same for himself. Inside he was jelly.

Rob said, "Anything else before we adjourn?"

Jim raised an index finger. "I assume you're contacting the families with condolences and appropriate support?"

"I started a doc for Mr. Bostwick's family." Rob managed a wan smile.

"I don't mean to seem callous, but please have your attorneys check it over carefully so nothing can be interpreted as an admission of wrongdoing."

"If we're responsible, I'll do right by their families."

"That's fine." Jim nodded. "But don't say so in public until we know where the responsibility lies. In fact, I'd like to preview your proposed statements."

Bertrand grumbled, "I move that each of us approve Rob's statements—any one of us having veto power."

Rob lowered his head. "I will *not* have my ethics dictated by committee."

Jim smiled warmly. "We're not trying to dictate your ethics. We only want to approve your public statements. That doesn't seem unreasonable considering what we have at stake."

Bertrand scowled. "Thanks for the sugar, Jim, but Rob only gets one vote on this board. If we decide we have control over his statements, he has to comply. Either that or we can find a new president—or CEO."

Jesus. Charlie almost winced.

Rob worked his jaw muscles. He spoke through clenched teeth. "Fine. Any other discussion?"

No answer.

"All in favor?"

All but Rob said, "Aye!" Charlie had no vote.

"Opposed?" Rob paused, then hissed, "Abstained. Motion passed."

Jim said, "I'll put you in touch with my lawyers. They handle this kind of thing a bit too frequently, I'm afraid. They'll have some boilerplates to get you started."

"Thank you," Rob said flatly. Then in quick succession, "Anything else? No? Meeting adjourned."

They all signed off leaving Charlie and Rob looking very small at the end of the very large table.

Charlie still felt some of the board members had been acting. *Why couldn't I read them?* The meeting had the feel of a card table full of professional bluffers, one expression on their faces and a subtly different story told by their body language. He put the thought aside. Right now he had bigger worries.

Charlie turned to Rob and said dismally, "That went well."

Rob seemed to waken. He let out a sigh and put his hand on Charlie's shoulder. "Son, I don't think you could have asked for a better outcome. Every one of them chose to stay with us. They believe in you. They're giving you a chance to get N up and running again. This could be a blessing. What if we had gone public and then found out there was a problem? Thousands of people could have been killed. No, this is far better."

Charlie nodded and shuffled back to his office.

They believe in you. That stuck in Charlie's head. *Jesus, if only I believed in me.* He felt almost as bad as he had after losing Barbara. At least he might be able to do something about this. If only his integrity came up to the level of their trust.

Charlie sent a message to the remaining testers. They already knew about Gary Billings and were winding down their N-dependent projects. Over the next hour they all terminated their connections.

Charlie went to Rob's office. *This is going to be tricky.* He tapped on the doorjamb.

Rob looked up. "Come in, son."

Charlie stepped in and closed the door quietly. "I have to ask a favor." He sat.

"Sure, what is it?"

"I want to keep using N-hanced."

Rob stared at him for a long moment. Then slowly and quietly he said, "Charlie, it's out of the question."

"But, sir—"

"No, son. We've seen N kill three people in just two days. You're not going to be the fourth. No... Absolutely not." His resolve gathered strength with each word.

"Please, Rob, hear me out."

Rob looked at him doubtfully. "OK, I'll give you that courtesy. But my mind is made up. I'm not having any more blood on my hands. I am *not* losing you."

Even though Rob tried to sound tough, Charlie could see the wetness in his eyes. *This is going to be harder than I thought. How do I begin?*

Charlie leaned in, face set with all the sincerity he could pull out of N. "The reason I'm pushing so hard is right now everything points to this being my fault. If it comes to prosecution, I'll have nothing more to say than, 'Gee, it looks like I did it. Not only that, but my PAs told me so.' "

Rob's lips stayed tight, his gaze steady.

Charlie pressed on. "Without N, it would take me ten years just to destush the code. I need my eight PAs, and I need N to coordinate it all. Once I find out who did this, we'll be able to move the program back into testing. But only if I'm N-hanced."

Rob spread his hands. "So how does that make you any safer?"

"Let me work here where I'm away from danger. Heck, I don't even have a virtual stapler in my office. What am I going to do, jump into the air and fall on my face?" Charlie was applying all the persuasion N could muster.

He could see Rob's resolve weakening. He hoped Rob couldn't see Charlie wasn't so sure about his own safety.

Rob clicked his tongue. "I'll tell you what. I'll let you try as long as someone is with you at all times. How about Milo? But I don't want him using N-hanced or doing any programming. He'll be there strictly to keep you from hurting yourself."

"Perfect!" Charlie nodded enthusiastically, getting up from the chair.

"That's not all. I want you to shut off N before going home."

That's not gonna be so easy. "Um—"

"No! Those are the only conditions under which I'll let you move ahead. It's *not* negotiable."

Maybe I can act as if... No. Good grief. How desperate can I be? I must be an N addict—and a loser. "Deal," is what Charlie said, trying to sound happy about it.

"All right then. Get Milo over here, and get started. But don't play games with me on this. You stick with the rules."

"No problem." Charlie headed for the door. "You won't be sorry, boss."

"I already am."

Looking back over his shoulder, Charlie saw the concern in Rob's eyes. *What a great guy. I've got to do right by him. But how can I do it without getting myself killed?* He ran down the hall—adrenalized with fear and excitement.

CHAPTER 23

Charlie wheeled another chair into his office for Milo. The room appeared in VR as the high-ceilinged warehouse module hanger. Milo stared open-mouthed into the huge room past the Real wall where Charlie's eight PAs flipped through modules like an old-time movie on high speed, leaving streaking ghost images of themselves. "Wow! I like what you've done with the place."

"Listen—" Charlie put his hand on Milo's shoulder to get his attention. "—you're here to watch my back. It'll be boring. You can't do anything but watch to make sure I don't leave my chair, not even listen to music. If you need coffee, grab it now, because you can't leave me alone for a minute. OK?"

"No problem. What's this all about? Does it have something to do with the suicides?"

"What the Hell—? I mean... yeah. Sorry. I'm just so frustrating. I forgot you've been out of the loop."

"I understand. So what do you think is causing it?"

"Well, first we found some antique code in the program. It's the old 'User Abort ON' line."

Milo frowned. "I'm... not familiar with that one."

"And that reminds me. I want to check that line right now."

Charlie drew a shared IS cube. Scrolling to the line of code, he shouted, "Whaaaat?!" His eyes bugged out.

"What is it, man?"

Charlie pointed. "It's set back to ON! We turned it OFF after Chad died. This is bad. Very, very bad." Charlie set it back to OFF and pressed his fingertips into his temples. *Why bother? This guy'll turn it on again.*

Milo said, "So... why is it there in the first place?"

"It shouldn't be. Nobody uses that code any more—not even me."

"Just take it out."

"I can't without a major rewrite. This guy's got us locked in, at least for now."

"So what does it do?"

"In the old days, we used it while testing a project. It lets the developer stop a process. But even if we accidentally included it, when we compacted the code, that bit would have been set to OFF. So it not only had to be inserted manually and intentionally, but *after* compacting. And I think it was done to make me look guilty."

"Guilty?"

"It's a programming error I used to make over twenty-five years ago. I would turn it on and forget about it. It's as if somebody looked at my old work and put it in to point the finger at me. Hell, it makes *me* suspect me."

Milo nodded slowly. "Jesus."

"Yeah. I've been calling on Him a lot lately myself."

"OK. So... all you want me to do is watch you? That's it?"

"That's it."

Milo scoffed. "Easy."

*   *   *

For the next hour and a half Charlie and his PAs finished examining the security layer on the last of the modules without discovering any problems. "Milo?"

Milo jumped. "Yeah. Uh... sorry. Daydreaming." He wiggled his fingers next to his head.

"That can be dangerous around here. Anyway, we didn't find anything."

"But that's impossible. I mean, in order to take advantage of that code, somebody needs a way in, right?"

"Absolutely."

"Maybe your security system isn't robust enough."

Charlie nodded. "That's what it looks like. I don't know what else to do. Any suggestions? We're out of ideas."

"What about bringing in an outsider like one of your investors suggested? Maybe a hacker?"

Charlie frowned. "How do we keep them from running off with the program?"

"Get one with a good rep."

"Got somebody in mind?"

"Ssssort of."

Charlie curled his fingers into the 'gimme' sign.

"HackerMeister."

Charlie rotated his head like a dog hearing a silent whistle.

HackerMeister was an enigmatic name which had been in and out of the news for more than a decade. He had broken into government and financial institutions all over the world, starting with the Department of Defense when he was supposedly eleven years old. He had never been prosecuted. Instead, he was often hired as a security consultant for astronomical paychecks. Since he kept his identity secret, the biggest rumor surrounding him was that he wasn't one person at all—but a team of hackers.

Charlie said, "How would we get hold of him. It's not like he's listed anywhere."

"Post a message on HackNet, same as everybody else who hires him."

"I don't know. I need answers now. And how do we filter out the slimeballs?"

Milo spread his hands. "What you got to lose?"

Charlie composed a simple message.

To: HackerMeister,

I'm interested in a security consultation.

Charlie Noble, creator of N-hanced

Corridor CyberDynamics

He held his hand in the pre-Send position, wondering if he was being too desperate. *I already have access to the best traditional experts and it's not enough.* Gritting his teeth, he flicked the message on its way. He sighed. "So, how long you think it'll be before we hear something?"

"Who knows. Could be—"

Charlie raised his hand to silence Milo. A comm labeled <undisclosed caller> made it past his executive PA. He frowned. "That can't be him already." Flicking the line open he said, "Charlie Noble here."

"I know who you are." It was an audio only comm. The voice was low and ominous, and obviously mechanically altered.

"And who are you?" Charlie flicked his fingers sideways toward Milo, opening the audio to him.

"You already know that."

"HackerMeister?"

"Tell me your problem."

"How do I know it's you?"

"It's me."

Charlie glanced at Milo who shrugged.

"Look, anybody could have answered my post. I need to know you're not some punk."

Silence.

Charlie shook his head and waited. Five seconds. Ten seconds. "Are you still th—?"

"Your banking password is G0rg0nz0la. The Os are replaced with zeros."

Shit!

"You also use it for two Net accounts. Not a good idea. What can I do for you." It was a command, not a question.

"Three of my testers have died—"

"I already know that. I won't keep this comm open for more than another sixty seconds. What do you need from me?"

"Uh… There's an opening in the N-hanced security layer. But my expert systems can't find it. Will you have a look?"

"Yes."

"So… you wanna come here?"

A cynical snort whipped their ears. "Absolutely not."

"What will this cost?"

"I think your work is going to change things. I'll do it for free."

"You need a user name and password?"

"Is that a joke?"

"No. Uh… OK then. H-how can I reach you?"

"You can't. I'll get back to you."

"How soon?"

"Don't push it. I'm working for free."

"OK. Sure. Sorry. I…" But Charlie found himself disconnected.

Milo's eyes were big around. "That was spooky."

Charlie sighed. "What'd I just do? I invited the most notorious hacker of all time to come into our system. He could take down the whole system, steal twenty years of my work, and waste billions in investor money. Worse yet, what if he's the one who killed my testers?" He saw his hand shaking and pressed it on his leg to stop it.

Milo sucked air through his teeth. "I don't know what to tell you, Charlie. But they say he's trustworthy, even if his methods are a little unconventional. And he usually charges a bundle."

"That's another thing's got me worried. Why's he doing it for free? "

Milo winced. "He said he likes what you're doing. But after the way he came up with your bank password—" he chuckled. "Sorry. But I don't think you could stop *that* guy anyway. Besides, nobody else is likely to find a way in."

"Yeah. Except whoever broke in in the first place."

Milo nodded slowly. "Right."

PART TWO

CHAPTER 24

There was a knock on Charlie's office door. He jumped. It was a surprise because he always got an alert when anyone came to see him. Pulling his awareness back from the server, he glanced at Milo who shrugged. Charlie knew it was 7:15 PM. "Come in."

The door opened and two men in dark suits and overcoats strode through.

"I'm Special Agent Lott, and this is Special Agent Mortensen. We're from the oBI." Their credentials checked out. "We'd like you to come with us, Mr. Noble."

Rob appeared behind them. "Sorry, Charlie. They made me block your alert."

Stern-faced, Mortensen held up a silencing hand. "You've got some answering to do, Noble. Let's go." He lunged for Charlie.

Lott put a hand on his partner's arm. "We'd like you to come to our office to answer some questions about a death that occurred earlier today at the Grand Canyon."

Oh, God, not now.

"Mr. Reynolds said you'd know the most about what happened."

"Actually, I'm working on it right now. Come in and sit down. I'll be glad to tell you what I know."

"Please, sir. We need you to come to the office."

"I need to stay here. My own life may in danger."

"I understand, but we need to handle this at our office."

Charlie reared back. "Am I a suspect?"

"Really, just some questions."

"Are you arresting me?"

Mortensen squinted at him. "Do we *need* to arrest you?"

If they arrest me, they can hold me for up to forty-eight hours. If I go now, I'll bet I'm out of there in less than an hour. He put on his famous smile. "No problem.

Let's go." N-hanced was already building a profile of their personalities, watching their body language and grabbing everything it could find about them off the Net.

As they passed through his doorway, Charlie remembered his promise to Rob about turning off N-hanced. *Uh-uh. There's no way I'm facing these guys naked. Besides, Rob said to shut it off before going* home. *I'm not going home. Right?* But another little voice argued with him.

Isn't that what addicts do?

Oh, shut up.

He imagined a cartoon angel on one shoulder and a devil on the other. He flicked them away. Flicking was so easy to do with N. *Flick off. Flick you. Get flicked. Go flick yourself.* He smiled, and turned his attention to the agents and to getting control of the situation. He soon found his N-hanced charm didn't work with these men.

CHAPTER 25

Charlie, Rob and the two agents were partway down the hall when a band of men strode around the corner.

Charlie glanced at Rob who shrugged back.

A tall, stocky, confident man with a blond buzz cut led the group. As they got closer Charlie recognized him. The man marched ahead of the other, ignored everyone else, and stuck out his hand to Charlie. "Mr. Noble, I'm Police Chief Will Hosley." He grinned like a politician.

Mortensen hissed, "We were here first."

The chief held up an index finger, still grinning. "And we're got two dead bodies that need to be explained. Questions will to be asked, timelines accounted for." He shook his head. "No, sir, Mr. Noble isn't leaving here unless it's with us." He pointed a thumb over his shoulder indicating the dozen uniformed officers behind him.

Lott stepped up. "Hello, Chief. I'm Agent Tom Lott." They shook hands. "We don't normally investigate homicides, but earlier today a man dove to his death in the Grand Canyon. Since it's a government reservation, his death is a Federal issue. I don't know if your deaths are related to ours, but there's no need for us to get into a jurisdictional—"

A young officer tagged Gorman sprinted down the hall. "Chief. There's a crowd gathering down on the plaza."

The chief turned. "What kind of crowd?"

"Mix of NewsDogs and looky-loos trying to catch a glimpse of the serial killer." He gave a furtive glance in Charlie's direction.

Charlie winced.

"And there're some demonstrators, too."

Chief Hosley seemed amused. "Demonstrators? What are they protesting?"

"Looks like some Luddites and a religious group with posters saying N-hanced is the end of world."

Charlie and Rob glanced at each other.

Hands waved in IS cubes as they searched for vid. People streamed in, filling the area. Strings of oCars choked the streets, dropping off more gawkers. Occupants of other vehicles slowed to see what the fuss was about, then inched on. A dozen protestors lined the southeast edge of the plaza waving VR signs which cycled through "No N" and "End N Now." One displayed moving text that read, "...false prophets, and shall show great signs and wonders. Matt 24:24." Another featured the N-hanced 'N' logo with a slash through it.

Charlie zoomed in to see if the Ken Doll was among them. He wasn't.

The chief pointed to a group along the west side. "What about this group?"

Gorman expanded the image. "Disciples."

Scanning their faces, Charlie saw one he recognized. *Oh, God. It's Matthew.* The group of eight clearly looked to him for instruction. They held aloft signs that scrolled through the slogans "Gimme an N" and "N-hance Me" and "Noble is Messiah." "N-Times Now" and "Charlie Noble = 2nd Coming." Charlie cringed.

The chief eyed agent Lott accusingly. "How the hell did they find out you guys were coming after him?"

Charlie had a pretty good idea. The chief was rumored to have his sights set on a mayoral run.

Lott balked. "We didn't tell anybody. The only one who even knows we're here is our boss."

The Chief glanced at Gorman. "Any trouble yet?"

"Seems reasonably calm so far. But you know...."

Lott turned to Rob. "Is there another way out of here?"

The chief held up a hand. "I have an idea."

Here it comes, Charlie thought.

"I'll bet we can turn this to our advantage and avoid something similar over at your place. Let's go out through the square. I'll talk to them and get them to disperse."

Lott shook his head. "Sounds like trouble."

"Trust me."

Lott frowned.

"Go along with me on this and I won't fight you on jurisdiction." The chief turned. "Captain Thomas, scan the crowd to make sure there are no weapons and nobody with a record. Gorman, keep monitoring the mood of the protestors. Let's try to avoid any confrontations."

Thomas said, "It's already done, sir. No problems, not even among the demonstrators."

Lott turned to Charlie. "You mind going out through the crowd?"

Charlie was working on an idea that would keep him here. He pasted on a smile. "Huh? Uh, no."

The Chief said, "Good. Thomas, you go down and make sure everything's set up, then comm me." He waved him away. "Ouderkirk. Get four officers and clear the lobby. When you're ready, send up an elevator."

When they reached ground floor, they crossed the lobby. Two police officers stood on either side of the invisible curtain. Someone outside shouted, "Look! Here he comes!" A ruckus arose, people pushing and shoving, trying to get a better view. Chief Hosley led the way followed by the two oBI agents flanking Charlie. The police officers on door duty brought up the rear.

When Charlie saw a podium and stage, he knew the Chief had planned the event—maybe even the protesters. Charlie was merely a photo-op.

Protesters and disciples moved to opposite corners of the stage, the protesters staring daggers at the disciples. The Chief climbed the stairs, stepped up to the podium and checked his body mic. "Testing." Tiny cams zoomed overhead like ravenous mosquitoes at a Red Cross picnic, and the sound from the crowd swelled.

"People! People! Please, please, calm down!" His hands patting the air for quiet, he waited. "I'm Lansing Police Chief, Will Hosley. The oBI is taking over the investigation into the deaths of three men who were testing a new product called N-hanced, which Corridor CyberDynamics manufactures right here in our great city of Lansing. Our police department will assist the agency in any way we can.

"Mr. Noble here—"

At the mention of his name, a disciple tagged Simon shouted, "We love you, Lord!"

A red-faced protester spat, "Go back to hell, Demon!"

Hosley raised his voice. "Please. Mr. Noble is only wanted for questioning. He doesn't have a criminal record, he's not under arrest, and you'll notice he's not in handcuffs. He's going with these agents from the oBI over to the Federal Building just a few blocks away. With his permission, we brought Mr. Noble out front here in order to show you he doesn't have anything to hide."

Charlie had to admit, the guy knew how to milk it.

"Now look here, you NewsDogs—" He squinted into the crowd. "—I realize it's not much fun for you these days, now that crime has dropped to a trickle. But don't blow this all out of proportion. Lansing is a wonderful place to live, and I want to see it stay that way. So don't embarrass yourselves by making up a bunch of lies. And remember this—" He raised a finger and an eyebrow. "—we have laws against libel in this country, and we *will* enforce them. You understand me?" Nobody answered.

He continued. "All right, show's over. Let's clear a path down here." He spread his hands as if part the crowd in front of a black van at the curb.

People moved a little, but the crowd was dense. The disciples surged closer, while others cursed them for pushing. The officers led the way holding back the crowd. The agents motioned *after you*, and Charlie started toward the van. A swarm of Skeets followed, and the crowd pushed in again. Disciples at the edge of the path reached out to touch Charlie.

Halfway to the van, the giant LED lamps brightened until the plaza seemed in full daylight. People looked up, and one of the LEDs burst with a loud *Pop!* A woman screamed. Voices murmured a fireworks, "Ooo." A few, including Charlie, ducked down, raising their hands to protect their faces. A flame shot up a couple yards and went out, and a stream of thick, black smoke curled skyward. Some kids clapped and cheered. A disciple shouted, "Praise the Lord!" Others added, "Amen."

The remaining lamps returned to normal brightness, and nobody seemed hurt. Recovering, the group continued on to the van. The agents and Charlie got in, and the vehicle drove off. No one left the plaza. They stayed to see what would happen next.

CHAPTER 26

While oBI Agents Lott and Mortensen were making it clear they were not leaving CCD without Charlie, Charlie decided *he* was not leaving with *them*. He saw the square full of people as an opportunity.

I need to create a diversion. What about those lamp poles? He zoomed in on the grid that powered CCD's block. In seconds he was in the system with direct control over the LED lamp. *Push that circuit and something'll blow.*

Now, find someone in the crowd who's built like me. He tagged a few matches.

As the plan gelled in Charlie's mind, Agent Lott asked if he had a problem going through the square. *Please, Br'er Fox, don't throw me into the briar patch.* Charlie smiled inside. "Uh, no."

After the Chief's speech, the crowd opened up just enough to let them through. It was a tense moment for Charlie. *OK, it's Gerald Collier, then. Almost ready— Oh, shit!* The disciples surged forward, pushing Gerald back. *I've got to get closer.* Charlie nodded encouragement to a couple disciples, who broke through, opening the path to Gerald. Two officers pushed the disciples back. Charlie slammed the circuit, flooding the square with light. When one of the LEDs exploded, the agents let go of Charlie to cover their faces. Charlie left his oMe2 with them and grabbed a copy of Gerald's ID. Ducking down and crawling through the forest of legs, he called for a face morph. The rush of electric facial twitches startled him. When it finished, his cheeks felt bloated. He crept on until he found an opening big enough so he could stand up. At the last second he transformed his clothes.

As far as the agents were concerned, he was still with them. And indeed he was—virtually.

Charlie's luck was about to get even better.

Now posing as Gerald Collier, Charlie shimmied through the crowd, ninety-degrees to the path the agents took. He was making progress when he noticed an attractive teen girl jostling her way toward him.

Her tag read Kimberly Collier. "Daddy!" She waved.

Oh, God. It can't be. Charlie lowered his head.

She put her hand on his shoulder. "Daddy! What's the matter with you?"

He smiled, trying not to appear as worried as he felt.

Kissing him on the cheek, she swung around to his side, put her arm through his and yanked him through the throng. "Let's go. We're late. Ooo, it's cold. Let's hurry." She hunkered down, holding more tightly to his arm.

Charlie glanced at the building. Only ten feet from the door, he was now headed in the wrong direction.

Kimberly's tag said she was a college student, but her privacy settings revealed nothing else. Charlie looked back and saw Gerald facing the other way, talking with someone next to him. *How'd his miss his own daughter?*

Kimberly answered him. "I forgot to comm you that I was coming early. But I saw the arrow over your head, and here you are. I don't want to miss any of the game."

Game? Charlie tapped into the Skeet swarm and hired one near Gerald. He angled it to pick up the man's voice. Ts in Charlie's throat and nasal passages reorganized to imitate the shape and resonance of Gerald's. But it didn't comfort Charlie. It was one thing to adopt someone's face, voice, and carriage, and quite another to know his or her mannerisms, speech patterns, and word usage, not to mention their life history. He had no idea what he would do when he had to talk to the girl. He kept the Skeet on Gerald as it absorbed more data.

"Now listen, Daddy, I'm shutting off my comm. This time is just for you and me."

If Gerald can't comm her, this might work. Charlie hoped he could get away before Gerald got desperate and contacted authorities. But he had no idea what game she was talking about. There were dozens in the area.

She had an oCar waiting curbside, and they climbed in. Charlie broke into a cold sweat when he saw Kimberly had them seated face-to-face. *When she figures out I'm not her dad, will she scream? Call the police?* He gave her one of Gerald's smiles. They turned off Elm Street and headed north on South Cedar—further away from CCD.

"So what was going on back there?"

Charlie's heart thumped, afraid to answer, but she was already Netting it.

"I see. Charlie Noble is accused of multiple murders. Ooo! Look how violent they are. God! One guy burned to death." Her eyebrows crinkled. "Ohhh, and that little boy. Now, that's just wrong. This is creepy; he's from Lansing. And he looks like a regular person. But you know those serial killers. Whenever Dogs interview the neighbors, they always say 'he was a quiet young man.'" She laughed. "Bet *I'd* know if I met someone like that."

Charlie caught his breath. *Oh, God!* He looked to see if she heard him. A sinking thought tugged at him. *Will other people use N this way to break the law?*

He watched the Net feed. Seeing his oMe2 smile at the Skeets while he sat here wearing somebody else's face, with somebody else's daughter, gave him the creeps.

That's when he got the comm from HackerMeister.

Oh, God. There was no way he could answer it, and his oMe2 was busy entertaining the agents. He waited for it to go to voice, and read the transcription.

I got what you need. --HM
<No return path.>

Great! How do I get back to him without a path? Kimberly chattered on. Charlie tried to listen, while fighting the urge to jump out and run away to make himself available for HackerMeister's next comm—if he ever tried again.

"God, I thought crime was bad in Chicago."

Chicago?

"Oh. I— I don't want you to worry, Daddy. I mean, where I stay on campus is really safe. Really. Besides, there're cams everywhere. Nobody gets away with shit any more. Oops. Sorry. I didn't mean to say the 's' word. It's just everybody says things like that at school."

Charlie almost said, 'I see.'

"I don't mean everybody's all loose or anything. And I don't mean loose like with sex and all, you know. It's just college is a more relaxed lifestyle. The guys call us bellas, which is like beautiful in Italian, and we call them bellers like the sound a bull makes. Funny, huh?" She laughed. It was innocent and sweet.

Charlie himself hoping she would stay that way. He smiled her daddy's smile.

They were on Michigan Avenue, passing Frandor Shopping Center. *Are we going to MSU?* Charlie noticed her studying him.

"Daddy, what did you do to your hair?"

Charlie's pulse quickened.

"You never parted it on the left before." She laughed and ran her fingers through it.

In the old days, Charlie might have jumped out of the car at a traffic light. But the oCar network eliminated stop lights. They hadn't even slowed since they'd left. *No. Better just ride it out and see what happens.*

"But there I go, jabbering on and on. Enough about me!" She flung her hands out dismissively. "What have *you* been doing?"

Charlie tried to look calm, but inside he scrambled. Grasping at nothing, he turned it around. "I *like* hearing about you, hon. Tell me about school." *Uh-oh! What if Gerald's pet name for her is sweetheart, or apple blossom, or Kimmie?* He watched her face but didn't see a hint of suspicion.

"I love my art class. The teacher is so good with watercolor. Oh, and in music history, we're studying Rock and Roll, past and present. You know, there are people writing songs now that sound like the ones from the '60s. It's really cool how long that music has lasted. It's almost like classical." She gave a quick turn. "Wait a minute! One of the modern guys we studied is named Charlie Noble."

Charlie coughed.

"You don't suppose it's the same guy?"

He watched her Net it.

"It is! Holy shit! It's the same guy! Oh. Sorry. Anyway, I like his music. It doesn't seem like something a murderer would write. More like— something from a quiet young man." She giggled. "Anyway, after hearing his music, I went back and listened to some of the bands he copied. They're really good. I like them better than the music now. I tried to show it to my friends, but they say it's old fogey."

Charlie was stunned. He was used to an occasional fan comm, but he had no idea anyone was studying his music. Of all the people who could have grabbed his arm back at CCD. It was a bit too much. He tried to keep his face calm and fatherly, but it was an effort.

CHAPTER 27

The oCar took the gentle curve onto the MSU campus. *That's it. Basketball at the Breslin Center. It should be fairly easy to lose Kimberly in the crowd. Then I need to connect the Real Gerald up with Kimberly.* Charlie could see the mob had broken up at CCD Plaza, but Gerald still talked busily to his friend and didn't look in any hurry to leave. *I'll counterfeit a message from her saying there's been a change of plans, and have him meet her at the game.*

Since most fans attended the games via VR, it meant traffic was light as the oCar dropped them off curbside. *But I've never tried to get in anywhere using somebody else's ID.* No matter what he told himself or where he put the dial, Charlie was not calm. He began sweating again as they approached the gate. As they passed through, an alarm went off. Charlie froze. *Oh, shit!* A guard brandishing an oWand came toward them. "Excuse me, sir. Would you please come with me?"

Charlie dropped his head. *Now what'll do?* He twitched as the guard brushed his shoulder, but the guard didn't stop. Charlie looked up, and saw him grab the man behind them. The guy shouted, "Let go of me, asshole!" The guard lifted the oWand, but the guy raised his hands before he could use it. "OK, OK. No need to get rough." Now he whined, "It's just so hard to buy a ticket these days."

Charlie and Kimberly hurried on. She whispered, "What an idiot. They can spot a phony a mile away."

Right. Charlie nodded. *Right.*

They stopped at concessions. He hadn't eaten since his pizza the previous night. Breslin made a big deal out of still frying in RealOil, although the foods themselves were fabbed. He ordered nachos, a hot dog and a root beer. Kimberly got popcorn with salt and butter. They went off to find their seats, Kimberly talking the whole time.

Charlie set the nachos on his knees and ate the hot dog in four bites. The pep band came in and warmed up with the MSU Fight Song. Nearly naked cheerleaders, pom-pons flying, lead the enthusiastic crowd in singing.

Done with the dog, Charlie started on the nachos. They came with a napkin, plastic knife and fork and a Handi Wipe. *Funny, after all these years they're still the best for fast cleanup.* He put the plastic ware in his pocket and indulged his OCD by eating carefully with a thumb and forefinger. He glanced at Kimberly, but she gave no hint his eating habits were unusual.

He stopped as he got a second urgent comm from HackerMeister, but he still couldn't break away from Kimberly. Clenching his jaw, he waited for the text version.

What the hell? You dead or what? Maybe this isn't that important to you. --HM
<No return path>

Charlie's heart sank. *Dammit! Don't give up on me, man.*

Breslin filled up. VR attendees simply appeared in their seats. Then, with a sudden burst of drum cadence and an explosion of fireworks, flying saucer platforms descended from the ceiling. Smoke and flames shot out the bottom, and multi-colored lasers sliced the air. The crowd roared as the teams circled the discs, performing trick dribbles and passes. Charlie found himself caught up in the spectacle, jumping, applauding and hooting along with everyone else.

Buzzers blared and referee whistles shrieked, but they could barely be heard above the cheers of the crowd. The pep band lit into a funky number featuring booming bass drums. Fun aside, Charlie had to make his escape. He sent the message to Gerald and waited. MSU played well against their archrival U of M, and the game was eleven to nothing in the first five minutes. Charlie tracked the hijacked Skeet as it followed Gerald's oCar until it turned onto campus.

"Say, hon. I have to go to the restroom. You'll be all right, won't you?"

"Oh, sure." She squeezed his hand. "It's so great to see you, Daddy." She kissed his cheek.

Tears welled in Charlie's eyes, but Kimberly didn't see them. She was already looking back at the game. He stood, shimmied down the row and hiked up the steps. He hoped there would be no awkward moments between Kimberly and her father over the switch he'd pulled. He had come to like her.

CHAPTER 28

Charlie came out on the Concourse level. Calling up a 3-D blueprint of the Breslin, he found the ramp where trucks brought in the big shows. He switched his ID to anonymous in order to prevent the real Gerald from running into any problems with the entry system. Tapping the security system, he instructed the area cams to stay away from him as he moved around. He took the stairs down to the Arena level, looking for a quiet place to check in. The lower lever also reduced the chance he'd bump into Kimberly—or the Real Gerald.

Following the long curve around until he found a quiet bench, Charlie sat down and reconnected with his oMe2. Rolling back to the first marker at 7:15, he looked through his double's eyes and gasped. The oBI conference room smelled of his favorite fragrances of cinnamon rolls and coffee and was filled with familiar objects from places where he'd lived in the past. *How do they have so much information on me?* It was impressive and scary. A lot *1984*. Charlie ran a fast integration, playing back all the events since he'd left the Plaza. In the van, the agents had been very cordial, but they didn't respond to his double's sense of humor. In fact, he wasn't able to manipulate them at all.

Moving forward in time, he saw through Charlie2's eyes as he asked, "Why do you have all this stuff from my past?"

Agent Lott said, "It's something new we're trying. We want to make people feel comfortable. And these personal items give us insight into the person we're working with. Is there anything you'd like to add?"

"Not that I can think of. Thanks." Charlie caught the smell of pork roast and onions. He licked his lips and smiled.

"Can we get you something to eat or drink?"

He knew he could look as if he were eating or drinking in VR, but there was no way to actually consume anything. "No, thanks." *Can they tell what*

I'm thinking? C2 accessed the server and tapped the acting module. Since the agents were likely using an eye pupil scanner, he let N take control of his autonomic nervous system to mimic the truth.

Agent Lott stood. "I'm getting coffee. I'll bring you a Coke."

After he left, Dylan said, "Tom is what we call the 'lead.' He'll ask most the questions. I'll take notes. Well, I don't actually *take* notes. I watch to make sure the transcription is accurate." He sounded friendly enough, but Charlie felt anger rustling just under the surface.

When Tom returned, C2 waved his hand over the Coke and a circle dissolved in the top producing the familiar "Fizzzzz." He pretended to take a sip, but he had to work to keep his hand from shaking. Anyone observing in Real would see the can never moved from the table. Any cams would merge his VR feed with Real, using the same technology as VR business meetings, where they needed to be able to replay a vid and "see" all attendees. As far as C2 knew, at that moment a technician might be telling Tom and Dylan he was a double. Not that it was illegal to send an oMe2, but that was the last time he touched the Coke.

CHAPTER 29

Special Agent Lott began. "This can get tedious, but we'll probably ask you some of the same questions more than once. People often remember other details when they tell their story again."

"Happy to help." Charlie2 leaned forward. "This thing has me more upset than you can imagine. N-hanced is my baby. If I help you, and you find the culprit, it'll help me."

"That's the spirit. So why don't you start from the beginning." He smiled apologetically.

"All three of them were testing our software. The program lets people instantly understand whole bodies of knowledge, sort of like Keanu Reeves in *The Matrix*, except without having to jam a plug into the back of your head."

Charlie continued from the moment Rob notified him while he was at lunch with Jeff. He didn't mention having his memory erased.

Lott said, "Can you think of anyone who would benefit from the failure of N-hanced, or somebody who might want to hurt you or your company?"

The question caught C2 by surprise. "Now that you mention it, probably Orchard, although they haven't pursued us aggressively. But they stay away from sabotage. They usually buy companies out."

Lott nodded.

"Then yesterday, Erik Kozlovski made what might be interpreted as a threat to me. But he didn't seem to know enough about N for something like this."

"Is this the guy?" Lott drew a square in the air and flicked the image to Charlie.

"Yep. But he's a lot bigger than he looks here."

Charlie explained why he contacted Eric, that he seem well enough acquainted with code to have hacked N-hanced, and that he had friends in the Russian mod, some who probably had computer skills.

It crossed Charlie's mind that Jeff told him he'd stop N if he could. And then there were those mysterious Luddite friends of his, not to mention the Ken Doll and the protestors. But as quickly as the thoughts arrived, he shoved them aside. N kept his reactions steady.

Lott said, "It looks like these deaths are tied to N-hanced, but we can't ignore the possibility they could be unrelated incidents. Who might want to hurt your testers?"

"They all seemed clean. I'm pretty sure that biker Jonesy would have wanted Chad dead. But he couldn't have arranged the fire. Here's what I have on Jonesy and Chad if you think it's worth following up on." He flicked over the data.

"Thanks."

"And here's what I have on Wilford and his company."

"Anything on Gary Billings?"

"Sure. But I haven't had time to study his death yet."

"Let us know anything you do find out."

"He was creating new products very quickly. Maybe a competitor?"

The primary Charlie absorbed all of this in a few seconds as he sat on the bench at Breslin, but now he was up to Real time. He needed to work with the servers and see what else he could dig up. As he disconnected from his double, he told C2 to notify him if something important came up. Then he projected his awareness into the N-hanced servers to dig in.

Charlie2 squirmed in his seat as he said to the agents, "You know, I don't want to sound unpatriotic or anything, but I was wondering if the military might be involved. If they made N look bad, it would put us under financial stress and we might consider licensing the technology to them. The same could be true of foreign governments. Can you picture an army of soldiers who can fire new weapons at the speed of thought, who know the answers to complex questions by absorbing the minds of their superiors? They'd rule the world."

"Charlie, I've been working for the government for almost fifty years, and I still don't trust them. Believe me, that's something we'll look into. But if we turn up anything, don't count on it getting prosecuted."

"Right." It sounded logical, but C2 knew making a statement about distrusting the government was a technique agents sometimes used to build rapport.

Or maybe Lott was just loosening him up—because he was about to get a little more personal.

"Could somebody be sabotaging N-hanced inside your company?"

Charlie2 frowned. "I ... can't imagine that. No."

"Anyone jealous of your success?"

"Not that I know of. There isn't much back-biting at CCD."

"What if N-hanced has an irreparable flaw, or maybe it's headed down the wrong path? CCD has insurance to protect against those kinds of failures, doesn't it?"

"I never paid any attention to that side of the business." C2 tipped his head sideways and squinted. "I don't like where you're going with that."

"How about this; you mentioned you found an opening in the security layer. Could someone from CCD have put it there to help an outsider get in? Anybody who could be influenced by money or blackmail?"

"Jeez." The corners of Charlie2's mouth pulled down. "Not that I know of. But I don't know much about most of our employee's personal lives—who's involved in sex, drugs, gambling and whatnot. I've been on this project by myself for the better part of a year, so I haven't interacted with them. You have any evidence? If you do, I'd like to know about it."

"We're almost done. Now, I don't want to upset you, but I have to ask. Would you have some reason to want N-hanced to fail?"

Charlie2 exhaled in disbelief. "Are you kidding?" *Don't think about it. Don't.* "Why would I do something like that?"

"Maybe *you* know there's a flaw in the program, and you're looking for a piece of the insurance settlement. Nobody knows the program better than you."

"No way! That's ... that's insane. N-hanced is worth so much more than some measly insurance payout. Besides, N is going to change the world. Once it comes out, bad parents won't be able to bully their children. People will be able to negotiate win-win agreements in all sorts of arenas. I think it will eliminate war. Believe me, if there were something stushy with N, I'd fix it." His passion brought color to his face, but his pupils remained steady.

"I had to ask. You understand."

"Yeah. Sure."

"But you have a rock and roll past. And there were those anti-war demonstrations in high school and college.

Charlie2's jaw dropped. *Holy shit! Nobody knows about that except ...* He nodded and grinned. "Ah, my first wife. You probably didn't have to twist her arm too hard. So, what's that got to do with anything? Most of that stuff is what ... fifty years old? I mean, come on. I was a kid."

"People don't change all that much."

"Well, *I* have. And if you have that old crap, you should have some more recent data showing my adult behavior. My solid job history. My books, articles and inventions—some of them even sold to the government." He was a little hot, but he calmed down once he realized it was another oBI technique. Stir up the hornet's nest to see what flies out. "Sorry. I have a history of anger. But N changed that for me, too."

Lott said, "And as long as we're getting in your face, the file also shows you expressed an extreme interest in the 2022 burning of the United States Congress building and the public beheadings."

C2 laughed. "Extreme interest? Yeah. Me and about 300 million Americans. Weren't you interested?"

"I suppose." Lott nodded.

"Come on." C2 leaned forward. "You wouldn't even have a job if that didn't happen. Nobody would. The way the politicians were changing laws left and right to help their rich buddies…" He shook his head. "The whole thing was held together with baling wire and duct tape, like a Cuban Buick. If they'd succeeded defaulting on the national debt, we wouldn't even have garbage cans to eat out of. But let me tell you, if I'd been anywhere near those guillotines, I woulda been happy to pull the handle." He sat back in the chair. "That what you wanna know?" He paused a moment to cool down. "Once we started running the government with the Orchard computers, it all started making sense again. So what else you got in that file there? My Net porn viewing history?"

Both agents laughed. Lott said, "You'd be surprised."

Charlie2's eyes twinkled. "I doubt it."

Agent Mortensen took over and reviewed the discussion from the transcription summary. When he got to the part where he talked about Orchard's in buying N-hanced, the program had added the phrase 'corporate espionage.' Charlie2 almost missed the rest. Almost bolted from the room. Almost ran screaming back to Charlie. Because those were the words he'd used to explain Linda's death five months earlier. A death for which there was still no explanation. *Could these suicides have something to do with what happened to her?*

He finally tuned back into the review. When Lott asked if there was anything else he could think of, he found he could hardly think at all. His mind raced with everything they'd thrown at him. All he might be able to add were things he did *not* want to think about—Jeff with his possible connection to the Ken Doll, and Charlie's suspicions about himself. He kept reaching over to dial down his anxiety. *Is there ever a time when you dial anything up?*

He found himself lifting out of a numbing silence just as Agent Lott said, "OK. That's all for now. But get back to us if you think of anything else."

"Sure. Like I said, whatever you find is going to help me. We're both on the same side here." *I think.*

The agents led Charlie's double to the elevator.

CHAPTER 30

It was dark when Charlie's oMe2 trudged down the steps of the Federal Building. Streetlamps spilled blue pools of light down onto eight people, where they stood guard-like, evenly spaced on the sidewalk down the block. One tagged Simon Peter called out, "Matthew. Our Lord is released unto us."

The other seven turned toward Charlie2, and he recognized Matthew directly in front of him. *Good grief.*

Matthew smiled and started toward Charlie2. Then his face fell deadly serious. Reaching inside his coat, he came out with a gun. "Stop! Don't move!"

Charlie2 put his hands in the air and froze, eyes wide. Hot fear stabbed him before he realized he couldn't be hurt. *Crazy religious fanatic.*

"I said don't move."

"I'm not moving."

Matthew fired. *Blaamm!* The sound echoed off nearby buildings hammering Charlie2's ears.

I've got to stop him. C2 did a forward roll, arriving to the right-front of Matthew. Springing upward, he caught Matthew's right wrist in his left hand. A quick grab and twist with his right, and the gun lay on the ground. C2 kept hold of the hand and pushed Matthew back. He surveyed the disciples. They stood motionless, their mouths open. "Anyone else have any weapons?" They all shook their heads. *Controlling him like this in VR means he's a serious gamer.*

C2 looked back at Matthew. "Why'd you shoot? I didn't move." Matthew tried to pull his hand back. C2 twisted it inward.

"You're hurting my wrist."

"Tell me!"

"Ow! OK. I shot the guy behind you. The Ken Doll."

"What?!" C2 looked around. "The only people I see are you guys. Besides, I would've had a warning."

"He was there. Then he disappeared."

"Did the rest of you see him?"

They all nodded.

"Show me."

Matthew flicked open a vid. Sure enough, as Charlie2 walked down the stairs, the Ken Doll came from behind one of the pillars, knife in hand. He was within a few feet of C2 when Matthew shot. Then Ken and the knife disappeared. *What is it, some kind of projection?* C2 pulled Matthew to the spot where Ken had been, but nothing remained of either Ken or the knife. "Look, I don't know what's going on here, but I do know that gun of yours is illegal. Where did you get it?"

"My dad buried it in the yard when they were outlawed. I dug it up thinking I might need to protect you."

C2 sighed in disgust. "But I'm an oMe2. That guy couldn't hurt me."

"You are?"

"This is a Federal building. This whole thing got recorded. I'll see if I can't mess up their security system. In the meantime, get your gun, put the safety on and get the hell outta here." Charlie2 let go of him.

Matthew rubbed his wrist and picked up the gun. "Thank you, Lord." He walked toward the other disciples.

"No. You've got to get out of here *now*. Run!"

Matthew ran and the others followed.

"In different directions!"

They nearly fell over each other trying to decide who should go where.

Charlie2 shook his head. *Idiots!* He sent a message to his PAs. They cleared the security vid. Finally he reintegrated with Charlie—and disappeared.

CHAPTER 31

After Charlie2 left, Agents Lott and Mortensen went back to the interview room. "So, Dylan, what do you think?"

"Seems like a nice guy. Passionate. A true believer—and full of shit."

"OK, Dylan, you know how I feel about profanity. So let's try to cool it. Now tell me, what did you see?"

Dylan rolled his eyes. "Look at the readout. Not one lie anywhere. You ever seen one like that? Sure, he got riled, but his body language and iris scans never varied from the truth. Not once. So unless he's Jesus Christ, there's something phony going on."

"Good observation. So, how you think he did it?"

"Probably that N-hanced shit. He's got it controlling everything he does. I'm not saying he didn't tell us the truth. But nobody goes to that kinda trouble to control everything he's feeling unless he's hiding something. We're not getting the whole story."

"Agreed. But maybe he's just trying to control his anger. He said he had some issues with that. We shouldn't assume anything. Just be aware for next time we talk to him."

"Yeah, right." Mortensen's tone was sarcastic. He picked up the coffee cup. When he reached for the Coke, it spilled. "What the fuck? It's full to the brim. He drank out of this. I saw him tip the can and swallow."

"A double! He sent an oMe2."

"Now why would he do that? Nobody trusts a double with us."

"Why do you suppose?"

"It's bullshit, that's what it is. We can't trust the fuck."

Lott nodded. "I know we had the original when we came out of his office. Let's go to the lab and take a look at our vid, see when he pulled the switch. Might give us some idea about why."

"Then I say we go track down the original and have a heart-to-heart with a little different flavor."

"Look, Dylan, let's take it easy here. Let's not rush into anything without covering all the bases, just in case it goes to court."

"Yeah, yeah. You old-timers. Just a little too fuckin' mellow. I hope you don't think you're gonna sell any of that choirboy shit to me. Trust me, this is one murdering son of a bitch, and I'm not letting him get away with it."

Oh, boy. Why do they always send me the young firecrackers? Please, God, don't let this one turn bloody.

CHAPTER 32

After getting the shocking update from his oMe2, Charlie pulled his full awareness back to where he sat on the bench on the lower level of Breslin. *There are a lot of people who might want to see N derailed—including Rob. But, Rob? Noooo. No way... No!* His head was swirling. *And now with the Ken Doll, maybe it's not just about dreaming. But if I had anything to do with what happened to Linda... God, I can't even think about that. What is going on? All I want to do is make the world a better place. Is that really so bad—that people have to die?*

All right. This isn't helping. Let's see if I can find a common thread between thee deaths.

He heard a beep and jumped. *HackerMeister. Thank God!* He took a deep breath and opened the channel.

"Where you been?" It was that ominous, mechanical voice.

"I know. I'm sorry. What'd you find out?"

"Look at module 337, the crystal, on the facing surface, lower left quadrant. There's a single loose pixel. Push it and it pops out."

"I worked that module myself. I didn't see anything."

"You don't have my eyes."

"How can I fix it if I can't see it?"

"I already locked it so nobody's getting in. But here's a short piece of code that'll open your eyes." It arrived in Charlie's cube. "It acts like night vision. Look in that spot, you'll see. You still need to check the rest of the modules. I had to stop after 337."

"How can I repay you?"

"Make N-hanced a success. It changes everything. Lots of people need it."

"Thank—" But he was already gone.

Now more than ever Charlie wanted to have another look at the modules. Armed with HackerMeister's code, he and the PAs should be able to find any other holes and put an end to the whole mess.

God, Jeff, I hope this doesn't have anything to do with you. Then, with a sinking feeling about his renegade PAs, he added, *or me.*

CHAPTER 33

Agents Lott and Mortensen hurried into the oBI tech lab. The room was more secure than the rest of the building, and it was filled with a vast array of electronic surveillance equipment and computer analysis tools.

Lott said, "Let's start the vids from when we were at his office run them forward."

Mortensen drew two IS cubes, one for each of their recorders. He synchronized them from the time they entered Charlie's office. He merged them into a single 3-D image and let them run.

Lott said, "Fast forward."

The speed octupled, playing Keystone Cops-style. They watched themselves come down the elevator, into the lobby, through the doors and onto the busy plaza. People moved comically as they shifted weight from foot to foot in fast motion, while chief Hosley gave his speech, arms flailing like a demented Skeet. Then the three of them headed for the van.

Lott said, "Slow it down to normal speed. Turn off the demonstrator's signs."

Their group got halfway to the van when the demonstrators surged forward and the scene went white. Five seconds passed before the color returned to normal.

Mortensen said, "That's where the light blew."

"What if that wasn't an accident?"

"You think Charlie did it?"

"Yeah."

"How could he?"

"An accomplice?"

"Mother fu—"

Lott raise his eyebrows.

"Let's look at the Board of Water and Light log."

"I'm not so sure that'll give us what we need. Let's try something else first."

"Like what?"

"Let's look at the security cams in the plaza. They might not suffer from white out."

"OK." Mortensen took a couple seconds to get clearance. He found twenty cams in the immediate area. The software built an image they could view from any angle, but it was still burned out at the critical moment.

"Ya know, Lott, two cams are mounted on poles pointing away from the lights. Let's see what we get from just those two."

"Go for it."

They got a partial 3-D image, but it didn't have enough data to construct anything they could rotate. Mortensen scowled. "Crap! Let's try the Board."

"Wait a minute. Back it up."

"Where to?"

"The explosion. Then go forward one vid block per second."

Mortensen motioned. After a minute Lott pointed. "Look. Right there."

"I don't see anything."

"See that guy two people to the left of us?" Lott put his hand into the cube and touched the man's chest. "He's looking at his feet, and frowning and turning his head."

"So what?"

"It's like he's watching someone on the ground moving from right to left. Back it up again. Play it in real time and glue your eyes on him."

Mortensen exhaled. "Yeah, and look! The next guy's doing the same thing. Then it skips that lady but not the next guy. He's crawling out of there!"

"Yup."

"I'm turning on tags."

The square filled with ID balloons, making it hard to see anyone. Mortensen zoomed in and flicked until only one remained. It moved from right to left, unattached to anyone. "So who the hell is Gerald Collier?"

"I'll check." Lott double-clicked the tag, which brought up Collier's sheet and pictures. "He and a friend rented an oCar and went to the plaza. So what's he doing crawling around?"

"You said Charlie might have an accomplice."

"Yeah, but where's Charlie?"

Dylan shrugged, then brightened. "Follow the tag to see where this Gerald guy comes out."

They watched until a head popped up. Mortensen merged all twenty cams and blew up the 3-D until they found themselves staring into Gerald's life-sized face.

Lott walked around Collier, stepping through the ghostly projections of people nearby. "That's him all right. So why's he leaving when everyone else is trying to get closer to Noble? And what's he got to do with Charlie?"

"And who's that chickadee with him?" Mortensen tapped her head, bringing up her ID. "It's his daughter!"

The agents followed until Gerald and Kimberly drove away.

Backing out of the scene, Lott said, "Let me check the oCar database to find out where they went." It only took a few seconds. "This can't be right. It says Gerald and his buddy rented another oCar twenty minutes after he left with his daughter."

"Is somebody screwing with the database? And where's our dear Mr. Ig-Noble?"

"Let's check Whipped." Lott brought up the World People Tracking Database, a tool acronymed WPTD, that followed T IDs. Orchard licensed Whipped allowing everyone the convenience of VR tags. Lott flicked Collier's ID from the vid over to the search box. He zoomed in on Lansing and down to the plaza. Backing it up to Gerald's arrival, he touched Play, then Fast Forward. When it got to the place the light blew up, a duplicate ID tag appeared.

"Whoa!" Both agents said at the same time.

Lott said, "That's not an oMe2. It's a second guy."

"What the hell? Hey, look for Charlie on Whipped."

Lott couldn't move fast enough. When the light blew, Charlie's tag transferred to his oMe2. "If the Real Charlie disappeared, it means he became the second Gerald Collier—T ID, face, clothes and all."

Mortensen said, "That's not legal, is it?"

"Hell, no!"

"And what about the girl he took off with? Gerald's daughter?"

"If she's not an accomplice, we may have a kidnapping or hostage situation on our hands."

"Or maybe all three."

Lott nodded, eyes narrowing. After a moment his face reddened. "We're going after the bastard."

"Now you're talking!"

CHAPTER 34

Charlie logged on and called up module 337. Looking in the lower right quadrant, he splayed his fingers to magnify the area. Nothing. He turned on HackerMeister's code. There in the middle of the beautiful crystal was a tiny, dirty-looking dot. Frowning, he ran his fingers over it. He could clearly feel a rough bump, like a hangnail.

"What the hell?"

He flicked off code, and the spot disappeared. Running his fingers over it, the surface felt smooth as glass. It reminded him of the Picture Puzzler in *Highlights* magazine when he was a kid, where he searched for differences between two seemingly identical pictures. That was fun. This was not.

So that's how the murderer got in. He called his PAs, "When was the security finish applied to this surface?"

"October 13 of last year. Same day—"

"As the User Abort ON line appeared," Charlie finished. "Of course. And the vid?"

One of the PAs had anticipated his request and ran it. There was Charlie waving the security layer into place. The code scrolled down the right side of his cube. The PA highlighted the User Abort line.

"Makes me look like a rank amateur. And I suppose there's no way to verify the authenticity of the vid?"

"Right."

"Very clever stuff this person is laying down."

With so many unanswered questions Charlie barely knew where to begin. "I want you all to use the new filter and continue from module 338. I'll compare the data from our three testers to see if any common threads show up."

He lay the three streams on top of each other along with the vid, and ran a routine that looked for long strings of matching 0s and 1s, starting from the moment they died and working backward.

As he watched the tests flicker by, he felt a fly buzz near his ear and waved it away. He shifted the top stream one bit to the left and checked again, finding it disconcerting to watch his testers come back from the dead. If not for N the process would have taken more than a hundred years. Instead, he finished in five minutes—but without a match. The fly was back. This time he turned his head to look, but all he saw was a black fleck zip out of sight. *Where have I seen that before?*

He turned to his PAs. "I'm missing something with these data streams. Half of you work with me." They swung around to face him. "Look at the test, and tell me what I'm doing wrong."

"You did it right. What if we—?"

The black fleck appeared again off to his left. It twisted and turned, spewing a stream of roiling code through his work area, growing in size and length until it took on the shape of a snake.

"What the hell is that?"

"We can't tell. But it's definitely not part of N-hanced."

Ohmigod! Is that the killer? "Listen, whatever you do, don't let that thing touch you. And don't let it cross the Net back to me. And—"

The thing split in two and the second one wriggled off to the right, poking and probing throughout the room.

That can't be good.

As his PAs dodged the creatures' paths, their work slowed.

Charlie said, "Um, can you work while keeping out of the way of those things?"

"Yes. Once we know their pattern of movement, we can focus again."

The two snakes became four. The two new ones squirmed around behind Charlie.

That's when he realized he'd seen something like it in the dream he'd had the night Terra stayed with him—the thing that kept slithering out of his view. But that thing had eight arms and was more like—.

The four snakes split and became eight.

A black octopus.

The same fear that dominated his dream washed back over him. He dialed it down, but it didn't last long. He remembered his testers had died right after remembering a dream.

"OK, guys. How are you doing with that thing?"

"Still watching for patterns. If there are no more than eight legs it shouldn't be much longer."

"Give it all you got. And whatever you do, keep it away from me."

Charlie felt like he was tap dancing on hot coals.

His team reported back. "We know its pattern. We can go back to our projects."

Still uncomfortable, he pointed at four PAs. "You were about to make a suggestion."

"Yes. How about if we look at your data streams for anything at all out of place?"

"Do it. But keep your eyes on that creature."

Three minutes later a PA called out, "I've got something."

"Show me."

"Here, it's on the audio track."

"Looks like normal audio to me." Charlie had to fight to keep his eyes focused on the window. They kept straying to the twitching arms.

"It *is* normal audio. But there's one distorted sample accompanying some of the vid blocks."

"What difference would a little distortion make?"

"There's something else we need to report first."

"Yes?"

"The Black Octopus is learning."

Great! Well, now it's officially the Black Octopus.

"It adjusted to our dodge, and now moving more randomly. Staying away is taking most of our CPU."

"Stay safe first." Charlie swallowed. *So, where was I?* "Why does the audio distortion matter?"

"It's consistently incorrect on the amplitude axis by a single digit in the plus direction."

"And that means...?"

"It could be a code."

"You mean a code riding on top of our code?"

"Yes."

"What does it say?"

"We don't know without the key."

"Can you pound away at it until a pattern emerges?"

"We're doing that now, but so much of our computing power is devoted to the Black Octopus, we're operating at the level of a 1970s TRS-80."

"Estimated time to solve it at the current level?"

"A thousand years."

Christ! Charlie shook his head. "Too long." To his left he spotted a pair of tentacles closing in on him. "Uh, guys..."

"The Black Octopus is predicting our moves. You won't be safe in thirty seconds."

"Quick then. Pass me the tester data. I'll work with it offline."

They began the transfer. Once his team shut down N, they wouldn't be able to finish checking the security modules. The presence of the Octopus meant there was still a security breach. He watched the download progress bar, then caught his breath when he felt the air from a tentacle ruffle his hair. His feet moved as fast as a game of double-dutch jump rope. Fear reaching a peak, he crouched and took a final leap. He disconnected from

N without waiting for the *Download Complete* dialog. He found himself back on the bench at Breslin. *Jesus! Did I get it all?*

As the agents headed out of the oBI offices, Mortensen said, "So use Whipped, and find out where Charlie and the Collier girl are."

They stepped into the elevator, and Lott ran the vid fast forward. The two IDs raced east down Michigan Avenue, into East Lansing and onto the university campus. "Breslin Center. Why would he be going to a basketball game?"

"Let me see if we have any agents near campus."

Lott waved his hand. "Don't bother."

"Huh?"

"With all the tricks Noble's been pulling, how long you think it'd take to bring them up to speed?" They strode across the lobby.

"Point taken. But what if he runs off before we get there?"

"And what if some other team spooks him? Right now he doesn't even know we're after him."

Mortensen put his hand on Lott's arm, stopping him. "If he doesn't know we're after him, why's he running?"

Lott considered it, then nodded. "But why a basketball game?"

"Hide in plain sight?"

Lott jerked his thumb toward the oCar, and they got in. He ran a traffic-pattern-manipulating algorithm that put them in the middle lane to move them across town faster. Mortensen brought up Breslin's pay-per-view feed and rotated the scene until it matched the Whipped coordinates and time. He zoomed in, and there sat the girl and her counterfeit father eating junk food, time stamped 7:40.

Lott splayed his fingers to get in closer. The emotion graph filled in. "She's not stressed. That does *not* look like a kidnapping or a hostage situation."

"She could still be an accomplice. Only other thing I can think of is she doesn't know who she's with."

Lott shook his head. "That right there is why it's illegal to fake somebody's ID. Imagine if she was under age and he was a perv."

"I'll give the guy credit, he's got balls. I wouldn't have the guts to pretend to be somebody else in front of one of their family members."

"That N-hanced thing will be a menace if it gets onto the market. Our tools are almost useless against this one guy. What's gonna happen if millions of people start using it? The whole country will spiral into chaos. Criminals everywhere."

Mortensen stared at their cube. "OK, that was thirty-five minutes ago. Move it forward, and see what they do."

Lott flicked, and they watched as Charlie left Kimberly, went up the arena steps, out into the hallway and through a door to the staircase. Then all the cams lost track of him.

"What?! Where the fuck'd he go?" Dylan slapped his leg. "What's Whipped say?"

"He's right— Oh. Now will you look at that? He disappeared from Whipped." The timestamp read 7:55.

Mortensen shook his head. "Twenty minutes ago. Now what are we supposed to do?"

"Oh, I wouldn't get too worked up about it. He'll probably show up as a black hole in a few minutes."

"A black hole?"

"Yeah, it's what I call an *unidentified*. It's similar to the way physicists locate cosmic black holes, by measuring their influence on visible objects around them. When somebody goes off the grid, they keep showing up anyway, because they influence things around them. People have the right to be excluded from cams, but we get data telling us the vid had been overridden. A group of cams in override mode in the same area practically scream 'He's right here.' And other people move out of a black hole's way in a crowded space, or nod and smile at nothing, their heartbeat and respiration changing."

"Yeah, yeah, I get it. Silhouette Tracking."

"Is that what they call it now? Anyway, you just watch. He'll show up again."

"Why don't we have MSU's security system divert any silhouette or black hole alerts to us?"

"Perfect! If we're lucky, we'll know where he is by the time we get there."

Dylan set it up, and they watched the displays. Their oCar sped down the middle lane and the only sound was Dylan's heel hitting the floor as his knee bounced with impatience.

Lott raised an index finger. "I've got another idea. Let's sic the dog on him."

"The dog?"

"You know, the Terrier."

"Oh, that old thing? It doesn't work worth a shit."

"If we lose track of him with our other equipment, it might be our only lead."

Dylan shrugged indifferently.

Terrier—a tracking NetBot named after the breed of dog that would run down a dark hole after animals, with no regard for its own safety—would sit waiting for specific data streams, watching like a dog at a window waiting for a squirrel. Once it saw the data it was looking for, it would chase relentlessly across the Net.

Lott set the Terrier loose to track the data flowing in and out of CCD. It went to work like a group of ruthless private detectives with one goal; find out where Charlie Noble is. This dog could hunt. And it never got tired. Never.

CHAPTER 35

As soon as Charlie turned off N-hanced, he knew he was in for the now-too-familiar wrath of withdrawal. Up until now, he had always been able to choose when that happened and find somewhere he could be alone. But this was an emergency. To make matters worse, it was halftime at the basketball game. The halls were packed with people loading up on refreshments and using the restrooms.

First came the stabbing pain in his head. *Oww!* Then the nausea. He leaped up, and rushed toward the men's room, but he wasn't fast enough. Out it flew with a loud, wet *Splaaatttt!*

People turned toward the sound and backed away. For those nearby, it was too late. Some of the vomit splattered their clothes. People shouted. "Shit! Jesus!"

A little boy stared. "Mommy, what's he doing?"

"He's sick, honey." The woman grabbed her son's hand, pulling him roughly away from Charlie, her eyes big, frightened circles.

His skin a greenish-gray, Charlie put his hand out and moved toward the mother and her boy to calm them. "No, no. It's OK. My stomach is just a little …" He puked again, a long orange column of cheese nachos and pieces of hot dog gushing onto their shoes.

Someone howled a horrified, "Oh, my Gawwwd!"

More faces turned as the retreating inner circle of bodies surged against them. Some ran. A girl squeaked out, "He's green."

Another female voice said, "Is that what the Green Plague looks like?"

Someone else heard the magic words and shouted, "Plague!"

An older man caught the smell and threw up. Screams pierced the air. "Plague! Plague!" Folks ran in panic. Charlie watched helplessly as people knocked each other down and tripped as they ran blind. An entire wave of people off to his right fell like wheat in a field laid flat by a hard rain.

Charlie tried to calm everybody. "No! It's OK. I'm better now!" Nobody heard him above the shouts, screams and howls of pain and terror of the fallen.

Then as gradually as an oCar crests a hill, the panic subsided. People picked themselves up and helped others to their feet. A claxon sounded signaling one minute to the end of halftime. Folks made their way back into the arena, a few glanced over their shoulders at Charlie.

Charlie's head pounded. It occurred to him all this activity was being caught on cam. It would certainly tag as an emergency, and security staff would arrive at any second. If they detained him, there was no way he'd be able to keep away from the oBI agents. As if his thoughts had triggered them, a swarm of Skeets descended upon him. Disconnected from N-hanced, he couldn't demand privacy. *Now what? Restroom! They can't follow me in there.*

As he scrambled down the hall, a few straggling people pulled back, giving him a wide berth.

*   *   *

Their oCar racing toward campus, Agent Mortensen blurted, "This is driving me fucking nuts. Can't we get there any faster?"

"We're doing sixty, Morty. Any faster and we won't be able to stop for pedestrians."

"Shit!"

Lott rolled his hand palm up. "What's with this anger?"

"I hate criminals."

"You're not the first agent I've heard that from. Guys who talk like that usually end up dirty."

Mortensen shook his head, lips tight. "Not gonna happen."

"We don't always get the bad guys."

"I will."

"What if politics gets in the way? What if the boss says lay off, but you know the suspect is guilty?"

Mortensen screwed up his face, his eyes searching for an answer. "Lemme think about that."

"Do that. But it happens."

Dylan spoke in a near whisper. "My old man. Some punks..." He glanced away. "Never mind."

"I'm sorry, but whatever it is, you can't take it out on everyone else. You ever take down somebody innocent?"

"Everybody's guilty of something."

"Right. Even you."

Mortensen turned his head and fidgeted with his fingernails.

"Look, you don't have to be angry like this. There's a simple oGER treatment—"

"I don't want to be treated! I don't *ever* want to forget. I wake up angry, and I keep it going all day. That's what motivates me."

Lott sighed. "I think regular use of obscenities makes it easier to stay angry. It certainly inflames other people. But aside from that, you're going to make a mistake someday and maybe put us in the wrong place. You oughta think—"

The IS cube burst to life. Mortensen said, "Look. Commotion at Breslin. And guess who's at the center of it."

"Told you he'd show up. But why's he throwing up? Nobody gets sick any more."

"Well, if other people are dying from N-hanced, maybe it's his turn."

"This isn't good. If anyone gets hurt, we'll have to pull in campus security."

They winced as people panicked and fell over each other. In less than a minute, it was over. Nobody seemed any the worse.

Their oCar rounded the corner, and Breslin loomed in the distance.

Mortensen rocked in his seat as if to hurry the car along, his eyes on the cube. "What're the Skeets doing?"

"They can't go into restrooms."

"I *know* that. Can't we override it?"

"We're supposed to look out for people's rights, not violate them. You wanna work that way, maybe you'd better move to China."

"So let's just send our oMe2s."

"What's the point? They can't physically interact with Noble. I don't want to spook him any more than he already is."

"I'll send my guy in to hound his ass until we get there." Mortensen reached into his cube.

Lott put out his hand and stopped him. "You do and we make an arrest later, it'll get thrown out. Fruit of the poisonous tree."

"Goddamn fairness laws. George W. Bush was the last *real* president we ever had. He didn't give a shit who was ... taking a shit. We'd be in there right now if those limp-dick liberals didn't have their precious revolution."

"So, you want to get him and make it stick, or you wanna blow it?"

"Yeah, well the jerk can blow me."

Lott laughed. "I don't want to suggest anything here, but, uh, that sounded a little gay."

Mortensen shot him a look that could have fried an egg. Instead, steam exploded from his mouth. "Fuck, fuck, fuck!"

"Hey, partner. We're going into a public place now. Let's start toning down the language, OK?"

"Yeah, yeah. Whatever. Fuck!"

* * *

As Charlie hurried into the restroom, a few men rushed out to get back to their seats before the second half started. Heading to a sink, he cupped a hand under the water and sipped it to rinse the taste of puke out of his mouth, then fidgeted in front of the Nano-Dri. He went to the stalls and looked to see if any were occupied. It made his head pound, but he was alone in the room.

Using standard VR, he lay the blueprints he'd downloaded over the top of Real to see which of the metal wall panels might give him a Skeet-free exit. No luck. One little cubbyhole contained pipes, the other hid electrical. Not even a cockroach could get out of there.

Then he spotted a small panel in the ceiling above one of the stalls. The blueprint showed it opened into a space big enough to stand up in and led to an exit across the hall from the truck ramp. But the lock required a six-pointed star-shaped tool. Here he was, the designer of high-tech software, being pursued by the high-tech Skeets, and an old-fashioned, two-dollar lock blocked his escape.

He made a quick sweep of the room, the trash cans and each of the stalls, looking for anything he might be able to refabricate. Nothing.

He jumped when a man strolled into the restroom. Charlie slipped into the stall below the escape panel. When he crossed his arms, he felt the pocket with the plastic knife and fork left over from his nachos. *Bingo!*— maybe. He waited until the man left, then knelt and scraped the handle of the knife on the cement floor to shape it into a star tool.

It was hard, sweaty work. The new utensils were much stronger than the ones from just ten years ago. *Maybe it's strong enough that it won't break off in the lock.* He climbed up on the toilet seat to check the fit, then back down and scraped some more—all the while on guard for anyone coming after him. Finally he got it right, but the lock wouldn't turn. *Come on!* Then he got the idea to hold the fork tight against the knife for more leverage. No luck.

Wiping sweat from his cheek, he bumped his head on the panel and felt it slip sideways. *It's not flush.* Pushing with his head and turning the improvised tool, the lock moved. Lifting and twisting, little by little, it finally released.

He lowered the panel, let it hang down, and tested the strength of the panel frame. When it held, he lifted himself up until he had both elbows inside. Once he was all the way up, he turned and began to pull the panel shut. That's when he noticed the black powder on the cement where he'd shaped the plastic knife. *Shit!* oClean would eventually dissolve it, but it might take a while.

He lowered himself down and use wet toilet paper to dab up the evidence. *Hurry!* He dried the floor, threw the paper into the toilet and flushed. Climbing back up into the ceiling, he pulled the panel shut behind him.

He started to worry about how he was going to lock it again, when he remembered something he'd read when he was a kid in a book about the magician Harry Houdini. Locks are meant to keep people *out*, not *in*. Sure enough, the mechanism was open from Charlie's side. He twisted the gadget with his fingers and felt it click. *Like butter.*

Standing slowly, he took a few seconds to get his bearings. He tested the floor and found it solid.

Just ahead of him stood the door that the blueprint showed came out onto a steel stairway descending to the loading dock. As he reached for the handle, he caught his breath, realizing cams certainly covered the dock. But he couldn't stay here where human security workers already seemed too slow on his heels.

He turned in a circle looking for a place to hide. Over to his right he heard a loud *Thump*, which made his heart thump nearly as hard. A large electric motor whirred to life, followed by a *Shuuggg, Shuugg, Shuug* behind a steel panel. Looking over the top, he discovered a conveyor belt covered with trash headed for the dumpster, which the blueprints showed him was on the right side of the loading dock. *I can hide out in the dumpster. It'll give me time to think.*

He lifted himself over the barrier and onto the ramp. He could see that if he lay flat, he'd be out of range of the loading dock cams. But to be sure, he grabbed a piece of cardboard and pulled it on top of himself. He turned off all his Ts. *Shouldn't need a lot of smarts for this. Jeff would be proud.* In a few seconds he found himself falling into the bin. He prepared for the landing, intending to stay loose and roll. But his landing wasn't what he expected. Not at all.

CHAPTER 36

Charlie landed in the dumpster softly enough. In fact he found himself completely submerged in a warm, thick liquid. His arms flailed as he tried to find something to push against or grab onto to get back to the surface, but all he ended up with were handsful of more warm goo. The stuff was so thick, he couldn't get his feet under himself. He needed to breathe, and now! At the edge of panic, he got his hand on something that stayed in place. Jerking himself upright, his feet touched down and he pushed his head out of the gunk. He took a quiet gasp. The stench of the mystery liquid gagged him. *Jesus! Don't they use oClean?* He held his nose, but he could feel the harsh fumes in his throat, acidic and putrid. The stuff dripped down his face into his mouth. *Shit!* He tried blowing it out with a soft "Fffff." *Quiet. Digital ears are listening.* What he wanted to do was spit, and gargle, and wipe his mouth out with a towel, and then another towel.

The gunk coated his eyes, blurring his vision. Squinting, and blinking and shaking his head, he whipped around, scouring the area for something to wipe his eyes. Among the boxes and decaying food, he found a disgustingly stained paper towel on top of a piece of cardboard. *God!* He found the cleanest filthy corner and dabbed at his eyes. When he was done, a film remained, making rainbow circles around the lights.

The dumpster was mostly filled with a potpourri of cooking grease, and rotting food. Some of it had clearly been there for days. Charlie was obsessive-compulsive when it came to things sticky or greasy. The bin held a nightmare he'd never dared dream. He cringed and shivered. *Oh, my God! No, no, no.* He tried to calm himself to avoid turning N back on to dial down the panic.

Before he had the panic under control, he felt a tingling that raised a more real fear. Some garbage bins used nano to break down plant and animal materials. The process produced heat, and this stuff was warm. A new rush of anxiety swept over him, as he imagined being digested like the acid that had eaten Gary Billings. In terror, he tried to leap out of the bin, but found himself frozen in place. *Move! Move! Get out! What's the matter with you?*

As the next few minutes crawled by, he realized he wasn't in pain. Then he felt stupid. *Of course. If the dumpster were filled with that kind of nano, it wouldn't smell this bad.* It was odd to find comfort in the stench. As terror descended to OCD distress, he found he could move again.

He tried to focus on his next step. *I've got to get somewhere safe, and then back to the CCD offices. But I'm going to need help.*

As Charlie lay basting, he realized the only person he could trust was Jeff. Better still, Jeff lived only eight miles to the south. And there was something else; Jeff had some friends Charlie had never met. Based on their reputation he suspected they had ways of eluding the ever-vigilant eyes of the Skeets. But he was also afraid Jeff's mysterious friends might be involved in the sabotage of N-hanced; partly because of the Luddites centuries old reputation, and partly because Jeff said he would stop N himself if he had the chance.

So my plan is to ask Jeff to help get N-hanced back on track. His lips pinched into a thin white line. *Yeah, that makes sense.*

As shaky as the idea was, he needed to do something soon. Whoever controlled the Black Octopus software was probably trying to find him right now.

How hard can it be to find me? I left biologicals everywhere. But there's not way I can leave here now. The way I smell—if I came within ten feet of anyone— He shook his head, leaned back in the corner and slowly drifted off to sleep.

*　　*　　*

He was jarred awake when the conveyor came on, dumping more trash into the bin and splattering grease into his face.

Yeah, this is the life. Something made him think of Matthew. *The life of a Messiah.* He had to stop himself from laughing out loud.

CHAPTER 37

Agents Lott and Mortensen got to the Breslin Center at the same time Charlie landed in the grease-filled dumpster. The building read their credentials, and they walked in. Lott blocked a message that would have alerted the security staff of their arrival. They went down to Arena level and into the restroom where the cams had last seen Charlie as Gerald. Checking the stalls, they found no one.

Mortensen said, "Fuck!"

"Whoa, partner. What'd I say about the language thing? We're out in public now."

"Look, man. You're gonna have to lighten up on that for a little while. If a goddamn priest shows up, I'll cool it. But until then, let's just get this asshole."

Lott lowered his eyes and exhaled through his nose.

Mortensen pointed at the wall panels. "What's behind these?"

"Blueprints show electrical and plumbing access. He couldn't get through."

"He could be hiding in one of them." Mortensen walked to the one nearest him and stared at the lock. "Got any tools for that?"

"Sure. We've got a multi that'll fit anything."

"Well, break it out, brother."

Lott rolled the backpack off his shoulder, removed a tool from a pocket, and positioned it on the lock. A laser measured the six-pointed star, and the body of the tool fabbed the shape from carbon nano fibers. The gadget inserted the tip, turned it in the lock and signaled it was done. Lott opened the panel to reveal an array of pipes—and no Charlie. He closed it.

Moving to the second panel, Lott opened it. Just wires.

"Where's that go?" Mortensen pointed at the ceiling.

"Didn't they teach you how to work the blueprints at the academy?"

"Yeah, well that shit's a little boring."

"There's nothing to it. It's like having x-ray vision."

Mortensen opened the stall door and looked up at the panel. "It's the same lock as the others. Let's go."

"Hold your horses, Tonto. Let's use the 4S." Lott went to the backpack for the silver box and handed it to Mortensen. "I'll drop the panel and you open the kit."

Lott stood on the toilet seat, and pressed the tool to the lock. It wouldn't turn.

"C'mon, man. Let's move it."

"It's stuck."

"Well, push it up."

Lott did and the lock turned. *I hate it when he's right.* He let the panel down slowly, and Mortensen popped the lid on the kit. Hundreds of tiny winged devices gently lifted into the opening.

Lott stepped down to the floor. He drew an IS cube and they both watched the display.

The 4S kit used a four-pronged approach to tracking; sounders, scanners, sniffers and scrapers, all communicating with each other. Sounders went first, because echoes decay fastest. Scrapers went last, looking for solid evidence.

Lott said, "I wonder how those sounders work. They never explained that during our training, and you can't get it on the Net."

Mortensen scoffed. "It's just EHR, Echo History Reconstruction, like what happens when you toss a rock into a pond." He flicked a vid onto the cube. "See the waves go out in circles away from the rock? Even if you didn't see it go in, you can figure out the entry point. Now those waves keep going until they hit the edge of the pond, and then they bounce back. That's the same as an echo. You following this?"

"Sure. Keep going."

"The shoreline shapes the liquid echoes, so they're not in a perfect circle any more, and they lose some of their energy. As those waves come back into the middle of the pond, they bump into waves coming off the opposite shore, and it gets harder to tell where the rock went in. But you can still work out the splash point.

"Up in the ceiling there, some of the noise from the game, the whoosh from the ventilation system, and flushing toilets are all adding their own waves into that space. EHR grabs the audio from multiple security cams and subtracts those noises, leaving just the sounds Noble made."

Whatever other problems the kid has, he's certainly not dumb. I just gotta get him to act more professional. "So how come you know all about the kit, but not the blueprints?"

"That kit is some cool shit, man."

Lott nodded, smiling.

*   *   *

Charlie figured out how he would make the trip to Jeff's. Unfortunately, he'd have to turn N-hanced on to access the campus security cams and the roaming Skeets that populated the area between the university and Jeff's house. At MSU, he could send a static image to the cams for a few minutes. The county Skeets would be a little trickier. Their job was to roam, looking for patterns that might suggest criminal activity. That would include anyone without a T signature, someone like Charlie.

He'd need to access the software controlling those Skeets and insert a few lines of code to mimic disturbances in the area near his route, so the Skeets would be too busy to notice him. His confidence built as he rehearsed connecting with the N servers and delivering his orders while dodging the Black Octopus. But the thought of the creature triggered a new round of fear and cold sweat. He felt his jaws clenching.

CHAPTER 38

The agents watched as the 4S data came in and formed a 3-D vid, showing a character Charlie's height and build. It moved along a path from the opening in the ceiling to the trash conveyor. The image changed colors from normal to red and back again; the red representing incomplete data. A digital clock estimated he was there only ten minutes ago.

A dialog appeared on the cube. "Data collection and analysis complete." Lott opened the silver case and beckoned the 4S bugs back home. Mortensen climbed into the ceiling. Lott said, "Hey, wait up."

"Great idea. If he's armed he can take both of us out at the same time."

Where do the recruiters get these guys? Lott stepped into the stall, climbed onto the seat, pushed the backpack ahead, and pulled himself up. Mortensen was already by the conveyor. "Got anything?"

"Yeah. IR says he had his hands on this panel. I'm guessing he got onto the conveyor. Blueprints show it goes to the dumpster."

"Blueprints? I thought they were boring."

"Yeah, well… Looks like some of that training might come in handy after all." Mortensen chinned himself on the panel and peered down at the conveyor. "The 4S doesn't show any heat on the belt here."

"Maybe the belt moved."

"Dumpster." Mortensen dashed for the door.

Lott felt like a yo-yo; his emotions yanked from hope to hopeless as the kid flew from promising to insubordinate, within seconds. He shook his head and followed.

*   *   *

Muffled voices put Charlie on hyper-alert. *That sounds like the oBI agents. Great! Maybe they have an answer for me.* He heard a door open and thump as it

145

bumped up against the stop. That was followed by footsteps on the steel staircase.

As he leaned forward to stand up, Mortensen said, "I know that lying son of a bitch is here somewhere."

Charlie froze and his heart began to pound. *This does* not *sound like a friendly visit.*

Lott said, "Great. Well, if he is here, you just tipped him off we're after him. Who taught you Surveillance and Pursuit? I want to let them know they've been leaving out some of the finer points."

"Listen, I got my own style. Shoot first, ask questions later."

Shoot!? Charlie's head jerked back.

"Oh, so now you're Dirty Harry Mortensen. C'mon, think, Morty. Put the gun away. Even my cat knows you can sneak up on a bird by keeping quiet and moving slowly. And my cat's not all that smart."

Charlie held his breath against an eruption of fear. *What do they think I did? Maybe they contacted the military and they've got a different agenda now.* He scanned the dumpster for a better way to hide. Trash covered him, but all they'd have to do was pull it out to find his head sticking up. *Don't tell me I have to duck underneath this gunk.* His first thought was to turn a box upside down and pull it over his head. But that would just leave the box sticking up where they could grab it. Then he saw a cardboard tube.

Picking it up, he winced before putting it in his mouth. It was covered with God-knows-what. Deciding it was too big to get into his mouth, he set it against his upper lip just and pressed it tight around his mouth. Then he closed his eyes and slowly lay back into the corner until he was completely covered, with just a few inches of the tube sticking out. *Wonderful!*

CHAPTER 39

Mortensen inspected the handrail to the stairs before taking off his jacket, folding and hanging it there. He rolled up his shirtsleeves. He found a clean piece of cardboard, folded and hung it over the edge of the dumpster. Shimmying up the side, he peered in. "Bunch of boxes and grease and shit. Damn! Stinks, too."

"What about IR?"

"Looks like one solid block of heat." He pulled at the boxes, tossing them over the side, careful not to get grease on himself. Leaning in like a Dipping Bird toy, his feet tilted into the air and his head disappeared. Then a box flew out as his feet came back down.

A loud *Thump* shook the conveyor, followed by the sound of the electric motor. Charlie recognized it even though it was muffled in his grease-filled ears. The belt would soon pour new debris into his hiding place. *Oh c'mon! What else can go wrong?*

Mortensen heard the sound, too. "What the fuck was that?"

As if to answer, the belt jittered and rolled and trash headed his way. He had enough time to pull out one more box before the first piece dropped into the bin. It landed with a *Splat* on the grease, and a shiny plume flew past Mortensen's head. He leaped off the unit. "Whoa! Fuck, man! That was close."

Lott shrugged, "Hey, it's part of the job."

"Not when I'm wearing a thousand credit suit, it ain't."

"Lesson thirty-nine; don't dress like that on this job."

Mortensen stared at Lott under crunched eyebrows. "Whaddya want? I should show up in a rubber suit every day? Christ, Lott!"

Lott stared him down.

Mortensen exhaled through his nose with a long hiss. Then he gritted his teeth and kicked the side of the dumpster three times, *Bam, bam, bam*. It rang with a low, metallic "Chuunng!"

Charlie's eyes flew open, flooding them with burning grease. *Jesus Christ! He's shooting!*

Mortensen scanned the outside of the unit. "There's gotta be a shutoff here somewhere."

"Check the blueprints?"

"Oh, yeah." He drew cube and tapped a finger on the loading dock. Aligning the drawing with the conveyor, the machine appeared translucent. He said, "Emergency shutoff." The image zoomed and rotated showing the button on the underside highlighted in red. "Typical. Put the emergency button where anybody with an emergency wouldn't be able to find it. Dumb shits!"

He found the button and pressed. The conveyor stopped with a *Foomp*. Examining the cardboard shield he'd hung over the side, he grabbed the edge, shimmied up and continued removing junk. "Man, I want a desk job."

Lott nodded. *Now there's an idea whose time has come.*

After a few moments he called over his shoulder, "Hey, there's nothing left in here but grease and some other floating shit. You wanna send in some sensors?"

"They don't work under liquid. You're gonna have to probe by hand."

"Yeah, right, Rainman." Mortensen tipped his head and smiled. "Wait a minute. You're just fucking with the new guy, right? Funny." He let out a sardonic, "Ha. OK, your turn."

"Look, if we don't find Noble, how are we going to explain to the boss that we tracked him all the way out here, and then gave up because you were afraid of getting your fingernails dirty?"

"Well if I go in, you'll be the one talking to the boss, because I'll be walking back—unless you don't mind me sliming all over the car. Hell, you want into this gunk? I'll even give you a boost. Then I'll drive back and take the heat with the boss."

"Well, what if—?"

"No, wait. Give me that broom."

Lott followed Mortensen's finger, and passed him the broom.

Mortensen unscrewed the brush and kept the handle. He jabbed at the thick slurry.

Charlie felt a series of soft *chunk, chunk, chunks* as the stick tapped the bottom of the dumpster. He didn't know what the sound was, but he knew it was close. Then something glanced off his leg.

Mortensen felt a resistance and poked wildly trying to hit it again, but he never made contact. Finally he gave up and tossed the handle away. "Hey, man, he's not in here. And this smell is getting to me."

"Come on down and we'll try a couple other ideas."

"I'm telling you, he's *not* in here."

"No, no. Let's have the 4S check the room. He's not in the security vid. He might have spoofed 'em, but if he did, it's nothing I can see. Maybe he went *up* the ramp."

"I'm not going up there."

Lott gave a tired smile. "That's what the kit is for."

Mortensen steepled his hands into prayer position. "Thank you."

*   *   *

While Lott and Mortensen waited for the 4S report, Charlie was having his own problems under the grease. Some of the liquid oozed into his mouth. He pushed the tube harder against his face. The seepage slowed, but the edge of the tube was cutting into his lip. Even though the agent's voices sounded more distant, he didn't dare lift his head. But he knew he couldn't hold out much longer.

Finally so much grease leaked into the tube that he couldn't breathe. A rivulet ran down his throat and he almost gagged. After a minute white bursts of light appeared on the insides of his eyelids. He had to surface now or pass out and drown. Pressing his hands against the bottom of the bin, he pulled his legs under him, and lifted his head out into the air.

As he took that first desperate breath, he heard a door close. *Did they leave, or did somebody else come in?* The tickle in his throat returned, and he needed to cough. Clearing his throat made it worse. Giving up he let the coughs come, trying to muffle them with his sleeve. Once they subsided, he listened, but heard nothing. *Thank God. Now what?*

And what the hell was that all about? He thought about all the reasons the agents might want him dead. One thing was for sure, the next interview session was not likely to be as friendly as the first. He'd been right about Mortensen; he was a real hothead. *Great. Now I've got somebody else after me. But what if these guys are the murderers? Of course. Pretend to have a friendly chat at the Federal building, gather some info, then go in for the kill. Shit!* He made a mental note to have the system warn him whenever the agents got anywhere near to him.

He tried unsuccessfully to get the grease out of his eyes. *This is insane. I mean, running from the oBI?* A shiver went up his back and ended by standing his hair on end. A surprised smile crept onto his face as he realized it was the same shiver he'd felt when he came down the mountain on the snowboard. *Am I enjoying this just a little?*

*   *   *

After the 4S kit found nothing upstairs, Mortensen said, "So, are we going after the Collier girl and her old man?"

The agents came through the loading dock door and back down the stairs. Charlie froze.

Lott said, "What's the point? She clearly wasn't a hostage or an accomplice. Anything Noble would have said to her other than father-speak would have registered as anxiety." He smiled. "Besides, from what I could see, she did most of the talking. I almost felt sorry for the guy."

"So can I assume I get to go home now?"

"Yeah. But let's get this junk back in the bin." Lott tossed a box over the side.

Mortensen jumped as a glob of grease splattered near his shoes. "Hey, hey! Take it easy! Just ease them over, like this."

Charlie grabbed a box and covered his head.

Lott said, "Hey, you'd better turn the conveyor back on."

"What the hell, Lott? Can't you do anything yourself?"

CHAPTER 40

Charlie guessed more than two hours had passed since the agents left the loading dock. With his T off, he was clockless. But the basketball game had ended long ago, and he was sure the building was empty except for custodial staff. The grease was hardening around him, but it didn't feel as if he would be trapped.

He needed to reconnect to N-hanced for a few minutes to clear a security path to Jeff's. As he pulled his arms and legs from the glop, he heard a vehicle drive down the ramp. *Cleaning crew? Semi bringing in a rock show? C'mon, folks! I don't have time for this.*

Other than the whirring of the electric motor, all he heard was the soft crunching of tires rolling on pavement. As the sound grew closer, he guessed it might be a bus or a delivery truck, but nothing as large as a semi. He jumped when he felt a shimmy as something scraped against the side of his dumpster. He jumped again when something bumped the bin, moving it a couple inches. *What—? No, it can't be.*

The bin tilted. Charlie looked around for anything to hold onto. Maybe a handle or a bolt, but he found nothing. When the dumpster tipped up to ninety degrees, he slid onto its side, and looked down for a soft place to land. As the angle grew even steeper, he spotted a large flat box. He swung around feet first, aimed and landed. *No problem.* The truck bounced the bin a few times, and large globs heavy coagulated grease plopped down on top of him.

When aheavy steel door closed the yawning mouth on the back of the truck, he found himself in total darkness. The truck shuttered, jerked, and advanced up the ramp.

As he settled back, He heard a *Thunk* and a *Whirrrrr.* The pile of trash he sat on moved. A metallic screech stabbed his ears. He raised his hand and felt the overhead door pressing down. *Oh, my God! It's a crusher!* The prospect of having the life squeezed out of him sent his bowels into spasm.

But when he smelled ozone and noticed a soft-blue glow near the floor at the front of the enclosure, he gasped. *A matter dismantler!*

To a human, a dismantler was the equivalent of a black hole; if you went in, you never came out. Charlie had heard stories about people who had lost an arm or a leg to the things. Arms and legs were easy to re-grow. But not your torso—and certainly not your head.

Charlie scrambled backward. His foot shifted, and instead of retreating from the event horizon, he slid toward it. "No, no, no!" Crab-walking backward, this time his feet held. Pieces of trash shot from under his shoes and into the blue, where they disappeared with a mean *Hisss* and a burst of yellow light. He found his back against the truck cover, which nudged him toward the glow. He estimated he had about four minutes to live—unless he lost his footing. And slipping was a distinct possibility. "Hey, I'm in here! Stop! Hey! STOOOPPP!!!" He pounded the side of the crusher door. Nothing. *God. These trucks are computer driven.* "Heelllppp!"

Three and a half minutes to go.

*　　*　　*

The crusher door goaded Charlie toward the dismantler. He had to re-connect to the N servers now—to find the trash service that handled the university account and get the truck to let him out. It meant he'd have to juggle that along with setting up diversions in the Skeet system—and dodge the Black Octopus. Probably not impossible. Probably.

Charlie fired up T but left his ID set to anonymous. He knew WPTD might pick him up, but he had no choice right now. Flicking the cube into view, he double-tapped the N icon. He felt the usual sensation of lights coming on and his tension lifted, but he didn't take time to enjoy it. His vision now N-hanced, he could see better in the back of the truck, but it did nothing to stop the moving door or the beckoning of the dismantler. *Fifteen seconds closer to oblivion.*

His attention now inside the server, it took all of five seconds to find out that Granger handled MSU trash removal. The Black Octopus awoke, and its tentacles snaked their way toward him. He dodged into another part of the server. Every move ate up precious time, but he had no alternative. It was either death by black or blue. In another five seconds he was in Granger's computer. Octopus at his heels, he jumped up two levels. He found the truck schedule, but the truck that usually handled MSU was offline for repairs. He searched the database for Breslin and found the truck he was in, but he needed to tap the truck's computer.

One of his PAs reported it was inside the MSU security cams and ready to usher him to the edge of campus.

The county Skeet system was in the middle of a backup and wouldn't be available for five minutes. As he and the team considered how to handle that, the Black Octopus found him.

He constructed a dozen shell programs that, on the surface, imitated him as he appeared inside the system. He scattered them in different directions. The Octopus hesitated, then chased eight of them—none of them the real Charlie.

Two and a half minutes until blue annihilation. And how long until black annihilation? Arrggh!

The front of the trash pile sat sitting on disappeared. The truck hit a bump, and the rest of the pile tumbled forward in a rush. He gasped. What had been four feet between him and the dismantler, became three. Less than two minutes, and he continued sliding. He reached back and pulled trash and greasy gunk forward, around, and from under him, feeding the pit. He was looking for a clear place to stand on the floor instead of on the shifting pile. The halo hissed and crackled, and strobed flashes of yellow, white and green light. The door had finished its arc and was now vertical to the floor—still pushing.

A six-foot metal bar churned to the top of the roiling junk. Scanning the truck box, Charlie spotted a ridge set back a couple inches from the dismantler. He jammed one end of the bar against the upper ridge and the other against the bottom of the moving door.

In the server, he shot his county Skeet plan at one of his PAs to carry out—*if* he escaped the truck. He would have no way of knowing if the plan was executed, because he would have to turn N off as he exited the truck. It would be easy to tell if the plan failed—he'd be caught! There were so many shaky parts to this scheme, but he didn't see any alternative.

As the crusher door strained against the metal bar, the motor whined and lowered in pitch, and a metallic groan shook the container. Then with a screech and a *Claaannng*, the bar bent and flew past Charlie's ear and into the halo, dissolving in a flash of orange sparks. The door leapt forward six inches, slamming him in the back, throwing him off balance. "Shit!" He swung his arms in circles trying to keep from falling into the pit, his eyes wide with terror. The fingers of his left hand brushed the surface of the blue light. There was a *Fizzz* and three sparks. Charlie fell back against the crusher gate panting. His T system blocked the pain, but a warning appeared in his oEyes. He looked at his fingers. Three of them were missing the top joint. The place where they had touched the dismantler was clean, perfectly flat and cauterized, as if they had never been there. His heart pounded. "Fuck!" He watched for a second as Ts began reconstructing the lost fingertips. But only for a second.

One minute to go.

The N-hanced server wasn't able to maintain the speed of his dozen counterfeits while running all his other requests. The Black Octopus caught the copies it followed and one by one they dissolved. Each free tentacle shifted its attention to one of the remaining copies—and Charlie, sending him on the run again.

As he zigzagged and dodged, he finally got the information about the truck. The next stop was Spartan Stadium, but the truck should have arrived by now. Checking GPS he saw he was far south on Trowbridge Road. Multiple streets were blocked for repair, and the truck had been rerouted. He still couldn't to access the truck's controls. Granger's truck controllers were on a different computer from the scheduling software. His PAs hadn't broken the user/password combination yet. *It's only a garbage truck for God's sake. What kind of security system can it have?* "OK, guys. Any suggestions?" And he got one.

"Use your Wi-Fi to access the truck's computer directly."

Letting his PAs handle the Black Octopus, Charlie pulled his awareness back into the truck and transmitted up and down the spectrum until he found the truck's frequency. But his signal wasn't strong enough to take control. *I've got to get closer to the cab.* Propping his feet against the bottom of the moving door, he tipped forward until his hands reached the front of the container, leaving him leaning him over the dismantler. The truck lurched sideways. His right hand slipped, throwing his shoulder down, his hand dangerously close to the pit. Screaming, he yanked his arm back, cradling it protectively—the smell of ozone and crackle of the blue light terrifying. Wiping the grease from his hand, he reached out and tested the wall for friction. It held. The last of the trash disintegrated just a few feet below his face. He focused his Wi-Fi and got command of the truck's computer. *I can't believe it! People are still using 1234 as a password? What's the point of having a security system if you're not—* The wall pushed against his feet, his toes inches from the edge of the blue glow.

He spotted the dismantler menu and clicked the "Off" button. Jumping up a menu, he found the crusher controls and commanded the door open. Pushing off the wall, he stood up straight. The cold night air flowed in around him. Then he shot his awareness back to CCD's servers.

He found himself being jerked in random directions by his PAs as they kept him just ahead of the Black Octopus. Gathering his composure, the words came in a rush. "Run the routine for the campus cams. I'm taking Farm Lane instead of Harrison Road. Do your thing with the county Skeets. Once you're done, shut down the system. And give me my own face back." He felt twitching under his cheeks and across his forehead. "OK, gotta go. Good luck."

"Good luck to *you*."

Charlie curled what was left of his fingers over the edge of the truck box and chinned himself. He spotted a group of students walking with their backs to him. Moving to the other side of the box, he hoisted up and peered over. No one in sight. He took a deep breath and switched off N along with the rest of his Ts.

Disoriented, in the dark again, and off balance, the familiar nausea washed over him. He slumped, preparing for the usual N-hanced withdrawal. His head throbbed but the nausea passed. *Thank God.* Pulling himself up the inside of the box, he threw one leg, then the other over. Hanging down the side, he let go and dropped to the street.

And he ran.

CHAPTER 41

As quickly as Charlie's feet hit the pavement he knew he was in trouble. With his T off, his shoes no longer had instructions for foot support. They were now nothing but floppy material. But he was on a schedule—assuming his PAs had gained control of the county Skeet system. *Think about something besides your feet.*

He scanned the horizon, the buildings and the roads, looking for anyone on foot or vehicles that might spot and report him as unidentified. All clear. He made his way east on Trowbridge, to his right turn onto Farm Lane. But he was already had blisters on his feet. *Forget it. Think about... what? The run!*

7.9 miles from the truck to Jeff's. Average marathon speed is 8 miles per hour. That's almost an hour. It takes about 7.5 minutes to run a mile, or 1.42 minutes for every 1000 feet. I can do that!

What did my clock read when I signed off? Hope I don't need to get off the road to hide from anyone. Don't think about your feet. Yeow! Think about breathing. One breath in for every two steps, one out for the next two. One hundred twenty steps per minute. Nice even stride. Lock it in. Breathe deeply. He heard the three-quarter hour chime of Beaumont Tower. *12:45. Right on schedule!*

As he approached Mt. Hope, an oCar came from the east with its right blinker on. He climbed over the bank left by a snowplow and dove into the clean powdery fluff on the other side. It was cold, but he was warm enough from running that it felt good. After the car passed he lifted his head. He started to get up and stopped. Lying back down, he rolled like a crazy dog, trying to get the grease and stink off. Then he sat up and rubbed snow on his head, shoulders, and arms. He still smelled, but his skin felt better. *Let's go!*

He was in an open part of the university with few buildings and no dorms. Ahead sat the now-abandoned Pavilion for Agriculture and Livestock Education. He had seen Monty Roberts do a show there back in the '00s. Monty was known as a horse whisperer. What Monty taught his disciples was now part of N.

How's my pace? Feels just right.

He turned right onto Forest Road, then left onto College Road. *Almost two miles. Still two and a half before I'm off university property. Then I'll find out if my boys were able to divert the county Skeets. C'mon boys.*

Listening, he only heard the faint *Whoosh* of far off oCars and trucks on US-127 which ran north and south just a mile to the west, and I-96 running east and west two miles to the south. *Otherwise quiet. Somehow different from VR-filtered quiet. Somehow more pure?*

Charlie changed his focus from listening to smelling. His own smell reminded him of dumpster diving when he was a kid. He and his brothers used to find treasures in the alley behind the stores near their house. He remembered the smell of ink behind the print shop. The same smell inside the pulp science fiction books he used to read. The smell that only later he noticed was gone from newer books, probably replaced by something environmentally friendly. Orchard added the smell back into virtual books. He wondered if they weren't leaving something good behind now that VR filtered everything "objectionable" out of life.

He would have liked some VR extended vision at the moment, because the moon disappeared leaving the night unusually dark. He worried about stepping into a hole or on a stone and twisting his ankle. That would be the end of it all. But the cold air felt good—more solid and silver-blue and palpable somehow. It burned his nose and his throat and in his chest—making him feel alive.

He paused for traffic to clear on I-96 before hunkering down and scampered over the bridge, onto the final leg of the MSU journey. *Halfway.*

The oscillating *Whoosh* of the highway sang in his ears like the sound of ocean waves as he rounded onto Sandhill Road. University property ran alongside to his left, but he was officially off campus. He couldn't see the pavement beneath his feet. The lights from an occasional car lit the sky far overhead, but none of it carried down to him. All he saw was ghostly blackness. *Just keep going. If you get caught, you'll deal with it then. One mile to Hagadorn.*

He caught his foot on something and stumbled—*Shit!*—but righted himself. The extra pressure on his feet made the blisters scream.

Halfway to his next turn, Charlie heard a dog bark. A deep voice. *Big! And it doesn't sound friendly. German Shepherd? Rottweiler? Chihuahua? Yeah, very funny. It would be nice to have a little moonlight right about now. Uh-oh. It's getting closer.* He staggered blindly over the snow bank to his left, back onto MSU property. He remembered a barbed wire fence he could jump, to give him time to make friends with the dog. It's bark grew more vicious and loud as the fence caught him in the chest. He grabbed hold between the barbs and leaned over. That's when the dog grabbed hold of his pant leg. Charlie kicked, but the dog dodged and yanked harder, snarling. The barb between his hands dug into his stomach. Finally a kick landed on the dog's nose. The dog yelped and let go. The sudden release threw Charlie face first over the fence. "Shi—" Everything went from extremely dark to completely black.

CHAPTER 42

When he came to, it took Charlie a moment to figure out where he was. His forehead and nose were pressed into the snow with something hard against his head. *Rock.* Then he felt a goose egg at his hairline. *Owww!* It he didn't feel he'd broken the skin.

How long have I been out? I'm not shivering. Probably not too long. He got up. His neck and head hurt. Feeling a draft he reached down his right leg to find his pants torn and his leg was scratched and bleeding. *Great! Tetanus, lockjaw, and what time do you suppose it is? And where's the dog?* He whistled and waited. No dog. Climbing the fence, he trudged back to the road. Taking a few tentative running steps, he studied how his body reacted to the movement. Upper body seemed fine, but *Yeeoow!*, his feet shrieked bloody murder. He gritted his teeth, which made his head hurt worse. Wincing, he loosened his jaw and picked up the pace, limping a little. His head pounded to his heartbeat. *Don't be a wimp. Only a couple miles to go.*

*　　*　　*

He made a right onto Hagadorn, and had only been on the road for a couple of minutes when he heard the whine of a siren behind him. Turning, about a mile away he saw three lights coming toward him; two on the road and one in the sky. *A car—and a chopper!* His heart sank. *That's it.* He let out a big sigh, weary and relieved. Raising his hands he walked to the middle of the road. *I'll go in, tell the truth, and their programmers will look at my work and understand what I was doing, and— No! There's no way in hell they'll understand it unless they're N-hanced themselves. And they're not going to do that if they think it's killing people. Give up? Bullshit!*

He raced to the roadside, leaped over the snow bank, scrambled across the ditch and into the trees. Laying down, he scooped snow on top of himself. Then his body sagged. *Oh, what's the use? The chopper will see my*

159

footprints. And if the Skeets reported me, being covered with snow won't make any difference. Then some resolve. *Well, better they find me now before I get to Jeff's and get him into trouble.*

He held his breath. The siren grew louder, its scream swirled together with the rapid *Thupping* of the helicopter blades. The cacophony grew so loud he needed to cover his ears, but he didn't dare move. Then the roar softened and lowered in pitch as it passed him by. *Maybe they're after someone else. But who? There's nothing out here. What, maybe a cow mutilation?* "Ha!" At last—a laugh. But it was bitter. He was so tired.

That took about three minutes. I'm still be on schedule. Let's go!

He jumped up, slapped the snow off, and ran, watching the red taillights and the helicopter disappear to the south. *We're supposed to be so much smarter these days. But even with all the technology, I'm still being tossed around like a leaf in the wind.*

He remembered the song *'Til I Die,* which Brian Wilson wrote for the Beach Boys. It make him think of his second wife, who tried to commit suicide during a bout with depression. The third verse was about a leaf on a windy day, and the wind would continue to blow, "Until I die."

He hadn't understood at the time. But now he thought he might have some idea how she felt—so utterly helpless, waiting for the wind to stop, knowing it never will.

He had a lot of regrets about his first two marriages. He wondered what arguments he could have prevented if he'd had N. *But maybe that's wishful thinking. Enough! Think of something fun we did.* But nothing came to him. *There had to be good times. Otherwise you don't get married. Right?* But he couldn't remember any. *Maybe that's how you move on without being crushed; you hold on to all that was bad.*

Then he thought about his VR son, Robbie. *Right. Robbie and music.* Charlie smiled.

"Daddy, sing me one of your songs."

"OK. Which one do you want to hear?"

"The car one."

"Ah. You know, I wrote that before the oCar."

"Yeah. What does that mean, 'drive?' "

"Charlie flicked an old movie into his cube. "See how they held onto a steering wheel?"

"Why did they do that?"

"Because they didn't have computers that could do it. It was dangerous. Some people did other things while they were driving."

"Like what?"

"Like talk on the phone, put on makeup, type text messages. I had a friend who told me he played guitar while steering with his knees."

"Is that dangerous?"

"Ohhh, yeah. Hey, did I ever tell you how that song started?"

"With my cousin, Marie?"

"Right. She was only a few years older than you when she wrote the words. Did you know the original song was *I'm Gonna Rock*?"

"Yeah. Will you write a song with me some day?"

"Why not?"

"Good. I wanna do one about farts."

Charlie smiled and shook his head. Robbie laughed his forced little-boy laugh.

"OK, so you know it's called *I'm Gonna Drive* <http://n-hanced.com/gonnadrive.php> Sing it with me."

I'm gonna drive in the morning
Drive, drive all through the day
Gonna race down the sunset
Chase it til the sky turns gray
Cause when I drive I'm free
Ain't nothin' gonna take that away

Gonna drive up to Boston
Montreal, Ottawa, Thunder Bay
Cross the Bad Lands to Spokane
Then Seattle on down to L.A.
Cause when I drive I'm free
Ain't nothin' gonna take that away

I'm gonna drive, drive, drive
I'm gonna drive, drive, drive
I'm gonna drive, drive, drive
I'm gonna drive, drive, drive
Cause when I drive I'm free
Ain't nothin' gonna take that away

The song changed keys and went to the bridge.

Don't give me no bi-cycle
No public transport-jive
And if I gotta walk there
I don't wanna be alive - I gotta drive

The instrumental broke into a Chuck Berry lead, and Robbie played air guitar, strutting with arms flailing and lips pursed like Mick Jagger. The song jumped back into the original key and they sang together.

Gonna drive all my life
Gonna drive 'til my dyin' day
Promise you'll pick up my ashes
Drive 'em down the old highway
And then you'll roll down the windows
Let the wind just blow me away.

They sang the chorus again and finished with…

Jump on my chariot 'o gold
Gonna drive 'round Heaven all day.

Robbie laughed and clapped.

Was it just the cold making Charlie's eyes burn and tear up? There was a feeling in his chest that told him differently.

Robbie. Charlie felt a great weight of sadness and regret for things forever lost. *Shit. Sentimental old fool.* He wiped his eyes. That was one thing about the prospect of living forever; sad memories keep piling up. How old would you have to be before the weight becomes too much to bear? People would absolutely need N just so they could deal with it all. He wished he had access to it right now.

*　*　*

And then he saw it—or thought he did. Jeff's house. Still tiny and far away. Up ahead, on the right. Just a flash of black peeking between the dark triangles that indicated a stand of pines. Too dark to know for sure. Just a silhouette really. *A silhouette.* It reminded him of the nightmare he'd had with the skittering thing that ran away whenever he tried to look at it. And that reminded him of the groping Black Octopus. It returned his feeling of foreboding.

Another minute of running and he was close enough to know for sure. Yes, it was Jeff's all right. And none too soon. Charlie was sure he had blisters on his blisters—some of them probably torn open. He imagined taking off his shoes to find socks soaked with blood.

A minute later Charlie started the run up the long driveway. The house was completely dark. *What if he's not home?*

CHAPTER 43

There was no doorbell on Jeff's house, and Charlie didn't dare pound on the door. Even though Jeff's place was out in the country, too much noise might arouse the neighbors or their dogs and end up calling out the Skeets. *Damned Skeets!* He knew Jeff's bedroom was upstairs, but he didn't know where. He went around the house throwing pebbles at each of the second story windows. It took five minutes, because with more than a foot of snow on the ground, he had trouble finding pebbles. On his second trip around a light came on. When he saw the curtains move, he waved at the shadow and pointed to the front door. Then he dashed to the porch, watching other lights coming on, and waited until the door opened. The cold settled in and his teeth were chattered.

Jeff took a whiff and reared back. "Jesus Christ! You stink! What the hell happened to you?"

"C-c-can I c-c-come in? It's f-f-f-freezing out here."

Jeff made a face. "Hell no. I don't want any of that shit on my carpet."

"M-m-maybe you can get a t-t-towel and I can wipe off? P-p-plastic bags for my feet or something?" Charlie shivered wildly. Jeff seemed to take a disgusted pity.

"All right. Wait here." It was a couple minutes before he came back with a ratty old towel and some plastic bags. He'd also donned rubber gloves.

"Here, wipe your feet and put these bags on them. Then come in and use the rest of the towel to wipe off that other shit." He winced and put the back of his hand against his nose, apparently getting another whiff.

Charlie did as he was told, but he shivered uncontrollably. While putting a bag on one foot he lost his balance and leaned against the side of the house.

"Aw, don't touch the house. That shit'll never come off."

"S-s-sorry." Jeff and Charlie were certainly alike when it came to their obsession with greasy things.

After he was bagged, Charlie shuffled in and wipe down. Jeff's voice dripped with irritation. "Now look, I don't want any of my blankets fucked up trying to get you warm, so I'm gonna put you in the shower. Probably work faster in there anyway. And don't touch *anything*."

Charlie tried to nod, but it came out as one giant spasm. Jeff led the way to the first floor bathroom. Charlie said, "Wh-what t-t-time is it?"

"What?"

Charlie pointed to his wrist. "Time."

Jeff still wore a watch. "Ten after two. Why?"

"T-t-tell you later."

Charlie's goal was to arrive at Jeff's at 2:00. *That means I was probably only knocked out for a couple of minutes. Assuming my PAs took care of the Skeets, I might have done it.*

Jeff paused at the edge of the tub. "Don't get undressed out here."

Charlie reached for the shower curtain.

"No! Don't touch that. Let me do it." He pulled it back to reveal a shower/tub. "Get undressed in there. I'll grab another plastic bag for your clothes. We'll decide later whether to clean them or burn them."

While stepping into the tub, Charlie had another immense shiver throwing him off balance. He tipped backward and grabbed Jeff's arm.

"No! Now that shit's on my pajamas. Fuck!" Jeff's gaze fell to Charlie's hand. "What the hell happened to your fingers?"

"L-l-later. Later."

Charlie got the rest of the way into the tub, and Jeff closed the curtain. "Don't touch anything in there. Just get undressed." He left the room.

After a minute he returned and pushed the bag through the curtain. Charlie put the filthy clothes into the bag and handed it back. When he started the shower, Jeff shouted, "There's a towel just outside the curtain when you're done. Don't forget to wash your hair. I'll find you something to wear and try to wash your stuff." Charlie let the warmth of the water wash away the cold. He jumped at Jeff's voice. "And rinse everything down in there when you're done, including the handles."

Twenty minutes later Charlie limped down the stairs. His hair was dry, and he wore some of Jeff's old clothes. They were a couple sizes too small, and he felt ridiculous. Pulling the tight socks onto his blistered feet had been agony. Otherwise he felt much better, and the blue was gone from his lips. Jeff had changed into a shirt and jeans. He sat in an old-fashioned lounger chair, all the features of his face pointing downward.

Charlie said, "I need your help." He sat down on the couch at right angles to the lounger.

"Do ya think?"

"Remember when I had to leave Beggar's the other day?" Charlie tugged at a short sleeve.

"Yeah?"

"One of our alpha testers committed suicide. Have you seen anything about it on the Net?"

"Um, in case you forgot, I don't participate in that."

"Right. Sorry. I thought maybe someone would have told you. Anyway, since then, two more testers have killed themselves."

"Oh." Jeff said it with what looked like real concern. "I see." Then his face tightened. "You see? That's what happens when you start messing with tech shit."

Charlie wanted to jump up and strangle him, but the feeling dissipated quickly. *Don't kill your meal ticket, Charlie.* He was tired, grouchy, un-N-hanced, and feeling particularly vulnerable, now dependent on the one person most opposed to everything he stood for.

Apparently seeing Charlie's anger come and go, Jeff held up his hands and said, "OK. OK. So what brings you here? And why were you covered in that … gunk?"

"First the oBI brought me in for questioning." He continued to fill Jeff in on the details, beginning with his escape to Breslin, the interview of his oMe2, shutting off N, his ordeal in the dump truck, the run, and finally being chased by the dog.

Jeff peered out from under suspicious eyebrows. "So what you want from me?"

"I need to get back to my office in order to figure out what went stushy. As far as I can tell, I'm the prime suspect. I don't think they're even looking at anybody else. If they arrest me, I'll never be able to prove I'm innocent—assuming I actually am."

"Live by the sword—"

Charlie's eyes tightened.

"Never mind." Jeff held up a palm. "So why me? Why don't you get that girlfriend of yours to help you?"

The last thing Charlie wanted to do right now was discuss Terra with Jeff. He fumbled. "Um … I can't go to Terra."

"Why not?"

Charlie searched for a way to explain it. As much as Jeff hated technology, whatever Charlie came up with wasn't likely to go over well. "Uh …" His eyes pointed at the floor. "She's virtual."

"Yeah, so what? So you guys meet remotely. Why would that prevent you from going to her for help."

"No. She's not … Real." Charlie squinted, expecting Jeff to hit him.

"What are you saying?"

"Well … you know about computer dating?"

"Yeah?"

"I'm dating a computer."

"What? "

Charlie shrugged.

Jeff's face rolled through a range of emotions as he apparently played back all their previous conversations about Terra. Once he put the pieces together his face twisted in anger. "You sick fuck!"

"Look, I just needed an uncomplicated relationship."

"And that's not complicated?"

"No, it's not."

"You're fucking a cartoon. That's not complicated?"

"No. It's ... it's not. Not at all. She's right there. I can touch her. It's not even like looking at a vid. It's Real. I ... I mean, Virtually ... Real." *I need to get him away from this conversation.*

"So what do you...? How do you...? Never mind. I don't want to know." He waved a hand and rolled his eyes. "So how's that any different from prostitution?"

"It's not prostitution. Terra can be anything I want her to be. She's creative inside my fantasies. And she's not trying to steal my wallet. It's a lot less complicated than a human relationship. And why am I defending myself to you, anyway? You know what? You're prejudiced."

"Prejudiced? I'm not prejudiced. You have to be prejudiced against people. You can't be prejudiced against a cartoon."

"It's prejudging someone or some*thing* before you know anything about it. That includes a virtual person."

Everything in Jeff's face and posture exuded disgust. "I don't care what you say. It's sick. You're one sick son of a bitch."

That lit Charlie's fuse—

"Hey! You know what? *You'd* be a lot better off with somebody like Terra. It would probably take the edge off your constant anger. You know *exactly* what it's like to lose someone. You remember how I was when I lost Barbara. Same as when you lost Susan."

"It's *not* the same. Technology killed Susan."

"Right. And a car killed Barbara. A car is technology. So get off your high horse and look at Reality. We're in the same boat here. Only I'm a lot happier. Or I was ... until all this started up."

Jeff's face changed into a triumphant expression.

—And Charlie's fuse hit the bomb.

"OK, you hate technology so much. So what do you want to do? Go back to the Stone Age? Oops! Nope. Can't do that because stone tools are technology. So I guess you don't wanna go back that far. But it seems to me that bike of yours is technology. Maybe you'd better give it up. C'mon now, if you're gonna be a purist, get pure. So, just how far back *do* you want to go? Have you thought about that? How far back do we have to turn the clock to make you happy? Huh? Until you get Susan back?"

Jeff reacted as if he'd been slapped in the face. His right fist snapped around and caught Charlie on the jaw. Charlie's teeth clicked together. The world turned white like a flashbulb had exploded, and he fell back against the couch. It took a few seconds for his vision to clear, and he found himself looking at the ceiling. He raked his gaze down to find that instead of confronting Jeff's eyes of fire, his head was on his chest and his shoulders slumped.

Charlie watched anxiously for a moment while massaging his chin. Then he said, "All right, I deserved that. I'm sorry. Jeff? Really, I'm sorry. I didn't mean it like that." He reached over and put his hand on Jeff's shoulder.

Jeff jerked his shoulder away and brought his eyes up. The corners of his mouth were drawn down and his eyes brimmed. "That's it. That's it. Get out! Get the fuck outta my house!" The tears rolled down his cheeks and onto his shirt. He leaned forward and Charlie jumped back, thinking Jeff was going to hit him again.

Jeff stood. "I said, get the fuck out!" He pointed to the door.

Charlie didn't move. He had nowhere else to go. Finally he mustered a weak, "Please. I'm sorry. I really am."

Jeff grabbed the door and flung it open so hard it bounced off the doorstop with a loud *thump* and slammed shut again. Now even angrier, Jeff grabbed the handle and with exaggerated slow motion pushed it against the wall. Without looking at Charlie he pointed to the outside. "Go!"

Charlie's mind raced. Then he came up with something from the deep past. A quote from one of Jeff's favorite movies. He raised the pitch of his voice and said, "Help me Obi-wan Kenobi, you're my only hope."

Jeff stopped, slumped his shoulders, and slowly turned with an exasperated look on his face. "Oh, great. Now you're going to pull that Princess Leia shit on me?" But it looked as if it had worked. His demeanor had softened.

"I don't know where else to turn. The trip here was a one-time, one-way deal. If I go back out there now, I'll be back on the grid, and that'll be the end of my chances to clear myself."

"So what do you think you're going to do, live here for the rest of your life?" Jeff closed the door.

"I guess I was thinking maybe one of your Luddite friends would know how I could stay off the grid. Obviously some of them have figured out how to get around without being seen."

Jeff's brow seemed furrowed in thought rather than anger. His eyes scanned the carpet. Finally he said, "Yeah. You know, maybe I do know somebody who can help."

Realizing the inconvenience, Charlie threw Jeff a pained look. "I hate to say this, but every minute counts. I'm afraid these government guys are going to seize the servers, and that'll be the end of it."

Jeff's attitude changed as if a light switch had been flipped. "I'll go now. You stay here. It'll probably take me an hour. You can get some rest."

What just happened? "Will this friend of yours be awake?"

"They'd get up for something like this."

They?

Jeff got his coat. "I guess I'm getting any sleep tonight." He smirked. "Not that I sleep worth a shit most of the time anyway. Hey, there's some homemade beer in the fridge. And some other stuff in the cupboards. Whatever you find is OK. Oh, I gotta to get your clothes into the dryer." He started across the room.

"Wait a second, Jeff. How do you know these people?"

"One of my students thought I might want to meet them after he heard me bitching about how technology killed … Well, you know."

"Yeah. So what are they like?"

"I thought you said every minute counts. You want to sit around and chat, or you want me to get going?"

"No, no. You're right."

"Don't worry. They're good people." He said it over his shoulder as he headed down the basement stairs.

Charlie looked in the fridge, but wasn't really hungry. With his T off and no bacteria in his gut, his stomach complained miserably.

Jeff came up from the basement. "Your clothes'll be dry by the time I get back. See ya."

Charlie flung himself around and shouted, "Wait! Don't go yet!"

Jeff jumped and turned toward him. "Jesus, man. What the hell's wrong?"

"We need to check to see if any of the Skeets followed me here. If they did and they start following you… Well, I don't want to get you and your friends into trouble for harboring a fugitive."

"Yeah? Well fuck those government jerks. They're just a little too far up our asses with those goddamned Skeets, anyway."

Ah, that's *what got him going.* "OK, but let's at least take a look."

Jeff shrugged.

"Bring me your strongest flashlight."

"Will a focused-beam super-LED do?"

"Perfect."

Jeff went to the kitchen and brought it back. "So how you gonna see them? They're so small."

"I should be able to see the glint from their wings." Charlie went to the front window, lifted a corner of the curtain and turned on the light. "Shit!" He gasped and fell back on the floor, dropping the flashlight.

"What?"

Charlie's face was a mask of terror. He whispered, "They're everywhere."

Jeff went to the window, pulled back the curtain and peered out. He started to laugh, a high, cascading cackle.

"What's so funny?"

"It's snow."

Charlie found the flashlight and pulled back the curtain. Big flakes sparkled everywhere. "OK, funnyman." He shook his head and smiled. "Too little sleep. Too much paranoia."

"Snow's a good thing. Kicks the shit outta the damn Skeets. I'm outta here. See ya." And Jeff was gone.

He seems almost excited to help. Activated, and on my side. That's something I haven't seen in a long, long time. If everything else is going to hell in my life right now, at least maybe I'm getting my friend back. Then just as quickly his optimism faded. *And maybe he can come visit me in prison.*

CHAPTER 44

Charlie fell asleep on Jeff's couch and dreamed fitfully.

Skeets swarmed around the house. He found himself looking into a control room filled with faceless government people watching an array of old-fashioned computer screens. They zoomed in on a farmhouse that Charlie recognized with growing anxiety as Jeff's. As the Skeets swooped closer, he could see his own face in the window. He tried to look at the faces of the people in the control room, but they were all in shadow. One man shifted in place, and his face fell into a shaft of light. It was Jeff! He pointed to the screen. "See? He's right there where I told you. You won't say I told you, will you?"

The scene faded and Charlie found himself back in Jeff's living room. He heard a crunching of stones as vehicles rolled into the driveway. He crept to the window, lifted a flap of curtain, and looked out. oBI agents in combat gear with assault rifles spilled from oCars and a truck. Someone using hand signals directed a group around back to block Charlie's escape. The leader approached the door and called out, "Mr. Noble. We know you're in there. The house is surrounded. Come out with your hands up." But Charlie couldn't move. He was frozen stiff.

There was a thumping of booted feet. With a loud Foompp! the door was ripped from its hinges and crashed to the floor in a cloud of dust and black powder smoke. The leader rushed in and grabbed him by the shoulders. "Charlie! Charlie!"

Charlie gasped and threw his hands into the air. He found himself staring into Jeff's surprised face.

Jeff jumped back. "Whoa! Sorry, man. I was calling your name, but you didn't wake up."

Charlie sat up and held his head in his hands, feeling the goose egg again. He mumbled, "Bad dream." His jaw ached. When he realized where he was, his gaze snapped up at Jeff. "What'd you find out?"

"They want you to come and meet them."

"When?"

"Now."

"How am I going to do that?"

"They gave me this." Jeff dipped his fingers into his shirt pocket and unfolded an eight-and-a-half by eleven piece of electronic paper. "They said I'd need it to program your T, since I don't have a VR ... anything." He touched a small black square in one corner, and a simple black and white control panel appeared on the paper.

"Now what?"

"They said I just hold it up to your chest and press Start."

"How long do we leave it there?"

Jeff shrugged. "They didn't tell me that."

Charlie rolled his head. "Greaaaat."

"How long does it take to activate your T after you've had it off?"

"Just a few seconds."

"Well, let's try it and see what happens."

Charlie nodded. Jeff pressed the paper to Charlie's chest and touched the button. It pulsed for a few seconds and chimed. Charlie looked down, but Jeff's hand blocked his view. "Now what?"

Jeff moved his hand and pointed at the paper. "It says cloaking activated, so I guess we're ready to go."

"Where are we going, and how we gonna get there?"

"They're at the abandoned Cyclotron on campus. I'll give you a ride on my bike."

"Can you do that?"

"Hey, I got Real muscles. Not that artificial shit like you VRs ... Uh, never mind."

"No problem. So what's this thing do?"

"I guess it makes you invisible to all security cams. They said it doesn't make you invisible to other people though. If anybody sees you, the cams will pick up their reaction, and the security systems will send out an alarm that somebody's using a cloak. Apparently it's illegal?"

Charlie cringed. *So why don't we just send up a flare? Jeez. Is he setting me up?*

"You're gotta stay close to me, so anybody who looks at you will seem like they're looking at me. Don't make eye contact. Shouldn't be a big deal this time of night."

"OK. Let's go." Charlie headed for the door.

"Uh, maybe you want your nano clothes?"

"Oh, yeah. And maybe a coat?"

"I've got an old coat and some boots from my dad that should do the job."

Jeff brought Charlie's clothes back from the dryer and he dressed himself. He was surprised to see his fingers had grown back. *Must be more than cloaking in the stuff they gave me.* He wiggled his toes and could feel his feet were healed, and his stomach had stopped gurgling. *Thank God.* Hope rising, he pulled on the boots, fastened the buckles and said, "Now."

"Let's go." Jeff slapped him on the shoulder.

It was a good slap. It said, *We're a team again.*

As he climbed onto the back of Jeff's bike he couldn't help but wonder, *Will the cloak work? And what about my dream? Is he really turning me in? He swore he'd stop N-hanced if he could. If he really meant it, that would be the way. And what about his Luddite friends? Would they kill me in order to stop N-hanced?* He found himself chewing the inside of his cheek and stopped. *Into the jaws of the beast.* Then, *Naw. C'mon. He's excited to be helping me, right?* He started chewing again. This time he tasted blood.

CHAPTER 45

Charlie asked Jeff, "So, your friends work here?"

"Well ... sort of."

"How do you mean?"

"Their work isn't what you'd call ... official. They hang out in the old Cyclotron, which was deserted after the university finished building the Facility for Rare Isotope Beams next door in 2018. One of my friends used to be a student. She hacked IDs giving all of us special access. You're already cleared."

Charlie's anxiety notched up, and he scraped his index fingernail against his thumbnail.

Jeff tilted his head. "You OK, man? You look as nervous as a canary at a cat convention."

"Yeah, yeah," Charlie lied, thinking about what he was heading into and glad Jeff didn't have lie detector software. "Just tired."

Just as Jeff predicted, the student at the desk smiled and waved them through. They walked straight ahead down a hall for a hundred feet and then paused in front of a pair of "No Access" doors.

Jeff said, "The FRIB is further down that way." He pointed toward a hall to the east. "But we're going in here." The doors verified his identity and opened. "This used to be a shop where they built the machinery—" Jeff swept his hand indicating a large, two-story room with a giant yellow crane overhead. "—but now they use it for storage. On the right here is where the second stage of the old Cyclotron still sits. These walls are six feet thick and made of interlaced concrete block. There are a number of chambers throughout this area set up the same way. The walls stop radiation—and the noise my friends make."

He pointed down at an opening in the wall. "That floor in the doorway is a six-foot concrete slab. It can be raised and lowered like an elevator to seal off the chamber. You'll see quite a few of those in this place."

And if they kill me, they could seal me inside one of these rooms and nobody'd find me for years. Just like in Poe's "The Cask of Amontillado."

They walked down endless hallways and around corners until Charlie felt completely lost. Finally Jeff stopped. "This is the machine shop where my friends do their work."

Passing through the door, a cold breeze gave Charlie a chill. Blinking until his eyes adjusted to the light, he guessed the space was nearly fifty yards long with a thirty-foot ceiling.

"And here they are now."

Jeff gestured toward a young lady, but a stocky, five-foot-ten-inch man with dark hair and a trim beard took over. "I know Mista Noble here." He shook Charlie's hand, pulled him in and gave him a back-thumping bear hug. "How you be Bro?"

Remembering the Ken Doll, Charlie felt a rush of panic. When nothing happened he returned a stiff hug. "Uh, what—?"

"Big fan, my man. Big fan."

"From the snowboard promo?" Charlie's gaze bounced from face to face. His chest squeezed, making it hard to breathe.

"OK, yeah, that be cool," the guy shrugged. "But man, I be following your work since that acoustic echo-canceling voodoo you put in your office building. You the top, man."

Nobody knows about that. "How—?"

"I was one of the MSU engineers on the gig, man. 'Member me?"

"... Sorry. No."

"Name's Anton. Think of me without the beard."

Charlie looked and it clicked. "Holy shit!"

"Yeah. Holy shit is right, dude."

Why's he talking jive?

The other two strangers shifted awkwardly. Jeff said, "This is Janice..."

"Pleased to meet you Mr. Noble." She didn't offer her hand and didn't make eye contact.

"You can call me Charlie." Her reticence added to his growing anxiety. *Is she acting that way because she knows what they've got planned for me?*

She stared at the floor. "OK ... Charlie."

Jeff swept his hand toward a slim, six-foot, twenty-ish-looking man with red tonsured hair. "And this is Dexter."

"How do you do, Dexter?"

"Not so good." His cheek twitched below his left eye.

"Sorry to hear that."

Anton snickered. "Don't listen to the dude. He's a liar."

"I am not."

"And he's lying now."

Charlie's eyebrows bunched. "Wait a minute. Which is it?"

"A pathological liar."

"Am not."

Charlie looked to Jeff. "What?"

"Yeah." Jeff nodded. "He is."

Charlie whispered toward Anton, "Why do you work with him?"

"He be good at what he do. Fact, he the best. His lying don't mess us up none."

Charlie, his face pinched into a question mark, turned to look at Dexter.

"It's true, I'm a pathological liar. I always lie." His cheek twitched again.

Charlie tilted his head. "But if you always lie, then you're lying now when you say you always lie. That would mean you sometimes tell the truth?"

"That's right."

Which means he never tells the truth. Charlie turned back to the others and tapped his temple. "Wait a minute, I've heard about this. But it was before I had perfect memory."

Anton said, "Yeah, it be Epimenides paradox. We know all about that, thanks to brother Dex here." Dex's mouth twisted into a crooked grin. "But don't you worry none. You can trust us." He pointed at himself and Janice. "You got a question, you ask us."

Trust was far from the top of Charlie's list. The whole thing felt way off center. *We have a liar, a lady who can't make eye contact, and a white guy who talks jive. I definitely gotta watch my back.* "So what does everybody do here?"

Anton continued. "Janice take care o' resources, research, and acquisitions. You need information or any hard-to-find physical object, ain't nobody better."

Charlie raised his eyebrows and nodded to her. Her sandy brown hair was pulled back in a ponytail. Although an attractive five-foot-five who looked in her mid-twenties, she wore a loose fitting lumberjack's shirt and baggy jeans. But as she moved, her clothes pulled across her body showing she was slim, yet nicely rounded. *Stop looking, you idiot! She's probably dangerous as a black widow.* He turned back to Anton. "What about Dexter?"

"Hardware, big n' small. Nothin' he can't fix or build. And me, I'm programming. Like you, only sneaky. And hacking. I make money hacking Orchard products, so's they can patch 'em. Good exercise. Also means I know everything what's in 'em." Anton beamed a smile at once conceited and warm.

Dex said, "Naw, Anton sucks."

Charlie smiled. "Another lie, right?"

"No." Dexter's face denied humor. His eye twitched.

Anton scowled. "Brother better be lying."

Dexter said, "Hey, lighten up, man."

Anton roared, "I'm 'bout as light as a brother can be, fool!"

Everybody tensed and looked at Anton.

Anton's scowl melted into an impish smile, and then he laughed, throwing his head way back. "Shoulda seen your faces. Ha, ha." He slapped his leg. "Lighten up. That's precious."

Charlie looked at Janice and rolled his eyes. She glanced away. Dexter grinned. *What is going on with these people?* He noticed a wire mesh covering the ceiling and walls which seemed embedded in the floor. "Uh..."

Anton raised his eyebrows. "What?"

"What's all the wire on the walls?"

"Faraday cage."

"I've heard of that, but I don't—"

"Ever see the old flat vid *Enemy of the State*?"

"Yeah, a long time ago."

"Blocks electromagnetic radiation including radio waves. The Gene Hackman guy lived inside one."

"Oh, yeah. With his cat, right?"

"Now you got it."

"If I remember right, he blew his place up. Um ... you got any plans for that?"

"You don't wanna know, bro. You do *not* wanna know."

CHAPTER 46

"Umm ... this may be a little personal." Charlie glanced at Jeff, then back at Anton. "You can tell me to get lost if you want. But, uh, you're white. Why do you talk jive?"

"What chu mean jive? Tryin' a say I got some kinda accent or sump'm?" He shot Charlie an offended frown that melted into amusement. "OK, man, I tell ya the truth." With a perfectly white and 'Steiny accent he said, "I was born ... a poor black child." He burst into another of his big laughs. "Steve Martin said that in the *The Jerk*. Honestly, I *was* born black. My folks oGERed me white. Thought they was helpin' me out. But didn't stop me from hangin' with my bros in the hood. Guess the sound just kinda got burned inna my brain, man."

Dex raised his hand and shook his head. "Now tell him the the truth, Boss."

Anton's grin turned to ice. "So when did tellin' the truth get so damn important to you?"

Dex shrugged and Charlie could see a bump in his cheek where he'd stuck his tongue.

Anton tapped his foot on the floor. "OK, here goes. When I was seven, I was into this VR game set in the seventies called *In The Ghetto*. Ever hear of it?"

Charlie shook his head.

"I was damn good, too. Pert' near best in the world. But I couldn't beat the top three guys. At the time we was using electrodes glued to our scalp to control the avatars. I figured I could beat 'em if it was connected directly to my brain. I soldered a long needle to one of the electrodes and shoved it through my temple."

Charlie felt his stomach surge.

"I know, I know. But what the fuck? I was seven, man. I got the cerebellum mixed up with the cerebrum, what controls speech. I turned on the game and my guy wasn't movin.' Them cats was kickin' my ass, so I cranked up the voltage.

"When I woke up in the hospital I sounded like my avatar. My folks was pissed."

Dex had his hand over his mouth laugh and his shoulders shook.

"Yeah, well fuck you, Dex." Anton turned back to Charlie. "Anyways, I can change my talk when I got to, but it take a whole lot o' concentration. 'Sides, I got me more important battles to fight, know what I mean?"

I do, but I hope I'm not one of them. "I don't remember hearing any accent back when you were with the engineering team at CCD."

"Like I said, bro, I can pass when I need to. But you on my turf now. Don't gotta be nothing but what I am around my 'Stein partners here. I accept them, they accept me, and nobody don't like it don't stay around long, see?" He shot a cold glance at Dexter who gave a deferential nod.

"Yeah, I got it." Charlie smiled. "You know, the way you just said that … you ever do any rappin?' "

"No way! I *hate* that shit. Beethoven. Now, that's my man. The dude got it goin' on. Now sister here, she into that modern shit."

Charlie looked at Janice who looked away. *Damn! What is going on? Maybe she's shy.*

A big grin blossomed on Anton's face. He snapped his fingers and pointed at Charlie. "Man, I been meaning to tell you sump'm ever since I knew you was coming to see us. You ever hear about them Echo History Reconstruction machines? That's me and Dex's patent, man. I came up with the idea based on your noise-canceling app. Brotha, we made a stack o' green offa the EHR. I love yo ass."

"Um hum. Well, then do me a favor, OK?"

"What's that?"

"Never stand behind me."

Anton paused and then laughed big and broad with his head back. "Yeah, man. You funny, too."

"You know, a couple agents from the oBI nearly caught me last night, and I'll bet they were using your software."

"Yeah, they probably sicced a whole 4S kit on your ass. You lucky you here. That 4S some powerful shit."

"So why would you license the EHR technology to the government? You're just helping them do the surveillance you guys hate."

"The money we made offa that got us all this beautiful shine you see around you. Can't fight a war without ammo. 'Sides, Jack, you gotta know I left some special code in my little babies that I can activate whenever I want. Motherfuckers ain't gonna use that shit on us."

Charlie gave the place a second once-over. "Uh, speaking of your gear, I just realized I'm not seeing any virtual equipment. Can I reactivate my VR?"

Dexter said, "Sure."

Anton held up his hand. "Whoa. We gotta be a little careful with that, my man. Dexter developed some special juice for the T we use. It can't be tracked the same way as that standard shit. You turn yours back on now, and it'll be like pointing a big spotlight down on this place."

"Can you reprogram mine to remove that code?"

"I was gonna suggest sump'm a little different. Course it's as illegal as hell." Anton smiled proudly. "But no matter what, you best not turn your N-hanced program on in here."

"So what's your code do?"

"Well, Janice here built up a stash of counterfeit IDs. Why don't you 'splain it, girlfriend?"

"OK." Janice spoke with confidence, but her gaze darted away whenever it neared Charlie's. "These ID's have history going back to when everybody's cams were integrated into Whipped. My program creates a whole background including family and personal histories with photos and documents scattered all over the world. Dex will program one of the IDs into you, and I'll make a few changes to Whipped. Then you can walk around as … how about Sebastian Pearlman?"

"Sure." Charlie performed a sweeping, courtly bow. "Sebastian Pearlman at your service." He watched as her gaze skittered away again. *Did she blush?*

Anton pointed at the IS cube. "Your fake ID will have a life that started when the cams went into service. She'll fuck with the history so it'll show how you got here to our place, and Whipped will welcome you back on your journey through life." He turned to Dexter. "How long it take you to get him fixed up?"

"Sorry. Can't do it today."

Anton turned back to Charlie. "Just a couple minutes."

Dexter's hands flowed through his cube like a butterfly ballet. After a moment he swept a two fingers toward Charlie. "This won't hurt a bit." His eye twitched.

Charlie jumped. "What?"

Anton laughed and Janice covered her mouth. Anton said, "It's OK, Charlie. That's how he makes a joke—he tells the truth."

Is this it? Is this when they paralyze me and turn me in? Or kill me? Charlie remained tense as Dexter made a few more motions. Finally Dexter said, "Go ahead."

Charlie fired up three levels of T. With his VR on, the place looked very different. The Faraday cage disappeared behind a covering of VR wallpaper. An impressive stash of gear and IS cubes cluttered the lab. He only recognized about a third of the tools.

Charlie's gaze settled back on Anton. "Well, I suppose you should take me on a tour of the place now that I can actually see it."

CHAPTER 47

Dexter's area was closest. He had a scaling workbench to magnify nano particles and work with them at human scale. On it was something that looked like a basketball cracked open, revealing machinery and circuits.

Charlie turned to Anton. "I don't get it. How can you be opposed to technology? You've obviously got all the latest stuff."

"No, some of this shit's newer than the latest. Some of it's our own invention. And we ain't opposed to tech. We love it. But we don't think them rich fucks, big corporations and the go'ment should have it first and keep it from everybody else."

"What about Orchard? They're benign. The whole company's built on helping people."

"That what you think? Let me axe you; they make money from it?"

"Well ... yeah."

"Long as they making money and human beings involved, it's gonna get used for power and control. And even if they ain't doing that today, you wanna be sitting there without no defense when sump'm changes? I don't."

Charlie nodded slowly.

Moving clockwise around the room, Anton's workspace held blocks of code similar to the ones Charlie worked on. But his work with security systems looked unfamiliar. Anton didn't want to talk about that just now. Instead he continued on his Luddite rant.

"If you need any more evidence about why we do this, think of all the cams you see—and don't see—everywhere you go. On buildings, flying 'round, in people's clothes and all—they just gifts to the powers what be. You suppose there mighta been any go'ment money helping with their development—and their low prices—and everybody adopting 'em so quickly? It's more than a little stushy, you axe me."

Charlie shrugged. "Aren't you being a little paranoid?

"Hey, just 'cause you paranoid don't mean they ain't after you. Know who said that?

"I don't know … Phillip K. Dick?"

"No. Joseph Heller in *Catch-22*. And it's true now more'n ever. Hell, man, you gotta know that much after what you just been through."

Charlie thought back over the last two days. What Anton was saying made more sense every minute.

Anton must have thought Charlie's silence meant he disagreed, because he shook his head and waved his hand dismissively. "Yeah, you and Kurzweil. Fuckin' optimists to the bitter end."

"Come on. There were plenty of visionaries who said we wouldn't make it this far. And come to think of it, things didn't exactly go the way George Orwell predicted in *1984*."

"Yeah, pretty clever of them, huh? Once they knew we was watching the front door, they just snuck around back. However you look at it, bro, they got us."

"OK, but I *want* rapists, murderers and thieves put out of business. And when you came right down to it, I *am* on the run. Which reminds me, if I don't get some help from you guys, there's a good chance I'm gonna go to prison for something I don't think I did."

Dexter said, "No you won't. They don't have anything on you."

Oh, great! Charlie dropped his chin onto his chest and blew out his breath with a defeated "Ffffff." Then he snapped his head back up. "You been tapping their systems! You know anything that can help me?"

Anton glanced at Janice and gave a quick nod with his eyes. She beckoned and everyone followed to her workstation. It was a mass of floating flat screens and 3-D cubes. She pulled one forward.

"I've been watching the reports filed from your oBI agents to their superiors. It's not so much that they have anything on you as they don't have anything on anybody else—but they haven't been looking. There was a report that you posed as Gerald Collier. That's illegal, which we frown on around here, of course."

Anton, Dexter and Jeff smirked, but Charlie wasn't amused.

Janice pointed to another report. "For a while they thought you might be holding his daughter hostage, which is why they chased you to MSU. They haven't had time to check on any other leads. After the way you escaped, you became their only suspect."

"Oh, that's great. Anything about the military?"

"Yeah. They're watching you all right, mostly to keep tabs on the advances of N-hanced. They've got some guy at the Pentagon keeping track of that, but it's not his full-time job, so my guess is they're not involved in your current troubles."

Janice continued to demonstrate her setup by rearranging the cubes in various preset configurations; some shifted back while others came forward and still others disappeared altogether. Most of the data streams looked proprietary, a few Charlie recognized from various government agencies. She finished by arranging everything the way it was when she started, the Whipped cube in front showing his Sebastian Pearlman alias complete with a walk-around construct of Charlie.

Charlie flicked a sideways glance at Jeff. "You know, for the last couple of months Jeff's been making me turn off N-hanced and my T when we get together. He says I manipulate him." Charlie lowered his eyes "I suppose there might have some truth to that."

Anton turned to Jeff. "Hey, tight ass, cut him some slack. This guy about to level the playing field for everyone. You trying to be so lily white pure Luddite. It ain't about *using* technology. It about *ab*-using it. Einstein shit his pants over what those military fucks did making bombs with his E=MC². That the kinda shit we against."

Jeff seemed offended. "But that happens with everything!"

Janice said, "Maybe not any more. Maybe with N it'll be different."

Are they are on my side?

Jeff continued. "Yeah, they said T would be different, too. But look what it did to Susan."

Charlie decided to force the issue. "You know, Jeff told me he'd stop me if he could. I figured all you Luds would be against N-hanced. How do I know you're not trying to stop me?" He watched their faces.

Anton smiled. "You don't. But we think N is pretty cool. At least the three of us do." His finger circled around from himself to Dexter and Janice.

Dexter shrugged. Janice looked away.

Charlie chewed his cheek. *I still can't read these people.*

Beides, our boy here," Anton rolled a thumb toward Jeff. "He be kinda extreme. He don't represent us. What you gotta remember is Luds are like vegetarians; there be all different varieties."

CHAPTER 48

All this tech talk and philosophy was interesting, but Charlie felt time slipping away. He tore his gaze from Janice's floating screens and settled it on Anton. "I don't mean to be pushy here, but about the help I need ... I don't know how much Jeff's told you—"

Anton nodded. "Yeah, sorry, man. We know what they been saying on the Net about you killing those guys." He gestured toward an arrangement of brightly-colored oChairs and ambled toward them. Everyone else followed and sat. "Jeff told us you think somebody mighta set you up. How can we help?"

"It started when my PAs skipped a security test."

"Wait a minute. You got more'n one PA?"

"Yeah, with N-hanced, you can have up to eight. That's what I've been using for the last five months."

"That's cool, man."

"They said I told them to erase my memory of how to perform the test. That freaked me out because it almost makes sense."

"Except it'd be dangerous."

"Exactly. Then I found out someone left an invisible hole in the program. When I looked at the code, it used a programming error I'd made thirty-five years ago."

"Yeah. If I was gonna fuck you up, I'd make it look like your mistake."

Charlie felt a wave of suspicion washed over him. *Is he telling me something?* "Except I haven't made any errors for over fifteen years. I invent things and test them in virtual environments, like everybody else."

Anton nodded.

"I rechecked the vid from the guys who died. All of them were remembering a dream in their last moments. When I told my PAs to look for anything odd, they showed me there were tiny distortions on the audio track. And I mean tiny. It would only be off by a single digit."

Anton's face lit up. "Was it always in the same location with reference to the vid block?"

"No."

Janice frowned. "I'm not following this, guys. But maybe it's not important that I do."

Anton said, "It might be, case we need you to research sump'm for us. Try to hang on, girl." He turned back to Charlie. "It might be a hidden code. I love that steganography shit. How can we get a look at that vid?"

"I've got it right here." Charlie flicked and the first vid filled the team's cube.

"OK, bro, show me the distortion"

"Here, look at the second block. My PAs marked the suspicious sample. You see that little bump circled in red? It shouldn't be there. The white line just below the bump is where the waveform belongs. If you advance to the fourth vid block you'll see one there, too, but in a different spot in the audio. Then it skips the next block. The blocks with these distortions seem random. I ran out of time before we could assign it any kind of meaning."

"When it comes to sump'm like that, I don't believe in random. Bet there's a key somewhere in one of the vid blocks, but it's a lot of data to check. I'll take a look. What else you need?"

"I'd like to physically get back to the N servers in my office as soon as I can, but I don't know how I'm going to get there. All the tricks I know for getting around without being followed depend on being N-hanced."

"You talking to the right crew now, bro." He lit up with one of his superior smiles. "If we can't get you there without bein' seen, ain't nobody can. Me and Dex got some hardware you gonna dig. Take us a little while to get it ready for you, and I wanna spend some time on this vid. Anything else?"

"Yeah, the reason I had to shut off N was because something was after me inside the server. It definitely came from outside. It had black tentacles, like an octopus. You ever heard of anything like that?" Charlie watched Anton's face for a clue his group might be involved.

"Don't sound familiar."

"I need to check all this out before anybody gets a court order and confiscates my system. If some forensic programming investigator gets in there and screws things up permanently, I'll be toast. If I'm going to defend myself, I'll need to know exactly how the rogue code works and who did it—if it wasn't actually me. And one other thing."

"What's that?"

"I could sure use some sleep. When I'm using N, I only need a couple hours a night. But right now, I am dragging. If you don't need me for anything, I'd like a place to lie down for a while."

"Hell, yeah, bro."

Janice looked away. "How about my room. It's a lot cleaner than theirs. They live like they're in the swine fraternity."

Dexter's eye twitched. "We do not."

Charlie now thought of the twitch as a half wink. "Dexter's word is good enough for me—if it won't put you out too much."

A shy smile crossed Janice's mouth. "No trouble at all."

"Show me the way." Charlie got out of the oChair. "Oh, Anton?"

"Bro?"

"Don't be afraid to wake me if there's anything you have a question about. Since I suspect the wheels of *in*justice are rolling pretty swiftly in my direction, I don't want to be sleeping while you're twiddling your thumbs waiting on me."

"Gotcha."

Janice led and Charlie followed. He was anxious because he still wondered if her job was to execute him. Then he caught himself watching to see if the movement of her clothes betrayed any more about her shape. He shook his head. *Good grief! Will we ever take people for who they are and not just the body they choose to live in?*

CHAPTER 49

The trip to Janice's room was a surprising distance of nearly fifty yards. As they passed through the door, Charlie noticed it had the same thick walls as the rest of the Cyclotron. It was set up like a large efficiency apartment with a kitchenette, decorated in a spare contemporary feminine style with a giant VR window looking out onto a breathtaking black-sand Hawaiian beach with palm trees. That caught Charlie's attention. "Wow, this is beauti—"

Janice grabbed his shoulder, whirled him around and pushed him against the wall with a dull thud.

Charlie's eyes flew open. *This is it!* She kissed him. *What?* As it became clear she wasn't going to kill him, he relaxed and joined in. *Is this why she couldn't look me in the eye?*

Finally she stepped back and said, "Do you have anyone?"

"Anyone?"

"You know. Anyone you're involved with." Janice's eye contact was solid.

"Oh, well, yes. But she's virtual and not subject to jealousy."

"You mean someone you see remotely, or—"

"No. A sim."

"Ahhh."

"She doesn't know I exist until I turn her on." Charlie leaned against the wall.

Janice's smile came easily. "I've known guys like that."

Charlie laughed. "And how about you?"

"Nooo."

"And you don't have anything going with Anton or Dexter?"

"Oh, hell, no! Shit, they're 'Steins."

"Uh, so are you? So am I?"

"OK. I guess." She came around beside him and leaned her shoulder against the wall.

Charlie looked at the floor, then at Janice. "You ever feel like everything happens to you by accident? Like you're just a leaf in the wind?"

Janice's eyebrows bunched together.

"Like when you look back on your life, all your careful plans didn't have much to do with where you ended up?"

"Uh, what does that have to do with the number of nanobots in Nantucket?

"Oh, I don't know. I'm … so tired, I'm getting batty. It's been a strange week. I'm thinking about how out of control things have been." Charlie looked away. His cheeks felt warm. "And us meeting like this."

A little smile crept onto Janice's face. "Hey, you're not going to get all mushy on me, are you?"

"No, no. Nothing like that. Do you believe in fate?"

"You mean like everything is predetermined?"

"Yeah."

Janice pursed her lips and shook her head. "No."

"Well, whatever's going on, I sure don't feel as if I have much say in it."

"I think with enough computing power, you could predict just about anything with a high level of probability. You know, like how the weather forecast keeps getting better." Her expression changed to sly and seductive. "Or who you meet."

"Maybe that's why we always want faster, more powerful computers." He smiled back. "You know, to improve our love life."

"Anyway, back to my partners, Dexter's kinda out there about sex. He's doing some kind of weird Tantric chastity thing. That's why he's got that monk haircut. But he cheats on the discipline by using T castration. Very fucked up. And Anton has his own girl, Clemencia." She giggled. It was a contagious, bubbling sound. "Dex and I call her Chlamydia to mess with him."

"Chlamydia?" Charlie laughed.

"Anton says, 'Ain't no goddamn VD no more,' and acts mad. But I can tell he thinks it's funny, too."

"So if I were to ask Dexter, he'd tell me you two were an item?"

"Oh, definitely." She laughed again and unbuttoned her flannel shirt. "I'm going to take a bath. Join me?"

Charlie felt a longing in the pit of his stomach. "I just took a shower. I was a mess after that dumpster."

Her jeans off, she was down to red bra and panties. The baggy clothes hid a carnival midway full of attractions.

"Right, but you're also pretty tired." She unclasped her bra and dropped it to the floor. "I'm afraid if I leave you out here, you'll be asleep by the time

I get back." Her panties came off. She took the band off her hair and shook it loose.

Charlie was excited, but he turned his eyes away. "Uh, yeah. You're probably right." The words to one of his songs played in his head. *Mama said, now don't you look.* He gave in and ogled her up and down. *But I just had to.* "The way you look right now, I'm not sure I can wait until the tub is full."

She grabbed the front of his shirt, pulling him gently in the direction of the bathroom. "Let's see how it goes."

"Uh ... shouldn't we light some candles or something? You know, to make it more romantic?"

"Come on. This is the twenty-first century. Ah, but I forgot." Janice tapped her temple. "You were born in what, 1950?"

"'49."

She shook her head knowingly. "Old fogy with a Sir Galahad complex. You've got a macho hangover. Know what? I'm going to help you get over that." She yanked him close and pulled his hands around her until they were on her butt cheeks. "Grab hold of me here." She put her hands around his head and kissed him hard again, but it soon melted like butter.

Modern, yes, but still a woman.

*   *   *

Afterward, Charlie went to sleep and Janice went back to work with her partners. He slept fitfully, twisted fragments of dreams about his shaky situation skittered through his mind. Without the benefit of N and Fas-Sleep, he awoke after two hours, feeling unrested and too anxious to go back to sleep. Trying to think positively, a melody flitted around in his head. He summoned up a VR guitar and worked on it, simultaneously thinking about how he was going to get back to CCD where he could study his security problem with all his wits about him.

The melody molded itself around the name Janice. He consulted a rhyming dictionary. *Nothing much rhymes with Janice. How about "yes?" Yes, yes, Janice. Not perfect, but it has a nice sound with all those Ss.* He sang the words slowly with a melody that stair-stepped down. *Sounds a little like David Gates. I always liked his stuff with Bread.* He played an E chord and alternated it with a mournful A9. Then he sang, "Why'd it have to take so long to find you?"

So the story is going to be about someone who waited a long time to find the right person. I can relate to that. Uh-oh. That's a question. He remembered a book he'd read on songwriting by Al Kasha and Joel Hirshhorn titled *If They Ask You, You Can Write A Song.* They suggested making statements instead of asking questions. *What if I write it as a series of questions, and then make the chorus into a positive statement, pushing all the questions aside?* "Yes, yes, Janice. Nothing's better than the best." Mmm. *"yes" rhymes with "second guess."*

Charlie shook his head with a start. He was getting so involved with the song he wasn't thinking about how to get back to the office. Then he relaxed. *Let's just see what these people come up with. Sneaking around seems to be their specialty. I can trust them.* He went back to the guitar. But a little worm of doubt wiggled around in the pit of his stomach. *What if they're the ones framing me?*

CHAPTER 50

Janice came into her room and found Charlie looking out the VR window onto her black-sand beach. "Oh, good, you're up. The guys said they'll be ready for you in about fifteen minutes."

"Excellent!"

"So, you want to make love again?" She had that look in her eyes, her hands already working her shirt buttons.

Charlie blushed. He put his hands up and laughed with embarrassment. "Whoa. Just a minute." He liked her boldness, but it was still a surprise. "I've got something I want to show you."

She looked at him, her eyelids at a seductive half-mast. "I've already seen it."

Charlie laughed again. "No, no. Not that." Then he grew serious. "It's a song I just wrote. Now listen, I don't want this to change anything between us. I mean, it's kind of romantic." *Shit. I'm probably gonna explain all the romance right out of it.* He raised his eyebrows apologetically. "But it's ... not like ... a marriage proposal or anything."

"Good. Cause I wouldn't marry you anyway. I don't mean it that way. It's just that it takes time to get to know somebody. I gotta know if you fight fair."

"What?"

"Some people fight dirty when they get into an argument. They get mean and say things to hurt you. Besides, I'm not so sure I'm in favor of that whole marriage thing anyway."

"Well, that's probably more than I need to know. But rest assured when I'm using N, I'm really good at fighting fair. So uh, just take this for what it's worth; inspired by your name and the very nice time I spent with you. And in the spirit of fighting fair." He strummed the virtual guitar. "Oh, wait a minute. I still don't know all the ins and outs of you guys' VR system. Can you see and hear this guitar?"

"Yep."
"OK then. I call it _Yes_.
<http://n-hanced.com/yes.php>
Here goes." As he played the intro she knelt on the floor, sitting on her feet.

Why'd it have to take so long to find you
Now that there're so many scars around my heart?
And how is it our paths were always crossing
But we missed like two ships passing in the dark?

What makes us think we're not like other people?
And how long can we make that fire glow?
Maybe I just ask too many questions
We're prob'ly better off if we don't know
So I'll say...

CHORUS
Yes, yes, oh, Janice
Nothing's better than the best
Forget all of that second-guessing
Yes, yes, oh, Janice
When you finally get it right
Don't question and don't fight it
Just say yes

The pieces seem to fit without much trying
Can it be good if we don't need to work so hard?
Is there something wrong with us and what we're doing?
And tomorrow will the whole thing fall apart?

Could it be we're meant to be together?
Or is it just that now we're older and more wise?
There I go again I'm asking all these questions
I'll stop talking now and look into your eyes
And just say, yes

CHORUS
I'll just say yes

When the last notes died away she crawled catlike toward him on her hands and knees and kissed him. "Thank you. That was very sweet. Nobody's ever written a song for me before." She pushed him back over onto the bed and lay on top of him. "Now, according to my clock we still have about ten minutes. I'm sorry to say that in spite of the song, I still don't want to marry you. How about we fuck instead?"

They were a few minutes late back to the lab.

CHAPTER 51

As soon as Charlie came through the door, Anton called out. "Hey, bro, sorry we had to get you up so soon."

"No problem. I didn't sleep very well anyway." Charlie hurried over to Dex's workbench. "What you got?"

"Dex here got you set up with some nice T shit that'll get you where you gotta go. And I figured out what be going on with the vids you brought along. That's some top-shelf shit somebody trying to lay on you, my man."

"So what is it?"

"Well, it's a little deep, and time be getting short. Let me summarize it for you. Somebody be 'cryptin' a message on your audio track all right. Turns out that distortion equal to a digital one. Every vid block without distortion is a zero."

Janice raised an index finger. "What about the key?"

"Right. I ran the files though my analysis tools and told them to look for any sequence of numbers what matched them funky coordinates. It found a string of colors in the first vid block of each dream." His finger swept the audio graph in his cube. "There be a minus one distortion when the code start and a minus one when it end. Take every zero and plus one in between, and you got yourself a string of a hundred and four characters what spell out 'User Abort ON.' You axe me, that ain't no coincidence. That's your rogue code."

Charlie felt weak and put his hand on the table to steady himself. "Which leaves the door open for a hacker to walk right in."

"You got it! Don't know what happens once that door gets flung open. My guess be it come through your N system and drill down to the VR program. It probably trip a switch in the brain that tells the user to move his body instead of simulating movement in VR. Normally we be looking for long lines of code to accomplish what you got here. You coulda wasted a whole lot o' time going down that road, and I'll bet that's where you was headed next."

"Exactly."

"No shame in that. 'S what I woulda done. It's sort of like epigenetics; it don't do the work, it just flip the switch. Whoever put this thing together, it be brilliant, partly 'cause the key be the data what already on the first vid block with no change at all. But not as brilliant as me. I'da used a single bit. Nobody woulda found mine 'cause where there ain't no repetition, there ain't no pattern." He slapped his hand on his shoulder. "Ouch! Hurt my arm patting myself on the back. Ha!"

Janice rolled her eyes.

"'Course the bad news is that User Abort ON makes you look bad."

"Dammit!" Charlie pounded a fist in the air.

"Right. Wish I had better news for ya, bro. Least now you know what be going down, even if you don't know who doing it. It's zakley what I would 'spec somebody to do if they was framing you. I mean, what more could they do than make you doubt yourself?"

"Yeah." Charlie ran his gaze across the floor for a moment. Then he looked up. "If you were me, what direction would you take next?"

"I'll bet there be sump'm in the system what erase the code. You might look for lines what deal with time, dates or counting down. If nothing show up, check your logs for changes."

Anton tapped his temple and pointed at Charlie. "Find out how the code get carried to the user and executed. Uh, no pun intended. Look for a digital fingerprint." He shrugged. "But I wouldn't 'spect much from that. Anybody clever enough to pull this off ain't likely to leave his home address. Now if you could watch it being triggered from the outside... But that could be risky. If these people get wind you know what they doing— and they prob'ly already suspicious—you likely to be the next one dead."

"Great!" Charlie shook his head in disgust. "So why didn't it get *me* when I was having a dangerous dream?"

"They wanna make it look like it be your fault. That way nobody looking for them. I don't think the killing be a automatic thang. Whoever set it up prob'ly get alerted whenever one o' your testers be in a unsafe situation. That way they can decide on the chances for a successful kill and who it gonna happen to—maybe looking for sump'm dramatic like what them NewsDogs like to eat up. So far it working pretty good, don't you think?"

Charlie pursed his lips and nodded.

"This hack got Erik Kozlovski's fingerprints all over it. Know who he is?"

Charlie spread his hands. "Do I? I tried to get him to sign with us last Thursday. Instead, he tried to knock my head off."

"Yeah, that sound like him, all right. I VR-ed into some conferences where he give a talk. Whenever anybody ask anything 'cept the most expert question, he humiliate them so bad you could practically watch them melt. I seen Erik make grown men cry. I would *not* wanna get on the dude's bad side. And that pretty much be only side he got."

"And he has some even rougher friends who would probably come along for the party. Could anybody else have made this code?"

"Well, me, of course."

Charlie shook his head. "Don't say that. I don't want you connected with this in case the heat gets worse. Anybody else?"

"Naw."

"What about Terry Slattery or Boz Wharfman?"

Anton scoffed. "Maybe. But only if they put they two shrunken heads together. Even then—"

"What if I took their knowledge and combined it in N-hanced?"

"I guess so. Yeah."

"Great!" *Nuts!* Charlie dropped his chin to his chest.

"But wouldn't you know it if you done it?"

Head still down, Charlie raised his eyes and tightened his mouth. "Not necessarily."

"Oh? Ooooh. You thinking 'bout that erased memory shit, huh? But why don't you think 'bout who stands to gain the most from having N-hanced look bad? Don't ignore one of the oldest pieces of advice they give private investigators."

"And that is…?"

"Follow the money. It's still a hell of a motive."

Charlie nodded.

"Hate to say it, bro, but hanging with us don't help your case none. Now you could make a argument we in favor of N-hanced, and you be right. But our general history with oGov ain't zakley pretty."

Charlie pursed his lips and blew out a long "Ffffff."

"Yeah, sorry. But that ain't all. Worse, you got a long time 'sociation with one of the most anti-tech people I know."

"Who's that?"

"Brother Jeff here."

Charlie and Jeff looked at each other. Jeff winced an apology.

It took Charlie a moment to recover. "How do you know all this stuff?"

"Well, you could call it paranoia. Or you could say it's on accounta I come from a long line o' folks who got a reason to think people was trying to fuck 'em up."

A pained look crossed Charlie's face. "Oh, Jesus. I never thought about that. I'm sorry, Anton."

"Aaa, don't worry 'bout it. Long's I can help you out, bro, maybe it all be worth it."

Charlie choked up and turned away, hand covering his eyes. He didn't know if it was because he felt bad for Anton's family, or because Anton was willing to put his own safety on the line for him. *Maybe I'm afraid for my own future, or maybe I'm just tired.* He wiped his eyes and coughed to clear his throat. He turned back with an angry resolve. "All right. So I'm fucked. Now what? Didn't you say Dexter has some special T apps for me?"

CHAPTER 52

"Yeah, man. This stuff is gonna blow you away." Anton angled a thumb over his shoulder. "Take it from here Dex. Uh ... and we'll interpret for you, Charlie. But Dex tend to be pretty straight when talking 'bout his babies."

Dexter turned to his bench and pointed. "This first app'll give you a new face." He brought up a playback of his own face morphing into eight different people. "And you'll be able to switch any time you need to. I know N-hanced does that, but you're kinda N-less right now." The final morph changed Dex's body into the shape of a woman. "Whoa. That's freaky."

Janice poked Dexter. "Hey! It looks like me."

"Right. Only six feet tall. Like I said, freaky." Dex grinned. "This next one is very cool."

"Wait a sec." Charlie put a hand on Dexter's arm. "How do you activate that?"

"Oh. Pretty much just think about it—with a little ... oomph. It's kinda hard to describe."

"You mean like...?" Charlie imagined Dexter's face.

Something clearly changed, because Janice stared at Charlie. "Now *that's* freaky." She dodged as Dexter tried to poke her in the ribs.

Charlie relaxed and shook his head. "Normal again?"

"Thank God," Janice said, keeping her eye on Dexter.

Dexter flicked at his cube. "The second one is OxyT. It'll let you hold your breath underwater for hours, or run miles effortlessly." A playback showed him using both. "Just hyperventilate for a minute and it'll load up with oxygen and store it for when you need it."

Anton said, "Hell, man. I never seen that one before. Gimme some of that."

Dexter grimaced. "I apologize for the working title of this one. Uh, it's the Harry Potter. It makes you invisible. You know, like his cloak?"

197

Anton and Janice moaned.

"Hey, come on guys. Look, it really works."

"Yeah, yeah, I know." Anton rolled his eyes. "But the name?"

"It uses a technology the military's been chasing since the beginning of the century, only theirs sucks. This one is perfect. It covers every surface of your body and clothes with billions of nano-cam/projector modules. The secret's in the projectors." Dexter spread his fingers, which brought up an image of something that looked like an array of BBs cut in half. "They're hemispheres that display multiple images so there's no apparent warping regardless of where the viewer stands. The nanos reorganize themselves any time you change clothes, and they cling like crazy so you don't have to worry about them brushing or washing off."

He ran the demo vid. A 3-D cam swung around him as he disappeared. "Oh, yeah, and your hands are free. You don't have to hold it over your head like that Harry Potter cloak piece of crap. Just turn it on and you're gone. But don't fool yourself into thinking you're not really there. If anybody touches you, they'll know. And if you're moving fast or breathing hard or farting, they'll hear you."

Janice scoffed. "Farting? Nobody farts any more."

Charlie smiled at her and thought of Robbie. He turned to Dex. "You could make a mint off that."

"Yeah." Anton sniffed. "With the military. Fuck 'em! Right, Dex?"

"Well..." Dexter's eye twitched.

Anton said, "That means 'Fuck 'em!' in case you couldn't tell, Charlie, baby." He smiled until all his teeth showed.

Charlie shook his head. "Man, Dex, you are the Q of Luddites."

Dex said, "Q? What ... like from *Star Trek: The Next Generation?*"

"No. Q from British Secret Service."

"What?"

"Q. You know," Charlie switched to a British accent, "Bond. James Bond."

"Who's that?" All three of them looked confused and gestured in their cubes.

"Oh, come on! You know *Catch-22* and you don't know James Bond? How old are you guys?" He pointed at Anton.

"Twenty-seven Real."

Janice said, "Twenty-two Real."

Dexter opened his mouth, his eye twitching.

Charlie raised a hand. "Never mind." He turned back to the others. "James Bond. Bookmark it. It's classic. Trust me, you'll love Q."

Dex pointed at the cube. "This is a Focused Beam Distracter or FBD. It's a little weird and takes some getting used to, but it'll make you seem as if you're somewhere you're not. Once you're using your Harry Potter, you may need to lead your pursuers away from you. You hold your arms out and aim the two beams with your palms. Any tracking device will pick up convincing human activity wherever the beams converge."

The vid ran. "You have to make the convergence point move so you're creating a convincing decoy path. But here's the cool part; it works through walls. That way you can give your stalkers the impression you're in another room and send them on a wild-goose chase. It projects sound and heat profiles. It even sends an image to public VR so you show up in the cams. Give it a try."

Charlie raised his hands, palms out and saw two red lines streaming away from him. He rotated his hands until the lines converged. A tilted projection of him appeared across the room. It took a few seconds of rotating his hands until he got the image upright. "So how's it any different from an oMe2?"

"This thing makes Real noise when it walks. And it doesn't have an oMe2 ID."

As Charlie maneuvered the beams, a thought flashed through his mind; *Just like when the Ken Doll appeared and disappeared at the Federal Building.* Then just as quickly, *Could Dex be responsible for that?*

"Now you're getting the hang of it. The trick is to keep the beams together. If they move apart, your ghost disappears. Oh, and this thing can't open doors. Nobody'll be fooled if you walk it through a wall."

Dexter twirled a finger and the image changed. "OK, now Shield is a program that protects you from physical harm. If anything approaches you quickly, Shield will turn hard based on your fear level."

Janice chuckled. "Can it make something turn hard based on your pleasure level?"

Anton frowned. "Girl, you gotta get yourself laid."

"What makes you think I haven't been?" She clucked her tongue. "You guys. You make comments like that before, during and after sex. But let a woman say the same thing and she obviously needs to get laid. Wake up little boys. It's the twenty-first century. Time to be twenty-first century men."

There was a momentary silence while all the men stood slack-jawed, seeming to consider tens of thousands of years of that particular injustice.

Finally Dex broke the silence. "Uh, boys and girl— Sorry, Janice, make that *woman.* If you'll direct your attention back over this way, please. We've even included some internal structure to protect your brain. That way if your body stops fast, your brain won't keep going and squash like what happens to a lot of people who play sports—especially football and boxing." The vid showed Anton trying to stab Dexter. In some trials the knife bent, in others it deflected. Then came a slow-motion 3-D MRI of Janice in boxing gloves hitting his jaw. The structure appeared and dissipated while holding his brain rigid.

Charlie pivoted around to Janice, his face radiating exaggerated amazement. "Quite a punch. Remind me not to piss you off."

She threw him a smug smile and a Kung Fu jab.

Charlie chuckled and turned back to Dex. "Didn't that hurt your jaw?"

"Nope, and I didn't even bruise. IgotYour6 will activate it, no special action required. And that, my friends, is the end of my little show and tell."

"Amazing. Thank you."

Anton leaned in, his eyes sparkled. "Most of this stuff is highly illegal. So if you get caught, you don't know where it came from. Maybe you can get your PAs to erase *that* shit from your brain."

"Erase what?"

"Dex's T tools—" Anton paused, then smiled. "OK. You got me. Which brings me to sump'n else. The go'ment don't want people having this stuff or N-hanced. They say it makes it easy for terrorists to pull a bunch a shit. Fact is, they don't like nobody off the grid. Once N hits the streets, things gonna get pretty stushy for the Feds. You best consider that the go'ment have they own reasons for setting you up. If they think rich folks gonna get hurt, no way they gonna let you keep on keeping on. You rockin' the boat, brotha, and they will do anything to stop that. And I do mean *anything*."

The idea deflated Charlie in one long sigh. It made perfect sense. He'd just never thought about it that way, even after talking with the oBI agents. He had always seen himself as a white knight arriving on horseback to save all of mankind from pain, suffering, and drudgery. *Shit. Talk about a one-track mind. I'm such a fool.*

CHAPTER 53

Charlie shook his head and backed away from Dexter's bench. "I can't thank you all enough. But I'd better get started. It's a long walk to CCD."

Janice said, "What? You're walking?"

"Well, yeah. I mean, I think the oBI'll be watching for any oCar coming from the university heading for CCD. I figured I'd walk using Dex's Harry Potter thing."

Janice turned to Anton. "What about one of the delivery trucks?"

"Hell, yeah! FRIB got access to MSU robot trucks." Anton looked over his shoulder. "Hey, Dex? Why don't you bring one around to the loading dock?" He turned back to Charlie. "You better comm ahead so somebody at your place knows to expect a *special* delivery."

Charlie opened a comm and got Rob immediately.

"Ohmigod, son. Are you OK?"

"Yeah. It's a long story. I'm coming back to CCD in an MSU delivery truck in about—" He turned to Anton.

"Thirty minutes."

"—a half hour."

"A delivery truck?"

"I'll explain when I get there. I'll have a different ID, and I'll look like this." He showed Rob the face of Sebastian Pearlman. "Can you arrange to have somebody let me in?"

"Yeah. But using a false ID is illegal—"

"Please, Rob. I'm just trying to solve this without endless interruptions from the authorities."

"You know how I feel about that, but I'll play along for now. Then what?"

"Then I need to figure out this alpha death puzzle."

"Will you have to use— Aw, never mind. We'll talk about that when you get here."

Dex came back through the door. "Listen, Rob, I gotta go. See you soon."

"OK. Be safe, son."

Charlie flicked off the comm.

Dex led the way to the truck and raised its back door.

Charlie shook hands all around. "I hope I get to see you soon, hopefully under different circumstances." He gave Janice a hug. "If I get this thing figured out so it's safe, you're all welcome to be testers."

Dexter said, "Yeah, well, maybe version two."

Charlie smiled. "Thanks, man." He climbed inside.

Janice said, "You'd better change identities now."

"Right." Charlie winced and his face seemed to melt until it settled in the shape of Sebastian Pearlman.

Dex pulled the door down and latched it. With a wave of his hand, the truck drove away.

CHAPTER 54

It was 8:45 AM when Charlie arrived at CCD.

Rob met him at the loading dock. "Whoa. You look tired."

"Maybe it's the face I'm using." Charlie shook his head, changing it back. "How's that?"

"Still pretty bad."

"Yeah, well, it's been a hell of a night." Charlie gestured and they walked.

"Maybe you should go home. Get some rest."

"There's no time for that. I've got to log onto the N server and keep working."

"Uhhhh ... I don't think that's such a good idea."

Charlie stopped. "Look, Rob, I'm *not* in the mood." His hand chopped the air to make his point. "Getting back here is all I've been thinking about since those agents hauled me out of here. No way I can figure out what's stushy with N without using it. I'm just not smart enough on my own." They walked again.

"Seems to me everyone who's using N is dying. I can see how it puts you in sort of a bind, but death is not what I call an alternative."

"I think I'm safe if I'm not using the Net. When they worked remotely, some other program used the same connection. That's why I have to be here. This morning I talked to a steganographer who showed me where some rogue code is hidden. I need to find out who's behind it."

"I don't like this—at all."

Charlie cast his gaze down the hall. "Is Milo around yet? We were doing fine until the agents showed up."

Rob put his hand on Charlie's arm. "Now, just a minute. Before you run your little bulldozer over me, there's something that doesn't make sense. You disconnected N from the Net before. But Gary died after that."

"Right. But the Alphas were still connecting remotely via the Net. When I worked with Milo internally, I didn't have any problem. When I tried to connect remotely last night, I got chased by some weird multi-threaded program that I think would have killed me if it caught me."

"And what if the killer code is already in the server just waiting to take you out?"

"If it's there, believe me, I'll be able to see it. It's this big black octopus-like thing. It doesn't even pretend to hide. That's why I want Milo. He can watch out for me."

"And what if it mutated into something else—something invisible?" Rob put up his hand and shook his head. "No. It's too dangerous."

"I'm doing it, Rob."

Rob's eyes narrowed down to two angry slits. "Now you're pissing me off."

"Look, Rob! Somebody is fucking with us, and I don't think we should just bend over and take it!" Charlie's frustration had hit a peak. Tired and grouchy, not yet connected to N, not able to dial it down, take it easy, cool his jets, he let it out as good old-fashioned anger.

They stood nose to nose. Rob scowled, lowered his eyes, and rubbed his chin. After a minute he said, "How long do you think it'll take?"

Charlie stepped back and hissed out a disgusted "Huh." Then, "Jeez, Rob! I still don't even know what it is. How the hell can I tell you how long it'll take?"

"Yeah, yeah. All right. I'm just worried about you. OK. Get Milo and see what you can find. But have him report to me on your health every five minutes. You got that?"

"How about every fifteen minutes?"

Rob looked askance.

"OK. Absolutely. Thanks!" Charlie turned to go.

"Oh, one more thing." Charlie stopped and turned to see Rob holding up an index finger. "Jim Higgins called. He's offering legal assistance if we need it."

Charlie shook his head. "Yeah, I remember the letter-writing assistance he offered you at the board meeting. Seemed more like an order than an option. Can you handle that? I've got more pressing issues."

"Already done. I just wanted you to know."

Charlie tightened his lips. "Yeah, the guy makes me feel all warm and fuzzy."

"Well, at least Bertrand Wilson's not on our ass."

"It's not going to matter who's naughty or nice if I don't get this straightened out." Charlie leaned his head toward the door with eyebrows raised in a question.

"All right, go. But report back."

Charlie nodded and strode out leaving a heavy silence in the air.

Charlie lay back in his chair, and Milo sat next to him in guard mode. "OK, Buddy, you know what to do. If I see that octopus thing, I'll shut her down. Just make sure I don't leave this chair. Oh, and report to Rob every five minutes to tell him I'm still breathing. In fact, touch my arm every five minutes and make sure I answer you, in case that thing tries to mess with my brain."

Milo nodded in answer to everything, a crease between his eyebrows.

Charlie rolled his head, loosening muscles and popping a few vertebrae. Taking a deep breath and exhaling, he summoned his IS cube and double-tapped the spinning N. The sun came out, and his body relaxed as his Real anxieties, self-doubts, fears, obsessions, and exhaustion turned to a harmless mist that blew away like a wispy morning fog. *There's a reason they call smart people bright. There's more light in your brain, your eyes, your ears. You're just brighter.*

"Hello, boys," he said to his PAs.

The oBI received notice of a university truck delivery to CCD. The agents' software made the logic jump. Charlie Noble's last known location was MSU's Breslin Center. They applied for and got warrants for a search of CCD and the arrest of Charlie Noble.

Wet chunks of snow fell from the churning gray sky when they arrived at the front door of the office. When building approved their credentials, the receptionist commed Rob. He huffed into the lobby.

"What's this all about?"

"I'm Special Agent Lott and this is Special Agent Mortensen. We're here for Lester Charles Noble. You need to show us where he is."

"Why do you need to talk to him again?" Rob's hands fluttered in exasperation.

"We've developed additional information that he may be involved in some homicides."

"Homicides? Impossible. He's my best employee."

"Mr. Reynolds, it would be so much better for everyone if you would just take us to him."

"Let me see the docs."

Lott flicked.

Rob sent them to legal while his PA summarized it in laymen's terms. In thirty seconds legal replied. He clicked with his tongue. "Come with me." He led them across the lobby under the rotating N and arrow icon.

*   *   *

When the agents first entered the building, Charlie heard a gentle beep and saw the blinking icon. He knew exactly what it meant; his research was over. "Oh, for crying out loud." He let out a weary sigh and brought his focus back into his office.

Milo looked up. "What?"

"Federal agents are coming to arrest me."

"What for?"

Charlie got up from the chair. "For the death of three of our alpha testers and evading arrest earlier."

"But you didn't do any of that ... did you?" Milo's eyebrows crept upward.

Charlie gave a dismissive wave. "It's not important."

"Uhhhh, it's important to me."

"No. What I mean is, what's important right now is that I'm going to run, and I don't want you to help me in any way. You don't want to be tried for harboring a fugitive."

"Holy crap."

"Yeah."

Charlie's sensors told him the agents were twenty feet from his door. He stepped across the room and into the hall. Catching their eyes, he waved. "Gentlemen." Then he took a deep, courtly bow and—disappeared.

Mortensen gasped "What the fuck?"

CHAPTER 55

The agents ran forward and swept the air with their arms high and low, stepping front and back and left and right, finding nothing.

"It was probably just a nano projection." Mortensen turned to Rob. "Is this his office?"

Rob nodded and pointed to the doorway Charlie had exited. Mortensen dashed in with Lott behind only to see Milo standing there.

Lott beckoned. "Where'd he go?"

Milo's eyes were big around. "He walked out the door and then ... vanished."

"Was that *really* him, or some kind of double?"

"Him."

Mortensen smirked, "We're supposed to believe you? He didn't have an ID tag."

Rob raised an index finger. "Milo's all right. Besides, don't you guys have lie detectors?"

Lott said, "We do, but we've been tricked by somebody from here before."

Mortensen gritted his teeth. "Fuck! Fuck that motherfucker! What kind of illegal shit are you people making here?"

Both Milo and Rob's mouths fell open.

Lott touched Mortensen's elbow and opened a PC, "Language, Dylan, language."

"Fuck that, and fuck all these guys. They're making us look like idiots. Let's just get on with it."

Lott shook his head and closed the channel. Taking a box from his pocket, he lifted the lid and waved. A swarm of winged sensors scattered in all directions looking for heat signatures and unidentified personnel. The reports came back. Nothing.

Lott pursed his lips. "We were too slow. But he couldn't have gotten past us, and I'm betting he can't walk through walls."

Mortensen mumbled. "I might just take that bet."

Lott started down the hall. "He had to go this way. Look in any room with an open door."

The entire wing was full of rooms with open doors and many large, open areas.

*   *   *

Once he had activated the Harry Potter, Charlie turned and walked swiftly but quietly down the hall away from the agents, holding his breath as he went. He reached the far end of the hall in time to see them waving their arms as if swatting flies. When they stepped into his office, Charlie opened the door leading to the exercise facilities. His idea was to hide in the building while giving the impression he had left it. *I've already wasted a whole day running around the city. I am* not *doing that again.*

He passed through the exercise room and into to the pool area. His first thought was to hide in the ceiling, like he had at the Breslin, but changed his mind when he thought of the dumpster.

As he walked along the edge of the pool, he looked down into the water and had an idea.

*   *   *

The agents tested their way down the hall and through the large open meeting areas with Rob following. Their sensors found nothing. Finally Lott remembered a technique he'd read about. He ordered the sensors to check the hinges on the three doors exiting the area for elevated temperature, indicating which had recently been opened. The report came back. "This one." They passed into the exercise area, Rob trailing and wringing his hands. The door opened onto a hall leading to the locker rooms with another door straight ahead. Lott dispersed the sensors to test the door hinges. Glancing up from his display he pointed. "This way." Gripping the handle of the door to the pool, he smiled. "Now we're getting somewhere."

*   *   *

Charlie took a few deep breaths to activate Dex's OxyT. He walked to the pool stairs and slowly lowered himself into the water. He didn't want any waves ricocheting around the sides of the pool once the agents got there, and he expected them shortly. Blowing the air from his lungs, he took a final step and let the water wash over his head. He shivered from the cool water. *God, I hate being cold!* Then he waited anxiously to see how the OxyT worked.

When he was a kid, he could hold his breath for up to three minutes, but it was a panicky struggle during the last minute. OxyT was different. His lungs still demanded movement, so he tamed the feeling with N. *God bless you, Dexter.* Sitting on the bottom of the pool, he watched the door, N correcting for the visual distortion of the water.

* * *

As they stepped into the pool room, Special Agent Lott directed the sensors to check the hinges—his new favorite trick. The display showed no recent movement except for the door they had come through. "He's in here."

Mortensen smirked. "Or he doubled back. Have them check in here for heat and whatever else it is they look for."

Lott scattered the devices into the room. "No heat and no unidentifieds."

"Where the hell is he?"

"How about in the water?"

"Check it out."

"They can't do water."

"Je-sus!" Mortensen rolled his head. "So now what?"

"We wait. If he's in the water, he'll come up to breathe."

Mortensen stood tapping his foot. After a few seconds he patrolled the edges of the pool squinting at the water. In the gutter he found a long aluminum pole that lifeguards use to help floundering swimmers.

Lott straightened up. "Whoa. What're you gonna do with that?"

"Sweep the bottom until I hit the son of a bitch."

"But if he *is* in there and you start making waves, we'll never see him if he tries to sneak out."

"Waves ain't gonna matter. He'll come out screaming when I swat his ass."

Rob looked horrified.

Lott shook his head. "Right. Because that technique worked so well at the dumpster."

"Well, shit, man. What are we supposed to do, just sit here?"

"Unless he can walk through walls, he's still here."

* * *

Charlie saw the trio come into the pool room. His N-hanced hearing adjusted for the muffling effect of water, letting him understand everything they said. Once he heard Mortensen's plan for the pole, he decided to move things along. He spread his arms and aimed his palms at a spot the other side of the far wall into the women's locker room and focused the beam.

Mortensen straightened. "You hear that? He's in that room."

Lott said, "It doesn't make sense."

"What do you mean? Somebody's in there."

"So tell me, how come our sensors can't get anything on him in room after room, and then all of a sudden he shows up out of nowhere?"

"Maybe he ran out of tricks."

"Those doors haven *not* been opened. I'm telling you, he's in here."

"He doubled back like I said. C'mon. Let's go."

"I don't think so."

"I'm going without you."

"We shouldn't split up."

"Aarrggh!" Mortensen threw himself down into a deck chair.

"Hey, Buddy. It's not all that bad. Ten years ago we would have needed a whole team to do this."

"Yeah? Well, we're not doing all that great if you ask me."

"Trust me, it was worse then."

The movement of Charlie's arms loosened a bubble of air caught under his clothes. *Nooo! Not now.* He froze, hoping to keep it from moving further. It crept on, tickling as it ran up the groove along his spine. Hunching his shoulders only moved it faster, so he rolled his shoulders back. No matter how he contorted himself, the bubble kept rising. Feeling it around his collar, he grabbed the material, pulling the fabric tight against the back of his neck. The bubble split in two, brushed past his cheeks and up to the surface. *Bloop! Bloop!*

Mortensen shot from the chair. "What the hell was that?" Looking in the direction of the sound he pointed. "There!" He yanked off his overcoat and flung himself into the pool, thousand-credit suit and all, on top of the waves that formed around the bubbles. Thrashing his arms back and forth and up and down, he howled and cursed.

CHAPTER 56

When the bubbles broke the surface, Charlie crab-walked across the bottom of the pool toward the shallow end. He backed up the steps in slow motion, only to glance down in shock at the bizarre sight of waves breaking around the torso-shaped hole he left in the water and the rivulets sheeting off his body. Snapping his gaze toward the agents, he saw Rob staring, mouth open, in his direction.

Rob shook his head as if to clear it. He turned and pointed toward the deep end. "Look! Over there!"

Mortensen's eyes followed Rob's finger. "Here?"

"Yeah."

Mortensen slashed at the water with a terrifying fury.

Bless you, Rob.

Now fully out of the pool, Charlie dashed down the short hall to the men's locker room. The door at the end lay out of sight of the agents, but he noticed he was dripping water onto the tile. With a sweeping motion, he turned his oClean on **DRY**. He pushed the door open a crack and slid out.

Mortensen yanked himself out of the water, dripping and yelling at Lott. "He's not in here!"

"What about the bubble? He could have snuck by you, come back around, and still be in the water."

"Fat chance."

"Will it make you feel any better if I do a hinge check?"

"Hell yes."

In a moment Lott pointed. "Down that hall."

Mortensen's wet shoes slipped on the tile and he went down, smacking his elbow. "God dammit!" He jumped back up and waddled, rubbing the elbow. His face was a jigsaw mask of pain, anger, and embarrassment.

When they got to the far side of the pool he pointed "Look! Wet footprints. I told you so."

Lott's lips tightened. *I'm beginning to hate it when he's right.*

As Charlie passed through the men's locker room, his mind raced. *I've got to get out of the building.* Stepping into the main hallway, he carefully closed the door behind him, turning the handle to avoid a click. Just as it latched, Mortensen yanked open the door from the pool side of the room. The pressure change made the handle jerk in Charlie's hand. He jumped. He decided to create another distraction. Stretching his arms, he aimed for the women's locker room again, making a ruckus that sounded as if someone were running. Then he hustled down the hall toward the exit.

"I *told* you he was in the locker room!" Mortensen dashed out the door Charlie had just gone through, heading in the opposite direction.

Lott shook his head wearily. "Why don't we let the sensors tell us where he went?"

"I was right about him getting out of the water, wasn't I?" He jerked open the door to the locker room.

Lott sighed and followed, the sensors and Rob fluttering behind. *Too late to test those hinges.*

Charlie waited until Tom, Dylan and Rob came out into the hallway and into the ladies area. He pushed opened the exit door, and gasped. The twenty-degree weather was a shock. Picturing his coat on the hook in his office, he ran. Looking back, he saw he was leaving a clear trail of footprints in the new snow. *Now what? Hey, Dex, can you make me fly?*

As he rounded the corner of the building, he saw oCars moving up the street. *I can't call one without giving myself away. Wait. I'll bet I can hack the rental computer.* He set his PAs to work on it while he watched for an empty vehicle.

As he hustled along the front of the building, he noticed an oCar sitting next to the curb with four passengers in it. One displayed a familiar profile. *Matthew? Oh, no. That's the last thing I need right now.* He turned away, then stopped. *Wait a minute. This could be a good thing.* Turning back he dashed the few yards to the car. *It is Matthew!* When he knocked on the window, all four occupants jumped, then turned their heads back and forth in his direction. *What's the matter with them? They act as if they can't see— Oh, good grief!* He gestured and watched as his own hand appear in front of him. All four of them jumped—again.

Matthew waved his portal open. "Teacher!"

Mary, the blonde girl he'd seen before, whispered to the others. "He appeared from nowhere. He *is* the Son of God."

"Listen, Matthew, can I have your car?"

"We'll take you anywhere you want."

"No. Some Federal agents are after me. I don't want to get you into trouble."

The girl whispered, "The temple guards."

Matthew straightened. "We're not afraid. We'll take care of you, Lord." The door dissolved and his seat rotated out.

"Look, if you don't let me have the car I'll leave now."

Mary said, "It is his fate. He cannot let the cup pass from his lips. We must do as he asks."

"OK. It's yours." Matthew flicked and the walls dissolved, delivering the other three onto the street.

Charlie saw the two remaining men were tagged Simon and Peter. They all wore biblical robes. *This is getting weird.* He lowered himself onto Matthew's seat. As it moved him into position, he gestured to keep the portal open. "Do me a favor."

"Anything." Matthew's face lit up with an expression far too eager for Charlie's comfort.

"Stay here, and if anyone asks if you saw anything, tell them you saw a ghost get into an oCar. Tell them it went south."

"Yes, Master."

"And quit calling me that."

"Yes, Lord."

Charlie rolled his eyes. The portal irised shut and the car made a U-turn to head north. Another wave of his hand and he was invisible again.

Within a few seconds he got a comm from he PAs. He opened the channel, which dropped him into the VR warehouse in his office. "I've already got an oCar..." Then he saw his PAs dodging tentacles.

"We know. But the Black Octopus is back."

Charlie's heart sank. *Of course. Now that I'm out of range of the CCD's Wi-Fi, I'm on the Net again.*

CHAPTER 57

Rob and Agent Lott stood in the doorway to the women's locker room.

"Shit!" Mortensen shook his fist. "He's not in here either."

Lott spread his hands. "Now can we use the sensors?"

Seconds later they headed out the exit.

"Jesus! It's colder than hell!" Mortensen gestured for his T to wring him dry. The process started at his hair and hissed as it worked its way down.

Lott pointed a set of footprints. "This should be easy."

The three of them ran along the sidewalk and around the side of the building to the street. The prints headed south along the front of the building. They men followed a few yards until the prints ended near four people huddled at the curb.

Lott flashed his credentials. "How long you been standing here?"

The guy tagged Matthew said, "About five minutes. What's up?"

"You see anybody get into an oCar?"

"No. But something weird happened. An oCar pulled up and opened the portal like it was waiting for somebody. We told it we didn't order it, so it just closed and drove away."

"Which way did it go?"

"That way." Matthew pointed down Washington. "I think it's that one there."

"Thanks."

Mortensen had called for their agency vehicle, which rounded the corner and headed toward them.

Lott turned to Rob. "Thanks for your help."

"I'm coming with you."

"Sorry, it doesn't work that way. And thing might get dangerous."

"I've known Charlie for nearly fifteen years. He's not dangerous."

Their car pulled to the curb and Mortensen traipsed to the far side. Two portals opened.

Rob held up a hand. "I don't recall anyone telling Charlie that he's under arrest. Right now he's just a guy you're tailing."

Lott shook his head. "You are *not* coming with us."

"I'm a citizen. I have a right to be on the street."

"Do I have to arrest you for obstruction?"

Rob's shoulders fell. He turned and headed to the main entrance.

The agents' car drove south as fast as the system allowed.

Charlie sat facing backwards, watching the CCD building. His heart thumped when he saw the agents and Rob come around the corner of the building. After they talked to Matthew's crew, he boosted magnification in order to see the agents get into their oCar and head south. He felt relieved for a second, but when he shifted his awareness into the server, his heart sped up.

Lott opened a comm and targeted the oCar in the center of his vision. "This is Special Agent Lott of the oBI. Lester Charles Noble, you are under arrest."

Mortensen put his hand on Tom's arm. "Wait, Lott."

Lott held up his hand signaling for silence.

A woman's voice came back, "Are you talking to me?"

"Who is this?"

Mortensen whispered. "Lott—"

"My name is Theresa Miller. What did I do?"

"Lott, it's not him. Look at the tag above the car. She's who she said she is." He flicked for the view from a security cam, zooming in to see the woman.

"Sorry ma'am. My mistake." Lott terminated the comm. "Well, that was embarrassing. So where the hell did he go? There're no other cars headed in this way."

"I'm gonna reverse the vid from the security cam near CCD." Mortensen found the feed. A car made a backwards U-turn and parked at the curb where the kids were standing. He continued until Charlie appeared. Running it forward, he saw the kids get out and Charlie get in. "They lied to us."

"Forget about them. We've lost too much time." He gestured in his cube. "Follow that car!" He turned back to Mortensen. "Move the vid forward and find out where he's going."

"I got those kids' IDs, too. They're not getting away with this."

Lott rolled his eyes—again.

CHAPTER 58

Inside the white VR warehouse that Charlie chose as his interface to the N server, he saw a movement and jumped. It was a tentacle. *That was close!* His eyes vigilant, he turned to his PAs. "What happened with the Black Octopus after I left that garbage truck?"

"It disappeared. It seems to want only you, or at least somebody live."

"Good. Then here's the plan; I want you to give this oCar priority in the oCMAD Master Assignment Database. I'm going to sign off, and you keep me away from the agents. Slow them down or send them somewhere else. Get all other vehicles out of my way and speed me up. That's it. I gotta disconnect."

Too busy making decisions, he forgot about the effects of N withdrawal. "Not again." He leaned over and threw up in the footwell just past his shoes—mostly. Little clouds of oClean appeared and attacked every spot with a sizzling foam. oCars had armies of the little buggers optimized for readying vehicles between customers. Other nano swept the air erasing all traces of the pungent odor. The headache swept in. "Arrgghh!" He pressed against his forehead.

His oCar sped up, nearing the one in front of him. Then his swerved into the left turn lane, passing an entire row of vehicles. Now un-N-hanced, panic swept over him. As he crossed over I-496, he checked his IS cube to find the oBI vehicle falling behind. *Good work, buddies.* It helped to busy his mind, but only for a moment.

Mortensen pounded the dashboard. "He's getting away. That's not supposed to happen."

Lott frowned. "He must be overriding the system."

"Can we get access to it from here?"

"You bet." Lott brought up the main control and pointed at a sub-menu off to the right. Before he could get to the traffic computer their vehicle swerved into the turn lane and cornered left onto St. Joe Highway.

Their voices chorused. "Whoa."

Lott touched the oCMAD interface and blew up the map showing the vehicles in their vicinity. Mortensen slapped his hand on Charlie's oCar, but it skittered from under him. "What the hell?"

"System override. Stop this vehicle." Lott snapped a finger at Charlie's car on the map.

The answer came back, "You do not have authorization to control that vehicle."

Mortensen said, "Like hell we don't. We're the fucking oBI. Who has higher clearance than we do?"

"That vehicle has programmer clearance."

Mortensen shook his head. "Damn programmers."

Lott said, "Give us programmer clearance."

"Clearance granted."

"Now *stop that car!*"

"Only one programmer can control any given vehicle at a time."

Mortensen spat. "Oh, for Chrissake!"

Lott's brow furrowed. "Take our vehicle and move it on a path to meet that one."

"I can't do that. Your vehicle is also under the control of another programmer."

Mortensen snapped his fingers. "I've got it!" He reached over and grabbed the oCar neared Charlie's. He slid it into Charlie's path. Charlie's car performed an evasive maneuver, swerving across the lanes of oncoming traffic. oCMAD diverted vehicles to prevent a collision.

Lott shook his head. "It looks like a Dodgem bumper car ride."

Charlie's oCar made a wide arc, sending it back south toward the agents. Mortensen smirked. "Now we're talking."

Lott slapped his hand on top of their vehicle's icon, but it broke away.

Mortensen said, "Bullshit." They approached the intersection at South Capitol Avenue, just one block west of where they'd lost control of their car. He touched a few vehicles on the map, freezing them in place. Then he grabbed still others and shuffled them, until they blocked the entire roadway. Their own vehicle slowed, and some of the oCars in the intersection pulled back to clear a path for Charlie. "Like hell!" Mortensen slapped his hands on the icons to hold them in place. Their oCar came to a stop a couple yards from a row of stalled vehicles. Passengers leaped out, waving their arms in anger and confusion.

Mortensen gestured for the portals to dissolve. Lott started to get out. Mortensen put his hand on his arm. "Wait. I just did that so the car wouldn't start up again. Put your foot out onto the pavement to keep the portal open. I'm gonna stop Noble."

The engine to Charlie's engine roared, trying to get back up to speed. Using their cube, Mortensen guided other vehicles into Charlie's path. Then he spotted a semi, which he nudged into the intersection at St. Joe. Charlie's car was going too fast to stop.

Charlie gasped as his car swerved to the right to avoid an eighteen-wheeler that appeared out of nowhere. With no street left, his vehicle jumped the curb and bounced off a light pole. With a loud *Shoonk* and a metallic screech, it plowed through a snow bank. He grabbed for a steering wheel, and his foot searched for a brake, but the car had neither. Rocking wildly, the wheels screamed, desperately trying to keep the car from spinning out of control. A large tree loomed dead ahead. Charlie put his arms out. "Shit!" The computerized wheels tried to compensate for the snow, but kept slipping. At the last second two of them caught and the car veered.

Two tires hit a snarl of raised tree roots, tipping the car onto the other two wheels. Eyes wide and mouth open, Charlie leaned his weight to set it back down. He braced his arms against the dashboard. "Whoa!" Now in a snow-covered garden, the wheels bounced on a boulder and went airborne again. The grounded wheels skidded in a patch of gravel and the car rolled over as the air bags deployed with a loud crack and hiss. The vehicle rolled over a second time.

The agents watched as Charlie's oCar landed on its roof, sliding and spinning like a helpless turtle on its back. A metallic screech brought it to a stop just a half block from them.

Mortensen hooted. "Gotcha, fucker!" He jumped from their car and ran. Lott was close behind. *Maybe the kid's gonna be all right after all.*

Charlie's heart pounded and his ears rang from the adrenaline, but he felt fine. "Damn!" During the bouncing and flipping, he felt Dex's Shield close in to protect him. When his head hit the airbag, he had a vision of his brain being protected by a grid of tiny red laser cubes. He felt better than before the crash. The N-withdrawal headache was gone, and he didn't feel any ill effects from the airbag impact. *Way to go Dex.*

Out his window he saw the agents racing toward him upside down. "Open sesame!" The wall dissolved, and he scrambled out. He stood and sucked in two deep breaths to replenish the OxyT. With the agents only a few yards away, he turned and ran.

For every ten feet the agents ran, Charlie ran eleven.
"This is bullshit." Mortensen opened his coat. "I'm gonna use the gun."

Lott said, "You've got to give him a chance to give up."

Mortensen huffed. "Fine." Yanking his gun from his shoulder holster he shouted, "Stop or I'll shoot."

Charlie stayed on the pavement where the snow had been cleared so he wouldn't leave any footprints. He felt as if he could run all day. With his arms pumping, he noticed they were white. *What? Airbag powder!* He sent T scurrying to clean it. He was nearly transparent when he heard Mortensen. "...or I'll shoot!" Charlie zigged sideways. He heard the shot. *Blaammm!*

His head jerked when something hissed past his ear, and a blast of air slapped the side of his head. He waited for the pain, but it never come. *Missed!* He leaned into the run—and then he fell onto his face. *Ohmigod! They got me.*

Trying to lift himself, he found he could barely move. *But nothing hurts.* He rolled over slowly, looking for blood. All he saw was the last of a patch of the airbag powder as it disappeared from his chest.

The agents seemed huge as they loomed over him, a crowd gathering behind them. "How do you like our new oCuffs, asshole?" Mortensen smirked. "I think we oughta call it oShit."

Charlie's heart pounded. He could barely speak. "What happened?"

"You're not the only one with new tech, dickwad. It resets you muscle T for slow movement only. You're not going anywhere. Now make yourself visible or I might accidentally step on you."

Charlie lifted a finger and reappeared.

Mortensen braced his feet against Charlie's shoes. He bent and jerked Charlie by his arms. Standing him upright, Mortensen stepped back and looked Charlie in the eyes. He his arms spread and beckoned a challenge. "Go ahead, you fuck. Take a swing."

Lott leaned in. "Dylan—"

Mortensen put out a hushing palm.

Charlie looked confused. "I don't think—"

"C'mon. If you can do it, I'll let you go."

Charlie paused then tried to pull his arm back, but all he could manage was something that reminded him of slow-motion Tai Chi.

"Yeah, you're pretty scary all right." Mortensen raised his hand and Charlie cringed, but the agent beckoned for their car. It didn't move. "Shit!" He drew an IS cube and ordered a public vehicle.

Lott spoke in a monotone. "Lester Charles Noble, you're under arrest for the negligent homicide deaths of Wilford Bostwick, Chad Rodriguez and Gary Billings. And after today there will probably be some other charges for evading arrest, destruction of public and private property and use of illegal T tacked on as well. You have the right to remain silent. Anything you say can and will be used against you in a court of law..."

PART THREE

CHAPTER 59

"Baxter Goodman to see Charlie Noble."

"Sure, counselor." The officer pointed to the VR panel with Baxter's picture and file. "Your credentials and ID are accepted. Please remove everything from your pockets."

"My pockets are empty."

"Permission to scan?"

"Granted."

Baxter proved weapon-free. "OK. He's already waiting for you in meeting room seven. Officer Mullinex will take you back." He motioned to the woman standing near the door.

She lifted her chin, calling Baxter her way and waved the two-inch-thick acrylic door open. It slid back with a "Whoosh!" that echoed down the halls. Baxter followed her along a glossy, institutional-green passage until she flicked two fingers at the door of the meeting room. It hissed open. "I'll be right outside if you need me."

Baxter nodded. "Thank you, officer."

The room was windowless and empty except for a plain metal table bolted to the center of the floor. The walls were the same drab green.

Charlie got up in slow motion, reached across the table and shook the man's hand.

"I'm Baxter Goodman, Mr. Noble. Jim Higgins sent me. He tells me he's one of your investors."

"Of course. Thank you for coming. Chicago, right?"

"Yes."

"Pardon my movement. They're using some new technology on me. Keeps me from moving quickly. I can't even yell or talk fast. At least I don't have to wear restraints. "

"We'll see if we can't get it turned off. It makes you look stoned. It would prejudice the jury."

"So you think this'll go to court?"

"Speaking hypothetically."

Baxter reached into the outside pocket of his jacket. He took out a small rainbow-striped cube and set it on the table. Charlie sat back. "How'd you get that in—"

Baxter held up a palm and put the index finger of his other hand to his lips. He made a magician-like wave over the device. Three Skeets fell out of the air, landing on the table between them. "Now we can talk."

"They'll know you did that."

The corners of Baxter's mouth curled up pointing to the sparkle in his eyes. "It's illegal for them to use those things in these private rooms. We'll never hear a word about it. And they won't dare try it again. They know I'll sue their ass." He slipped the cube back into his pocket. "So, how are you?"

"How am—?" Charlie shook his head. "Can't complain."

Baxter chuckled.

Charlie studied Baxter. The man was overweight and disheveled with graying hair, slicked straight back and held in place with reading glasses. "You don't look the way I expected. So how old *are* you?"

"Sixty Real. But I'm oGERed to twenty-five. The rest is for effect. I don't need glasses, and I can afford better suits. But I found out a long time ago witnesses and juries trust me more this way, and my opponents relax and don't work as hard. About the time they think I'm not too bright, I have one more question that sinks 'em. Kinda like Peter Falk in the old *Colombo* TV show."

"I remember *Colombo*. Glad you're on my side."

Baxter let out a deep sigh. "I looked over the charges. It's pretty serious, but I don't see any hard evidence. Some minor stuff about the chase and illegal T, but I'm pretty sure we can get that tossed out. You might have to pay some fines."

Charlie leaned in. "Hey! Thoth guyth moved the carth—" The cuff kicked in, so he took it down. "Sorry. Those guys moved the cars around, not me."

"They'll claim they had to because you were fleeing arrest. But don't worry." Baxter waved dismissively. "We need to concentrate on the negligent homicide charges."

"Right."

Baxter smiled and shook his head. "And we've *gotta* get that slow-mo thing turned off."

"Did Jim tell you I intend to represent myself?"

"Yes. But you know what they say—"

"I know. A fool for a client. I'll ask the court to let me use N-hanced. It would be ten times more powerful than the best team you can assemble. No offense."

"None taken."

"You know about N-hanced?"

"Yeah." Baxter nodded. "And if the judge turns you down?"

Charlie winced. "There's no way I could handle it without N."

"Mr. Higgins instructed me to offer my services either way. I'll be glad to help you defend yourself or act as your counsel. There are a number of issues about your case that are groundbreaking and could lead to an appeal."

"That's nice, but I don't find the idea of an appeal—well, appealing. I don't want to lose."

"Me either. But you raise the odds defending yourself."

"See what you think after we go over what I know and what they don't know. Unfortunately I'm not allowed to use N-hanced right now, so I'm at a slight disadvantage."

"Then you'll need me to handle things during the arraignment, unless you want to give it a go."

"Oh, no. But I do want to move this along so we can go to trial tomorrow, if they'll let us."

"Usually we like delays in order to gather as much evidence as we can."

"The prosecutor thinks they have all they need. I think he's wrong. I want to get out of here. I've got a product going to market. Which reminds me, will you see if I can post bail and go home today?"

"You might have some trouble with that, but we'll try. The arraignment's at 3:00. That gives us—" Baxter glanced up at the time. "—a couple hours. My team'll submit some arguments, and see if we can't get the whole thing dismissed. So, now's the time for you to give me as much ammunition as you can."

Charlie slid his palms onto the table. "All right. Here's what I got..."

CHAPTER 60

The bailiff brought Charlie through a back door into the courtroom and helped him oCuff-waddle across the floor and into the jury box. The walls were traditional dark oak panels, the room arranged like many courtroom programs he'd seen. For someone coming in the front doors, the bar with the swinging waist-high gate divided the room in half, the front section contained the jury box off to the right, court reporter, clerk, and bailiff on the left and the judge's stand in the middle. The only nod to anything modern was the sunlight-tinted LED lights in the ceiling and a set of simple hanging Art Deco lamps, also LED.

Charlie scrutinized the upper edges of the room and spotted an array of wall-mounted cams that would capture the proceedings from all angles. He tried to imagine how court would change ten years into the future, once N was everywhere. People would share information at the speed of thought, but still probably lie in unimaginable new ways. *Eight or more copies of a person could integrate memories of separate events—truthful versions from one covering the lies of another.*

The bailiff called out, "All rise."

A woman tagged 'Honorable Judge Valerie Brennan' and dressed in judge's robes entered, climbed the two steps to the bench, sat, and rapped a gavel. "You may be seated. Next case."

"oUnited States District Court for the Western District of Michigan, Case number 967392, The oUnited States vs. Lester Charles Noble."

An officer helped Charlie to his feet and led him to the defense table. Baxter Goodman came through the hinged gate from the gallery and joined Charlie.

The judge eyed him. "Are you Lester Charles Noble?"

"Yes, Your Honor."

"The Federal Prosecutor has submitted his complaint to the oLaw computer and your counter-arguments have been considered. It has not been able to come to a conclusion, so your case must now be analyzed by humans. First, you are charged with three counts of negligent homicide. Each count carries a maximum sentence of five years. Second you are charged with evading arrest and destruction of public and private property. And third you are charged with use of illegally programmed T. Do you understand these charges?"

"Yes, Your Honor"

"How do you plead?"

"Not guilty on all charges."

"Is this your attorney, Mr. Noble?"

Charlie turned to Baxter with a questioning look.

The attorney raised his hand. "Your Honor, if I may. I am Baxter Goodman of Goodman, Barclay and Thompson in Chicago. We would like to address the details of representation during pretrial motions, but for now I will act as Mr. Noble's attorney."

"Very well, Mr. Goodman." She turned to the prosecutor. "Mr. O'Neil, what's your evidence for negligence?"

The tall, slim, fortyish prosecutor with dark hair and dusted gray temples stood. "It is our contention that Mr. Noble knew there was something wrong with his product before the first death. He chose to ignore in a rush to get the app to market. We believe any reasonable person would have called a halt to the testing at that time. We have a vid of the CEO of his company urging him to do just that. Mr. Noble ignored Mr. Reynolds. We contend that the second death demonstrated a pattern. At the very least the third death was totally unnecessary and proves negligence. We will provide witness testimony and recorded evidence that Mr. Noble acted with reckless disregard toward both his testers and himself."

"That's reasonably compelling." The judge turned her gaze to Baxter. "Mr. Goodman?"

"We believe the first death could easily have been interpreted as a coincidence. There was nothing connecting it to N-hanced. All testers knew about the tragedy and had no interest in withdrawing from the project. Mr. Noble provided each tester with a PA to watch out for them so that—"

"Because he knew there was a problem."

The judge's eyes shot a sliver of ice in the prosecutor's direction. "One at a time, Mr. O'Neill."

O'Neill nodded and looked away.

"Continue Mr. Goodman."

"Thank you, Your Honor. Mr. Noble launched an investigation to see if the system was compromised. Mr. Rodriguez was killed during that investigation. Mr. Noble immediately contacted his testers and told them they could continue only at their own risk. We have copies of that comm and there is no question about which risk he spoke. These people were unanimous in their desire to continue using the system. If the prosecution's entire case is that Mr. Noble didn't notify his testers, we can all go home."

"Mr. O'Neill?"

"The prosecution will provide testimony that Mr. Noble knew about the problem and attempted to cover it up. That he actively prevented experts from examining the system for the same reason. We believe he suffers from sleep deprivation, which led to messianic delusions of—"

"Messianic delusions?" Charlie tried to leap up but only managed to lean forward. "Where the hell are you getting that bull—?" His voice carried an angry tone but the oCuffs prevented it from reaching the volume of a shout.

Baxter put a hand on Charlie's shoulder.

Charlie looked at Baxter and whispered, "He's full of shit."

The judge aimed a pinched smile at Charlie. "Mr. Noble, we are a little less formal during arraignment. But that language may work against you with the jury. If this does make it to trial, we'll go out live to hundreds of thousands of homes. Profanity certainly won't help you represent of your product."

Charlie looked at her sheepishly. "Sorry, Your Honor."

"Anything else, Mr. O'Neill?"

"That's it, Your Honor."

"Mr. Goodman, aside from the arguments you've already given me, do you have any other reasons we should not go to trial?"

"Yes, Your Honor. It's the EULA."

"Will you define that for the record, please?"

Baxter stood. "It's an End User License Agreement, the long list of stipulations users agree to when they get new software. There was a clause in CCD's EULA protecting the company against claims in case of health issues or loss of life. Every tester signed it."

"Yes. I'm not a big fan of those, but that's not my call." She turned her head. "Counterargument, Mr. O'Neill?"

"Your Honor, every user should have a reasonable expectation of safety for his or her own well being."

Baxter raised a finger. "Your Honor, there is some precedence for physical safety and EULAsy. For instance, there are EULAs for devices that plug into a wall socket which warn against operating them while bathing. There are other examples."

Harrison shook his head. "Using software that's supposed to increase your knowledge is not plugged into a wall socket. There has to be some room for common sense here. People shouldn't be expected to know they might be killed by— oh, say something like reading an eBook. Death by 'learning tool' is beyond reasonable expectations for such a product. These are three lives we're talking about here. Adding a clause to the EULA does not absolve Mr. Noble from responsibility."

The judge looked at Baxter. "I'm inclined to agree with the prosecutor on this one. Anything else, Mr. Goodman?"

"No, Your Honor."

Apparently scrolling notes in her IS cube she said, "I think there's enough evidence that I'd like to hear what both your witnesses have to say. I'm granting the prosecution's request and ordering Mr. Noble bound over for trial."

Charlie dropped his head to his chest. *Shit!*

"Mr. Goodman, I assume you would like to discuss bail?"

"Yes, Your Honor. Mr. Noble is primarily being charged with negligence, which is neither an intentional nor a violent crime, and he has no criminal history. He is not a flight risk and seems to look forward to his day in court. I ask that he be released on his own recognizance."

Harrison raised his hand. "Your Honor, Mr. Noble led oBI agents on an intense chase that lasted for nearly an hour, resulting in the destruction of public and private property. He was found in possession of illegal T, which allowed him to travel without identification. He has already shown a—"

"Your Honor—" Baxter jumped up. "—Mr. Noble had reason to believe the agents threatened his life—"

Harrison interrupted. "Are you claiming he's paranoid and delusional? Because it sounds as if you're laying foundation for an insanity defense."

"Gentlemen, please." The judge held up her hand. "Let's save it for the trial. I'm going to deny bail for now. We'll try to iron out some of those other issues as we go along and see if I can give the defendant a break later on."

She turned her gaze toward Charlie. "You said you're prepared with your case, Mr. Noble. Thanks to computerization, pretrial preparation doesn't need to drag on like it used to. We'll keep you here in this building, which means you won't have to contend with a cellmate, or anything resembling a prison population. Based on the witness lists, your stay should be less than a week—assuming you're innocent."

Charlie nodded, but his spirits were sinking.

"Attorneys may submit written motions overnight to be handled by computer. As long as everyone is amenable, we'll reconvene for Pretrial tomorrow morning at 9:00 AM." She raised her eyebrows, and both attorneys nodded. "All right then. See if you can work out a plea bargain by then." She banged her gavel. "Next case."

CHAPTER 61

Charlie lumbered stiff-legged around the bare-bones conference room. He would rather have paced, but the oCuffs wouldn't let him. He did *not* like the way the conversation was going.

Baxter shrugged. "You never know with a jury. It's better if we work out a plea bargain for temporary insanity. It doesn't fly much these days, but I think you have a good case because your erased memory."

Charlie looked dubious. "Has it ever been done before?"

"No, but—"

"Then it's a crapshoot. Without a precedent my odds too low."

"But it could mean the chance to change law in a higher court."

Charlie looked askance. "This isn't about your career. I want this over with, not turning into a series of trials crawling their way up the steps of the Supreme Court."

"If it works, you'd probably only do two years in an institution with some follow-up evaluations. Put that up against fifteen years, it's no contest."

"But it could go longer than two years, couldn't it?"

Baxter raised his eyebrows as a silent "Maybe."

"And if I go along with that plea, everything I've worked for will come to a screeching halt. Afterward, I'll have the nut-case stigma to live down. Look, I did not do this thing. And I'm beginning to think someone in government has it in for me. The oBI guys mentioned that when they questioned me."

"Keep talking about a conspiracy, and you really will have a shot at an insanity defense."

"I told you, I don't want to go that way. The jury will see I'm OK. Plus I've never even been arrested before."

"What do you mean, 'the jury will see?'"

"When I tell them."

"Oh, no. You're not going on the stand. Bad idea."

"Now just a minute." Charlie flushed. "You work for me."

"And you're not screwing up my perfect record."

"If the judge lets me represent myself, you won't have to worry about that, will you?"

Baxter sighed. "I apologize. You're right. I do work for you. But there's a reason I get paid so well; I give excellent advice."

"And because you defend well in court. As far as I can tell, they don't have a case. Innocent until proven guilty."

Baxter shook his head. "All the prosecutor has to do is plant doubt with the jury. And he *will* get rough with you. You gotta know that."

"Uh— I guess so."

"No, I mean he *will*. He'll bring up things from your past. Your anger issues. Your ex-wives. Your Techno Grouch website."

Charlie's mouth fell open. "You know about that?"

Baxter smiled just a little. "Research. But the prosecutor's gonna do his homework."

"Shit!"

"What'd you expect? And it would probably be best if you got into the habit of watching your language from now on."

"Oh. Sure." Charlie eased himself back into his chair.

"And there are the death threats you made against people who practice identity theft."

"Wait a minute. Nobody knows about that."

"Did you tell any of your friends?"

"Oh, hell—" Charlie grimaced and held up a palm. "I mean, I guess so. But that stuff was before oGER and T nano and N-hanced."

"Have you had T deactivated any time in the last five months?" Baxter stood and leaned on the table straight armed, fingers splayed.

"Ye-ah. Every Thursday, but—"

"The prosecutor will claim you had an episode of anger when it was off and made a mistake while programming."

"He does have to prove that, doesn't he?"

"Technically, yes. But all he really has to do is let the jury hear it."

"Damn." Charlie tried to pound his fist on the table, but it floated down and landed with hardly a sound.

"Hey, I'm only getting warmed up. Want me to stop now?"

"No— No, I guess not. But listen, I *liked* my testers. They're like family to me."

Baxter came around and sat with one leg on the table. "How much sleep you getting?"

"Couple hours a night."

"He'll bring in experts to say lack of sleep makes people psychotic."

"You don't need sleep when you're N-hanced."

"Um-hum. Has Corridor CyberDynamics done any clinical trials along those lines?"

"No, but—"

"That's negligence. You sure you wouldn't rather go with insanity?"

Charlie threw him a pained look. "You think I'm insane?"

"You're still talking about representing yourself. That's nutty. But hey, it's not what I think that matters."

Charlie's shoulders slumped.

"Just think about it. I've got a meeting with the prosecutor in a few minutes. As long as you're not going along with a plea bargain, I'll see what I can do to get the lesser charges dropped. If you change your mind about the plea bargain, yell for a guard and have 'em come get me." He looked at Charlie's beaten-down posture. "And think again about letting me represent you."

Charlie waved him away. "Yeah, yeah. I'll be thinking."

CHAPTER 62

Charlie sat on the edge of his jailhouse bed, head in his hands, exhausted. He thought he'd have time to sleep, but he was wrong. Hounded by worry and nightmares, when the guard brought his breakfast, he'd already been awake for hours. His eyes were dry and red, his head ached, and his skin felt tight as he picked at his meal. Pushing the tray aside he got up and washed his face, used the toilet, and did his best to make himself presentable.

Just before 9:00 the bailiff and a guard escorted him down a series of hallways and through barred doors, and past the meeting rooms to the courtroom entrance.

The noise level dropped as people recognized him and shifted from talking to pointing and staring. A group of grim-faced protestors sat on the left side of the aisle. Matthew and the disciples sat on the right and looked in his direction with adoration. He heard someone say "Hallelujah." That was followed by a deep voice that mumbled, "Blasphemer."

Ah, my fans. The protestors glared at him. Charlie smiled and nodded.

The court clerk handed Charlie a bulky set of vid/phones gamers used to wear. She said it would let him see and hear the VR interactions.

Jeff sat in the front row wearing an identical headset. He tipped his head toward three apparently empty seats to his left. Once Charlie had his headset on, three people who vaguely resembled Anton, Dexter and Janice occupied the chairs. They were tagged as Walter Bratton, Toby Hodges and Anne Conley. All the previously empty seats were now filled with VR visitors, as was every square foot of standing room. The noise level in the phones soared, and a wave of stage fright made Charlie catch his breath. He spotted investor Jim Higgins' oMe2 half way back on his fans' side, near the center aisle.

Jim nodded and mouthed, "Good luck."

Charlie gave him a nervous nod back. "Thanks." His voice echoed hollowly inside the headset.

When Charlie spied a row of cams high on the back wall, he shook his head. *Great. Get it all on vid for the whole world to see.* His stress level soared. *This is it. This is the day that defines my fate. I'm not rested. And without N, I'm not smart enough to handle it. I can hardly wait.* He didn't have to.

"All rise." Everyone stood, even the oMe2s. "oUnited States District Court for the Western District of Michigan, Case number 967392, The oUnited States vs. Lester Charles Noble, pretrial hearing. The Honorable Judge Valerie Brennan presiding."

The judge climbed onto the bench. Without a glance she sat and waved her hand. "You may be seated." After a moment she lifted her eyes and aimed a sweeping scowl at the gallery. "Many of you think this is an entertainment event. You're wrong. This is a court of *law.* I will not tolerate *any* disruptions from the gallery. And that goes double for you NewsDogs. Being in the gallery is a privilege, not a right. I will gladly empty the gallery if everyone cannot maintain proper courtroom decorum. Everybody clear?"

A few heads nodded. The judge clicked her tongue, sighed, and shook her head, apparently expecting she would be both babysitter and judge.

"Also, you protestors—" She wiggled a finger in their direction. "—turn off those VR signs."

Charlie swiveled in time to see them disappear amidst a flurry of hand motions.

"First up; have the prosecution and defense reached any agreement as to the extent of the charges since yesterday?"

Harrison stood. "We have, Your Honor. The State has agreed to drop the lesser charges of evading arrest, the use of illegal T, and—for reasonable fines and appropriate compensation to the city and the injured parties—the destruction of public and private property—all with no admission of guilt."

In the gallery, agent Mortensen's oMe2 gave Lott's oMe2 a disgusted sidelong glance. Lott2 shrugged.

"Have you been able to come to a plea agreement regarding the three charges of negligent homicide?"

"We have not, Your Honor."

"Then we'll go to trial. Does the prosecution have any motions not yet submitted?"

Harrison shook his head.

"Please, Mr. O'Neill, a verbal response."

"No, Your Honor."

"Then we'll hear the defense motions."

The judge seemed to study her IS. "Mr. Noble, I understand you want to act *pro se.* You know what they say about someone representing himself?"

"Yes, Your Honor."

She shook her head.

Harrison raised a hand. "Your Honor, Mr. Noble intends to use the very program suspected of causing these people's deaths, as an expert system to provide him with legal knowledge. Do we have to watch the defendant commit suicide here in the courtroom?"

"What do you have to say to that Mr. Noble?" The judge held a palm out.

Charlie smiled. "I can assure you I have no intention of committing suicide. Beyond that, I believe I'm entitled to the best legal representation I can get, and right now that would be me using N-hanced."

"You are indeed entitled to the best. But you'll have to admit, it is without precedent."

"Your Honor, N-hanced will provide me the knowledge of a team of lawyers, and instant access to all of legal history. It is my contention that not being allowed to use N-hanced will provide me with inferior defense." He half-turned toward Baxter to apologize, but thought better of it. "I should be allowed to defend myself regardless of the court's concern for my safety. N-hanced will also let me handle my case unemotionally, as if I were someone else."

"Mr. prosecutor?"

"This stuff about emotion control sounds a like mood-altering drugs to me."

Charlie came back, "Not that N-hanced is anything like a drug, but I don't believe it has ever been illegal for defendants, lawyers or even judges to use anti-depressants or even caffeine."

The judge smiled. "Point taken."

Harrison said, "Your Honor, Mr. Noble has used his app in recent days to manipulate people's minds and evade authorities. There is no place for that in a courtroom."

"Mr. Noble?"

"I thought we already dismissed the issue of flight. But as to manipulating people, I can say N does have modules based on entertainers, sales people and, dare I say it, politicians. Now, as far as I know, lawyers are not required to check their personalities at the door. I don't see why I should. Maybe the prosecutor's afraid of a little competition."

There was a round of laughter.

The judge shot an icy stare at the gallery. "Thank you Mr. Noble. I have to admit I am fascinated by the prospect of watching you use N-hanced in my courtroom. But this specific form of self-representation would be a very big step—one just a little too big for me to go along with. And I have never had one of my verdicts overturned because we were too old-fashioned."

Charlie said, "Your Honor, I would argue that the main difference between N-hanced and standard computer technology is that it simply takes gesture and voice input and moves it up the nerve network, directly into the brain, thereby speeding data entry and retrieval. Otherwise, it's essentially the same."

"I understand, Mr. Noble. But I am not prepared to let you use a technology that could result in your death. And this court is not going to take the chance that it or any of its witnesses might be manipulated—any more than they usually are by counsel."

That brought a few chuckles.

"You yourself are on record saying N-hanced is revolutionary. So in effect you admit you would have an unfair advantage over the prosecution. Therefore I'm denying your petition."

"Your Honor, I don't believe there's any law against one attorney being smarter than another."

"Nice try, Mr. Noble. But you'll have to find another way to argue your case. Do you need more time to prepare?"

Charlie had to fight not to hang his head. "No, Your Honor. I'm ready now."

"Unless you have anything to add, you will not be allowed to reactivate N-hanced during the course of this trial. I presume Mr. Goodman will now represent you?"

"Yes, Your Honor." As Charlie sat down he thought, *Arrggh! Beaten by my own sales pitch.*

With sagging shoulders, Charlie turned in his chair to look at Anne/Janice. She rolled her hand dismissively as if to say, "You'll be fine." He shrugged and gave her a pained look. Then he turned back. Not being able to use N to defend himself—that was a big blow. Now his fate was in someone else's hands entirely. Someone he barely knew—and might not even be able to trust.

CHAPTER 63

Baxter took over, "Next, Your Honor, is the issue of the oCuffs."

By the time Baxter was done, the judge agreed to remove the cuffs and restore Charlie's T to level three. No more helmet. But they were minor victories, paling when compared to the denial of a forensic analyst to examine N-hanced from the inside. Charlie understood the judge's argument about the risks. But he was sure an outsider wouldn't have any idea what they were looking at. Anyone testifying about it's dangers would be testifying blind, like guessing at the workings of a grandfather clock without opening the case.

The judge consulted her notes. "Anything else?"

No response.

"Then unless anyone has a reason to change our proposed schedule, we'll advance to trial this afternoon."

The lawyers nodded. Charlie did too, but without enthusiasm.

"Your jury will be selected based on the stipulations both of you submitted. Most jurors will be oMe2s, but in this jurisdiction you can expect about thirty percent Real. All right then. Court recessed until 1:00."

*   *   *

Charlie stared at the floor. He was glad they were moving forward, but he felt severely crippled. His most important motions had been denied. The only consolation was that Baxter seemed to know what he was doing. If Charlie couldn't have N, Baxter was definitely number two. But he felt like the gap was more like a chasm. For a second he wondered if he should reconsider the temporary insanity defense.

Baxter tapped him on the shoulder and signaled for a PC. "Before arraignment you said you knew someone friendly to our side who could have generated that code. Now that we're going to trial I'll need that card in my hand."

"He's here in the courtroom. What do we have to do?"

"Who is it?"

"Walter Bratton." Charlie pointed into the gallery.

"I'll connect you." Baxter flicked in Walter's direction and again at Charlie. "You're on your own, gentlemen."

"Anton— I mean, Walter, I need to ask a favor."

"What can I do you, dude?"

"I need a steganography expert to testify on my behalf that someone could have broken into the system and inserted that code."

Somehow Anton managed to swagger even while seated. "Who zackly you got in mind, bro?"

"Who do you think?" Charlie chuckled. "But I'm worried about your identity. It's one thing to have you in the gallery as Walter. But once you're on the stand, there'll be all kinds of people checking out your credentials."

"I be cool. Janice got it covered."

"You sure? Seems every time I stretch the truth, the brown line gets higher on my pant legs. I'd hate to drag you through the poop, too."

" Stay loose." He waved at Charlie dismissively.

"OK. I appreciate it."

Anton nodded and they closed the comm.

Turning to the gallery, Charlie looked at his friends. *And they are my friends now, aren't they?* He was worried and it showed on his face and in the way he held his body. But there they sat with encouraging looks on their faces; Jim Higgins nodding, Anton as Walter giving him the thumbs up, Janice as Anne smiling and Dexter as Toby shrugging—which made Charlie smile. He felt a friendly hand on his shoulder and turned. It was only the bailiff. Charlie raised a palm to his friends as the bailiff took him away.

CHAPTER 64

The courtroom was filled to the rafters. The jury had filed in—four Real and eight oMe2s—and Judge Brennan came in and gave them preliminary instructions. Finally she said, "What you will hear in the next few moments are the opening statements of the lawyers. After hearing all the evidence, you will determine whether the prosecution has met its burden of proving the defendant guilty of the charges, beyond a reasonable doubt. I caution you that what you hear in opening statements is not evidence. The evidence will begin when the first witness begins to testify. We will now hear those opening arguments." Turning to the prosecutor she said, "Mr. O'Neill?"

"Ladies and gentlemen of the jury, Thursday of last week, Wilford Bostwick dove to his death in the Grand Canyon in front of his family. Here are Vs of the family at the park." He let them play as he continued. "Notice his demeanor. According to the emotional data collected from Mr. Bostwick by the defendant, he was not depressed, and in fact was having a wonderful time—until he hit the rocks." The point of view changed showing a little puff of dust as Wilford landed. Some of the jurors winced and looked away. "Why does the defendant have these special emotional data streams? Because Mr. Bostwick was taking part in the testing of an experimental new software called N-hanced. Software invented by the defendant, which the prosecution will prove was not ready for testing on people—and was in fact—deadly.

"After Mr. Bostwick died, did the defendant, Mr. Noble, call a halt to the testing of N-hanced—even though his boss begged him to? He did not."

Harrison waved his hand. The vid of Chad playing 3-D Pool in The Sportsman's Bar began. "The following day, a happy-go-lucky programmer named Chad Rodriguez went into a burning house to rescue five-year-old Andrew Bellows." The vid changed to a view just over Sara's shoulder as she sat on the motorcycle watching Chad go into the smoking window. Time moved forward and *Kawhoom!* the side of the house blew out. The courtroom shook and half the attendees jumped, some gasped. "We will show that something in the N-hanced software made him believe he could walk into that fire with immunity. After Mr. Rodriguez died, did the defendant call a halt to the testing of N-hanced—even though his boss begged him to? He did not.

"Later that same day, Gary Billings, a brilliant chemist and programmer…" Harrison began a vid of Gary kidding with his receptionist, "…while working on a product to protect children and adults from poisoning…" The scene changed to one inside the lab. "…he fell under the spell of N-hanced and tried to reenact a memory of a side show performance he had seen when he was a boy, causing him to drink a beaker of an extremely dangerous version of sulfuric acid known as Piranha solution, which ate a hole right through his stomach and the floor below him." The vid showed him drinking and then moved forward until smoke rose from his body, with a view down through the floor. In the courtroom people looked away and moaned. Baxter remained stoic.

"After Mr. Billings died, did the defendant call a halt to the testing of N-hanced? This time he did. But by then it was too late for Gary Billings and Chad Rodriguez and Wilford Bostwick and their families." He played a montage of their faces and their grieving wives and children.

Baxter watched the jurors' faces and checked their reactions with his software. He sent a message to his team.

Harrison continued. "We will prove that the defendant was in a hurry to get N-hanced to market. That it was a 'make it or break it' product for his company. We will show that his ambition made him careless. That he suffered from sleep deprivation, which caused him to make deadly mistakes." The family vids faded away.

"You will hear expert testimony that the N-hanced code is so complicated nobody can understand it—let alone hack it—unless they invite the deadly code into their brains. In other words, there is only one person who could possibly be responsible for these deaths and that person is the defendant himself." Harrison pointed at Charlie.

"We will show, by the defendant's own admission, that his program contained a coding error he had made on numerous occasions.

"You are going to hear testimony that the defendant had a special section written into the software agreement—an agreement his testers were forced to sign before using N-hanced. A section that deviously attempted to protect Mr. Noble and his company from being sued if using the product resulted in their death—which indeed it did.

"We are not saying Mr. Noble murdered these people. What we are saying is his carelessness and ambition made him negligent. And we will show you all this beyond a reasonable doubt. That is why we are asking you to convict him on three counts of negligent homicide." He played the three men's faces again. "One count each for Gary Billings... Chad Rodriguez... and Wilford Bostwick."

Harrison stood facing the jury and as the vid faded, they found themselves looking at him. He took his time making eye contact with each one of them. The room was absolutely silent, stunned faces everywhere.

Finally, he nodded. "Thank you." And returned to his table.

CHAPTER 65

Baxter Goodman rose and buttoned his one-size-too-small jacket. Walking slowly to the center of the floor, head bowed, brows arched in pained sympathy, his demeanor somehow conveyed sorrow, thoughtfulness, empathy, respect, humility and confidence all at the same time. He began.

"Ladies and gentlemen of the jury, on behalf of my client, Mr. Noble," he gestured toward Charlie, "and myself I want to express our deepest sympathy to the families and friends of the three men whose lives have come to such a sad and tragic end. These were vibrant and creative people, and active in their communities. Our hearts go out to their families.

But we also think it would be tragic if the wrong person were sent to prison for their deaths while the real culprit went free—very likely to kill again. And we hope you agree." Baxter walked around behind Charlie's chair. "It is the opinion of my team and myself that Mr. Noble—" His hands rested on Charlie's shoulders. "—is no more guilty of these deaths than any one of you." He spread his arms wide and turned to take in everyone in the courtroom.

Baxter took his time walking back to the center of the floor. "I want to take you back a few years. Back to the time when people still drove their own cars. Some of you remember those days, right?" He looked at the jury to see a dozen nodding heads. "If there was an incident of hit and run, the state would do everything in its power to track down that driver and bring him to justice. They would not mount a lawsuit against the manufacturer of the car. So consider this; my client is a software manufacturer. My team and I believe someone else may have used his software to murder the three victims. We'll get to that in a moment. But remember, my client is innocent until proven guilty. It is the prosecutor's job to prove he's guilty, and he will not be able to do that. So the first thing I want you to keep in mind is my client—" He tipped his head toward Charlie. "—is no more responsible for these murders than is the manufacturer of that car."

Harrison raised his hand and spoke quietly, "Your Honor, defense counsel seems to be arguing his case."

Baxter tipped his head. "Then let me just say that the evidence—or should I say, lack of it—will show Mr. Noble had nothing to do with the deaths of these men." Baxter strolled a few steps and paused as he caught the eyes of each member of the jury. Then he scanned the gallery.

"The prosecutor is focusing on Mr. Noble because he can't figure out who really did murder these men. And make no mistake about it—these were murders. As we begin to hear testimony from the witnesses, you will see that contrary to what the prosecutor has said, there are many possible suspects for these murders. So many in fact, that it would be a *huge* task to track them all down and question them. A task that would take an enormous amount of time and money. Now, I don't want to say the prosecutor is lazy—"

The judge straightened to attention, ready to stop Baxter.

"—but it certainly is easier and less expensive for him to blame those deaths on my client.

"Remember when the prosecutor spoke to you about my client's ambition? Well, I would like to point out that even though Mr. O'Neill's is an appointed position, it can do nothing but help his own career whenever he saves the taxpayers enormous amounts of money and makes them feel safe—even if he does so by putting the wrong person in prison."

The judge pointed at Baxter. "That is out of line, counselor. Let's move it along."

Baxter didn't acknowledge her. "Even though it is not my responsibility, it is nevertheless my strongest desire to prove to you Mr. Noble is not to blame for these deaths—" He rotated slowly, hands out, sweeping the entire room with his eyes. "—and in so doing, to help protect all of you by moving the investigation in the direction of finding the *real* culprit.

"But—and this is very important—I can*not* do that."

Murmuring.

"And the reason I cannot do that is because the evidence I need is inside a computer that the court will not allow you to see."

"Objection. Assumes facts not in evidence."

The murmuring turned into a low rumble. Charlie clearly heard someone behind him say, "What?"

The judge smacked her gavel against the block. "Order!"

* * *

After a moment the commotion subsided.

The judge said, "The objection is sustained, Mr. Goodman."

Baxter paused for a moment, getting his bearings. "Ladies and gentlemen of the jury—" He walked over until he was in front of them and rested his hands on the railing. "—the burden of *proof* is on the prosecutor." He pointed at Harrison.

"Over the next few days you will see a parade of witnesses who will give you their opinions, and speculations and inferences. Remember, those things are *not* proof. They are what is known as circumstantial evidence. Since the prosecutor has no proof, he will try to use circumstantial evidence to draw a picture making it look as if Charlie caused these deaths. But he needs to be able to show that no other explanation is possible, and I can assure you, he will not be able to do that."

Baxter took a moment to let the words sink in as he scanned the jurors' faces and gave them a chance to see his sincerity. "A few minutes ago the prosecutor showed you a very touching vid of the victims and their families. Now I want to show you a vid of some people." The images began. They were sweet faces, softly highlighted in joyful family settings. They cross-faded one to the other. "These are all men who were falsely accused of crimes, and long years of their lives were wasted as they were taken away from their families and imprisoned before finally being exonerated."

The pictures changed to the same men behind bars, sad-faced, fading to their families just as sad, gathered around spaces left empty by the absence of the prisoner.

The judge leaned forward, a disapproving look on her face.

"Now I want you to imagine what it would be like for you to be in that chair, right there, right now—" He pointed to where Charlie was sitting. "—picked out of the crowd and accused of a crime you did not commit, fighting for your freedom. How frightened would you be? How would you feel if it were you who were taken away from your family?" He pointed to one of the male jurors and a sad version of his face appeared in the vid on the body of the man holding onto prison bars.

The juror's mouth fell open.

The judge said, "Mr. Goodman."

"Or you?" And a woman juror's face replaced the first, the prisoner's body changing to female under the uniform.

The lady sat up in her chair.

Someone said, "Look, it's her." The gallery rumbled.

Someone else said, "Lord, have mercy."

"Objection!"

"Mr. Goodman!"

"Your Honor, the prosecutor was allowed to show a vid that created empathy for the victims. I think it's only fair the jury members feel empathy for my client and the gravity of their decisions."

"No, Mr. Goodman. It is outside the bounds of—"

"Or you!" Baxter pointed at the judge. A sad version of the judge's face appeared on the prisoner.

"Oh, for cryin'..." The judge rolled her eyes and head. "That's enough!" She reached for her gavel and bumped it just out of reach. She slapped the desktop with her hand. "Shut it off! Chambers! Now!"

CHAPTER 66

The judge strode around and stood behind her desk, arms crossed. The two attorneys remained standing.

Harrison started. "Your Honor, I want to call for a mistrial and get a new set of jurors."

"Just you shut up, mister! You started it with that sympathy vid of yours. And you, Mr. Goodman, when I say stop, you *stop*." Her arms flew high into the air, robe sleeves flapping like angry bird wings. "That is not the way to win points in my courtroom."

With a hint of a smile, Baxter said, "I don't know judge. My software tells me most of the jury is with me."

The judge's face turned red. "That is *not* what I am talking about and you know it! Listen! I can make your life hell in there if that's what you want."

Baxter cocked his head and an eyebrow. "Maybe I should file for a mistrial."

Face bordering on purple, her mouth fell open, but no sound came out.

"I'm sorry, Your Honor. I was trying to lighten things up a little. But I am serious about this; my client is innocent. This case should never have come to trial. I will do everything in my power to clear his name."

Harrison glowered. "Well, you've got a fight on your hands, fat boy."

Fat boy? Baxter stood taller, smiled at the insult and nodded. Flicking his fingers toward himself he said, "Come and get it." *Oops. Must be this age-reversal testosterone.*

The judge recovered enough to say, "Get the hell out of here, both of you!"

Baxter said, "Will I be allowed to finish my opening statement?"

"Go!"

*   *   *

As Baxter got back to the table, he had the JuryBox software reassess his status. The numbers rolled across his IS and the graph filled in. There was a green plus sign over each juror's head. *Ah, ha! Fat boy, eh? We'll see about that!*

Charlie waved his hand in front of Baxter's face and signaled for a comm. Baxter opened a PC and the room went silent for them.

"Are you in trouble with the judge?"

"You should have seen her in there," he snickered. "She'll get over it."

"Can she make things bad for you?"

"Naw." Baxter put a calming hand on Charlie's arm. "She doesn't like the idea of having her cases reviewed by the appellate court. It's really the jury we've got to worry about."

"Well, that was an amazing vid you put together."

"Had to do something. Harrison practically had the jury weeping—and *you* convicted."

"That bad?"

"Weren't you watching them?"

"I was watching the show."

"JuryBox says we're ahead, but we've got a long way to go." Catching a movement out of the corner of his eye he nudged Charlie. "Judge is back. She still looks a little angry."

"All rise."

The judge sat down and took a deep breath. Turning to the jury she said, "I want to remind you about what I said before. The evidence begins with the testimony of the witnesses, *not* the speeches made by the attorneys." She aimed a stern eye first at Harrison, then Baxter. "I'm going to allow Mr. Goodman to finish his opening. But before I do, I need to ask you this: does anyone on the jury feel they were so traumatized by Mr. Goodman's vid that they will have trouble participating in the rest of the proceedings?"

Heads shook and everyone said, "No." Stats confirmed it as true.

"All right then. Mr. Goodman will finish. Then we'll move on to the first witness." Without looking at Baxter she said, "Mr. Goodman?"

"Thank you, Your Honor." He stood and moved back to the center of the floor near the jury.

*   *   *

"In conclusion, I want you to remember three points.

"First, Mr. Noble is merely the manufacturer of N-hanced. And some unknown person—one out of many identified by the oBI—caused the death of Wilford Bostwich, Chad Rodriguez and Gary Billings.

"Second, my client and his company went to extraordinary lengths and expense to provide superior safeguards to their software and protect their testers. Quite the opposite of negligence, Mr. Noble displayed extreme diligence in his work. These three men made their own decisions and took calculated risks—risks of which my client informed them." Baxter strolled along the bannister next to the jury, his gaze settling on one after the other.

"And third, once you've heard all the *lack* of evidence presented here, I want you to think about how secure you'll feel knowing the person who committed these murders will still be out there roaming your neighborhood. And while you're doing that, think about what it would be like to sit in the defendant's chair—racing toward prison—knowing information about someone else's guilt—information that would prove your innocence—" Baxter noticed the judge lean forward. "—hasn't even been investigated, yet. And I want you to find Mr. Noble not guilty—the same as you would want the rest of the jury to find *you* not guilty."

He flicked two fingers at the jury. "Here's a copy of those final three points to keep in the corner of your oEyes." Each copy included a personalized, highly-improper vid of the juror behind bars. "And one for the court record." He flicked a copy to the court reporter and the judge—minus the vid.

Harrison sighed and shook his head.

Charlie thought, *We're ahead at the end of round one. Right! But ahead is not the same as a KO.*

CHAPTER 67

"The prosecution calls Dr. Owen Larson to the stand."

"Dr. Owen Larson." The doctor had that homogenized oGER look, but he was a little on the short side. He wore a white lab coat, undoubtedly at the request of the prosecution.

"You are an expert on sleep, is that right, Doctor?" Harrison walked casually toward the stand.

"Yes, sir." The doctor seemed proud and perhaps a little conceited. "Last year my co-researchers and I turned out the most comprehensive study on sleep in history, dispelling dozens of myths and advancing the field immensely." Then, as if he realized he might be bragging too much, "Of course it was a team effort."

"Of course." Harrison turned toward the jury. "So tell us how sleep deprivation affects people."

The doctor explained how it can mimic psychosis and post-traumatic stress disorder and cause hallucinations and delusions.

"Could sleep deprivation like that cause a programmer to make mistakes in his work?"

"Without a doubt. You would not want a person like that doing work of any importance."

"Like creating a program that affects the way people think? A program that might even be considered a form of... brain surgery?"

"Oh, my, no. That would be extremely dangerous."

Charlie wondered why Baxter hadn't objected. *Maybe he's got something in mind for cross.*

"Thank you, Dr. Larson." He passed the defense table with something Charlie thought looked like looked like a sneer. "Your witness."

Baxter stood, buttoned his artificially rumpled coat, and strolled toward the witness stand with his head down and brows in deep thought.

Removing the reading glasses from the top of his head, he ran his fingers through his hair. When he glanced up at the witness, his face beamed a welcoming smile.

"Good morning, Dr. Larson."

"Good morning." Larson looked wary.

"This work you've done is very impressive."

"Thank you." The wariness faded to smug.

"So sleep is kind of a mystery then, isn't it?"

"Oh, no. We've learned so much about it in the past few years, before long there won't be any secrets left."

"I see. That's impressive. What about helping people sleep better?"

"That is one of my team's greatest accomplishments. We created oSleep. It helps induce and maintain sleep. And best of all, it works for people who've had insomnia all their lives. It's a best-seller." He leaned back in the chair, relaxing.

"oSleep is wonderful. I use it myself."

Larson's smile broadened.

"Have you examined the defendant, Mr. Noble?"

His smiled evaporated. "No…"

"I see."

"But he is a human."

Baxter turned to the gallery. "Well, thank you for confirming that, Dr. Larson."

There was some laughter and muttering in the gallery. The judge looked up, her eyes tightening. As Baxter turned back, the judge caught his eye and his smile faded.

"Did you know Mr. Noble gets only two hours of sleep a night?"

"Mr. O'Neill told me that."

"I'll bet he did."

There were some chuckles in the gallery.

"But you've never studied Mr. Noble or anyone else using N-hanced?"

"No. But I'd like to."

"And yet you feel confident saying he's probably psychotic and a danger to other people and should be locked up in a mental institution."

"Objection." Harrison stood, palms up.

"I'm simply repeating what the witness said."

"No, you're paraphrasing and making conclusions."

"Let me rephrase the question."

O'Neill sat down slowly, lips tight.

"So you really don't know whether he's psychotic or careless when operating on those two hours of sleep, do you?"

"Well—" Larson glanced at the prosecutor. "—no."

"Your team has been able to get the sleep cycle down to five hours, is that correct?"

"Yes. People do better using our five-hour program than those who sleep far more without it."

"Would you like to condense those benefits down into two hours?"

"Of course."

"And if N-hanced goes on the market and everyone only needs two hours of sleep, oSleep will stop selling, and you'll be out of business, won't you?"

Larson's mouth gaped. He looked scared. "Uh... Yeah. I guess I would."

"Well, good luck with that study of yours, Dr. Larson." Baxter turned toward the judge. "I'm done with this witness."

Mumbles rippled through the gallery.

Harrison said, "Redirect, Your Honor?"

"Of course."

"Now, Dr. Larson, had you even thought about N-hanced as a competitor to oSleep?"

"No. Not until he mentioned it." Larson pointed at Baxter.

"So your testimony wasn't influenced by that?"

"No."

"Since you're a sleep expert, have you ever heard of anyone who was able to operate effectively on two hours of sleep for days on end?"

"We've heard anecdotal stories. But when we investigated, we found they took catnaps without knowing it, and they were inattentive and demonstrated psychotic symptoms."

"Do you think Mr. Noble is in that category?"

"Objection."

"Withdrawn. Thank you, Dr. Larson."

After Harrison sat down, Charlie asked for a PC. "That didn't go too badly."

"It's a pretty weak start for the prosecution, but we'll need a lot more before we can shake off—" Baxter held up a finger. "Oh. The prosecutor wants to meet with us in the judge's chambers. Pretty early to offer concessions. Maybe we're doing better than I thought."

The judge called for a fifteen-minute recess and beckoned the attorneys and Charlie. They followed her through the door.

The judge sat and indicated the other chairs. They shuffled awkwardly and finally got themselves seated.

The judge said, "OK, Mr. O'Neill, you called the meeting."

"The state is willing to take the first death off the table believing Mr. Noble could have seen it as a coincidence. But he has to plead guilty to the other two counts."

Baxter said, "Why not retract the second count? If the first death was a coincidence, it would have taken a second to establish a pattern. We're not agreeing that Charlie was negligent. I'm just trying to establish what you're offering.

"I can't go that far. What would the families of the first two say?"

"So apparently the Bostwick family doesn't matter. It's only when you write off two families that forgiveness becomes inappropriate?"

"N-no. I-I'm just offering this in order to... save the taxpayers the cost of a full trial."

"Come on. You know trials aren't that expensive now."

The judge shot Baxter a glance.

Baxter caught it and spoke directly to her. "No, Judge. I want to establish what level of moral high ground Mr. O'Neill thinks he's parading around on."

"Mr. Goodman—"

He waved a hand to cut her off. "I think this deserve an answer."

"Mr. Goodman!" The judge leaped up, her face glowing. "This is *my* office! You do not *shush* me in my office! You got that?"

He put up a palm. "Of course. Sorry, Your Honor. It won't happen again."

"It had better not."

"Please give me a moment to consult with my client."

She sat, still ruffled, as Baxter opened a PC to Charlie.

Charlie said, "I'd still have to serve up to ten years, right?"

"With time off—"

"No. I didn't do this." He set his jaw.

"Charlie, maybe you haven't heard this before, but it's only a coincidence when the law and fairness occupy the same universe. Sometimes you have to accept the best deal you can get."

"No."

Baxter shook his head and they closed the channel.

"No thank you, Mr. O'Neill. May we be excused?"

The judge waved them away.

CHAPTER 68

"The prosecution calls Robert Reynolds to the stand."

Rob was sworn in. He clutched a handkerchief and kept mopping his face.

Harrison said, "Mr. Reynolds, would you please tell the court your occupation?"

"Yes, I'm the CEO of Corridor CyberDynamics."

"And you work closely with Mr. Noble?"

"Yes, that's right."

"All three victims were using N-hanced at the time of their deaths, is that correct?"

"Yes."

"Is it possible N-hanced was responsible for those deaths?"

"Well, N-hanced is just a program that—"

"I'm sorry, Mr. Reynolds—" Harrison looked like he was trying to be gentle. "—I'm really just looking for a yes or a no. Let me ask again. Is it possible N-hanced was responsible for those deaths?"

"Well... I suppose... it's possible, but—"

"Thank you. "

Harrison tried to get Rob to say that Charlie was under stress because the company had so much riding on N-hanced. Rob did reasonably well to avoid answering in ways that would make Charlie look bad, but Harrison pushed on.

"Is it your opinion Mr. Noble should have stopped after Mr. Bostwick died?"

"Well, in retrospect... But I didn't think our decision to continue was a bad one at the time. And let me make one thing clear; I had the final say. I made the decision to move forward."

"What about the vid?"

"You can play it if you want, but you'll see we're just discussing it. Our testers knew what was going on. They didn't see a link between N-hanced and Wilford's death any more than we did."

Harrison said, "I'd like to look at the vid of the two of you talking after Chad Rodriguez's death." He drew a public IS cube and splayed his fingers until it was big enough for everyone. Rob was speaking.

"It sounds to me as if N-hanced has been compromised in some way. I think we'd better shut it down until you can figure out what's going on."

Harrison flicked his hand, and the vid jumped ahead.

"Rob, let's contact the alphas, tell them we've made some changes and give them two options. They can disconnect from the servers or we can leave them connected and shut down the Net access."
"I don't know. I thought continuing was risky after we lost Bostwick yesterday. But now I think we need to stop. This whole thing's got me spooked."
"Me, too. But we'll let them decide. We'll remind them they're being recorded. We'll make it clear if they elect to stay connected, anything happens is their responsibility."

Charlie was surprised by the desperation he displayed in the vid and held perfectly still, trying not to draw attention to himself. But his ears burned.

"Charlie, is this you I'm talking to? You sound like one of our goddamned lawyers. What about doing what's right? I'd feel terrible if anybody else were hurt and we could have prevented it. I'll tell you what. We'll let them decide, but I want you to lay it out for them honestly. Be clear about the dangers, and be specific about the things we don't know—especially that there could be some stush on the servers."
"That's more than fair, Rob. Thank—"
"It's more like irresponsible. But I'm going to trust because you're N-hanced, you have a point of view I couldn't have. I'm also hoping it has an equal amount of wisdom attached."

Harrison pinched the cube closed. "What made you go along with Mr. Noble there?"
"Like I said, I thought his N-hanced point of view would be better than mine."
"But it wasn't, was it?"
"It seemed reasonable at the time."
"You said the decision was irresponsible."

"It was my decision. If you want to come after me, fine." Rob was red-faced and rings of sweat darkened his shirt.

"It was Mr. Noble's advice that was irresponsible, wasn't it?"

"It was my decision."

"Your Honor…"

The judge said, "You must answer the question, Mr. Reynolds."

"It was something I said, but it's not how I meant it."

Harrison said, "How else could you have meant it?"

"It's more like a joke. I… I mean, a play on words. Charlie and I do that sometimes. It was sarcastic, not literal. I felt terrible that our company might be responsible for their deaths. I still do."

"You let your employees keep the patents for the products they create, don't you?"

"Yes, I do." He straightened, obviously proud of the generous arrangement. "CCD only *licenses* their creations."

"Mr. Noble is the owner of N-hanced?"

"That's right."

"So regardless of your saying the decision to continue was yours, and regardless of the EULA, the liability is really Mr. Noble's, isn't it?"

Rob gasped and the color drained from his face. His eyes searched wildly.

"Mr. Reynolds?"

Rob's voice was barely above a whisper. "Yes." He threw a pained glance in Charlie's direction.

Harrison seemed to check his notes, but it may have been a stall to extend Rob's suffering for the jury. "Is it your opinion that Mr. Noble thinks he's creating a new world?

Rob's eyes had turned steely. "I won't hire anyone unless they think they have something unique to contribute. Is Charlie unusual in that way? Not at all. Brighter than most? You bet. Does he think N-hanced is going to change the game in a big way? Absolutely. And so do I. And so do a lot of other people. Does he think he's the new Messiah?"

One of the disciples said, "Amen!" Everybody looked. It was Simon. Instead of being embarrassed, he lifted his chin as if to say 'Yeah, that was me.'

Rob picked up. "I've known Charlie a long time." He smiled and nodded, remembering. "I've seen him create other products and get very excited about them and watch them become successful. Is he proselytizing about this one more than the others? Absolutely. And I want him to. Oh, he'll change the world all right—if we ever get out of here."

Laughter.

"But the Messiah? No."

Harrison walked near the jury. "How close are you to Mr. Noble?"

"I've known him for over fifteen years. He was one of the reasons I started the company."

"And he was married to your daughter."

"Yes."

"Your daughter who passed away?"

Rob's gaze fell and his voice grew quiet. "Yes."

"Would you say you consider him a part of your family?"

"Of course."

"So you might have reason to lie for him."

Rob pushed back, eyebrows bunched. "No!"

If everyone is so enthusiastic and productive with N-hanced, why aren't you using it?"

"Well, I always wait until all the bugs..." A shadow of fear swept his face. "Uh, what I mean is, m-my job is different. I... I don't use all the products we make."

But the damage was done.

"Thank you, Mr. Reynolds. That will be all."

CHAPTER 69

Baxter moved quickly. "Were you aware Mr. Bostwick used an oCar before he jumped to his death?"

Rob looked confused. "Nnnnnno."

Harrison leaned forward like a cat ready to pounce.

"Were you aware Chad Rodriguez and Gary Billings also used oCars earlier on the days of their deaths?"

"No."

"Would it surprise you to learn that all three of them ate breakfast, drank coffee and went to the bathroom on the days of their deaths?"

Laughter.

"Objection."

"Your Honor, the prosecutor has been trying to show cause and effect by saying N-hanced caused the men's deaths. It does nothing of the sort, any more than does their use of an oCar, eating breakfast, drinking coffee and going—"

"Thank you, Mr. Goodman." The judge gave Baxter a tired smile. "We get the idea."

More laughter.

"Objection overruled."

Baxter asked a few questions to establish that Rob didn't think Charlie wasn't afraid of using N-hanced, and didn't seem sleep deprived or psychotic.

"Negligence means someone was careless. Was Charlie carless about his work?"

"Never. He's incredibly devoted."

"Does your company have insurance to protect against large losses if a product should fail?"

"Yes."

"Now the way this insurance works, aren't there different payouts depending on the problems that occur with a product."

"Yes."

"For instance, if there were a death involving one of your products, there would be a higher payout because of the negative publicity. Is that right?"

Rob frowned. "Yes, but—"

Baxter raised a palm to stop him. "So if something made it unmarketable—let's say it was deadly—that would be a lucky break for your company, wouldn't it?"

"Now listen here—"

"Objection. Mr. Reynolds is not on trial here."

"Your Honor, the prosecution says these deaths were caused by negligence. I'm simply trying to show there are other parties who might have their own reasons for wanting N-hanced to fail."

"The objection sustained."

Baxter glanced at the jury, noting their surprise, and tried to push a thought into their heads. *There's your reasonable doubt.* Nodding at Rob, "Thank you, Mr. Reynolds." He turned to the judge. "I'm done with this witness."

The judge said, "Mr. O'Neill?"

"No redirect, Your Honor."

"You're excused, Mr. Reynolds. Let's take a fifteen minute recess."

Rob came off the stand. As he passed the defense table he gave Charlie a pained look and mouthed, "Sorry."

"It's OK." Charlie smiled with understanding.

Swinging around toward Baxter, Charlie's eyes turned cold. He demanded a PC. "What the hell was that? That's Rob you were disemboweling!"

Baxter's face was all sympathy. "I'm sorry, Charlie. I don't think Rob did anything wrong. But I needed the jury to see that there are other ways those men could have died. Rob'll be OK."

"Couldn't you have warned him?"

"And have the jury miss that look on his face?" Baxter gave his head a slow shake. "I didn't want him to look like he was covering up for you."

Charlie huffed. "I don't like it."

"So, if the judge had let you be your own lawyer, would you have done that?"

"Hell, no!"

"Then, it's a good thing you got me, because with your N-hanced multi-lawyer plan, you'd have sucked, and Harrison would have kicked your ass. Everything I do is in the service of my client's freedom, even if he doesn't like it. That's why I hate this job. That's why I live in Alaska."

"What? I thought you lived in Chicago?"

"That's my legal address. When I started out I thought I'd be helping people. But I found out everybody hates you. So once I had enough money, I moved to Alaska."

Charlie stared as Baxter flashed a picture of himself—bearded, long hair to his shoulders, rifle in hand—standing over a twelve-point caribou in three feet of snow with blue-gray mountains in the background.

"Whenever there's a case they need me for, they send in a tracker to find me. It's not too hard with all this T shit. But I turn off all my comm, so they have to want me pretty badly."

Charlie searched the Net. "I don't seem to find anything personal about you at all."

"Nobody has anything on me—except my case record."

"How—?"

"I started opting out of everything way back when. I refused to use my Social Security Number for anything. Look it up; they don't have the right. But then I guess you're finding out about all the rights you've given up."

Charlie was dumbfounded. *Who is this guy?* "But... you came from Chicago the other day."

"Sure. I just finished another case. I'll be going back north after we get done here."

"Sorry I kept you from it."

"Aw, don't worry about it. I like what you're doing. I hope it does away with lawyers. Then I can stay there permanently. So now you know I'm fighting for you. Get ready. It'll probably get worse."

Charlie nodded slowly. He looked back in the gallery at Rob who stared gloomily at the floor. *Jesus. I didn't think winning would feel bad. And we haven't even won yet.* He thought again about pleading out. *No! No way!*

CHAPTER 70

"The prosecution calls Erik Kozlovski to the stand."

"An oMe2 will substitute for Erik Kozlovski."

"Do you solemnly swear that the testimony you are about to give will be the truth, the whole truth, and nothing but the truth, so help you God?"

"Dah."

The judge turned toward him and said, "Please answer, 'I do.'"

Erik frowned. "I do."

"You understand this oath applies the same as if you were here in Real?"

"Dah, I do."

Harrison took over. "You are the oMe2 representative of Erik Kozlovski, is that right?"

Erik spread his hands and sighed. "I just say so."

"Please tell the court your profession."

"I am mat'matician professor at UCLA."

"And you are also a specialist in cryptology?"

"Dah." He glanced at the judge. "I do. And I invent VGP—Very Good Privacy. Is best algorithm in da world for encrypting and decrypting data. Government no like it because when you use it, dey can't read your comms. Ha!" He thumped his chest with one of his big fists and leaned back in the chair, chin high.

Harrison said, "Your Honor, I'd like to state that Mr. Kozlovski has been granted immunity so he can speak freely on the facts of this case without incriminating himself because of his legal difficulties over VGP."

The judge said, "So noted."

"Now, Mr. Kozlovski, did you have a discussion with Mr. Noble last week?"

"Dah."

"And what was the nature of that discussion?"

"He want what Erik have here." He tapped his head. "Erik is best."

"He wanted your expertise for N-hanced?"

"Dah."

"And what was your response?"

"I tell him go fly kite."

There were chuckles throughout the courtroom.

"Why?"

"I no like him."

"Why's that?"

"He tell stories how Erik make money, like that. He make big blow job."

The gallery erupted with laughter.

"Order."

Erik's face clouded over. Then his eyes shifted as he understood. "No, no. I mean he a blow hard."

Harrison covered his mouth and pretended to consult his VR notes. Finally he continued. "Are you familiar with the specific steganography referred to in this case?"

"Of course. You send to me yesterday."

"You know just about everybody in your field?"

"Erik slapped his chest. "Dey know me."

"Who might have been able to create the steganograph used here?"

"One person."

"And who is that?"

"Me."

That brought out another disturbance in the gallery.

Charlie thought, *Oh, sure. Now that he has immunity he admits it. But that might be all I need.*

The judge whacked the block with her gavel. "Order."

Erik turned his head and glowered at her.

Harrison said, "And did you create that code?"

"No."

More noise in the court.

"Order."

Again Erik gave her a dirty look.

"You understand N-hanced gives Mr. Noble special abilities."

"So he say."

"That he might be able to do steganography."

"Objection. Speculation."

"Sustained."

"Could an advanced computer could create ciphers?"

"Maybe."

"And if that computer were hooked into someone's mind, could they create those codes?"

"Objection. Your Honor—"

"Sustained. Do you have anything else, Mr. O'Neill?"

Harrison paused, then shook his head. "I'm done with the witness."

Erik pointed at Charlie. "I tink he do it."

The judge said, "You may only answer the questions. Do not offer your opinions, Mr. Koslovski."

"He do it with computer. He kill doz people."

She smacked the gavel block. "Silence, Mr. Koslovski." She pointed the gavel at him and scowled.

He glared right back.

The judge looked away. "The jury will disregard the witness's last comments." She turned toward Baxter. "Mr. Goodman?"

CHAPTER 71

Baxter walked to the witness stand and smiled. "You told the prosecutor no one else could have written this code except you, is that right?"

"Dat what I say. What, you no listening?"

"What about Terry Slattery or Boz Wharfman?"

"Ha! Those numb nuts."

The judge said, "Mr. Kozlovski, I won't have that kind of language in my courtroom."

"What? You want I should say dumb fucks or dick heads? Dat's what dey are."

Laughter.

"Just leave out the obscenity."

"I not talk very good English. Dis is only way I know how."

"Well, you seem to have mastered our bawdy language. Please, just try to hold it down."

He sneered. "OK, judge lady."

Baxter continued. "You don't like Mr. Noble very much, do you?"

"No. He is assho…" Erik looked at the judge. "Butthead."

More laughs circled through the court. The judge frowned but had to cover her mouth to hide a smile.

"Aren't you mistaken when you say no one else could have written that steganograph?"

Erik scowled. "You tink I stupid? If I have immunity, den why I lie? I can tell truth and even say I make dis cipher. But I no say dat."

"You might try to make it look like no one else could have created the code, and that Mr. Noble made a mistake."

Erik appeared to consider that possibility. Then he nodded and raised his huge hands. "But I no do dat."

"Why should we believe you?"

"Because I swear on Bible."

"And being Russian, of course you're deeply religious."

Erik smiled and shrugged.

"Objection."

"Withdrawn. Isn't it true you have connections to organized crime?"

"Where I come from, you need people to look out for you. It like insurance policy. Only dat."

"I see. But you yourself have a history of violence."

"No. No-ting like dat. I big pussycat."

A few chuckles trickled out of the gallery.

"Isn't it true you took a swing at my client?"

"I no do dat." Erik lifted his eyebrows in mock innocence.

"My lie detector shows that's not true." Baxter turned toward the gallery. "Anybody else?"

There was a low mumble and heads nodded.

"Objection."

"Sustained. Please direct your questions to the witness, Mr. Goodman."

"Let's take a look at this vid." Baxter drew an IS cube and everybody watched as Erik threw his fist into Charlie's cheek. Then another. And then a backhand.

Erik scowled and worked his jaw.

The gallery reacted with muttering.

"Order." The judge whacked the gavel block.

Erik snapped his head toward her, his eyes slits. "Stop wit dat fucking hammer."

The judge pointed it at him. "Language, sir. I'm not going to tell you again—"

Erik stood and yanked her gavel-less left hand. "Fuck you, beetch!" Gripping her wrist, he pressed down, forcing her fingers to splay across the tabletop. With a flick he held his own VR gavel and pounded around and between her fingers in a series of quick, furious whacks. "Bam, bam, bam, bam, bam, bam, bam, bam, bam, bam, bam, bam, bam," thirteen times, missing her flesh by a hair. He threw down the gavel, which bounced off the stand and evaporated. "I SAY NO!" He released her wrist, and she fell backward off the side of her chair.

The bailiff pulled her weapon and people threw themselves to the floor.

Her voice shaking, the judge stood and shouted, "Bailiff, arrest that man!"

Oozing with contempt, Erik sneered, "Women should stay home. Men would have no-ting to do wit you if not for da pussy."

The bailiff said, "I can't arrest him, judge. He's an oMe2."

"Well, turn him off then! Do it!"

"Yes, Judge." The wide-eyed bailiff motioned in her IS and he was gone.

The judge shook out the hand Erik had grabbed, then straightened her robes. Pointing at her clerk she said, "Have him arrested in his jurisdiction."

"He's got immunity."

"Not for *that*, he doesn't!"

"Yes, Your Honor." She waved inside her cube.

The judge strode through the door to her chambers.

People got up from the floor, and loud babble filled the room. Nobody seemed to know what to do.

Baxter strolled calmly to the defense table.

Charlie signaled for a PC. "Whoa!"

"Yeah." Baxter sighed a deep, "Whoofff. I guess you could say his credibility's in the crapper."

Charlie frowned. "But he couldn't have hurt her. It was a VR gavel. Why was her interaction level set so high?"

Baxter smiled. "Maybe she's got something kinky going on during the breaks."

Charlie laughed. "I told you that guy was trouble. Now I know it wasn't just me." He paused and looked suspiciously at Baxter. "You knew he was going to blow, didn't you?"

Baxter gave a quick nod, the corners of his mouth repressing a small smile. "The jury's leaning your way, but Harrison will be counting pretty heavily on that oBI agent. He'll have a lot of credibility."

The clerk came out of the judge's chambers. "Ladies and gentlemen, court will resume tomorrow morning at nine AM."

Baxter said, "All right then. See you back here tomorrow."

Charlie nodded as the still-rattled bailiff led him away.

CHAPTER 72

At a few minutes before 9:00 on Tuesday morning the bailiff dropped Charlie off at the defense table. Baxter's changed from 'Hello' to 'Oh, hell.' He opened a PC. "You look terrible."

"I wish I could at least use N-hanced to get some restful sleep."

"I guess you know that's not going to happen."

Charlie pursed his lips and nodded.

The judge came in and the court day started.

"The prosecution calls Metodi Rosenberg to the stand."

Metodi took the stand and was sworn in.

"Please tell us your occupation."

"I am chief counsel for Corridor CyberDynamics." Metodi sat upright but appeared completely relaxed, even smiling.

"You're the one responsible for the EULA—the End User Licensing Agreement, is that right?"

"Yes."

"Did you recently make a change to your standard EULA?"

"Yes."

The questioning went on for several minutes as Harrison tried to corner the unflappable Metodi into saying Charlie ordered changes in the agreement to protect the company.

"Is it your opinion your company should have stopped testing N-hanced after Mr. Bostwick died?"

"Mr. Reynolds and Mr. Noble did consult with me about that, and I didn't think it was necessary."

"Because of your EULA?"

"Objection."

"Overruled."

Metodi said, "Uh, no. Not at all. Because I couldn't see how the death was related to the software."

"Because Mr. Noble told you so?"

"Well... Yes. But—"

"Thank you, Mr. Rosenberg. Your witness."

Charlie watched as Metodi leaned back, and shook his head almost imperceptibly, a tiny curl remained at the corners of his mouth. *What's that smile?*

Baxter stepped out onto the floor. "You already told us Mr. Noble did not ask you to insert the new section. Is that right?"

"Yes. I did it on my own."

"Did you tell him about it?"

"No. I just put it in, and the new version went onto our shared server so the next time anyone needed an agreement for one of our products, that would be the one they used."

"So it wasn't specific to N-hanced?"

"No. It's for everything we sell—and test."

"Did he—Mr. Noble—ever mention the clause to you?"

"No." Metodi tugged lightly on one cufflink.

"Did you even discuss it with anyone in the company?"

"No. I didn't think it was a big deal. Other companies were using that phrase, so I just updated our contract. Until now I thought the whole thing was perfectly innocent. That I was doing my job, keeping us up with the times."

"Thank you, Mr. Rosenberg."

Harrison said, "Redirect, Your Honor?"

"Proceed."

"Mr. Rosenberg, do you know if Mr. Noble can read?"

"Objection."

The judge frowned. "Mr. O'Neill, we can do without the sarcasm."

Harrison kept his eye on the witness. "You said the new version was on the shared server—a server everyone in the company has access to. Is that right?"

"Yes."

"Isn't it possible Mr. Noble could have read the new section?"

"I suppose so."

"Well, let's see when that might have happened. Since the time you added that section, Mr. Noble has had a number of testers and expert system providers sign the agreement, right?"

"Give me a second." Metodi's fingers fluttered. "Yes. He personally had five new experts sign the agreement since that section went in, although others in the company have used the agreement as well."

"Which means they might have mentioned it to him?"

"Possibly."

"So Mr. Noble could have begun testing, knowing the company couldn't be held liable?"

Baxter opened his mouth to object, but Metodi knew the procedure and remained unruffled.

"I can't say what Mr. Noble was thinking, and I never had a conversation with him over the issue."

"Thank you, Mr. Rosenberg."

The judge looked at Baxter who shook his head. "The witness may step down."

CHAPTER 73

"The prosecution calls oBI agent Tom Lott."

"Objection. I thought we agreed to do away with the issue of flight."

Harrison lifted his chin. "We'll be covering other issues, Your Honor."

The judge nodded. "Overruled."

Harrison started from his chair. "When did you first see the defendant?"

"Last Friday evening at Corridor CyberDynamics."

"How did the defendant behave?"

"He was resistant to coming with us for questioning. We had to threaten him with arrest—"

Baxter half stood. "Objection. Prejudicial." He sat.

"Sustained. Less inflammatory, Mr. Lott."

Harrison stood and took a couple steps onto the floor. "In your opinion, does an innocent person send an oMe2—"

"Objection. The witness can't know what the defendant was thinking."

"Sustained."

"What did you think about the fact that Mr. Noble sent an oMe2—?"

"Objection. Your Honor, there are at least a dozen other ways to phrase the question."

The judge faced Harrison. "You know better, Mr. O'Neill."

Palms up and face innocence, he said, "Your Honor, I just want his opinion. Apparently it is unusual for anyone to send a double to an oBI interrogation session—"

Baxter said, "It was an *interview*. An *interrogation* implies he was under arrest, which he was not. And it is perfectly legal to send an oMe2. Your Honor, prosecution is still trying to prejudice the jury."

"Understood, Mr. Goodman. But I'd like to hear this. Members of the jury, you will note that this is an opinion, not a fact." She turned to Harrison. "You may continue."

Baxter looked away and pushed back into his chair.

"Was there anything unusual about the interview?"

"Like you said, he sent an oMe2. In all my years as an agent, nobody I've questioned ever did that—and I've participated in over 600 since oMe2s went on the market."

"And why do you suppose he did that—uh, in your opinion?"

Baxter shook his head. He couldn't believe the judge was letting the jury hear this.

"We think it's because he wanted to avoid incarceration. An oMe2 can vanish, leaving us empty-handed."

"Anything else unusual about the... interview?"

"Yes, it was the way he tricked us."

"And that was...?"

Agent Lott crossed his arms and lifted his chin. "He blew out a street light on CCD Plaza to distract us so he could send us off with his oMe2."

"Oh, he destroyed pub—"

"Objection. Beyond scope and prejudicial." Baxter's mouth tightened into a thin line.

"Sustained."

Agent Lott said, "He did it so he could get away."

"Objection. Opinion, not fact."

"Sustained. Strike the question and the answer. Jury, you are to ignore the last exchange."

Harrison said, "Anything else?"

"He changed his face and ID and got away through the crowd."

"That's unusual, isn't it?"

"Very. Very new and high tech—and illegal."

"And he went to all this trouble in order to escape."

"Ob-jection!" Baxter shook his head wearily.

"Sustained. Mr. O'Neill, please."

O'Neill sighed. "Anything else unusual?"

"He pretended to drink a Coke. He tried to convince us he was there in Real. When we went to pick up the can later, it spilled because it was still full."

"I see. That *is* suspicious."

Baxter shook his head.

Harrison looked at the jury. "Anything else?"

"I... don't think so."

"What about his reflexes?"

"Objection. Leading the witness."

Agent Lott took the cue. "No, no. I remember now. He used this N-hanced thing to control his reflexes."

Baxter rubbed the back of his neck.

"Really?" Harrison turned a surprised expression to the jury. "And how was that?"

"We monitor suspects to see if they're telling the truth. All during the interview, his heart rate and pupils were perfectly steady. That is not natural."

"I see. Did you ask Mr. Noble's double if he knew about a flaw in his program?"

"Yes."

"That maybe he was getting a piece of the insurance settlement to murder the three—"

"Objection!" Baxter stood. "Is the prosecutor now going to change the charge to murder?" He remained standing, arms crossed.

The gallery rumbled.

"Sustained."

Harrison said, "Three counts of murder. Why that would carry the death penalty, wouldn't it?"

The noise in the gallery jumped up a notch.

"Objection!" Baxter's hands raised in a wide shrug.

"Withdrawn."

Billy Bostwick pointed at Charlie. "You killed my daddy!" His sister started to cry. "Mommy."

Baxter plopped back into his chair and sighed.

"Order! Order in the court!" *Tap, tap, tap.* "The jury will ignore the prosecutor's comments. And you, Mr. O'Neill... Any more and I'll find you in contempt."

"I said withdrawn, Your Honor." He looked comically innocent.

"Very funny. Your fined a thousand credits. Another word and you'll spend the night in jail."

He opened his mouth. With eyes widening, the judge pointed at him with the gavel. He turned and motioned to Baxter with a silent *Your witness.*

Through clenched teeth the judge said, "No, Mr. Goodman. We will have a fifteen minute recess."

*   *   *

Baxter opened a PC and Charlie began. "You looked pretty frustrated."

Baxter chuckled. "Yeah. Well, a lot of theater goes into this." He put his hand on Charlie's arm. "Say, that friend of yours, can he get me a soda?"

"Sure. Oh... wait a minute. He's purged. No credits."

"Jeez. How's he get by?"

"Rides a bike and goes to a store that still has an iris scan."

"Rustic. He a Luddite?"

"Yeah."

Baxter's face shadowed. "You don't suppose—?"

"No."

"Well, I'll go. Want anything?"

"No, thanks."

"OK." Baxter ambled down the aisle.

CHAPTER 74

Baxter began speaking before he was out of his chair. "Agent Lott, did you ever find any direct physical evidence Mr. Noble murdered anyone?"

"Um... No."

"Nothing about any insurance settlement?"

"No."

"When you began your investigation, didn't you determine the three deaths were likely murders?"

"Yes."

"And there were multiple suspects?"

"Noble was our number one suspect."

"So there *were* others?"

"Yes."

"I see. How many total?"

"I don't recall a specific number"

"Would you be surprised if I told you there were four individuals along with Orchard, the Russian mob, the oUS military and nearly every other government in the world? You have access to the same vids I do. You made them."

"OK. That sounds right."

"Looks to me like you were pursuing a murder case."

"Well, at the time—"

"Were you, Agent Lott?"

"Objection. Badgering?"

"Sustained."

Baxter plowed ahead. "In fact, when you came gunning for my client at his office, you were upset because he'd gotten away from you and your partner twice, making you look like fools." He was in front of the witness box.

Agent Lott leaned back and glanced side to side. "No, uh… that wasn't it at all. We-we had a warrant."

Baxter was now invading his space. "Sure you did. Because it was a lot easier for you to get a negligent homicide charge against this really smart guy who ticked you off, rather than chase down all those murder suspects. After all, that's a whooole lotta work."

"Objection. Is there a question in there somewhere?"

Baxter turned to the judge. "Your Honor, may we speak via PC?"

She signaled him to come closer and opened a comm, which included Harrison.

"Your Honor, this witness establishes reasonable doubt. I would like to ask the court to dismiss the case on the basis that there are more than a few *hundred* suspects who could have committed these murders. The prosecutor filed charges on the premise that these could not be murders, therefore the deaths must be due to negligence on the part of Mr. Noble. That is clearly not the case, as the prosecutor's own witness has just made clear. I move for a judgment as a matter of law. The prosecutor simply does *not* have enough evidence to support his claims."

"Motion denied."

"What?! On what basis?"

"On the basis that we have not established these were murders at all, but instead look like accidents caused by unsafe software. The fact that these deaths might have been intentional does not mean they were. This trial will continue."

"Your Honor, this is *exactly* what reasonable doubt is all about."

"We'll let the jury decide that." She waved him off.

Clearly disgusted, Baxter turned away with a huff.

He trudged back to the table, drank from his Coke and took a moment to compose himself. Finally he turned. "Mr. Lott, does the fact that Mr. Noble sent an oMe2 in his place prove he's guilty?"

"Not exactly."

"Please explain."

"Our data shows everyone who has ever done that has eventually been found guilty."

"I see. And how many times has that occurred across the whole oBI?"

"Four times."

"Only *four* times? Is that statistically significant?"

"How do you mean?"

"I mean, out of all the thousands of interview sessions and interrogations done by the oBI since oMe2s have been around, you only have *four* cases to look at. Is that number enough to form a statistically significant pattern?"

"I don't have the expertise to answer that."

"Your Honor, if I may?"

Baxter took a few minutes to explain the math. When he was done the judge warned the jury they were not to conclude Charlie's guilt based having sent his oMe2.

He turned back to the witness stand. "Now Mr. Lott, why do you think Mr. Noble would have sent a copy in his place?"

"Objection. Calls for speculation."

Baxter turns his head slightly over his shoulder toward Harrison. "Strategy worked for you."

The judge shot Baxter a glance.

Baxter looked right back at her and spread his arms. He turned to Agent Lott "Let me ask it this way; if *you* were going to be questioned, why might you send a copy?"

Harrison said, "Your Honor?"

"Well, Mr. O'Neill, he is asking what the witness would do. But it is a little off center, Mr. Goodman."

Baxter said, "Mr. Lott?"

"Well, maybe if I were busy with something else really important?"

"You mean busy perhaps trying to find out if something in an application you created might be hurting people? Something important like that?"

"Objection! Your Honor."

"That's enough, Mr. Goodman. Let's move along."

"Is there anything in your interview room that disables the oMe2 tag?"

"What do you mean?"

"I mean that an oMe2 is clearly tagged in red in the corner of my vision. I can look around this courtroom and tell you every double here. Why didn't you know you were interviewing Mr. Noble's oMe2 until after the session?"

Lott's face turned red. "You just get so used to... You stop checking..." His face changed from embarrassed to angry. "Nobody ever trusts us with an oMe2."

"So neither one of you noticed?"

Lott's lips tightened.

"Hmm. Wonder what else you missed. Withdrawn." Baxter went to the table, took a long drink from his Coke, and smacked his lips. The judge frowned.

Baxter put down the can and turned back to the witness box. "I understand your partner said some things which could have been construed as a threat to Mr. Noble. Let's take a look." He drew a cube and the courtroom watched along with a few hundred thousand Net viewers.

The agents came through the door onto the shipping dock at the Breslin Center. Mortensen said, "I know that lying son of a bitch Noble is in here somewhere."

Lott said "Great. Well, if he is, you just tipped him off we're after him. Who taught you Surveillance and Pursuit at the academy? I want to be sure to let them know they've been leaving out some of the finer points."

"Listen, I got my own method. Shoot first, ask questions later."

"Oh, good. So now we're using the Dirty Harry method. C'mon, think, Morty. Put the gun away. Even my cat knows you can sneak up on a bird by keeping quiet and moving slowly. And my cat's not all that smart."

People in the gallery chuckled.

Baxter stopped the vid. "Well, agent Lott, is there anything else we should see?"

Agent Lott's face continued to glow red. "No. That's pretty much it."

"Do you think Mr. Noble might have had a reason to be a little nervous about meeting up with the two of you after that?"

"Maybe."

"Maybe? It sounded as if agent Mortensen was threatening to kill him. Yes or no?"

"You'll have to ask my partner that question."

Baxter moved his index finger and vid showed agent Mortensen inside the oBI lab through Lott's eyes.

Lott said, "If she's not an accomplice, we may have a kidnapping or hostage situation on our hands."

Mortensen said, "Or maybe all three."

Lott nodded and his eyes narrowed. "We're going after the bastard."

"Now you're talking!"

Lott was on the edge of his chair, his face now ashen. "Whoa, whoa! That's from my personal recorder. Where'd you get—?"

"I can play some other selections if you'd like."

"No, no." Lott's eyes scanned the floor. "Wh-what was the question?"

"Did it sound to you as if agent Mortensen was threatening Mr. Noble?"

Lott's glanced up. "My partner can be a little… over-enthusiastic."

"I'd call it hot-headed—" Baxter raised a palm toward Harrison. "—but over-enthusiastic will do for now." He turned toward the jury. "So when you claim Mr. Noble was evading capture, isn't it possible he thought he was running for his life?"

"I don't know…" Lott's voice trailed off.

"I couldn't hear you."

"I said I don't know what he was thinking."

Baxter turned and looked at the jury. "I'll bet the members of the jury know what *they* would have been thinking if they had been in Charlie's place."

More than half of them nodded.

"Oh, and one more thing before we leave this issue of fleeing arrest—which we're not even supposed to be discussing." He glanced at the judge. "If Charlie really were trying to flee, would he go back to his office? A place where anyone could find him?"

"I disagree. That would be the best place to hide."

Baxter let out a half-laugh. "Ho, really? Well, if we use your logic I suppose an even better hiding place would be *your* office." He turned and eyed the jury, shaking his head. "But then again, probably not."

Baxter flicked in the air, reading his notes. "Now about this controlled reflexes thing. Have you ever interviewed anyone who tried to control their reflexes?"

"Yes."

"Anyone who attempted to fool a lie detector?"

"Sure."

"Were all of them guilty?"

"Well, no."

"Why would anyone do such a thing?"

"Uh… Maybe they just had something personal they wanted to hide. Maybe from their wife or family or, if they were a public figure—the public."

"I see. So the fact that Mr. Noble was trying to control his reflexes doesn't mean he's guilty, does it?"

"No."

"Thank you, Mr. Lott."

CHAPTER 75

It was so close to lunchtime that Harrison jumped up. "Redirect, Your Honor?"

She looked at the time. "Will this take long?"

"No longer than five minutes."

"Proceed."

"Thank you." Harrison rolled one hand toward agent Lott. "Why did you decide to turn your investigation away from murder and in the direction of the defendant?"

"Everywhere we looked there was no evidence of murder. That left only negligence. And of course there was Mr. Noble's odd behavior."

"And do you still think the deaths were caused by negligence?"

"Objection. Calls for an opinion."

"Sustained."

"Now about Mr. Noble's sending an oMe2. Are there any other reasons someone—I mean, *you*—might do that if you were being questioned?

"Well... maybe to see if I could get away with it."

"Objection!"

"Sustained. The jury is not to infer that Mr. Noble was trying to get away with anything based on agent Lott's answer."

"One more question, agent Lott. Were any of the people you've questioned over the years who tried to fool a lie detector later found guilty?"

"Yes."

"What percentage?"

Agent Lott made some hand motions. Then he passed the result to public view. "Very close to ninety percent."

Turning to the jury with raised eyebrows Harrison said, "Ninety percent. I see." He made a slow pivot back toward the witness. "Thank you, agent Lott. No more questions."

Baxter was halfway out of his seat with his hand up. "I'm sorry, Your Honor. If I may?"

She sighed and nodded.

"Agent Lott, did you investigate any of the people or governments mentioned earlier as murder suspects?"

"No."

"So, no one other than my client?"

"No."

Baxter turned to the jury with raised eyebrows. "No." He gave it a few seconds to sink in. Finally he turned back. "And yet you're willing to say he's the only one who could be guilty of anything." Shaking his head he clicked his tongue as he headed back to the defense table. "Thank you for all your *hard* work."

"Objection."

"Sustained."

Baxter sipped from his Coke. He took a couple steps back toward the stand and said, "Uh, one more thing—" The can fell from his hand, hitting the floor with a *Bang!* He shouted, "Oh!" A number of people in the jury and the gallery jumped at the noise. Nothing spilled. Picking up the unopened can, he looked at agent Lott and said, "Well, lookey here. I was *pretending* to drink. I suppose that makes me guilty of negligent homicide."

"Objection!"

The judge gave Baxter a dirty look and leaned forward, finger pointing. Before she could say anything, Baxter waved a hand high. "I'm through with this witness."

"The witness may step down. Everybody back here at one o'clock." *Whack!*

Baxter and Charlie went PC.

Charlie said, "Whoa! Impressive. And that Coke thing—brilliant! I was hoping you were going to get the whole thing dismissed when you brought up all those other suspects."

"No. The judge was right about that."

"What do you mean?"

"The agents just threw the other suspects at you to see if they could get you to admit something. That's why I didn't bring it up."

"I don't remember that."

Baxter shrugged and smiled. "At least I was able to neutralize his testimony. If I can keep it up, you might have a shot at walking."

"And if not?"

"You want to take the prosecutor's offer? Or maybe think about the temp-insan?"

"Hmmm… Can I make up my mind later?"

"Sure. But you have to decide before the jury comes back with a verdict."

"Right." Charlie smiled.

CHAPTER 76

"The prosecution calls Jackson Masters to the stand."

"An oMe2 will substitute for Jackson Masters."

Harrison started the questioning. "Good afternoon, Mr. Masters."

"Oh, you can call me Jack."

"OK, Jack." Harrison smiled. "What is your job?"

"Programming and procedures for Orange Computers, Inc."

"I asked you to look into the problem with N-hanced. But you don't know anything about its programming, right?"

"Well, actually, we do."

"Oh? How's that?"

"We have Vs made by various people who program N-hanced. They show Mr. Noble and his tester's interaction with the server. The audio was transcribed and stored in a database."

"I see. So you do have evidence from the N-hanced?"

"Yes, sir."

"You could essentially look over the shoulder of the team to see what they did, is that correct?"

"Yes."

"These past twelve months, the only programmer on N-hanced was Charlie Noble, is that right?"

"Well, actually he worked with two other programmers until about four months ago. Once he was N-hanced, he worked by himself."

"Is there any part of his work that was unavailable to you?"

"Yes, a lot of it."

"Why is that?"

"Much of it is proprietary. If they let anybody outside their company see it, we could possibly create our own version."

"Is that type of secrecy unusual?"

"No. We do the same thing at Orange."

"Anything else that was kept from you?"

"Yes, the security layer. Anyone who knows how it works could get the code."

"The defense has stated that someone may have hacked their security and altered the code. Could *you* do that?"

Jackson flashed a smug smile. "I'm not a hacker."

"But you were able to see a line of code known as the 'User Abort ON' command, is that right?"

"Yes."

"Can you tell us what the code does?" Harrison turned to watch the jury.

"It's a code developers once used that allowed them to stop a computer procedure. It's something that would certainly be removed before alpha testing. Leaving it in would let anyone who knew about it to stop whatever process was running and perform other action."

"I see. Could the other action be something like telling the user that a dream is reality?"

"Objection. Calls for a conclusion."

Harrison turned to the judge. "I intend to make the connection."

"Sustained."

Unfazed, Harrison went on. "Was there a way to tell when that code had been added?"

"That was the strange thing about it. There was absolutely no timestamp or programmer associated with that code. It was as if the information had been erased."

"Are changes usually attributed to programmers and timestamped?"

"Always."

"Is removing the timestamp the kind of thing someone might do if they were covering up a mistake they made?"

"Objection."

"Your honor, I'm only asking if *someone* might remove that information to cover up, not if the defendant did it."

"I'll allow it."

Baxter winced.

Harrison said, "Mr. Masters?"

"Absolutely."

"Interesting."

The jury seemed to find it interesting, too.

"You and your team also studied some of Mr. Noble's programming methods all the way back to 1985."

"Yes."

"Did that User Abort ON command appear in any of his work?"

"Yes it did, quite often. We also looked at some invoices he issued to clients where he credited money back to them for having forgotten to turn it off."

"So he made this error before?"

"Yes."

"How often?"

"We found a half-dozen instances."

"Is it your opinion Mr. Noble should have stopped testing after the first death?"

"Objection. This witness is not an expert on policy."

"Your Honor, Mr. Masters is an expert on computer programming procedure and has made similar decisions about software readiness."

The judge said, "I'll allow it."

Baxter threw his hands out. "Your Honor, this is another opinion, far too many of which are making their way into this trial."

"I said, I'll allow it, Mr. Goodman."

Baxter shook his head and tightened his lips.

Harrison turned back to his witness. "Mr. Masters?"

"When we discover a problem in software, we evaluate its impact on users, assign it a priority and act accordingly."

"Something affecting people's lives, what kind of priority would that get?"

"Priority one."

"And a one is…?"

"It gets our immediate attention."

"So let me ask again; in your *opinion*—" He held up a finger for emphasis. "—should Mr. Noble have stopped the testing after the first death?"

"Absolutely."

CHAPTER 77

Baxter took his time getting to the witness stand and presented a warm smile to Jackson. "You comfortable?"

"Yes, thanks."

"Just so everyone is clear, you're here by way of Virtual Reality? Is that right?"

"Yes."

"An oMe2?"

"Right."

"Can I get you a Coke?" He looked over at the jury as the gallery laughed.

The judge's eyelids tightened to half-mast. "Mr. Goodman."

Baxter paused a moment. "You examined some of my client's code from as far back as 1985, is that right?"

"Yes."

"Have you seen instances where he used that specific code in the past thirty-five years?"

"No."

"Anything similar?"

"No."

"So it looks like he learned his lesson after all—and a long time ago at that." Baxter turned to see if Harrison was going to object. Harrison stared straight ahead.

"If you were going to frame a programmer, wouldn't you try to find an error he made and add it to his code?"

"I would never do that."

Baxter smiled at the dodge. "All right then. If some *other* programmer were trying to frame Charlie, might *they* use an error he made in the past?"

"I suppose so."

"The prosecutor said removing the timestamp and the programmer name from the code could have been done to cover up a mistake. Is there any other reason someone might do that?"

"I can't think of one."

"Well, let me suggest one and see what you think; If someone were trying to make a programmer look incompetent, would that be a reason?"

"I... guess so."

"So it's possible someone could have added the code to make Mr. Noble look bad?"

Jackson looked at the prosecutor and answered with a slow, "Yyyyes."

"So Mr. Noble might not be responsible for the security breach at all."

"He... might not."

"And as far as you've been able to tell, there's no proof he forgot anything."

"No." Jackson shifted uncomfortably.

"Now, you told the prosecutor you actually *do* have evidence from the server, is that right?"

"Yes, sir."

"Do you know the capacity of the N-hanced server?"

"It's one hundred yottabytes."

"I see. So based on your analysis, what percent of the total capacity of the server do you have access to?

"Oh..." He looked desperately at Harrison. "Uh, I-I don't really know."

"Oh, come on Mr. Masters. You can easily get to your data from here. Just tell us how many Terabytes of storage it takes up.

"Um... It would take a little while..."

Everybody's lie detectors flashed. People in the gallery pointed, whispered and smiled.

Baxter clearly enjoyed the moment. "Really? I know the amount of data from this trial up to this very second." He drew a cube and pointed to the flickering numbers. "Why, lookey here. Two-hundred-fifty-seven terabytes. Not much when you consider how important it is to Mr. Noble."

"Objection."

"Sustained."

"So, you mean a computer scientist like yourself doesn't have as sophisticated a system as a li'l ol' country lawyer like me?"

Jackson looked at the prosecutor who closed his eyes in defeat and nodded ever so slightly. "I guess it would be about three-hundred-twenty-three terabytes."

"There we go! Good for you! And what percent is that of one-hundred yottabytes—just in round numbers?"

Jackson answered sheepishly, "About point three billionths."

"That little?" Baxter made sure his surprised face was in view of all the jurors. "So this so-called evidence you're talking about is really a very tiny percentage of what's on the server. Would that be correct?"

Jackson shifted in the witness chair. He whispered a dry, "Yeah."

"I'm sorry, I didn't hear you."

He cleared his throat. "Y-yes."

"Less than one billionth. Wow! That's statistically pretty nearly zero, isn't it?" Baxter turned three quarters of the way around, speaking as he faced the gallery and finally the jury. "I wouldn't want my fate determined by so little evidence. Would you?" He stood near the jury box, but his hands requested an answer from everyone in the room.

A couple of the jurors shook their heads, a few others looked at the judge. The gallery buzzed.

There was no need to torture Jackson any further. Wearily Harrison raised one finger. "Your Honor, the prosecution will concede that we have access to almost no information from the N-hanced server."

Baxter said, "Thank you, Mr. O'Neill. And thank *you*, Mr. Masters."

Leaning in to the jury he whispered, "Jack Masters. Jack of all trades, master of none."

All of them smiled, a few giggled.

The judge frowned. "You will not belittle the witnesses."

"Of course. Sorry, Your Honor." He knew she was watching him. It was the jury that mattered. He almost winked at them, but thought better of it.

Baxter paused to consult his notes. "Now, that line of code—that User Abort ON—it's just a switch, is that right?"

Jackson regarded Baxter icily. "More or less."

Baxter took a few minutes to have Jackson confirm that the line of code was not a kill command. Then he said, "Any evidence that anyone at CCD mounted these attacks?"

"No."

"Once the switch was open, could the attacker be from a company other than CCD?"

"Yes."

"Even your company?"

"Objection."

"Withdrawn."

"Now, you work for Orange, a subsidiary of Orchard. You mentioned you analyzed all this data. I understand your company volunteered the time. Do you know how much that cost?"

"About a million credits."

"Wow. That's very generous. Now, help me with this, Mr. Masters; Orange is a competitor of CCD, is that right?"

"Well, in a friendly sort of way, yes."

"Uh-huh. And if my client were to go to prison, it would probably slow down his project, wouldn't it?"

"Yes." Jackson shifted his shoulders and rolled his head, popping the bones in his neck.

"Are you aware your company offered to buy Corridor CyberDynamics on a number of occasions?"

"I've heard rumors."

"Oh, come on, Jackson. You were on the committee."

"OK, then. Yes."

"And if N-hanced had to be back-burnered because its creator were in prison, that might put financial pressure on CCD to sell N-hanced to your company, mightn't it?"

"It might."

"So your testimony here today could actually lead to your company acquiring CCD, isn't that right?"

"Um..." Jackson's shoulders fell an inch. "Yeah."

"N-hanced is projected to be world-changing, isn't it?"

"I guess."

"You guess? Well, here's something I guess; I guess Orchard would give you a big fat bonus if your testimony helped them acquire the biggest-selling product of all time!"

"Objection."

Baxter smiled and flicked his hand over his shoulder at Harrison. "Withdrawn. Thank you Mr. Masters. You have been *very* helpful."

CHAPTER 78

"Redirect, Your Honor?"

"Yes, Mr. O'Neill."

"Mr. Masters, the defense counsel suggested that an attack could have come from an outside source. Is there any evidence it might have come from *your* company?"

"No. In fact, there's no evidence of an attack at all. Nobody knows what happened."

"Isn't the opening left in N-hanced a security risk?"

"Absolutely. We would never allow any of our software to go into testing like that."

"Now, for the record, Jackson, have you been offered any compensation for testifying in order to make Mr. Noble look bad in this trial?"

"Absolutely not. Please, you've got to believe me." He looked at the jury, eyes pleading. "I would *never* do anything like that. It's not what our company is about."

"The defense pointed out you and your company volunteered to do the analysis for free. Why was that?"

"We wanted to find out if the problem was in our VR."

"And was it?"

"Not that we could tell."

"Does that mean the problem is in N-hanced?"

"Objection. Calls for speculation."

"Sustained."

"Thank you, Jackson." Turning to the judge he said, "That's all for this witness."

Baxter stood and said, "Re-cross, Your Honor?"

"Yes, Mr. Goodman."

Baxter jutted his chin toward Jackson. "Are you aware Mr. Noble and his team use software to clean the code before it goes into use?"

"I imagine they would."

"Really? Then why would you accuse him of skipping that step?"

"I didn't. I said that's what *our* company does."

"Indeed, you did. Would you now look at the CCD N-hanced log and see if they ran a similar check?"

"Sure." He made a request and answered in a few seconds. "Yes, they did."

"So would that indicate the line was added after code lock down?"

"I guess so."

"Now tell me, why on God's green earth would Charlie add code to make it look like he didn't know what the hell he was doing?"

"I can't imagine."

Baxter looked at the jury and shook his head. "Neither can I. Neither can I." After a moment he turned to the judge. "I'm done with this witness."

The judge said, "Do you have any other witnesses, Mr. O'Neill?"

"No, Your Honor. The prosecution rests."

"Let's take a fifteen minute—"

Baxter raised his eyebrows, his index finger and his voice. "Your honor?"

She lifted her chin toward him.

"Permission to approach for a PC?"

The judge said, "With the prosecutor?"

"Yes, Your Honor."

She beckoned them forward. Raising her palm she said, "Everyone else please remain seated." Once the lawyers reached the bench, the judge drew a small circle with her index finger, encompassing the three of them in PC. "OK, Mr. Baxter."

"Your Honor, the prosecution has not established negligence. Again, I move for a judgment as a matter of law. There is no evidence to support these claims."

"Your request is noted and denied."

"On what basis?"

"That if the N-hanced system were compromised, then its security was not adequate, which constitutes negligence. Not that my job is to argue the prosecutor's case for him." She glanced toward Harrison.

Baxter blew out his breath. He wanted to argue but didn't have any ammunition. Instead he said, "Thank you, Your Honor," and headed back to the defense table.

The judge said, "We'll have a fifteen minute recess and begin the defense case." She tapped her gavel and the noise level went up in the courtroom. Four jurors stood and filed out while the eight oMe2s went into pause mode.

As soon as Baxter opened a PC, Charlie said, "What was that about?"

"I was trying to get the case dismissed. But the judge wants to keep playing her game, God knows why. So on we go." He sounded disgusted.

Charlie nodded. "Jeez, you really lit into Jack. He seems like a nice guy."

"Yeah, but he'll be fine if Orange and Orchard are as benevolent as they pretend to be."

"So where's that leave us?"

He called up the graphs. "Some of the jury members question Jackson's testimony, so I did a good job. But most of them see the whole exchange as irrelevant. They know there's no proof either way. And it took me down a notch in likeability. I have to be careful so they don't turn against you because of me."

"You're gonna have to put me on the stand."

"No, I'm not."

"But agent Lott left the jury thinking I'm a sneaky SOB. They need to see I'm not like that."

"Harrison asked Lott those questions to prejudice the jury and to get you on the stand. Don't play his game."

"You think the jury's going to forget what he said because the judge says so? You know what our odds are."

"Yep. About sixty-forty, your favor. But you could make it a lot worse."

"How?"

"Trust me. The jury has seen your sincerity in the Vs. That's all they need. If Harrison questions you, he'll find a way to get you into a corner and rip your head off."

"I know enough to keep from letting that happen."

"I doubt that. Your honesty will be your enemy."

Sixty-forty isn't good enough. I've gotta find another way.

Baxter could see Charlie wasn't convinced. "Mark Twain said, 'It's better to say nothing and be thought a fool, than to open your mouth and leave no doubt.' I can make you look good. But Harrison can tear you a whole new asshole, same as I did with Jack. While I'm working with our first witnesses, you try to picture Harrison standing over your bloody carcass." He gave Charlie a pleading look and patted him on the hand.

It didn't make Charlie feel any better.

CHAPTER 79

"The defense calls Milo TwoDogs to the stand."

"Would you please tell the court where you work and your job?"

"I'm lead programmer at Corridor CyberDynamics."

"How long have you known the defendant?"

"Three years. Ever since I came to work there."

"How well do you know Mr. Noble?"

"Very well. I consider Charlie one of my friends."

Baxter went on to establish that as far as Milo was concerned, Charlie was not psychotic, rushing the product to market, or trying to get an insurance settlement. However, he *was* concerned about someone having broken into the server and was working hard to find out what went wrong when the oBI agents arrived.

Baxter said, "So do I understand *you've* been using N-hanced?"

"Yes, sir."

"What have you done with it?"

"Tried to find the hacker."

"And what have you found?"

"Sorry to say, nothing new."

"Any attempts on your life?"

"No." Milo chuckled. "But it's not connected to the Net."

"Do you think it's safe to have an analyst take a look?"

"Objection. The court has already made that ruling."

"Sustained."

Baxter turned. "Your witness."

Charlie was shocked. *He didn't ask shit. At least he didn't attack him as a spy.* Charlie signaled for a PC. Baxter shook his head, pointing at Harrison headed for the witness box.

Harrison spent ten minutes failing to get Milo to say either Charlie or N-hanced were dangerous. "Is it possible Charlie discovered the faulty code and disabled it?"

"You have access to the Vs."

"But isn't security an illusion? A game hackers laugh at?"

"I guess you could say that."

"So an authenticated vid might be hacked and still look authentic?"

Milo shifted in his seat. "I... guess so."

"N-hanced has a number of hacker modules doesn't it?"

"Yes."

"So someone using those modules would in effect be an expert hacker, wouldn't they?"

"Yes."

"How about Charlie?"

"Objection."

"I'm only asking if he *could* have hacked the vids."

"Overruled. You may answer the question."

"I... guess so."

"Have you experimented with the hacking modules?"

"I've been busy. And besides, my regular work is in another department."

"Do you know if Charlie experimented with N-hanced hacking?"

"That's not his style."

"Let's look at some vid." Harrison drew a cube. There was Charlie hacking into the power grid to blow the LED lamp on CCD Plaza. He broke into the Skeet system to assume Gerald Collier's identity and then the security at Breslin Center. Harrison paused the vid. "Need more?"

Milo, mouth open, shook his head slowly.

The judge said, "We need an audible response."

"Uh, no. I don't need any more."

"Did you know he was hacking this way?"

"No."

"So isn't it possible he might have used those skills to authenticate vid that was in fact false?"

Milo's eyes scanned back and forth, trying to find a way out. Finally he said, "I suppose."

"Thank you, Mr. TwoDogs." To the judge, "I'm done with this witness."

Baxter said, "Redirect, Your Honor?"

"Yes, Mr. Goodman."

He stood and buttoned his coat, which left a starburst pattern of wrinkles radiating from his bellybutton.

"Let's assume hacking is a game. Wouldn't it be a lot of fun for a hacker from outside CCD to break in and mess with the system?"

"Yes." Milo's face relaxed and he sat back.

"Wouldn't Charlie's snowboarding run be an invitation for hackers to break into N-hanced?"

"Yes." Milo sat taller.

"Probably a lot of hackers?"

"Yes!"

"Just a few more question. When we looked at those Vs of Charlie hacking, didn't they take place while he was desperately trying to get back to solving the puzzle of how his testers were being killed?"

"Yes!" Milo beamed.

"And half the Vs were of events that took place after he thought his life was in danger."

"Exactly!"

"Thank you, Mr. TwoDogs. That is all."

The judge looked at Harrison. He just shook his head. "The witness may step down. That's all for today. We'll reconvene here tomorrow morning at 9:00." She smacked her gavel on the block.

CHAPTER 80

Milo was all apologies to Charlie. "I'm so sorry. That guy had me saying all kinds of stuff."

"Don't worry about it. Harrison's amazing in a sick sort of way."

"Really, I'm sorry."

"Enough already." Charlie smiled and waved his hand. "Listen, I'm gonna try to get a room for a meeting in a few minutes. Can you stay around and join us?"

"Hell, yes."

"Hang on." Charlie signaled Baxter for a PC. "So how did the Vs of me hacking go over with the jury?"

"Your stock dropped a couple notches. But you're just above fifty-fifty."

"Shit." Charlie looked grim. "Can you arrange for me to meet with my friends in the conference room?"

"Sure. And I'll need to meet with Walter to prep him in the morning."

"No problem. How soon can I get in with them?"

Baxter took a second with the bailiff. "Now good?"

* * *

"Thanks for being here. I want you all to meet my friend from work, Milo TwoDogs. Milo, this is Ja— uh, Anne Conley." He shot a quick glance at Milo. A rush of sweat rolled over him for nearly blowing their cover. "Walter Bratton, and Toby Hodges." They all shook hands.

Milo smiled. "Nice to meet you."

"Now, in case you haven't noticed, things aren't going so good. Baxter says my chances are about fifty-fifty.

Anne/Janice put her hand on Charlie's shoulder. Even though it wasn't Janice's face, he could feel the sympathy flow from her eyes.

Walter/Anton said, "Sorry, friend. So what can we do?" Apparently something his fake identity lowered his voice and rendered it jiveless.

"Baxter wants to meet with you to get you ready for tomorrow. So hang around after we're done here."

"Sure."

Charlie leaned in and lowered his head and voice. "So here's the thing, I can't leave my fate up to this jury. I'm working on an idea where you all can help me prove who caused these deaths."

Walter said, "Interesting. So what's your idea?"

"I'll probably have it figured out overnight. Milo, I'd like you to contact the remaining seven testers. See if they'll help us capture the Black Octopus. You need to let them know there may be some risk. I want them to work remotely in case we're tracked by the oBI." Charlie lifted an index finger. "Each of them should have someone they trust with them to make sure they stay sitting or lying down. I'll need to know first thing in the morning how many are willing. Can you do that?"

"No problem."

"Now this is for the rest of you. If I don't get enough of the testers to make a team of eight, would you be willing to go N-hanced and help out?"

Walter/Anton said, "We're in."

Anne/Janice nodded.

Toby/Dexter said, "Not me."

Walter/Anton looked at Charlie. "He's in. So, how are you going to coordinate it all from here?"

Charlie saw Milo watch the odd interchange, and hoped there wouldn't be a problem. Then he answered. "I've got an idea about that, but there's no need to talk about it until tomorrow."

Jeff said, "What can I do?"

"Would you be a spotter?"

Jeff nodded.

"I'll need all of you here in Real. Are you willing to change your physical appearance?"

"Absolutely."

"If court goes badly, I'll lay out the rest of the details. OK then. Thanks everybody. See you tomorrow."

As the rest of them started out of the room, Anne/Janice stayed behind and said, "Can I talk with you for a minute?"

"Sure."

The bailiff looked in and Charlie said, "Couple more minutes?"

She gave a quick glance at Anne/Janice and smiled. "No problem." She backed out and closed the door.

Janice took him by the hands and looked him in the eyes. "So what does Baxter's software tell you?"

"Like I said, not so good. I want him to call me as a witness."

"What does he say about that?"

"He thinks it's a bad idea."

She put her hand on his shoulder. "You should listen to him."

"Shouldn't I try to change the jury's opinion of me?"

"There must be a reason he's telling you not to."

"He says the prosecutor will trap me."

"He's been doing a pretty good job of that so far. I think maybe you should trust Baxter. He's good, right?"

"The best."

"Listen to him."

Charlie looked down. "I don't know—"

Putting her finger under his chin, she lifted until they were looking into each other's eyes. "What is it? You need the jury to... understand you?"

"Mmm. Maybe that's it."

"If you need someone to understand you, let it be me. But you should listen to him."

Charlie thought about it. Then slowly, "OK."

She smiled and moved her hand to the back of his neck. "Now kiss me, you idiot."

"It's... weird you not looking like Janice."

"Well put your lips here and see if you can tell the difference."

He kissed her. Then he said, "You always this pushy?"

"Yep."

"Probably excessive testosterone."

"Whatsamatter, afraid you might be gay?" She smiled.

"Afraid you might be a man trapped in a woman's body?"

Janice chuckled. "Let's find out."

Charlie liked the talk as much as the touch, and Janice proved equally dexterous at both. He pulled her close. "Too bad the bailiff looks through the window every couple minutes."

She danced him over to the wall, out of view of the window. "Can't see us now."

"Yeah, but next time she looks in and can't find us—"

She slid her hand down to the FasLatch on his pants, then walked her fingers down the outside until she found what she was looking for. She gave him a gentle squeeze.

He made a comical face with wide eyes. In a voice an octave higher he said, "Um, I guess she'll find us humping against the wall."

"Naw. I'm just trying to remind you I'm still here. You know, so you won't go back to that VR girlfriend of yours." She gave him a final rub, then took her hand back.

"Hey, you're not going to leave me like this, are you?"

"Um-hum." Her smile now cheeky. "You suppose they allow conjugal visits in prison?"

"Oh, you had to bring that up."

"I bring a lot of things up."

Charlie smiled and pulled her close, feeling her warmth and smelling her hair.

There was a tap on the door and the both jumped.

"Time's up."

When they saw how wide each other's eyes were, they laughed.

Still smiling, he kissed her one more time, noticing how she kept her eyes open. Stepping back he said, "Until tomorrow?"

"Right. Good luck." She squeezed both his hands.

"Thanks. I'm collecting those luck things right about now."

CHAPTER 81

When Charlie entered the courtroom Wednesday morning, he spotted Milo and lifted his chin and eyebrows to ask, *What'd you find out?*

Milo held up seven fingers.

Charlie nodded and mouthed *Thank you.* Every one of the remaining testers had agreed to help. *But if I'm lucky in here today, that won't matter.* Then he felt the exhaustion bulldoze over his shoulders. *C'mon, stay in the game, Charlie.*

"The defense calls Lucas Astor."

Charlie looked around. *Who?*

Charlie wasn't the only one who didn't know.

"Objection. This witness is not on our list."

"Your Honor, Mr. Astor only appeared last evening."

The judge nodded.

"Your Honor..." Harrison sighed.

"I'll give you some time before cross if you need it, Mr. O'Neil."

Harrison sat down and scowled.

A man Charlie didn't recognize stood and made his way from the back of the courtroom. His tag identified him as Lucas Astor in gray, indicating an alias. Below the name where people normally posted their public info was the word <undisclosed>.

Charlie swung around to see what Walter/Anton thought about being bumped, but the seat was empty. He gave Janice a questioning look. She tilted her head and flicked her eyes toward Lucas.

Charlie turned back to watch.

"Please tell the court how you make your living."

"I'm an independent contractor. I invent T programs and sell them to various companies and the government."

"Aren't you also a computer systems security expert?"

A smug smile crept onto Lucas's face. "You could say that."

The smile was one Charlie would recognize anywhere.

"What is your NetName?"

Anton paused a beat. "HackerMeister."

There were gasps and a ruckus arose in the gallery, especially among the NewsDogs.

Charlie's mouth gaped. *Anton is HackerMeister? No way!*

"If it please the court, Mr. Astor is here today with an altered appearance and an assumed name in order to protect his Real identity."

"So noted."

"Now Mr. Astor, aren't hackers criminals?"

"Nooo." He laughed. "Some hackers are criminals. But the Internet Engineering Task Force defines hacker as a 'person who delights in having an intimate understanding of the internal workings of a system, computers and computer networks in particular.' Some hackers debug security problems for a living. I've done some of that—"

Charlie thought, *No shit!*

"—And the World Wide Web and Internet were conceived and created by hackers."

"Now, have you been monitoring this trial?"

"Yes I have."

"On a number of occasions the prosecutor said no one could have broken into the N-hanced system, therefore the faulty code—the code that caused these three men to die—could only have been the result of Mr. Noble's negligence. Do you agree with that?"

"Absolutely not."

"Who could have broken into the system and changed the code?"

"Me."

There was another round of noise from the gallery.

"Are you confessing to this crime?"

Lucas/Walter/Anton laughed through his nose. "Hmm-No."

Charlie blanched.

"Does the fact that someone could break into the N-hanced system mean Charlie is negligent?"

"Absolutely not. There is no system in the world that can't be compromised. Not one."

"Thank you Mr. Astor." Turning, Baxter said, "Your witness."

Lucas looked surprised. "Hey, wait a minute. Aren't you gonna—"

Baxter spun around with his hand up. "That will be all."

Lucas recoiled as if he'd been slapped.

Charlie thought, *What?*

The judge said, "Mr. O'Neill, will you need time to prepare for a cross?"

"Uh, yes. Thank you, Your Honor. Fifteen minutes?"

"Court will reconvene in fifteen minutes." Her gavel came down.

*   *   *

As soon as the judge stepped down, Baxter signaled for Lucas, Anne, Toby and Jeff to join them in the conference room. Milo, looking a little forsaken, stayed behind.

Once the door closed Lucas got into Baxter's face. "What the fuck was *that*, man? I thought you were gonna nail me with the details of the steganography so you could get my man here off. You soft-soaped that so thin, if I was taking a shower I'd still be stinkin' dirty." Jabbing a finger at Baxter's chest, his language disintegrated back to street. "I went to a lotta fuckin' trouble puttin' my ass out here in public. And I don't like nobody knowin' my binis, specially no oUS fuckin' Federal court. So what the fuck *up*, Muthafucka?"

Charlie was amazed at Baxter's cool balance between attentive listening and subservience. *No wonder he's the best.* Charlie put a calming hand on Anton's shoulder, but Anton shrugged it off.

Baxter said, "I understand you're upset—"

"Fuckin' right I'm upset."

"—but while you were on the stand, one of my associates told me you're not who you say you are."

Surprise flashed across Lucas' face. He covered it with bluster. "Course not. You knew I was usin' that name to protect my HackerMeister identity."

"He says you're not Walter Bratton either."

Everyone in the group reacted differently. Charlie blanched and lowered his head. Anne's eyes widened, then searched back and forth on the floor. Lucas threw a furious sideways glance in Anne's direction, then squinted with more aggressive bluff.

Baxter had his hand up. "Whether it's true or not, if I'd gone with the testimony we planned, I think the prosecutor would have been desperate to discredit you. His team might have found the same information I did—if they haven't already. At this point we're better off leaving it this way. I think it gave us the reasonable doubt we need.

"I'm sorry I couldn't let you know earlier. But if I'd asked for a recess, it would have sent Harrison digging for the reason. Really, what you said up there was great. I think it moved us ahead."

"Shit, man." Lucas whirled away from Baxter.

Charlie said, "So what's next?"

"The prosecution will get to cross examine him." Baxter talked to Lucas's back. "I'd like you to keep from volunteering anything. Answer the questions with as few words as you can; just yes or no if possible. Don't lie. Which reminds me, have you ever used any other aliases?"

Lucas shrugged, back still toward Baxter.

"Well, if he asks you about that, don't deny it. But you don't have to reveal any of the names. If he pushes you, I'll object." Baxter glanced around the room. "Everybody else OK for now?"

Nobody said anything.

"All right then, I'm going back out to study the jury data and work up something for redirect."

After Baxter left, Anne leaned in. "I don't know what could have gone wrong. Maybe somebody on the Net figured it out. Or maybe the prosecutor planted some fake data. Baxter needs to know if that's what happened. I'll run a check and see what's out there."

Lucas/Anton paced the room. "Damn right you will, woman."

She winced. "I need to go and sit in the courtroom to work on it."

As she left, Lucas huffed, "That's fucked up, man."

Charlie said, "It's probably not so bad. Bax says the jury took you seriously. And by the way, you're HackerMeister? Unbelievable."

"What? A white black-man can't be smart?"

"No, no. I mean you never let on."

"Hey, dude, I'm humble." The tightness in his face melted as he rolled his head back and laughed.

Charlie felt relief. *Yep. Different face. Same guy.*

Toby/Dexter seemed to relax a little, too.

There was a knock at the door. "Two minutes."

Charlie said, "Um, you might want to back off on the jive."

Lucas straightened up and looked down his nose aristocratically. "I shall be perfectly appropriate, my dear man."

Charlie patted him on the shoulder. "Let's go, Mr. Star Witness. You gotta protect my ass."

"Yeah, I'll do sump'm wit'cho ass." He chuckled. "I shall be happy to accommodate your request."

Lucas and Toby went ahead. Charlie's face darkened. *Now let's see what Harrison does wit'cho ass.*

CHAPTER 82

Harrison got right to it. "You say you're HackerMeister. But there are rumors that's just a name used by a team of hackers and there's no such person. You're here under a false identity. How do we know you really are HackerMeister?"

Panic scalded Charlie. *Does Harrison know?*

Lucas/Anton leaned back and smiled. "You can't. But perhaps a little demonstration will help convince you. You name the system and I'll break into it."

"You mean right here? Right now?"

"Why not?"

"Your Honor?"

She turned to Lucas, "You won't do any harm?"

"No, Judge."

She rubbed her chin. Finally she shrugged. "You may proceed."

Lucas looked at Harrison. "You choose the system."

Harrison seemed to scramble for a moment. Then a touch of triumph appeared around his eyes and mouth. "How about the oSA? They should be secure enough."

Lucas's grin bordered on a smirk. He drew a public cube and expanded it until it encompassed everyone in the court. Using a series of gestures, he navigated a VR datascape, first from above, then diving down and between what looked like skyscrapers. He soared around corners and finally slowed once they were hovering in front of the Orchard Security Agency in Washington, DC.

Dropping to street level he walked up to what looked like a giant bank safe with a huge black wheel and gleaming steel bars. A rainbow grid of lasers crisscrossed its front. He stepped to the right and zoomed in close on a small box next to the door. Splaying his fingers, a wireframe diagram of the inner workings of the mechanism bloomed from the box, filling everyone's view. Mostly wires and computer chips, he pointed to a metal plunger.

"That's what I have to move in order to make the safe door open. But I can't pull it directly without setting off an alarm. I have to sweep past this outer panel and convince the system that my T carries the credentials of an employee. Those credentials can be anything from a sound bite, to a digital image, or a string of their child's DNA code. It would take weeks to try all the variations." He put his hand inside the box. "Or I can just pull this wire here." He gave it a yank. There was a click and the cylinder slid to the side. The lasers shut off, the black wheel spun and the gray safe door swung wide.

Some people gasped. Some laughed. Some applauded.

Lucas led them inside. The space was filled with sparkling columns of data crystals rising three stories high, set in rows that seemed to go on forever. "This is where they keep info on all of you. Your comms, your family images, and your Net viewing habits." Lucas reached and his hand penetrated a crystal. He plucked a large file folder and pressed his finger on the tab. "Shall we take a look at what they have on you, Judge?" Lucas winked. The folder opened with the words "Federal Court Judge Valerie Constance Brennan" above her picture.

The judge shook her head. "Um, I think the court is satisfied with your talents, Mr. Astor. Thank you very much. May we leave now?"

The attendees burst into laughter.

Lucas closed the file and flicked it back into place. Leading everyone out the front door, he closed it, spun the handle and replaced the wire. Then he banished the cube and everyone found themselves back in the courtroom. "Judge, even though millions of people saw that—" He made a few gestures. "—I reprogrammed it so the wire pulling method won't work any more."

Charlie thought, *What a monster talent! What will he be able to do with N-hanced?*

Harrison continued valiantly. "Even though we've seen your expertise, you can't say for certain these deaths weren't Mr. Noble's fault?"

"Of course not." He chuckled. "But you don't seem to be able to prove they *were*."

There were more laughs. Harrison frowned.

"Look, your argument is that Charlie was negligent. I'm here to show you that someone else could have run a computer attack that killed those people. You yourself said the oSA is as secure as they get. If someone can break in there, they can break into N-hanced." Looking out at the courtroom he said, "I think you'll all agree, *no— system—* is *safe*. Either all security specialists are negligent or none of them are. End of story." He sat back in the chair, arms wide.

Charlie scanned the gallery and the jury. People were nodding their heads vigorously.

Harrison looked deflated. "I'm done with the witness, Your Honor."

And he's done with you, thought Charlie.

"You may step down."

They all headed back to the conference room. As soon as the door closed everybody except Baxter and Anne danced, hooted and slapped Lucas on the back.

Charlie shook his head at Lucas. "How did you pull that whole thing off without triggering everybody's oLDs?"

"I told you I worked on those systems. Nothing is hacked more. People *need* to lie. Think about it; what would happen if you couldn't lie when your girlfriend asked you, 'Does my butt look big in this?' I mean, c'mon." He looked at Anne and said, "No offense."

She ignored him and glanced at Charlie with a tense look he didn't understand.

Anton said, "Anyway, as soon as a new version of oLD comes out, a couple minutes later somebody's got a hack-around. Most oLDs are updated a dozen times a day."

Baxter shook his head. "And that's what worked against you."

"Huh?"

"The jury agreed with you in principle, but the fact that you're a hacker means they don't completely trust their oLD. We're still at sixty-forty."

Lucas shoulders slumped. "You gotta be kiddin' me."

Charlie exhaled. "Ffff. Jesus! What the hell do we have to do to convince these people? I thought he was brilliant."

"He was. I couldn't have wished for better testimony if I'd questioned him myself."

Charlie said, "Which reminds me; isn't there a saying that a lawyer should never ask a question he doesn't know the answer to? What's with Harrison, anyway?"

"I don't get it either. Something funny's going on."

"Well, that's it, then. Put me on the stand. It's the only thing I've got left."

Baxter held up a hand. "I wouldn't say it's the only thing. You haven't seen me do a closing. I can dance pretty fast on that courtroom floor. I can probably get you up to seventy-five. But you go on the stand— I don't know if I can dance *that* fast."

Charlie shrugged. "Seems to me Harrison's not firing on all cylinders. After what we just saw, I'm not afraid of him." Anne was now in his line of sight, sending him desperate signals with her eyes. He stepped around near her, held up a finger to everyone else and whispered in her ear. "Is this about me going on the stand?"

"No. We need a few minutes without Baxter."

Charlie stepped away from her. "Bax, I'll make my decision about testifying in a couple of minutes. Can I have a couple minutes with my friends?"

"Sure. But we go on soon." Baxter's face pleaded. "I'd like to tell the judge that we rest." He turned and left, closing the door behind him.

Anne held up a hand and watched through the window until she was sure he was gone, then she faced them. "He's full of shit. There is no documentation showing a connection between Walter or Lucas with Anton."

Lucas said, "You probably didn't look hard enough."

"Hey, it's *your* software. If it can't find the link, there *isn't* one."

Charlie looked at Lucas. "You told me she's the best. You think they have a better researcher than Anne?"

Lucas shrugged. "Baxter must have something or he wouldn't a said it."

Toby nodded. "Good thing he would never lie."

Charlie said, "Of course not. Why would he—?" And then it hit him. He had almost forgotten Dex's little affliction. *What if Baxter is trying to lose?*

Charlie tried to think back over all the days of testimony and Baxter's questions. "Baxter seems like he's trying to win. But anybody who's really good would know how to pull back just a little at the right time; like an athlete throwing a game to win a bet, but not so much that it would show. But why would Baxter do that?"

Lucas said, "Can't tell you why. But I'll bet you can't name anyone who might have more of a need for a high-end, privately-hacked lie projector than a lawyer."

"Did you write something for Baxter?"

"I don't always know where my stuff goes."

Charlie tipped his head, eyes wide.

"Hey, don't look at me that way, bro. I do it for the cause. That shit we own ain't free."

Anne said, "And Baxter never *did* show us any documentation. We just assumed he had some because we knew *we* lied. We got bluffed and he didn't even know it."

Charlie looked at Toby. "Takes one to know one?"

Toby shrugged.

"Listen everybody, I think I may be in more trouble than I realized."

Lucas said, "Why not just fire him?"

Charlie's eyes searched the floor for a few seconds. Then slowly, "Nnnnoo. I don't think so. They say 'Keep your friends close and your enemies closer?' If he *is* trying to sabotage me, we'd be better off not letting him know we know. Whether it's true or not doesn't matter. At this point, he said my chances of getting out of this without being convicted are only about sixty-forty, and that's before his closing, which—if I'm right—he's planning to fumble."

Charlie stood tall, decisive. "OK, that's it. First I'm going on the stand to see what I can do for myself. But the plan I talked to you about last night? The one with the testers? It won't require Mr. Goodman's allegiance—or any help from a jury." He drummed his fingers on his forehead. "Meet me back here after I get off the stand. We'll almost certainly have a date with N-hanced tonight."

There was a knock at the door. "Two minutes, folks."

CHAPTER 83

As soon as he got back to the table, Charlie leaned over to Baxter. "I'm gonna testify. Make me look good."

Baxter sighed and nodded.

Charlie didn't expect any miracles, though, especially now that he suspected an ambush. *I'll be watching you, Buddy.*

"All rise."

"The defense calls Lester Charles Noble to the stand."

After Charlie was sworn in and settled into the witness chair, Baxter walked up to him as if he were his best friend. Facing the jury so they could see his affection, he smiled at Charlie with the warmth of the sun.

"N-hanced is your creation isn't it, Charlie?"

"Yes, but it's been predicted for some time. I just created the first workable version and won the patent."

"Would you give us a short summary of how it works?"

"Sure." Charlie ran it down for anyone who hadn't already heard about it.

"How long have you been using the app?"

"A little more than four months."

"And has it ever hurt you?"

"I haven't even stubbed my toe while using it."

There were a few chuckles and an "Amen" from the gallery. Some jurors smiled. Charlie relaxed a little and smiled back.

Baxter barely paused. "So how can being smarter hurt anyone?"

"I don't see how it can."

"If N-hanced isn't dangerous, what could be causing this problem?"

"Part of what my PAs and I were working on was a theory that it was a problem with Orchard's VR program."

Worried looks and mumbles returned to the gallery.

Charlie raised his voice and a hand. "I don't mean to upset anyone."

They quieted back down.

"It's only a theory I wanted to test, but I haven't been able to check it out. There haven't been any reports of accidents with VR like what happened with our testers."

"So is N-hanced causing this?"

"I still can't say. We began to suspect maybe some hacker was using N-hanced as a channel to tunnel into VR. N and VR are closely intertwined. But we need more time."

"What made you suspect a hacker?"

"We found hidden code that might have been used to provide an opening into the system."

"Wasn't that code really an error you made in your programming?"

"No. Well— yes and no."

A low rumble started again.

Charlie waited for it to die down. "What I mean is, the code we discovered imitated an error I made in some of my programming about forty years ago. But I haven't used it since then. And even if I had, my PAs would have eliminated it."

"Why didn't they catch this one?"

"That's another suspicious thing. They told me they were instructed to ignore it and erase it from my memory."

The rumble sounded like far away thunder. The judge raised her gavel, and the noise died away.

"OK then, help me understand this. The prosecutor said you were negligent and made errors in programming. What you're saying is someone else may have attacked your system and made it look like you made a mistake?"

"That's what I'm suggesting. But—" Charlie's hand was out in front of him again. "—I want to make it clear I really don't know."

"So it doesn't sound as if there's negligence at all. One way or the other, something intentional happened here."

"That's how it seems."

"Since you haven't been able to find an outside attacker, I can only ask you to speak for yourself. Why would *you* do such a thing?"

"I wouldn't. There isn't a single reason in the world I would sabotage N-hanced. I can't wait for it to get out into the world—as long as it's operating properly."

"Ah. But that sounds like ambition. Before the trial the prosecutor said you made mistakes because you were in such a big hurry to release N-hanced. What about that?"

"I can't tell you how excited I am about N-hanced. From the first day I used it I knew it would change the world."

Out of the gallery came a, "Tell it all, brother."

The judge shot a jagged glance in the direction of the voice.

Charlie went on. "But would I release it before it's ready? No way. And no matter what, it's not supposed to kill anyone. As I said, I was the first one to use it. I haven't had a single problem with it—unless you count the times I had to turn it off. I just hate going back to normal."

Charlie looked at Jeff in the gallery. His friend's face softened, as if he understood for the first time how much N-hanced meant to Charlie.

Baxter raised a palm. "What about Dr. Larson's comments that you don't get enough sleep?"

"Before I used N-hanced, I needed six or seven hours, and I was often needed a nap. Now I only need two hours of sleep and I'm never tired."

"What about the hallucinations Dr. Larson talked about? Weren't you suffering from paranoia when agents Lott and Mortensen came after you?"

"Well first of all, I had N turned off at the time. But let's face it, they *were* chasing me. So watch this and you tell me if I was paranoid."

Baxter said, "Just a moment, Charlie." Turning to the judge he said, "If it please the court?"

"You may proceed."

Charlie drew a cube and played the vid where Mortensen said, "Well, I got my own method. Shoot first, ask questions later." He closed the vid and looked between the jury and the gallery. "He threatened to kill me, right?"

People nodded and a few said, "Yeah," along with other shuffling and mumbling and an, "Amen, brother."

The judge pounded her gavel. "Order." Then turning to Charlie she said, "Mr. Noble? Please direct your answers to Mr. Goodman."

"Oh, sure, Your Honor." Charlie raised his eyebrows and stretched the corners of his mouth like a bad boy being lectured at school. Some people in the gallery laughed.

The judge shook her head and gave a dismissive wave, which only brought on more laughs.

Baxter said, "So what else do you want the jury to know?"

"I have done everything I can in order to figure out what happened to Wilford, Chad and Gary. I feel terrible they're gone. I got to know each of them during the testing. I just want to finish my investigation and find out what really happened and who really did this. That's all."

"Thank you, Charlie." Baxter walked back to the defense table.

The judge said, "Let's take a recess. We'll resume with the prosecution cross in fifteen minutes."

*   *   *

Charlie stood and stretched. Baxter's questioning had gone better than he expected from somebody who was trying to sabotage his case. He sat back down and scanned the jury. The looks on their faces gave him a good feeling. He'd have to check with Baxter, but he thought they were with him.

Now all he had to do was schmooze his way through the prosecutor's questions, listen to closing remarks and go home. Unless—

What if Baxter's trick is to give information to the prosecutor? It would look like he did everything he could for me, and there won't be any room for an appeal. Charlie was getting anxious. He wished he could dial it down. And he was tired. As tired as he had been in a very long time. Resting his chin on his chest, the noise in the courtroom faded away. There was a noise that woke him with a start.

The judge was back.

CHAPTER 84

Harrison began. "While you were a professional musician, isn't it true you had sex with hundreds of women?"

Charlie's jaw dropped. "What the—?"

"Ob-jection!"

The jury sat upright almost as one, eyes wide.

The gallery erupted.

"Order!" The judge whipped the gavel against the block, clearly as angry at the prosecutor as she was at having lost control of the courtroom. "Strike that from the record. The jury is instructed to ignore the question." She turned to Harrison, her eyes a pair of narrow slits almost as thin as her mouth. "Mr. O'Neill, you have stepped waaaay over the line. There will be no salacious grandstanding in my courtroom. Do you understand?"

"But Your Honor—"

"I said, *do you understand?*" She sat taller, her eyes now wide.

"Yes."

"Yes, what?"

"Yes, ma'am."

Her head snapped with a double-take. "What?"

There was laughter in the gallery.

"I mean, yes, Your Honor."

She waited for a moment apparently to let herself cool. Still frowning, she pointed her finger at him. "You may continue. But watch it, counselor."

He went back to his table, face red, clearly stalling until he could find a new place to begin. He waved a finger in the air as if he were paging through his notes, maybe even waiting for an assistant to suggest a safe place to start over. Finally he turned and faced the witness box.

"The product you invented, this N-hanced, it means the user is augmented with nano technology. Is that right?"

"Yes."

"Doesn't it mean you're part machine?"

"I— Well, I guess you could say that."

"Could you possibly be considered half machine?"

"Well, everybody who uses Ts—"

"Just answer the question."

"Objection."

"It's a simple yes or no question, Mr. Noble."

"Your Honor, the prosecutor is badgering the witness."

Charlie looked at the judge and raised his hand. "Your Honor. I would like to answer the question. But I need to be able to say more than yes or no."

She thought for a moment. "OK, Mr. Noble, but—" She turned to the prosecutor. "—I'm going to let Mr. Noble answer in his own words. You may not interrupt him. Do you wish to withdraw the question?"

The hint of a smile came to his face. "No, your Honor."

Baxter saw that smile and his heart flopped.

*   *   *

In all trials each side hopes to have a star witness. For Baxter, the prosecutor himself had oddly been the defense's greatest ally if not a star witness—with his weak, almost nonexistent case and poor line of questioning. Baxter barely needed any witnesses at all. Harrison did have that strong opening, but Baxter had beat it back. So who was Harrison's star witness? Didn't he know he needed one? Maybe there was something going on in his life right now distracting him. But if there were, Baxter's assistants hadn't been able to find it.

Baxter's team had examined the witness list over and over. Not one of them stood out, which he had proven during cross, crushing them one after another.

But Baxter never thought to look at his own list to find O'Neill's star. Now he turned his team on Charlie and there it was, cross-referenced with juror number four.

Charlie, Shut up!

And here was Charlie getting ready to speak with messianic certainty. Ah, there was that word again.

When Baxter saw the prosecutor's smile, he knew. *Charlie is the star witness!* He wanted to call a recess. Warn Charlie. Even though he didn't have a good technical reason, it was now or never. He stood.

"Your Honor, I'd like to call for a short recess."

"I'm sorry, Mr. Goodman, we just came back from a recess."

"But, Your Honor, I need—"

"No, Mr. Goodman."

"—to consult with my client."

"No."

And that was it. Two little 'nos.' Nothing out of line. Nothing worthy of a mistrial. Or an appeal. Nothing conspiratorial even. But no doubt about it, those two nos sealed it. If he hadn't pushed her buttons one time too many, she might have given him the recess. But now it was too late. Dazed, he found himself sitting again.

Shut up, Charlie! Shut up!

But Charlie couldn't read his mind. Charlie wasn't even looking at Baxter. He was getting ready for a brilliant speech. The speech of a lifetime. Brilliant and crucial and fateful. The speech that would finally convince the jury he was a man of honor and good intentions—that he should walk out of here a free man.

Shut up!

Baxter was at full attention, eyes wide, weaving cobra-like from side to side, trying to catch Charlie's eye. He cleared his throat. But it was too late. Charlie was already speaking.

"Ever since the Green Plague, all of us have been infused with protein computers—or Ts, as we call them." Then thinking of Jeff and those like him, Charlie said, "That is, most of us. We wouldn't even be here if not for nano-tech. And yes, they are machines. They're our partners like friendly bacteria had been in the past. Every day we use T to care for us and bring us information about the world. There are roughly ten-thousand times more nano computers on and in our bodies than human cells—nearly a quadrillion in our brains. They're so small they only take up a few teaspoons by volume."

Harrison looked interested, nodding, encouraging.

Shut up, Charlie.

"Previously when we wanted to use a computer, we went to a keyboard linked to a box under a desk. Later we carried handhelds and cell phones. Today these T computers are a part of us. So am I part machine? Even more machine than man? Absolutely."

There was a buzz in the gallery. The judge looked up and took the gavel in her hand, but the room quieted back down.

"And so are you." Charlie indicated the prosecutor. Then, waving his fingers to include the gallery and the jury box, "And so are all of you. We no longer simply use computers. We *are* computers."

The gallery began a buzz, which the judge dispelled with a glare and a tap of the gavel.

"N-hanced didn't cause that change. But N *will* make the tools we use work much faster. We'll be able to do away with the IS cube and the microphone input. N will shorten the wires between the input and the output. Between the CPU and the RAM. It bypasses your fingers and stays right up here in your brain." He tapped his temple. "So if this is what you're trying to get me to say Mr. O'Neill, here it is; yes, I am mostly machine. And so are all of you." Charlie let a sly smile pull at the corners of his mouth and eyes. "All of us here, we are the Borg."

The left side of the gallery erupted with angry expletives from angry faces. Some leapt up, shaking their fists at Charlie, shouting, "Bullshit!" and "I ain't no goddamn machine!" and "No fucking way!"

The judge shouted back. "Order!"

On the right side of the court his disciples yelled, "Leave him alone!" and "Preach it, Lord." One of the protesters glared across the aisle and caught the eye of a disciple and shouted, "He's the fucking devil! And you're the devil's disciple!"

"*You're* the devil!" the disciple roared back.

All the protesters and disciples turned toward each other, a mass of red faces, accusations, fists and pointing fingers.

Charlie watched in awe, his mouth open.

"Order! Order in the court!" The judge pounded her gavel. It flipped out of her hand and off the bench, skittered across the floor, and settled at the feet of the startled prosecutor.

One of the protesters burst out of his row and flung himself across the aisle at the closest disciple, fists flailing. Others from both sides followed until a full-scale brawl roiled in the aisle. People not involved pulled back from the melee, faces filled with fear or amazement.

The guard at the main entry lunged forward reaching for his holster shouting, "Halt now or I'll shoot!" But the fighting continued in a churning ball of body parts. The guard aimed and fired. A sticky web engulfed them, and they slowed to a gooey halt.

After she was sure it was safe, the bailiff walked over, retrieved the gavel and handed it back to the red-faced judge, who lifted her eyebrows and mouthed, *Thank you.* She tapped it three times. "Order! Officer, have those people removed from the courtroom."

Within a few seconds four more officers arrived. They worked their way around the mass, gesturing to release them one at a time, then handcuff and lead them away.

Real attendees returned to their seats. The chairs left empty by the brawlers immediately filled with people on the VR waiting list.

The judge adjusted her robe and glared. "If we have one more outburst—even a small one—I will *clear* this courtroom." She scanned the crowd long enough to look every one of them in the eye. Finally she turned to Charlie. "You may continue, Mr. Noble."

"Thank you, Your Honor." Charlie looked between Harrison and the jury. "I'm sorry. When I said 'We are the Borg,' I was joking. I don't mean to imply we're mindless automatons that go around assimilating the uninitiated. But think about it; all of you have a personal IP address. As far as the Net is concerned each of you is a computer."

Charlie turned his full attention on Harrison. "I know you're trying to get me to say I'm some kind of robot without a conscience. What I'm saying is we're already infused with trillions of friendly machines, and it's all pretty harmless. Look at all of us here. Seems like nice, normal people—at least now that the demonstrators are gone." He smiled.

"Except some of the people who trusted you with their lives are now dead."

Baxter shot out of his seat. "Is the prosecutor going to ask—"

"Withdrawn."

Baxter sank back into his chair. He imagined slapping the back of his own head. *How could I have been so stupid? Harrison's the real Colombo. Shit. Shit! SHIT!*

"You said some of your N-hanced memory was erased. Isn't it possible you could have issued the deadly command yourself?"

"I—" Charlie wanted to say *I don't think so,* but remembered the oLDs. "—suppose it's possible."

"And since that memory's gone, you don't have any idea of the content of the missing material."

"Right."

"It could have been anything."

"Maybe my grocery list."

Laughter.

Harrison smiled, too. "Or your death list."

"Objection."

"Sustained."

"You keep saying someone else caused these deaths, but you really can't say who, can you?"

"You already know I can't. But I can tell you this; anybody smart enough to break in would be smart enough to make it look like I did it."

"Admitting it looks like you did it is not much of a defense, Mr. Noble. That's what we call a confession."

Baxter jumped to his feet. "That's what we call reasonable doubt!"

"Sit down, Mr. Goodman."

Baxter sat, sighed and pressed his fingertips against his temples.

"That snowboard event at Park City, Utah last Thursday, that was a big publicity opportunity for you wasn't it?"

"Sure."

"The Net momentum—the public interest—it's at a peak?"

"Yes."

"So if you delay the product, you lose that momentum, right?"

"Well— If you're trying to say—"

"I'm just asking if you lose the momentum."

"Well— Um—"

Baxter leaned forward, but Harrison changed directions.

"Let's take a look at the vids where you're discussing with Mr. Reynolds whether to shut down the project." The piece played and O'Neill stopped it. "Right there we clearly see he's trying to get you to stop. But you're arguing with him. If you had taken his advice, Mr. Rodriguez and Mr. Billings would be alive today wouldn't they?"

Charlie couldn't speak. Harrison had him backed into a corner. There was only one answer.

"Wouldn't they?" Harrison waited. "Mr. Noble...?"

Baxter sat poised to object, but Harrison stopped just short of badgering Charlie.

Harrison looked at the judge. "Your Honor?"

The judge turned to Charlie. "Answer the question, Mr. Noble."

Very slowly Charlie said, "Yes— Yes, they would." He put his thumbnail against his teeth.

"Now, let's look at another vid. This is right after Mr. Rodriguez was killed." He played, then paused it. "You're arguing with Mr. Reynolds to keep the system running as long as each of your testers agrees to take their lives into their own hands."

"Objection!" Baxter was on his feet, red-faced and frowning. "That is not what was said in the vid."

Harrison sighed. "Withdrawn. Mr. Noble, if you had taken your boss's advice right then, Mr. Billings would still be alive, isn't that right?"

Charlie's eyes searched the floor. Turning to the judge he said, "Your Honor... um... do I have to answer these questions? I mean, can I plead the fifth?"

"Yes, you can, Mr. Noble. But you wanted to appear as your own witness. You don't get to choose the questions."

Charlie settled slowly back in his chair. A chair that felt very hard and cold and unforgiving. *I killed these guys. Jesus. How am I ever going to live with that?* He put his fist against his mouth and lowered his head, trying to keep himself from crying. *What have I done?*

Harrison said, "Would you like a minute, Mr. Noble?"

Charlie held up a finger. After what seemed like a long minute he swallowed and with his head still down, spoke quietly. "But I kept using N-hanced myself. I didn't think it was dangerous. I would never have hurt them knowingly."

"Just accidentally."

Baxter stood, "Your Honor, could we have a short recess?"

Harrison turned. "I have no more questions for this witness."

"Court will recess for fifteen minutes." The judge smacked the gavel block and Charlie jumped.

* * *

Charlie went back to the defense table and caved in like a deflating balloon. Even though he still suspected Baxter, there was no question who was responsible for what he had just been through, and he needed to talk about it. He twirled a finger for a PC and Baxter opened the line.

They both spoke at the same time. "I'm sorry."

Charlie said, "What?"

"You first."

"Go ahead, say it."

Baxter looked confused. "Say what?"

"You know."

"What? 'I told you so?' I would never do that."

"You just did."

Baxter opened his mouth, but Charlie held up a hand. "It's OK. I deserve it."

"I'm only sorry I didn't fight you harder."

"I don't know what else you could have done."

"Oh, I don't know. Maybe shown you some vids of other cases."

"I killed them, didn't I?"

"Your testers? I don't believe you did. And you don't want to think that way. Look, you're a good person. You've just been ambushed by an expert. That's what I wanted to apologize for. I underestimated Harrison. Big time. Don't let what happened get to you."

"So, what's it look like?"

"Not good. Juror number four didn't like your Borg comment. But he fell all the way to guilty when you tried to take the fifth. Worse yet, he'll most likely be foreman. But let's not get ahead of ourselves. I need a little time. Why don't you relax for a few minutes? Do some meditation or something. I've got to wrap my mind around what I'm going to ask you on redirect. See if I can't do some of my magic and pull a rabbit out. Try to be positive for me. I don't want you acting guilty when you get back up there."

Charlie nodded. "OK."

I don't get it. He doesn't sound like a traitor. So what was the deal about Anton's ID? And he couldn't have known I would insist on taking the stand. Or could he? Maybe I've been Baxter's puppet all along. Ah, what difference does it make? After tonight I won't need him, anyway. After tonight this whole thing'll fade away like a bad dream.

He turned his head toward Harrison. *How could that innocent-looking man who just a few minutes ago looked so inept—how could he have been all teeth and claws, attacking me like a wildcat? Yeah, but all he really did was hold up a mirror to me. Those teeth and claws are my own guilty conscience. After all, if I hadn't invented N, those guys would still be alive.*

OK. Stop it! Baxter told me to be positive. Charlie tried to remember the good things Baxter asked him on the stand, back when the jury still liked him. But his guilt kept jumping in the way. That wildcat was ripping at his stomach. *If I don't calm down, I'm gonna mess up this next part, too.* He put his hand out in front of him. *Look at me. I'm shaking. I'm sweating. I should have listened to Baxter. Lord, give me a time machine so I can go back and fix it all.*

The clerk said, "All rise!" Charlie's head jerked up.

CHAPTER 85

Baxter radiated an air of deep empathy as he came onto the parquet floor. "Now, Charlie, we'll be going over some uncomfortable territory here. I want to establish what you were thinking at the time you decided to move ahead with the project after the first two of your testers died. Can we do that?"

"Sh-sure."

"What were you thinking after you heard about Wilford Bostwick's death in the Grand Canyon?"

"First I was shocked and upset. I liked him personally. But at the time I just thought it was a tragic accident. A number of people die in the Canyon every year."

"Then what did you do?"

"Once I looked at the data I could see it wasn't a normal accident, and he wasn't suicidal. That was a red flag. It made me very nervous."

"But you decided not to stop the project."

"That's right. It seemed as if it had to be a coincidence or perhaps something in Orchard's VR program. But we looked into it immediately."

"Now, after Mr. Rodriguez died, what went through your mind?"

Charlie brushed his hand along the wood railing in front of him, studying the grain. "This time I was sure it couldn't be a coincidence. I felt terrible, because minutes before I heard Chad was dead, we plugged a hole in our security. I figured any commands had to come from the Net, so I shut it down."

"Why didn't you shut down the whole program then?"

"All the testers wanted to continue with their projects. I thought it was safe. How could anyone attack without a way in?"

"What was your intent at that point?"

"Objection. Intent is not the issue."

Baxter spun toward Harrison. "Intent is very much the issue. For the past two days you've done nothing but argue that Mr. Noble was *intent* on everything from being seduced by ambition, to walking on water thinking he's the second coming of Jesus Christ—"

The judge waved a hand. "Mr. Goodman."

Baxter turned to the judge. "Sorry, Your Honor." He took a breath. "What I mean to say is, even though this is supposed to be a trial about negligence, Mr. O'Neill has repeatedly suggested Mr. Noble sabotaged N-hanced and attempted to cover it up. We now have the opportunity to ask the accused exactly what he *intended*."

The judge nodded slowly. "Overruled."

"Thank you, Your Honor. So, Charlie, what was your intent?"

"I only had one thing on my mind; figure out what was wrong and fix it. Whether it was N-hanced or Orchard's VR, or some combination of the two."

"That's it?"

"Well, I did want to continue providing service to my testers. But believe me, if I had thought they would be in any danger, I would have disconnected them in a second. I have no interest in hurting anyone. Ever since it happened I've felt terrible. That's what's driven me to the point where I've put myself in danger in order to solve this. I want to prove it wasn't something I did and make sure no one else can be hurt in the future."

"When Chad died, did you have any idea there still might be danger to your remaining testers?"

"Since I didn't know the cause—and still don't—I couldn't say I thought it was risk free. But even after Chad was gone I kept using N. I didn't think I could solve the puzzle without it. It's just too complicated."

"What do you say to those who claim N-hanced is addictive?"

"I would say it's seductive. I mean, who doesn't want to know everything right now? But there is nothing in the code we wrote that could kill people. I believe somebody used N like a weapon, fooling my testers into thinking they were doing something safe when they were not."

"What about those who say your security wasn't stringent enough?"

"Well, after Mr. Astor's demonstration I feel more than a little shaken." Charlie shrugged. "But at CCD, we exceed the industry standard for security—probably by more than any other company in the world. Rob—uh, Mr. Reynolds—is very big on safety and probably spends double what other companies do. And I have a friend whose fiancé was killed by sub-standard software, so I'm right there along with Rob." His gaze fell on Jeff for a second. "We're as obsessive about security as we are about the quality of our software."

Charlie took a breath. "I know Lucas said if one security specialist is negligent they all are. But that's not my attitude. I don't intend to leave my front door open to let just anybody walk in. If somebody's going to get in, they're going to have to work at it. It's going to take a very high level expert—someone like Lucas—to make it through. Maybe I can get him to lend his talents to us."

"So regardless of all the scenarios the prosecutor has paraded in front of the jury, you say you were not negligent."

"Yes."

"That you believe someone from the outside caused the deaths?"

"I do."

"That the only option left is these were murders?"

"Objection."

"Withdrawn. Your Honor, the defense rests."

The judge said, "All right then. I understand there's a memorial service this afternoon for the three victims. We'll reconvene here tomorrow at 9:00 AM when we'll hear closing arguments and send the jury out for deliberations." Her gavel came down.

Before Charlie was halfway back to the defense table, Baxter opened a PC. Charlie spoke first.

"So where are we now, Bax?"

"Juror number four is still locked and loaded. But three of them all the way on your side, and JuryBox says they're not likely to give in to any bullying. The fact you don't have everybody on your side could work for you. I think we have a good shot at a hung jury."

Charlie didn't like the talk about percentages and chances. And he still didn't feel as if he could trust Baxter completely. "Listen, Baxter, I need one more visit with my friends. It may be the last time in the next fifteen years I can talk to them without that prison VR."

"Sure. I'll set it up."

"Thanks."

Lucas/Walter/Anton didn't come to the conference room because he was concerned someone might be able to figure out a connection between him and the others. But once everyone else was there Charlie said, "I'm guess you can tell things have not gone well enough that I can leave it with the jury. So we're running the plan tonight the way I told you."

Milo nodded. "It's all set. Everyone will be on hold at 8:45 to get their final instructions. We go at 9:00."

"Perfect. I can't thank you all enough." He went around the group and gave each of them a hug. He got to Anne and gave her a long kiss, until Toby cleared his throat.

Charlie let her go and said, "Sheesh, Toby. I didn't mean to leave you out."

Toby said, "Hey, I don't really like you all *that* much."

Charlie moved in, and pulled Toby close. His friend hugged back. After a moment Charlie pulled away and patted Toby on the cheek.

Toby cleared his throat. "Thanks, Buddy. Really." He turned to the others. "OK, we're outta here." He opened the door. "Hey, bailiff, we're done."

Everyone filed out, leaving Charlie alone.

The bailiff came in, took Charlie's arm and led him away. Turning him over to the jailer she said, "Good luck tomorrow."

"I don't need any luck."

"Why you say that? It didn't look as if things were going so well."

"That jury loves me."

The bailiff scoffed. "You must be at some other trial."

"Guess so." Charlie gave the bailiff a little half wink.

CHAPTER 86

It was snowing like Siberia when their oCar slid to a halt in front of the CCD building.

Toby scowled. "I hate snow."

"I love it." Anne's face pointed skyward. "It's like a fairyland."

"Oh, it's beautiful. I just hate the cold."

Anton met them at the door, now looking like Walter. As they swept into the lobby, Milo said, "I took care of security for all of you, so we can go right up."

Toby said, "Can we all at least look like our Real selves until we meet with the testers?"

Walter and Anne nodded and projected Anton and Janice in VR.

"Damn, Bro." Anton shook his head. "That was one smooth switch you pulled with Dexter back there."

The man who looked like Toby became Charlie. "I'm glad Dex agreed to do that. There's no way I could have handled this from my cell." He turned to Milo. "I'm sorry to put all this on you, but you're a part of it now. You gotta keep all these aliases to yourself."

"Don't worry. I've been with you a hundred percent for a long time."

Anton spread his arms wide. "OK, so what we doin'?"

"I want to have you and Janice try on N-hanced. Some people need a little time getting used to it. Let's get that out of the way right now."

*   *   *

Neither of them had any trouble adjusting to N. Milo worked with Janice and showed her the research modules so she could experiment with the internal network and navigate the CCD file system. Anton played with security and worked with Charlie to see if he could find anything to account

319

for the breach. Jeff found a memory module movie he played on an old LCD.

Anton kept saying, "Shit, man, this is fucking amazing!" As they finished the tour, he gushed, "Anton does *not* wanna go back to normal."

Charlie nodded. "Now you know how I feel."

Janice said, "It feels like being in one of those English hedge mazes. When I'm normal I can't find my way out. But with N-hanced, I'm thirty feet in the air with a bright-green arrow showing me the path." Her face softened into a wistful smile. "And I can think of some more— intimate uses we could put it to." She shook her head. "Anywho, this *needs* to get go public. It's gonna be huge."

"Thanks, but here's what I need from each of you. Milo, I want you to go to your house and have your wife watch to make sure you stay in the chair. You'll be the decoy, and you'll grab the number one tentacle, like I told you yesterday."

"Sure," Milo nodded. "My wife'll be glad to help."

"Good. Anton? I want you to go to your girlfriend's place. Can she stay with you?"

"She s'posed-a be. Let me comm her."

"Jeff and Janice, you'll both stay here with me. Jeff, I want you to to make sure I stay in my chair."

Jeff snickered. "Yeah, I can do that."

"Janice, once the rest of us corner this thing, I need you to do the research so we know who's responsible. I don't mean to take you out of the action, but it is your specialty."

"No problem. Will I be able to watch the rest of you?"

"Absolutely."

She raised a palm. "That'll be enough fun for me."

Anton was back. "Big butt woman givin' me some shit, but she'll do it."

"Great. Now once we corner this thing, there will doubtless be secured systems all along those pathways to its source. I want you to crash the firewalls. With the modules we've just been testing and your experience, I can't imagine anyone who'd be faster.

"Man, I can*not* wait."

"OK. We have some time before log-on. Let's grab a bite."

They hustled down to the cafeteria.

By the time they returned from dinner it was 7:30. Milo got a comm. When he wrapped it up he looked grim.

"One of our testers backed out. His wife is stushing him because they've got kids."

"Sheesh!" Charlie rubbed his forehead. "I really wanted eight of us; one for each of the Octopus' data tentacles. If we divide our attention to cover missing guy, we might not have enough time. Janice, I hate to take you away—"

"I'll do it."

Charlie turned toward Jeff. "What?"

"I'll be your eighth man."

"Ohhhh, no. I know how you feel about tech. I can't ask you to—"

"You didn't ask me. I volunteered."

"But—"

"I said I'll do it. If having one more man on the team will buy you the time you need, I'm in. If it turned out you went to prison because I didn't help, I'd feel even more like the asshole that I've already been. I'm in!"

"All right." Charlie nodded slowly. "Milo, can you take him to the lab and load him up with T?"

Milo rolled his eyes. "Who you think you're talking to, Charlie?"

Charlie raised a surrendering palm. "OK. OK. Once you're ready, bring him back here so I can test him on N-hanced. But keep in mind, you and Anton have to get out of here in fifteen minutes."

"Gotcha." Milo put his arm around Jeff's shoulder, and they started down the hall.

Charlie jolted. "Wait a sec! Since Jeff won't be watching us, I need someone to guard him. Any of you know somebody we can trust?"

After a moment Anton smirked. "How about that Matthew guy?"

Charlie laughed, then his expression grew solemn. "That might not be such a bad idea—if he's not under arrest for that courtroom brawl. I'll check. Milo, you take Jeff."

Milo led Jeff away. "We're gonna bring you into the twenty-first century, Jeremiah Johnson."

Jeff said, "Who?"

"You don't know Jeremiah Johnson? It's this really cool old Robert Redford movie about a mountain man..." They disappeared down the hall.

"Hey, Matthew. Charlie here."

"Charlie? Who's Toby Hodges? I almost didn't answer."

"A friend. You in jail?"

"Naw, they just banned us from the building. Where you calling from?"

"It's a long story. I need your help. Grab an oCar, and don't bring any of your people with you."

"Don't worry. After today, they all went home."

"All right, then. Get over to CCD. Come in the front door, and follow the green arrows."

"It shall be done, Lord."

Good God.

CHAPTER 87

While Milo worked with Jeff in the nano lab, Charlie discussed the strategy he wanted Anton and Janice to use.

"I'll flick my plan to everyone else at 8:45. I don't want any of our crew tracked to their Real location. Anton, is there anything you can do about that?"

"That's more up Janice's alley."

Janice nodded. "Once they log onto the server, I'll doctor the ICANN database so the IP addresses associated with their bodies point to locations in the cloud. But you need to know it won't fool anybody for very long."

Anton raised his hand. "I can have their personal IP addresses increase with each outgoing request."

"Perfect!" Charlie shook his fist. "And I want everyone to use my T ID so they don't get into any trouble."

"Done."

"Ah. Matthew's down front. Look, I know the guy's a little whacked. but he tried to save my life the other day."

Anton smirked. "Yeah. Just make sure he ain't packin' today. No point in any us gettin' shot."

"Don't worry. Our security's good—uh, I think."

Milo and Jeff arrived. Charlie turned to Jeff. "You still OK with this?"

"Sure. But the VR's a little weird after not using T for so long."

"I'll bet." Charlie pointed to Anton and Milo. "OK guys, twenty minutes, you'd better get goin'. Wait! Anton and Janice, you'd better switch on your aliases. I don't wanna blow your cover with the testers."

"Right." Anton morphed and dashed off with Milo.

"Jeff, I've gotta get you set up with N-hanced."

Jeff nodded. Charlie held his hands near Jeff's head and beamed the program to him. Then he flicked two fingers.

Jeff's eyes opened wide and he rolled his head.

Charlie put his hand on Jeff's shoulder to steady him. "You OK, Buddy?"

Jeff blinked and answered slowly, "Yeah. It— just— got really bright in here."

"That's it all right."

"And I'm thinking a lot more clearly."

"Um hum. Maybe we should talk some politics."

"Don't push your luck, old man."

"Mr. Noble."

They turned as Matthew rushed in.

Charlie beckoned him. "Glad you're."

"I'll do anything you ask, Lord."

Anne caught Charlie's eyes. She tipped her head and an amused look scampered across her face.

Charlie introduced Matthew to Anne and Jeff, then he put his hand on Matthew's arm. "OK, listen. I've got to work with Jeff, here. Then you're going to go with him to keep him safe. OK?"

"You mean I won't be with *You*?"

"No. But this is really important."

"All right. If that's what you want."

Charlie ran a few of N's modules with Jeff, who caught on quickly. "In case we get raided I want you in the exercise room. Nobody uses it any more. Lie back on one of the loungers and don't get up."

"Where is it?"

"Other end of the building," Charlie flicked to set the green arrows blinking."

"Got it!"

"I'm telling you, Buddy, you shoulda been using this a long time ago."

"Right. And maybe I'd be among the dead."

Charlie could see Jeff was kidding, but he felt a jab and moved on. "OK, Matthew, go with him."

Anne said, "Since I'll be using N-hanced, too, who's gonna watch you?"

"Aw, I'll be fine."

She raised her eyebrows.

"All right. Why don't *you* watch after me? Your skills won't be required until after the chase anyway."

"Will I be able to see you in Real and VR at the same time?"

"Exactly."

"OK. I'll keep my hand on your leg." She smiled.

Charlie clicked his tongue. "Uh, maybe keep hold of my arm? I do *not* need you messing with my concentration. Ah! Time to meet with our testers."

CHAPTER 88

"Thanks for being here, everyone, seriously. This is very important to me—and to the future of N-hanced."

They offered a mix of nods and verbals.

Charlie flicked his plan into their heads. "Anne and Lucas will make some alterations to your IP addresses. You'll use my T ID."

One of the testers raised a hand. "Um, isn't switching IDs illegal?"

"Yes. But I've got it set to switch off before anyone can make the connection to you. If this plan doesn't work, I'll be in prison for a long time anyway. I couldn't care less about a few misdemeanors.

"Now, we'll be working with objects that represent the program code." Charlie played a section of Lucas' courtroom attack on the oSA, showing the data as a cityscape. "We'll be rushed. But pay attention to any fantasies that creep into your thoughts. Consider anything like that an attack and disconnect from N. There's no telling how this will play out. I don't know if the Octopus will turn on any of you once we box it in. You all have your spotters?"

"Yes."

"This is serious business. They need to focus. Eyes on you at all times. No kids running around. I'll give you a minute to talk to them."

Charlie scanned their faces and thought about the risk they were taking. His heart swelled and his eyes welled. He was struck with an awesome feeling of responsibility for their lives, and he swallowed. *What if I get one of them killed? All that to protect my worthless ass.*

He almost called it off.

Instead, he dialed it down and his inner voice came back with, *All that to change the future of mankind. That's the reason!*

Charlie waited until the last of them returned their focus to him. "Ready?"

"Yeah!"

"Let's do it!"

They found themselves standing in a large open city square surrounded by glass and concrete buildings. They spread out and acted like pedestrians casually enjoying the day, while Milo stood in the center of the space. He adopted Charlie's face and a bowed stance, his back to the main information boulevard. He requested massive amounts of data using Charlie's ID and imitated the calls Charlie had made each time he'd been hunted by the eight-tentacled beast. Dark clouds of data swirled in long sweeping streams from the sky, narrowing into tornado-like columns, which flowed toward his back and over his shoulders, into the IS in front of him. The sight added to Charlie's sense of foreboding.

They watched.

And nothing happened.

Charlie glanced at a large analog clock in the square as the second hand swung around to one minute. His anxiety crept up with each tick of the second hand. *It never took this long before. What if it doesn't come?* But he knew the answer. *Fifteen years in prison.*

And still nothing happened—at least not where they were.

Agent Lott played his weekly virtual poker game with four of his friends when he got the comm. "Sorry, guys. Gotta take this. My oMe2'll be happy to take your money."

"Yeah, very funny, butthead."

He found himself back in his living room. First he checked Charlie in jail, then he commed Mortensen.

"Hey, Morty, we got an alert."

"What is it?"

"Looks like your old buddy Charlie Noble is pulling down a data storm. Gotta go to work."

"Aw, please don't tell me that. The wife's in the mood for a change. She's been walking around in her underwear all night. I'm gonna get laid."

"Whoa. More than I need to know. Sorry, but we got work to do."

"Shit! Can't we just VR into his cell and see what's going on?"

"Already did. Practically flew the Skeet up his nose. He's there." He flashed Mortensen the vid.

"Yeah, looks like the asshole all right. Guess I'll be jerking it in the bathroom tonight."

"Ow! I'm gonna have trouble getting that picture outta my head. C'mon, let's move it."

Mortensen shrugged on his coat and pretended to listen while his wife whined. In the car he reconnected with Lott and they continued working.

Lott pointed. "I got an IP address."

"And?"

"It's a fictitious address in Duluth, Minnesota. Doesn't make any sense."

"Nothing with this guy makes any sense. Can't we just accidentally shoot him or something?"

"Cute. Ya know, the last time you talked like that, it made me look like a fool on the witness stand. Let's just do our jobs, OK?" Lott sent out a data sniffer.

A shiver rolled over Charlie. "We're being watched."

Lucas said, "Who is it?"

"I was hoping you could tell me. Here's what I got." Charlie flicked him the info.

"That's your friends from the oBI."

"Great. Can you throw 'em off?"

"If I change an IP address now, your monster might not be able to find us."

Charlie blinked. "Anne, can you do something with the ICANN address?"

"Yeah, but the oBI guys won't get an update."

Lucas said, "I can take care of that. I'll send a counterfeit message from ICANN. Something like; 'There's been an error. We have an update to your request.'"

"Perfect. But Anne, can you use a Real address this time? I'll bet they know the last one was fake. It'll probably slow them down if they have to check a physical location."

"Sure, but somebody's not going to be happy answering the door to the oBI at 9:00 at night."

"Find somebody in an earlier time zone." He waited until they made eye contact. "Make the switch!"

Lott read the message. "Ah, see? There was some kind of stush over at ICANN. Here's the right address."

"Let's pay them a visit."

"Um… My oMe2 is tied up."

"Tied up? What, you got something kinky goin'?"

"No," Lott said sheepishly. "Playing poker with the boys."

Mortensen rolled his eyes. "Well, reintegrate, asshole. If I can't stay home with the wife and munch the fuzz, you're not playing poker."

"Munch the fuzz? That's a new one." Lott shook his head and commed his buddies. "Sorry, guys. Gotta take my double back."

"No problem, big guy. Good luck and all that."

As he folded, Lott noticed over a thousand credits on the table. He held a straight flush. "Oh, you guys are *so* accommodating."

"Anything for a friend. See you next week." They smiled him off.

Seconds later the agent's oMe2s arrived on the front porch of Fred and Bea Neumann's house in Great Falls, Montana.

"Ding dong."

CHAPTER 89

Milo hunched over his IS drawing in the data. Everyone stayed alert.

And nothing happened.

Charlie ordered some Skeets to observe the agents' progress in Montana. The Neumanns let the agents check all the computer units in the house and in themselves. The couple had followed the trial and recognized agent Lott and seemed to trust him.

Charlie wanted to get up and pace, but he didn't dare leave his chair. He commed to the team, "This isn't right. The Octopus should have been here by now. We can only play these agents for so long."

Lucas said, "Don't get ahead of yourself, Charlie. Anne and I can keep throwing them bones. When they'll realize there ain't any meat on 'em, they'll give up and go home."

"Or come to CCD."

"Maybe. But we're not there yet."

They saw the agents come out of the house. Mortensen said, "What'd I tell you. He's still fucking with us. Let's go roust him out of his jail cell."

Charlie began to worry about Dex. *What'll happen to him if they figure out he's not me? One thing's for sure; no matter what they ask him, he's going to lie.* Charlie smiled and scanned the square for the first sign of a tentacle.

The clock ticked.

And nothing happened.

C'mon!

Motoring toward the Federal Building Lott said, "I'm still five minutes out. Let's go directly to Charlie's cell."

"OK. I'm gonna run this new trace they taught me at the academy. Instead of following the data, I'll insert a line of code in the request and ride the data back to him."

"Can't do much else for the next five minutes, anyway."

Mortensen sent the command.

"Wo-hoo!" shouted Lucas. "They musta hired some 'o my hacker brothers to teach those academy boys. Mortensen's trying to surf the data. Watch this."

He flicked up an image of a kid wearing Mortensen's face dressed in red flannel pajamas with a button-down trap door in the back. The kid slid down the banister next to a staircase. As he got near the bottom, Lucas made a sweeping motion with his finger, which divided the railing into a y-shape, like a side rail on a train track. Mortensen went sailing off in the wrong direction, up and away as the railing changed into a roller coaster. Lucas made him scream, "Mommie!"

"Bye, by— Woah! What the fuck is that?" Lucas pointed down one of the alleys as a black, sucker-lined tentacle snaked its way toward Milo.

Charlie said, "That's it! That's what we've been waiting for!"

Agent Lott was trying not to smile as Mortensen's VR roller coaster car came to a halt. "Hey, that was fun, Morty. Maybe you can teach me how to data surf."

"Yeah, I'll teach you how to go fuck yourself."

Lott covered his mouth to hide the smile. "Don't get sore. At least you tried. OK, I'm pulling up in front now."

"I still got thirty seconds. Wait for me."

They went through security and up in the elevator to the fourth floor jail. A guard took them back to Charlie's cell and let them in.

Charlie was lying on the bed. He closed his cube, swung around and put his feet on the floor. Looking up into their faces he smiled. "Hello, gentlemen."

CHAPTER 90

In the data square, more tentacles appeared and twitched their way down the spaces between buildings toward Milo's back.

Charlie whispered, "OK, Milo, use IGotYour6. Whenever one of the arms gets near you, swat at it like a fly and move a little further away."

The eight black arms snaked into the square until they were at their limit. The far end of each of them lifted until the head joining them lurched over the top of a building directly opposite Milo's back.

Jeff shivered, and Charlie watched the fear spread across his face. "What's the problem?"

"I hate octopuses. I thought it just as an analogy."

"It is. It's a computer program."

"I gotta get outta here." Jeff turned and ran.

Charlie grabbed his arm. "Here, let me show you something." He reached over and turned Jeff's fear knob.

Jeff's mouth fell open and his face relaxed. "What the hell is *that*?"

"It's the control for fear. Here're the ones for shame, anxiety and guilt. But I don't have time now."

Jeff plopped down and turned the knobs.

The Black Octopus slithered into the square, closing in on Milo. He kept swatting and dodging the arms until he was surrounded.

Charlie whispered, "Milo, when I say 'now,' leap straight up. When you come down, grab arm number one. The rest of you grab the arm you've been assigned." He checked Jeff who looked totally zoned out. "I'll take Jeff's place."

The tentacles writhed slowly. When they got within an inch of Milo, Charlie shouted, "Now!" and leapt on arm number eight. The others pounced and the creature screamed, thrashed and bucked, trying to throw them off. It was no match for the N-hanced team.

After a moment it came to a halt. Charlie flicked and it reverted to a data module.

"Ye-haw!" The testers leapt into the air slapping each other's hands.

Charlie waved them down. "Wait, wait! That was too easy. Lucas, can you open it and tell me what it is?"

"Sure. But now that I see it up close now, it doesn't look like much."

"What do you mean?"

"It's some old tech."

"Meaning what?"

"Well, let me get inside to see if I can tell you."

He opened a toolkit and hacked at the crystal ebony surface.

Charlie/Dexter stood and offered his hand to agent Lott. "To what do I owe the pleasure?"

Mortensen's lips tightened. "Don't get smart—"

Lott put a hand on his partner's arm "Looks as if somebody's using your T ID to access the N-hanced server. You know about that?"

"Nope. Sorry." His eye twitched a half wink.

"How about those friends of yours? The ones who came to court?"

"Naw. That's not their stush. One of 'em's a purged professor at MSU and the other three are students."

"Yeah, we know that."

Mortensen frowned. "Let me talk to him my way."

Lott opened a PC. "Look at your oLD." He pointed to a white sphere bobbling in the green truth zone. "Its' not like he can fake us out with N-hanced."

"All right. Fucking waste of time. Let's get outta here."

Lott closed the comm and turned back to Charlie. "Thanks for your time, Mr. Noble. Good luck in court tomorrow." He put out his hand.

Charlie shook it. "Thanks. I'm feeling pretty lucky."

Withdrawing his hand, Lott took another look at his oLD. *Maybe he's delusional.*

Lott motioned for the guard who let them out.

"Let's go up to the office and see if we can get a better picture on the power cubes."

Lucas twisted the tool into an indentation in the gleaming, black surface. The module popped open like two halves of a Russian doll. He poked his finger around at what appeared to be clockworks and shook his head. "Look at this." He splayed his fingers, zooming in on a micro label on the inside of the shell. It said, *Property of oBI.*

"Those sons of bitches!" Charlie spit it out. "But why would the oBI be killing my testers?"

"They're not. Or at least this thing isn't. It's a tracking device. No killer code in it."

"You sure?"

"Positive."

"You mean I've been running for my life from nothing? Shhhhit!" Charlie spun around in a circle and stomped his foot. "It's my own damn fault. Since it wasn't supposed to be in the system, I assumed it was the killer. I VR-ed the damn thing into a monster." His shoulders slumped. "Now what? I don't know what else to do." He glanced over at Jeff, who was completely withdrawn. When he noticed all eyes on him, he wondered, *Are they accusing me?* His faced burned with embarrassment. Quickly dialing it down, his eyes searched the ground for an answer, but all his mind seemed to do was throw accusations back at him. *So, you got these great people to risk their lives, and you didn't even do your homework. Dexter may be in legal trouble. And you got zilch to defend yourself against Baxter's betrayal. Nice going.*

He felt like crawling into a hole. Visions of his lies to Rob raced in front of his eyes, and how he'd tricked Jeff into helping him. He imagined huge amount of investor money butterflying away, and felt the weight of everyone's faith in him. And the deaths. Those deaths again. *They trusted me, and I let them down. All of it for nothing. Nothing but some crazy dream. Next stop; prison. I'll make one hell of a cellmate. Jesus! I hadn't even thought about that.* A series of violent images starring him as the screaming victim scrolled across his imagination. They made him catch his breath and lunge for his control wheels.

As he calmed down, he looked up and scanned the faces of his crew. "I'm sorry I dragged all of you out here tonight for nothing. I guess I got it all wrong, so you might as well—"

An air raid siren blasted from the building tops. Everyone winced and half the crew covered their ears. Charlie jumped and flicked off the noise.

One of the guys pulled his fingers out of his ears. "What the hell was that?"

"The pixel's been flipped!"

"The what?"

"The hole in the security layer where the killer code came in." He flicked them the image of the darkened pixel on the module. "This is the *real* thing. Any of you remembering any dreams?"

"No."

"Alert your spotters." Charlie paused until he got confirmation from everyone. "We're gonna chase down that pixel-flipping son of a bitch."

They followed Charlie to the entry point. The command had arrived in packets that reassembled at the server.

Lucas nodded. "We'll split up and follow the packets back to their source." He pointed each team member to their route.

Charlie flicked. "Let's go get him!"

They flew like falcons on fire.

CHAPTER 91

Lott flicked the gear awake. They needed to work in the office to avoid Wi-Fi interception. The data came up in their cubes. "Somebody pretending to be Charlie just dismantled our octo-locator."

"That thing's a piece of crap, anyway."

"Yeah, well— Whoa! Look at that!" Lott pointed at the map.

"Son of a bitch! Now there's eight of him. What're we supposed to do now?"

"Let's pick a couple and chase them. Maybe it'll give us a clue."

"This is bullshit. I could be home getting laid."

"Look, you want a nine-to-fiver, you picked the wrong job. Quit your bellyaching and let's get goin'."

Mortensen blew out a frustrated, "Fffff."

*   *   *

Even with Charlie's team spread far apart in the virtual datascape, they maintained contact as if they were in the same room. As each of them hit the entrance to a server farm, Lucas had to pierce the security layers and open the virtual door. The whole operation bottlenecked as they waited on him.

Charlie turned to Lucas, "You need more CPUs. While each of them waits on you, why not use their free cycles?"

That changed everything. The team rocketed across vast datascapes of glistening corporate skyscrapers and modest personal information houses. The process was like Milo's Hopi Indian tribe tracking an animal across terrain where there seemed to be no trail: looking for a streak of dust on the top of a rock, a strand of hair pulled from a pelt, or a wild scent left hanging in the breeze. On the Net it was a molecule of ozone or the temperature change left by the passing of electrons. Just enough to tell where the signal came from.

But they weren't the only ones tracking.

*   *   *

Watching their software creep along, agent Lott made conversation. "You know, this job isn't like the old days. Now it's all morphing faces and forged T IDs."

"Big deal. Back in your day the crooks burned off their fingerprints with acid and forged driver's licenses. Same story, different day."

"I guess you're right."

Lott tightened his lips as their program tracked first one then another of the people identified as Charlie Noble away from the CCD offices up to a firewall. Once each Charlie went through, their own software ran a password blast. It was painfully slow going.

Mortensen said, "Man, this is driving me nuts. I wish we could use N-hanced. Those eight Charlies are kicking our ass."

Lott rubbed his chin. "Using N-hanced—that's not such a bad idea."

"I'm kidding. You heard 'em in court. They've got security up the wazoo."

"I don't know." Lott shrugged. "If somebody else broke in, maybe we can, too."

"That HackerMeister guy said it could take hours—and that for a pro."

"Or maybe we can find a wire to pull."

Mortensen scoffed. "Yeah. So, uh, which wire you gonna pull?" Then his expression turned serious. "Or maybe *we* can get HackerMeister."

Lott smiled. "Dream on, my friend. Dream on."

"Why not? The guy's for hire."

"Well, first off, I don't think we can get clearance to spend that kind of money. Second, nobody knows how to reach the guy. And third, he's probably part of the group right there in our IS cube."

"I'll bet he is."

Agent Lott's face blanked to deep-thought mode.

"What you thinking, Lott?"

"Listen, you're an adventurous guy, right?"

Mortensen looked skeptical. "*Now* what you getting me into?"

"Well, I was thinking about that surfing trick of yours."

"Yeah?"

"Last time you tried to follow the data to him. What if you turned it around to follow their wake back to N-hanced?"

"What makes you think they wouldn't send me flying again?"

"He was trying to keep you from chasing him. This time you'll be moving away from him. Just a hunch. What do you think?"

"Well, I'm tired of sitting on my ass. Sign me up!"

N-hanced rebuffed Mortensen's first attempt with a curt <Access denied>.

He made a few changes to the code so it wouldn't look like the same hack. Scrunching his face in anticipation of being slapped down again, Mortensen sent the new line on its way.

Their space went black. Mortensen hissed and turned to look at Lott, but he couldn't see him. "What the hell?"

"Hey, what's going on?"

"I can't see."

"I know. My interface is black, too."

Mortensen flicked to Real. "No. Not just my IS, everything is black. Jesus Christ! I'm blind!"

CHAPTER 92

Something brought Charlie's team to a fast halt. The packets ended in a series of unrelated machines in different parts of the world instead of at a single source.

Charlie said, "What's going on?"

Lucas shook his head. "We just hit what's known as a brick wall, my friend. It's a bit thicker than a firewall."

"So what do we do?" Charlie's voice was frantic.

Lucas opened a PC to Charlie. "Don't go psycho on me. You got HackerMeister on your side. Each of the packets was sent to a separate machine a while back and fired off just minutes ago like a time bomb. I'll check the machine logs and look for similar data arrival times."

"Do it!"

Lucas waved the PC away and took off. He was back in a few seconds. "Got it! And get this; all the packets were sent from the same IP address."

"Who does it belong to?"

Lucas traced the address, "Aw, crap! It's only a router. Whoever this is can spin some serious stush. Gotta respect somebody like that."

"Let's save the hacker awards for another time. Can you get through?"

"Already done. But it's a server farm with a dozen computers on the other side, and each of them is a server with virtual servers on them." Lucas raised a hand. "Don't get all shook up. I'll check the sending logs just like before. Everybody?" He made a scooping motion with his arms and took their cycles. Then he blinked and shook his head. "Jesus, man! I thought N made me sharp before. Light is flowing into my head from everywhere."

"We can see. Now what can you do with it?"

Lucas closed his mouth and turned his attention to the network. Splaying his fingers, he sent Roman-candle-like bursts of databots down the lines to read hundreds of logs. It only took a few seconds. "Got it!"

"Good! What is it?"

"Well, it's a set of logs with matching times. But the IP addresses they came from don't match up."

"Which means—?"

"It probably means each of those packets was sent from a different machine. It's just another layer to deal with. Brilliant!"

"Jeez. So, now wha—"

Matthew shouted, "Something's wrong with Jeff!"

Charlie flicked the feed from the exercise room into view, but the room was empty. "Where are you guys?"

"We're at the pool, and Jeff's under water."

"What the hell is he doing there? I told you to watch him." He checked Jeff's data stream. It ended the same way the dead testers' had. *Why didn't I get a notice?* A white-hot rush of fear surged through Charlie. He played the data stream in fast reverse until it showed activity. There was Jeff dreaming about breathing under water. "Jesus! The sons of bitches got him!" Charlie leapt out of the chair and ran down the hall.

Someone said, "What? Got who?"

Realizing he wasn't sharing with the others, Charlie flicked the images to them. "You gotta take it from here. I'm going after Jeff."

Anne chased after him. "Hey, I'm coming, too!"

Charlie kept running and spoke into her head. "No, no! Stay there. They'll need you to do the research."

"I can research from anywhere."

His voice cracked with irritation. "All right. C'mon!"

Lucas said, "Hey, hey, who's gonna coordinate this?"

"I don't care! I'm not letting one more person die because of N!" *Because of me.*

"At least give me your oMe2."

Without a backward glance Charlie tossed it over his shoulder.

Lucas grinned at Charlie2. "Glad you could join us." And to Charlie, "Go get 'im, Buddy."

Charlie focused his attention on Matthew. "What the hell are you waiting for? Get him out of the water!"

"I can't swim."

"Jesus!"

As Charlie raced, he felt a thud of guilt. *This is all my fault. I forgot to check on him.* "Matthew, there's a long pole in there somewhere. Get it and try to pull him out."

"I can't. It's on the bottom of the pool."

Great! Thanks, agent Dirty Harry. "What were you thinking? I told you to make sure he stayed safe."

"I'm sorry, Lord. All he did was get up and walk. It seemed safe enough. I thought he was going swimming. I called you as soon as I thought something was wrong."

Shit!

Charlie bashed the door to the exercise room so hard it bounced back and slammed into his shoulder. "Oww! Shit!" He pushed it again and scanned the room. Zigzagging between the rows of weights and pulleyed equipment, he charged through the door to the pool. Jeff lay motionless on the bottom.

Charlie dove in. He grabbed Jeff's jacket and yanking him upward. Jeff was much heavier than Charlie imagined. *Dead weight* was all he could think. Getting Jeff to the surface, Charlie flailed desperately with one arm and both legs, gulping water, struggling to reach the side while keeping Jeff's head above the surface. Anne knelt, waiting to help. Matthew stayed back, clearly terrified of the water.

Charlie coughed and gasped. "He's not breathing! He's not breathing!"

Anne beckoned. "That's OK. We'll respirate him. Here, let me help."

Charlie lifted Jeff with such force his own head went under. He came up choking.

CHAPTER 93

Lucas reached the next layer of computers, but some were no longer available, and most were on the move—probably located inside people. "I've got the logs, but the entries look like bogus IP addresses. I think we've reached the end of the line, fellas."

Milo shook his head. "If a machine ran a backup before the log change, it might still show the original IP address."

"Kind of a long shot, but—" Lucas swallowed all their computer cycles and compared each log to its backup. "Nope. Nothing—wait! I only checked the primary backups. Almost everybody runs secondaries offsite." He eyed the backup schedule on each machine. "Got one! This guy backs up his T every five minutes. Kinda obsessive, but exactly what we need. Let's find him and hope it came through before the fake log entry."

*   *   *

Anne got hold of Jeff's shoulders and together they hauled him out onto the tile. Charlie lifted himself out and felt the sides of Jeff's throat. "No pulse. God! Don't tell me I killed him, too." His face wrestled a desperate grimace.

Anne shook Charlie's shoulder. "Hey, don't lose your shit on me now. Let's see if we can get his heart going and make him breathe." She skittered around, straddled Jeff's stomach and began chest compressions.

Matthew kneeled near the wall as far away from the water as possible. He prayed and watched their rescue attempts, then prayed some more.

Charlie recovered a little. "Should I give him mouth-to-mouth?"

Anne smiled. "You really are freaked out, aren't you? I'd slap you out of it, but I'm a little busy. Why don't you dial it down and consult your expert system?"

That did it. Charlie lifted Jeff's chin. There was a slight click as the airway opened. Charlie heard a soft "Huh" each time Anne compressed his chest. "OK, pause while I breathe for him." He pinched Jeff's nose and exhaled into his mouth, but he couldn't see his chest move. Then he realized he could watch through Anne's eyes. He breathed a second time and saw Jeff's chest rise and fall. Anne resumed the compressions.

After a minute Charlie felt for a pulse. All he could feel was a faint beat whenever Anne pressed. "C'mon, Buddy. Don't die on me."

*   *   *

Lucas ran an ICANN search using what he'd learned from Anne. "OK, I got the guy's info. Now let's see if I can find him." He checked the IP address. "Looks like he's offline. Let me try something else." The others watched as he scrolled a list of text.

"Now this is interesting. Looks like he's at a convention in Miami. And he's not hanging out at the hotel bar like he should be. The GPS before he went offline was at The House Uv Many Pleasures. They call it HUMP. Wanna guess what he's doing there?"

A few lecherous chuckles sounded.

"I wonder what his wife would think— OK, we got better things to do."

Milo grinned. "Do we?"

Charlie2 said, "Keep moving, please. I don't know how much more time we have."

"Let's see— Ah! I can get into the HUMP server and Wi-Fi directly into the guy." The rest of the crew found themselves looking through the eyes of Nathan Magnus, as three naked, twenty-something Asian women worked him over with peacock feathers. "OK. Well, that's enough of that. Um, where's the log?"

Milo stared. "Can't we watch while you look for the log?"

"No, you sick fuck," Lucas laughed. "Ah! Here's the log. And we have an IP address from the backup log, which is indeed different from the counterfeit. I think we're closing in on the bastards."

*   *   *

Charlie and Anne had been working on Jeff for three minutes, and it was five minutes since he'd lost consciousness.

Anne frowned. "I don't know, Charlie. Maybe we're too late."

"Don't say that! Jesus, he can't die! He can't! Keep up the chest compressions." Charlie's mind raced. "What we really need is a Heart Starter." Then he heard Linda's voice. "Use his T."

Charlie froze. "Did you hear that?"

Anne glanced at him. "Hear what?"

339

"Linda said, 'Use his T.'"

"Who's Linda?"

"Somebody who used to work for me. She's part of N."

"That's kind of— Wait! Use his T? You think she means as a Heart Starter?"

That was all Charlie needed. N showed him a diagram of how he could harness the T in and around Jeff's heart to imitate a signal from the brain. "I think I got it."

"Has it ever been done before?"

"Never. But N says it'll work."

"Do I need to move so I don't get zapped?"

"No. It's not like defib. Here, look for yourself." He flicked her the image. "Let me at his chest." Charlie put his hands over Jeff's heart and transferred the program to Jeff's T. He left his hands there and felt the first heartbeat. "Thump-ump." He gasped and waited as N showed him an EKG. It lay flat.

"It didn't take."

Janice said, "Can you up the voltage?"

"Right!" Charlie sent a stronger signal.

"Thump-ump!"

Charlie starred at the readout. "Shit. Nothing."

"If his brain isn't online, there's nothing to keep the beat going. Maybe you need—"

"Look!" Charlie pointed at the graph. "It repeated on its own. It's weak but it's there. You did it! You saved him!"

Anne leaned back and rolled her head and rubbed a shoulder. "Well, we both had something to do with it—and Linda."

Matthew stopped praying, but he still looked worried.

Jeff jerked and they all jumped. He coughed and blew a fountain of water onto Charlie. Then he drew in a rasping gasp and opened his eyes.

Charlie stared. "You OK?"

"Uhhh—" Jeff's eyes focused. "OK? You kiddin' me? I got a woman straddling my crotch and my best friend's been French kissing me. That's the most action I've had in years."

Charlie looked wide-eyed at Anne. "He's OK."

She nodded. "I can see that."

Matthew looked Heavenward and mouthed, "Thank you, Lord."

Charlie said, "I wasn't French kissing you, you shit."

"Call it what you want, it was my pleasure."

"Jesus, I thought we'd lost you." Charlie sighed. Then he remembered Matthew. "Don't go telling anybody I raised the dead, goddamn it. And you know for sure I don't walk on water. "

Matthew nodded his head, his eyes still wide.

Anne climbed off and Jeff started to get up, but faltered.

"Whoa," Charlie put out a hand. "Maybe you should rest a bit. Your heart was stopped for a few minutes."

"Yeah, I do feel a little weak. But that T shit'll fix me up, right? Hey! What happened with the rest of the team?"

Charlie couldn't answer.

CHAPTER 94

Charlie, Jeff and Anne rejoined the others. They found themselves in a dark, wood-paneled library somewhere in the VR universe.

Lucas said, "Glad to see you're OK, Jeff."

Jeff ignored the comment. "What'd you find out?"

"Something very interesting." Lucas turned to Charlie. "I'd like to introduce you to Christopher."

"Oh, Mr. Noble and I have already met. How are you?" The attractive blond man was dressed in a three-piece tweed suit, a high-collar white shirt open at the neck with an ascot. He got up from an overstuffed antique chair, holding a brandy snifter of a transparent brown liquid.

Charlie's mouth gaped. Christopher was the Ken Doll.

His eyes on Christopher, Lucas spoke to the team without going PC. "I think he's a projection. But I'm not sure what's beyond that. Could be the Wizard of Oz for all I know. Can you tell us, Chris?"

"I believe I'm the first successful sentient computer. Previous attempts seemed human according to your Turing Tests, but I actually think on my own. At least I think I do. But *thinking* and *being* are concepts you humans have been philosophizing about for much longer than I. When not working, I amuse myself by painting, reading and writing music. But where are my manners?" He waved a hand and a set of chairs appeared. "Please, have a seat."

The team started, but Charlie said, "I believe I'll stand," which sent everyone shuffling back into place.

"Have it your way." Christopher moved around to stand behind his wing-back chair.

Charlie's eyes narrowed. "And what exactly is your work?"

"My only assignment so far had been to stop development of N-hanced. After a couple of failed attempts, I made it seem deadly so the NewsDogs would eat it up. When one of your users remembered a dream, I studied his physical surroundings. If the setting was dangerous, I made him believe the dream. So far I've succeeded three times and failed once—with you, Jeff. It's been thrilling!" He lifted up on his toes with excitement.

Charlie wanted to choke him but he controlled his voice. "I thought robots weren't supposed to harm humans."

"First of all, I'm not a robot. Second, you're talking about Isaac Asimov's Three Laws of Robotics. He only created them for his 1942 story *Runaround* in order to break them in interesting ways. And third—" He lifted his eyebrows in amused defiance. "—Isaac is not the boss of me."

"I see. And can you tell us who is?"

With a perfect imitation of the Hal computer from *2001: A Space Odyssey* Christopher said, "I can't do that, Dave." His a wry smile lit his face.

Charlie forced himself to smile back. "Excellent impression. But really, we would like to know."

"I'm sure you would. But I don't know his name. I erased it."

That sounds familiar! Charlie forced disappointment into his voice. "Ohhhh."

"But I do have a vid you might be interested in."

The team members looked at each other.

Charlie enthused. "Yes, we would be interested."

The vid was dated Tuesday, October 2, 2034 and recorded in Christopher's library.

"Your job is to slow down the N-hanced project."

"I can do that. How slow?"

"Just stop it for now. But I need to be clear about something here. I don't want to know anything about what you're doing. From this point on, you're on your own. Can I trust you to handle it?"

"Absolutely! I've already penetrated—"

"Please! I don't want to know what you've done or what you'll be doing. My group and I need plausible deniability should anything go wrong."

"I understand. And, sir, you can count on me. I'm the absolute best there is."

"I know, Christopher, I know. Now, you're not to contact any of us for any reason after you and I are done here today. Is that clear?"

"Absolutely, In fact, I just erased your name and number, and in a second there will be no trace of your contact information anywhere in my memory."

"Good. All right then. I guess this is goodbye."

"I'm sorry. I seem to have had a lapse of memory. To whom was I speaking? Hello? Hello?"

"Very good, Christopher."

"I can't hear you. There must be something stushy with our comm. Maybe if you comm back we'll have a better connection. I'm signing off now."

The last image in the vid was the man nodding with a slight smile as he flickered and faded.

There was no question who Christopher was talking to. It was Jim Higgins, Charlie's biggest investor and supporter on the board of CCD.

Everyone looked stunned. Christopher said, "So, did you find that helpful?"

Charlie's mind raced so fast he had to shake his head before he could answer. "Unbelievably helpful. Thank you so much for showing it to us."

Christopher seemed pleased at the praise.

Lucas said, "Why didn't you erase the vid?"

"The man didn't ask me to."

Charlie and Lucas looked at each other.

Charlie paused. *If Christopher is sentient, living this way has probably been something like solitary confinement.* "Have you had any other contact with humans since you spoke with— what do you call him?"

"My creator."

"Yes, your creator?"

"No. But I'm enjoying this conversation immensely. I don't think it's good for me to be alone for so long."

Charlie opened a PC to Anton. "Is it just me, or does he seem emotionally immature?"

"He hasn't had any life experience. He's probably effectively a child. But he sounds eager to please."

"I've got an idea." Charlie closed the comm.

"Christopher, can I ask you a favor?"

"Certainly."

"Could you stop causing these accidents with people who are using N-hanced?"

"Why? Don't you think what I did was clever?"

"Oh, it was *more* than clever. It was brilliant."

Christopher beamed.

"But it's caused me a lot of distress."

"Distress. I know that word. It's a noun. It means great pain, anxiety or sorrow. Is that— like being lonely?"

Charlie had to think for a second. "It's— certainly in the same category."

"Oh. I'm sorry I made you feel like that. Yes. I'll stop." Christopher's face creased with what looked like worry.

Charlie felt a twinge of compassion, but trounced it. "Good. And for future reference, people don't like to be killed."

"That's not always true. Besides, I made sure your friends were happy. They were living their dream."

Jeez. "Yes, but their family and friends—the ones who are left behind—are— lonely."

Christopher's face clouded over again. "I— see."

Another idea came to Charlie. "But your hacking skills are exceptional. I'd like to include your knowledge in our database." He looked at Lucas who nodded his approval.

"How flattering. Let me think about that."

"Sure. But can you give me a copy of the vid and the code you used to kill my friends?"

"Of course. Here." Christopher flicked him the data with a flourish.

"Thank you. Say, when we first met, at Beggar's Banquet?"

"Yes?"

"How did you do that?"

"Simple. I took control of castoff nano in the area and networked them together to form an avatar of my favorite human. There are trillions of nanos everywhere, and a teaspoonful has the surface area of a football field. I think of it as animated matter, you know, like humans."

Whoa. That's exactly *what humans are.*

"As soon as my Ken Doll left you, I erased the programming and he disappeared into the floor. I did the same thing outside the Federal Building. I hoped that second threat would stop you, but you're not afraid of anything."

"Ah! Of course!" *Not afraid? If you only knew.*

"I've been thinking about creating a more detailed avatar complete with human senses as an extension of myself, so I can feel what you people feel. Then I could move around freely in the Real world."

There's a scary thought.

"And I did the Black Octopus, too."

Charlie gave a sideways glance to his team. "Uh, that was the oBI."

"Oh, it's their program, all right. But that little thing couldn't penetrate your security. I did that, and then I used it as a decoy to keep you distracted while I did my other work." Christopher's eyes twinkled.

Oh, my God. Charlie noticed his mouth had fallen open. He closed it.

"You're so smart. Every time I thought I had you beat, you came up with something new. It was such a challenge playing with you. I felt alive. Can we play again?"

Charlie blinked and spoke with stunned sluggishness. "Soon. Very soon." Then he straightened and snapped his fingers. "Oh! One more thing. You said you had a couple of failed attempts. I noticed the vid of you and your creator was dated October 2, 2034. Did you have anything to do with Linda Sullivan's death on October 3rd?"

"Yes. I went to her as my Ken Doll to explain that I wanted her to sabotage the project. She panicked and wouldn't stop screaming, so I covered her mouth while I talked. By the time I finished, she'd stopped breathing. I decided to make it look like an animal killed her, so I formed my hand into a claw. After that I devised the dream switch."

Charlie was furious, but he didn't dare let it show. *Bastard! I want this guy in solitary for eternity. See what lonely is really like.* He fought to keep his voice cheerful. "Well, I'm sorry to tell you this, Christopher, but we have to go now."

"Wait! Will you come and visit me again soon?"

Charlie threw a weighty glance at his team. "I'm sure someone will be coming to see you very soon. Probably later today."

"Wonderful! Oh, I have so much to do. Goodbye, then."

"Goodbye, Christopher." The Ken Doll faded away.

Charlie scowled. "We've got work to do, gang."

CHAPTER 95

Lott and Mortensen spent a panicked ten minutes and multiple T reboots trying to get their vision back. Gradually the flicker of a candle flame appeared in the upper left of their field of view, then below that some words. "Confucius say, 'The hardest thing of all is to find a black cat in a dark room, especially if there is no cat.'"

They both waved wildly in their IS cubes, trying to regain full control of their sight.

The text faded and was replaced with, "Confucius say, 'Don't fuck with HackerMeister.'" Their vision returned to normal. A woman's voice played in their heads. "Thank you for flying HackerMeister airlines. We hope you choose us in the future. If you enjoyed your trip be sure to tell your friends you flew HackerMeister. If not, tell them you flew Orchard."

Lott wiped the sweat from his forehead. "Shhhhit!"

"You know, Tom, you're not much of a talker. But when you finally say something, you nail it."

Lott steamed, but kept quiet.

"So, Lott, as much fun as this has been—and it's been a ton—there's one sure way we can put pressure on whoever the hell is running their project."

"I'm listening."

"Let's go down to the CCD offices and kick some ass."

Lott slammed his palm down on the table. "Hell yes! We shoulda done that a half hour ago."

"If everybody's working remotely, we'll shut down the server and see who screams bloody murder."

"What are we standing here for? Let's go!"

* * *

Charlie frowned. "I don't think that vid is going to be enough for the judge. Is there any way we can prove a link between Jim and Christopher?"

"Sure. We've finally got his IP address. Let me check ICANN." Lucas brought it up in his cube. After a moment he said, "This doesn't look right. The domain assignment says it belongs to Corporation Management Systems. The docs look phony. I think it's a sham. Anne, you wanna take this one?"

"My pleasure."

Lucas swooped her into the driver's seat and passed her the free cycles.

Her eyebrows flew up. "Whoa!" She blinked hard at the overpowering brilliance of the combined minds then got down to work. In a minute she said, "Got it! It goes through six layers of corporate shells and comes back to Global Industrial Coalition." Her expression went from pleased to pitiful. "Oh— Charlie."

"What? What is it?"

"Uh— You're not gonna like this."

"Come on. Flick it to me."

She gave Charlie a pained look. "It's a consortium of your investors headed up by Jim Higgins." She flicked him the documents.

Charlie devoured them. "What? Every last investor is on the list." He fell back into his chair. "Now that I can prove my innocence, I'll lose my funding. All that work and I'm still screwed." His head and shoulders slumped.

Anne put her hand on his arm. "I'm so sorry, Charlie."

"Why the hell would they do that? Why spend fifty billion only to sabotage the project?"

Lucas was the first to notice the alarm. "Can't tell you, man, but you gotta get your ass out of there. Your buddies from the oBI are closing in."

Charlie swung around to look. Sure enough, they were heading in a beeline toward CCD. ETA, four minutes, thirty-seven seconds—thirty-six, thirty-five...

"OK everybody. I can't thank you enough. Once we get the rest of this ironed out, if you still want to be testers, you'll be first in line. So—"

Lucas cut him off. "Do your speechifying later. Right now, you gotta move!"

Charlie disconnected and found himself back on the side of the pool with Anne, Jeff and Matthew. "Can you walk, Jeff?"

Jeff got up and took a few tentative steps. "Guess so."

"OK. Let's go."

Charlie stayed next to Jeff to make sure he was steady. He wasn't. He stumbled and Charlie caught him. With only three minutes left, he threw Jeff's arm over his shoulder. "Matthew, give me a hand."

Matthew came around to the other side, and they shuffled along with Anne following.

Charlie summoned an oCar, then called for three more. He broke into the city Skeet system and diverted all units in the immediate vicinity away from CCD. They stepped out the front door with two minutes to go.

The snow fell more heavily than when they'd come in. "Jesus! Nothing like being wet and cold."

The first oCar skidded to the curb and Charlie stopped Matthew. "Listen, Buddy, I want you to take one of the other cars." He shivered violently. "G-go a block in one direction, and tell the car to change routes a couple times. Then head on home. If we're lucky, the agents'll follow you."

Matthew nodded, then frowned. "What if they stop me?"

"Tell them you lost track of me and were d-driving around to see if you could f-find me walking nearby."

"Yes, Master." Matthew backed up onto the curb.

"And quit c-calling me that!"

"Yes, uh, Charlie."

Charlie slapped him on the shoulder. "Thanks. Gotta go." He waved the door closed, hacked into the oCMAD database and vanished the vehicle from the grid. His teeth chattered. "The oBI guys are too close. We gotta hide."

He ordered their car to cross the street and park behind the abandoned Consumer's Power building. As the other vehicles arrived, he made them drive over the tracks left by their car and head off in different directions, all the while fearing the agents had software to unscramble tire tracks.

Charlie flicked their car's heat on full blast. "We'll w-wait here until the agents go inside. OK, get ready now. We need to d-disconnect from the server. Brace yourselves." With a twist of the wrist their faces fell slack and white.

Anne dug her fingernails into Charlie's arm. "Uuhhh!"

Jeff said, "I think I'm gonna be sick." And he was. So was Anne.

Fifteen seconds later a Federal oCar pulled up to the front door of CCD.

CHAPTER 96

Agents Lott and Mortensen leapt out of their car and onto the snowy sidewalk in front of the CCD main entrance.

Mortensen pointed at the ground. "Well, see-prise, see-prise. Fresh footprints heading to the curb and away from the building." He surveyed the tire tracks. "Three vehicles stopped here." He paused for a quick flick in his IS cube. "Two look empty and the other's rented to that wacky disciple Matthew. I'm gonna check 'em all out." He fired off a set of Skeets.

"And check this out." Lott gestured at the map. "All the Charlies just disappeared."

"Except the one in jail."

"Of course."

The Skeets and the database reported two of the cars were indeed empty. Mortensen moved his hands in the IS, drawing his fingers apart until they were looking in the window of the occupied vehicle. "Sure looks like Matthew, and the car is weighted for a single occupant, so Charlie isn't with him."

"Unless he assumed Matthew's identity."

Mortensen rolled his eyes and his head. They chased down the car. After ten minutes of 'Our Lord' this and 'my Master' that, Mortensen PCed Lott. "I don't care what expert system Noble's using, this son of a bitch ain't him. Let's get the hell out of here."

As they drove off, Mortensen sighed. "That's it. Mission accomplished. We can go home now."

"Nice try, Morty, but as long as we're here, we should check out CCD. It'll only take a few minutes."

Mortensen pouted.

Pulling to the curb they stepped through the invisible curtain and hustled down the hall to Charlie's office. The door was open.

350

Charlie got up from his captain's chair, a bemused expression on his face. He extended his right hand to Mortensen. "Welcome, gentlemen. I've been expecting you."

Mortensen—eyes steely—ignored the hand.

Lott made the VR camera click. "An oMe2."

Charlie smiled, dropping his hand. "Get you a Coke?"

Mortensen spat a vicious, "Fuck you."

"If you're gonna be that way about it." Charlie snapped his fingers and disappeared in a wisp of gray smoke.

"Great. Can't wait to tell Gloria I spent the evening chasing ghosts."

Lott's face hardened. "Look, you—" He stopped and exhaled through his nose. "Just tell her you were doing your job. Then munch her fuzz and all will be forgiven."

Mortensen nodded and smiled. "Yeah. Yeah. That's exactly what I'll do."

They ambled out.

*   *   *

As soon as the agents went into CCD, Charlie ordered the oCar to the FRIB building where they could hide out until court in the morning. Nano scurried in a blur to clean up the puke.

Anne said, "What the hell was that?"

"You mean the dizziness?"

"Yeah."

"We think it's got something to do with turning the center of balance back over to the body. Same with the headache. We hope once people start using N, they won't want to go back."

"That's one way to make sure they don't. That sucks."

Charlie nodded while holding his head. "I'll work on it— if I ever get another chance."

At the Cyclotron everybody went to their rooms—Charlie with Janice—and right to sleep. It had been a long and intense day.

But Charlie never got it. He tossed and turned, worrying whether he had enough evidence to clear himself.

CHAPTER 97

At 8:40 AM Charlie stomped up the front steps of the Federal Building, face set in an angry mask.

"Hey, it's him!" NewsDogs and disciples shouted questions at him. Skeets jostled for position.

"What are you doing out of jail?"

"What words do you have for us today, Teacher?"

"How did you get away?"

"Can you raise the dead? I'll jump off Zhang Tower."

"Why did you come back?"

"Bless me, Teacher. It'll only take a second. No? OK, just sign an autograph for my girlfriend."

Charlie flicked them off. He hadn't slept and there was something else. The only person he wanted to talk to was Baxter Goodman, and it was going to be explosive.

At the front door, a security officer waited with weapon in hand. He escorted Charlie to the courtroom. Baxter was already at the table.

"Mr. Goodman? I found Mr. Noble at the front door."

"Front door? What the—? OK. Thank you, officer."

The bailiff saw Charlie and reached for her stunner.

Baxter waved her back.

Charlie growled, "We need the conference room."

"We can do a PC right here."

"Fine, but there's going to be a lot of arm waving."

"Do I need a guard?"

"Maybe."

The bailiff popped the button on her holster, but Baxter shook his head and held up a hand. "We'll be OK."

In the conference room, a red-faced Charlie poked a finger at Baxter's chest. "You threw the case!"

"What are you talking about?"

"I'm talking about you throwing the goddamn case. You held back on my defense so Jim and his cohorts could stop N-hanced, for God only knows what reason."

"I did not." Baxter's voice was firm, but soft.

Charlie threw up his hands. "Are you saying you didn't know about Christopher, the computer that killed my testers? You didn't know about that?"

"I have no idea what you're talking about."

Charlie looked away and spat through clenched teeth. "Lying fucking lawyers."

"I'm not lying to you." His hands were in front of him, pleading.

"What about when you pulled Lucas off the stand and told him you had proof he's not who he said he is?"

"I have an intern who went to school with him at MSU."

"Nice dodge." Charlie turned and looked out the window in the door.

"My guy worked at the reception desk on night shift at the FRIB and recognized two men and a woman going in and out of the abandoned Cyclotron. He figured it out when we ran our scan of courtroom attendees."

Charlie pursed his lips and gave Baxter the *liar* look.

"Look, I didn't want this case. I took it as a favor to Jim. But once I heard more about it, I saw a opportunity to change the law. I couldn't pass that up."

"That's a conflict of interest."

"Maybe. But me lose on purpose? That's impossible. I can't *stand* to lose. I know it happens to some lawyers." Baxter grinned. "Every lawyer I've ever been up against."

Charlie stared at him.

"Listen, if Jim had asked me to do that, I would have told him to go fuck himself. I've done it more than once. I'm not losing for anybody." Baxter saw Charlie wasn't convinced. "All you had to do was ask me."

"Why would I ask you if I thought you were lying?"

"You guys *were* acting a little squirrely after Lucas came off the stand."

"So why didn't *you* ask *me*?"

"Uh, we were a little busy, remember? As I recall, you asked me to leave the room."

Charlie continued to glower.

"Hey, point your oLD at me."

"You've got some kind of lie projector that beats it."

"I do not. Scan my T. You'll see."

"An honest lawyer?"

Baxter shrugged. "I wouldn't go that far. But I've been honest with you. And I stay that way as much as I can. It's not so easy in my job."

"Don't tell me this is that old thing they say about 'assume.'"

"What's that?"

"You know, whenever you *assume*, you make an 'ass' out of 'u' and 'me.' Damn!" *Especially when* I've *been the one lying.*

"Are we OK now?"

Charlie gave a resigned nod. "I guess so—" Then as if taking it back, "I don't know."

"All right, then. So what's this about a computer named Christopher?"

"Just turn everything over to me when we get into court. Everybody's in for a big surprise."

"I don't like surprises. Not when it comes to defending my clients."

"When I get done telling my story, you won't have a client. Let's go. It's two minutes 'til."

CHAPTER 98

After court was called to order the judge stared at Charlie. "Well, Mr. Noble, apparently you led the oBI on quite a chase last night. You're making a habit of that."

Charlie nodded. There was no apology in his attitude.

"Is there any reason I shouldn't have my people disable your T and have you attend the rest of these proceedings in handcuffs?"

"Your Honor, I can't deny I've been pushing the limits, but—"

"There's an understatement."

"But I could see my case was headed downhill, and I had to do something besides sit in my jail cell."

"So far I don't like what I'm hearing."

"I understand, and I hope what I have to say will convince you to forgive me, since I believe the courts are all about doing what's right and fair." He shot a sideways glance at Baxter, remembering what he'd said about law and fairness being a coincidence.

"Please take the stand, Mr. Noble."

Charlie was already moving.

"Let me remind you, you're still under oath."

"Yes, Your Honor." He settled in, took a deep breath and let it out. "After I switched places with a friend of mine—which reminds me, can we get him out of there?"

"Let's wait until I hear your story. As of this moment he's an accessory to a prison escape."

Charlie made a pained face. "I went back to the CCD offices and entered the N-hanced server."

"After I specifically ordered you not to use N-hanced?"

"You ordered me not to use it in court. And I'm not N-hanced now."

The judge's face soured. "What I *said* was, 'you will not be allowed to use N-hanced during the course of this trial.' The trial is not over yet." Her lips cut a thin line. For an uncomfortable moment she seemed to consider the significance of taking her words literally.

She was right and Charlie knew it. He found himself holding his breath.

Finally she flicked a finger. "Continue."

"A team of eleven of us linked up to the server. We set a trap for the person tampering with the system. After an intense chase and the near death of my friend Jeff—" Charlie glanced over his shoulder and pointed. "—we found everything had been staged by a supercomputer by the name of Christopher. My friend and world-class researcher, Anne—" He turned toward Janice. She raised a hand and gave the judge a nervous smile. "—plowed through an unbelievable stack of falsified documentation on a series of shell corporations. Christopher is owned by a consortium of company leaders who are all investors in CCD and that Jim Higgins gave him—it—orders. Lucas showed me Christopher is responsible for the killer code that caused the deaths of my testers."

"And you have proof of all this?"

"Absolutely." Charlie nodded at Lucas.

Lucas flicked his hand and all the documents and code transferred to the judge.

"Give me a moment," she said.

There was murmuring in the courtroom. Charlie heard none of it, his pulse pounding in his ears. Sweat rolled from his underarms and his hands felt like ice. He reached for the anxiety dial, then realized it wasn't there. He would have rolled his head around to loosen his neck muscles, but he was afraid he'd miss the second the judge looked up. Instead he sat frozen.

Finally the judge raised her head. "My team verified the authenticity of the documents, including the so-called 'killer code.' We will be launching a full investigation." She paused. "The court is convinced the prosecution has not proven the defendant guilty of criminal negligence, and hereby dismisses all charges against him."

Charlie said, "Yes!" yanking down his fists and elbows in victory. He caught Baxter's eye and sent him a virtual, hearty handshake.

Bedlam erupted across the courtroom, with shouts of "Hallelujah!"

The judge pounded her gavel. "Order! Order! We are not finished here yet."

After the room quieted, she continued. "As I said at the beginning of this trial, Mr. Noble, I am fascinated by N-hanced. I have high hopes for the positive changes it could bring to our court system. That being said, it doesn't mean your security is good enough. This thing you're doing requires extraordinary responsibility. As it says in the Bible, 'Of those to whom much is given, much is expected.'"

Charlie nodded. He thought about turning to look at Matthew but couldn't take his eyes from the judge. Then a vision of Spider-Man flashed across his mind as Peter Parker's Uncle Ben said, "Remember, with great power, comes great responsibility." *So that's where Stan Lee got that.* The corners of his mouth twitched, and he bit the tip of his tongue to keep from laughing. Luckily the judge's gaze shifted to Rob.

"And Mr. Reynolds, I can see you tried to do the right thing each time one of your testers died. But you didn't push back hard enough. You are the conscience of the company. You say you made the final decisions. But you need to make the right decisions, not turn it over to an unproven technology." She waved her finger. "I don't want to see either of you back in here except as visitors."

Rob bobbed his head solemnly.

"Now, Mr. Higgins? Until we get this ironed out, you do not leave the country."

Jim said, "Yes, Your Honor."

"And keep your little friend, Christopher safe. We'll want to talk with him."

Jim nodded.

As the judge picked up the gavel, Charlie raised his hand. "Uh, judge— I mean, Your Honor."

"Yes, Mr. Noble?"

"Permission to speak privately."

She looked irritated but beckoned him.

Charlie leaned in and whispered, "My friend Toby's still sitting in my prison cell."

Her eyes slitted, and her jaw came forward.

"You know, because it would be the right thing to do?"

Her gaze fell to the desktop, seeming to examine the wood grain. She dismissed Charlie with two fingers. In her courtroom voice she said, "In the interest of justice, I proclaim that the person sitting in your jail cell be released."

Charlie looked at Baxter who smiled and shook his head.

"Bailiff, you may unblock Mr. Noble's access to N-hanced."

Turning to the jury she said, "On behalf of myself and this court, I thank you for your service to the oUnited States of America." Facing front and lifting her gavel she said, "Case dismissed," and slammed it down with finality.

A variety of shouts blasted from the gallery—some positive, some negative. Charlie closed his eyes and let out all his breath, his chin falling to his chest. He sprang from the witness stand, turned to the 'Steins and bowed with hands steepled under his chin, mouthing "Thank you." He saluted Jeff, then stretched his arms out and smiled to the alphas. Crossing the courtroom floor to Baxter, Charlie shook his hand for Real. "An honest lawyer. Who woulda thunk it?"

Baxter smiled and patted him on the shoulder. "Congratulations. But you know, you got lucky. She could have given all of you time for the prison break."

"Yeah. I guess I got too desperate."

"I understand. Shoulda taken the temp-insan. 'Cause you were, you know." He smiled. "Oh, and when you get all the stush out of N-hanced, put me on the list of testers. I do not intend to move into the position of number two lawyer in the world."

"How about if you contract with us to for your expertise?"

"And give away all my secrets? I don't think so."

"You'll have access to everybody else's secrets—and I don't just mean legal."

"Hmmm. I'd rather be a subscriber."

"As long as you keep inventing, you'll stay one step ahead."

"Let me think about it."

"Better think fast. Times are a-changin.' Don't miss the boat."

Baxter chuckled. "Got any other clichés you want to throw at me before I head back to Alaska?"

"No. That's it. Thanks. Thanks big time."

"'Sall right. It was a pleasure."

"Hey, I never got to see your big closing."

"Did you go to prison?"

"No—"

"Then I won. Now, go see your friends."

Charlie shook Baxter's hand again, then gave him a hug.

The bailiff said, "You can turn on your N-hanced program at any time. Congratulations. It's been interesting knowing you."

"Thank you." Charlie smiled and nodded at her as he flicked his IS cube into view. When he double-tapped the N icon, streaks of light sprang from the edges of every object in the room. He squinted for a few seconds, then everything became clear—very clear.

He turned to the team. "Lunch at Beggar's. It's on me!"

Jeff said, "It'd better be!"

They headed out of the courtroom.

*   *   *

As they stepped into the hall, Anne held up an index finger. "You might wanna see this." She flicked and a blonde NewsDog appeared in her IS cube.

"In a dramatic turnaround in the case of oUS versus Lester Charles Noble, it was revealed that a consortium of wealthy investors built a sophisticated computer named Christopher to commit a series of murders made to look like suicides. Jim Higgins, leader of the consortium, claims they had no knowledge of Christopher's activities, only that they owned the computer. He said his last contact with Christopher was four months previous to the first death."

Not counting Linda, Charlie thought.

"We go live to Jim Higgins. Jim, what do you have to say about Christopher?"

Charlie pointed down the hall. "Look. He's right there." They all turned to watch in Real.

Jim talked to the cams. "We bought the computer and hired out the programming. I was the only person to have contact with Christopher, and I never told him to kill anyone. I suspect the problem will turn out to be programming stush. Our group will cooperate fully with authorities on their investigation. Our hearts go out to the friends and families of these brave soles and we will not rest until justice is served. Now if you'll excuse me, I have to talk to someone."

The NewsDog came back on. "In other news today—"

Charlie turned away. "What bullshit.

Everybody nodded and Lucas said, "That is one bold muthafucka."

Charlie noticed Jim heading toward them, waving. "Is that son of a bitch waving at us?"

CHAPTER 99

"Hey, Charlie. I need to talk to you."

Charlie's friends quickly formed a line and blocked Jim's path. Lucas lifted his chin. "Not gonna happen, asshole."

Jim craned his neck to look over their shoulders and raised his eyebrows.

Charlie scanned him for weapons and verified his calm body language. Satisfied, he sighed. "It's OK. Let him through."

His friends looked back at Charlie and stepped aside.

"Can we talk in private, Charlie?"

Charlie sniffed. "You've got to know I'm not one of your biggest fans right about now."

"I understand. But it's important. Can we just take a walk?"

Charlie frowned. He looked around and tipped his head toward a fairly quiet hallway to the right. They started walking, Charlie's friends keeping intense watch at a distance.

"First of all I want to apologize. I wanted to say that to you in person, because I'll have to deny everything in my public statements."

"Why, that is so *very* considerate of you," Charlie smirked, "and not very bright, either, because I record everything. If the prosecutor's office subpoenas me, they'll be able to use it in court."

Jim smiled modestly. "You're not recording this."

"Sure, I..." Charlie flicked his vid recorder into view. It said <blocked>. "How—?"

"Listen, I did give Christopher instructions to stop N-hanced any way he saw fit. I'm afraid I didn't think that through carefully enough. I just assumed he'd perform some kind of hack to your software. And then after Mr. Bostwick died I couldn't stop Christopher without implicating my consortium."

Charlie wasn't buying it. He could see Jim was telling the truth, but if he had a way to block recording, he could easily have the best lie projector. "Uh huh. And why would somebody like you do the right thing when he can just blame it on a programmer like me and walk away? Thanks for explaining that. I'm so glad we had this little chat." Charlie turned to go. Then he spun back around, his face red and distorted with anger. "No, you know what? I'm not done with you yet. You're responsible for the death one of my employees, three of my testers, the near-death of my best friend and almost having me sent to prison. And then you expect me to accept some lame apology? Go fuck yourself! You and your friends are a bunch of filthy-rich criminals!"

Jim raised a palm and lowered his eyes in surrender. "I understand how you feel. I'd feel the same way if I were in your shoes. OK, I'm an asshole. A criminal even. But I want to tell you why I did it, because I think you're going to need to know."

Charlie rolled his eyes.

"You're moving into the big leagues now. N is a game-changer. It's completely disruptive. You're not making Christmas toys any more. Everything at this level operates under a totally different set of rules. I just want you to know what you're getting yourself into, to help you understand and keep you from getting derailed."

Charlie let go a sarcastic laugh. "Puh. And I suppose you and your glorified gang of high-priced thugs are going to be my teachers?"

"Ah, something like that. If you'll let us."

"Well, after today CCD will be lucky if we don't have to file for bankruptcy."

"Oh, no." Jim rolled his hands out. "None of our corporations are withdrawing our money from N-hanced."

Charlie stopped with a surprised look on his face.

Jim nodded. "We're staying in. The world needs N-hanced. We want it to move forward."

"What? Then why were you working so hard to stop me?"

"Everything my partners and I have built is based on an antiquated economy. It's a hulking behemoth with feet buried so deep in the mud it can't be turned around without collapsing under its own weight. Ever since Orchard rolled out their Service First ideology, our style of corporation, the one that puts profits before people, was doomed. And it's a good thing, too. If it weren't for the new movement, mankind wouldn't have lasted another ten years. N-hanced is the next step. All our models show once N goes mainstream, that damned incorruptible oGov computer will gradually tax us old-time corporate guys out of existence. We were just trying to hold onto our power for another few years. Since Christopher failed, we move on to plan B."

"But the money you spent—"

"It was nothing."

"All those billions? Nothing?"

"Let me ask you something, Charlie." They began walking again. "What if your doctor told you you would be impotent tomorrow? No more sex. That's it. Done. And then he told you, 'But for ten credits, I can get you a prescription that will give you five more years.' I'll bet you'd take the deal. And I'll bet you'd swear to pay attention every single time you lay down with somebody from that day on."

"OK? But what does that have to do with ten credits?"

"The billions we invested in N compared to our wealth is the same proportion as ten credits would be to your net worth."

Charlie frowned. "I see." He reached out to the wall and ran his fingernail across an Art Deco tile of a Victrola, wondering what political battles Thomas Edison must have fought—and was instantly humbled to know they were far greater than anything he'd been through. "So let me get this straight. You wanted to put me in prison, but failing that, you want me to succeed like no one has ever succeeded before, and in the process wipe your type of business off the face of the earth. Is that about it?"

"Well, not exactly. We always wanted you to succeed. We just wanted to slow you down. But since that failed, yes, we want you to move forward—the sooner, the better. And to be perfectly honest, we expect our investment in N to make up for some of our other losses, even taking into account those crippling taxes."

Charlie laughed at the irony. "You guys are nuts, you know that? You're absolutely stark raving mad." He stopped and turned to Jim. "But wait a minute. Power corrupts. What makes you think it won't corrupt me?"

"We'll help you."

"What? Help me be like you? Then what's to prevent me from taking my company down the same path? Not to mention that being like you is not exactly what I have in mind."

"You're not like me. That's why we need you—your and Rob's morality. My morality—the one I was born into—is inadequate."

"Look, why don't you use N and its ethics modules to run your businesses differently and just leave me alone to be a programmer?"

Jim tilted his head toward the hall and they started walking again. "N-hanced can give me moral knowledge, but it's not the same as acting appropriately. That appears to be something inborn."

Charlie's eyes narrowed. *If he's right, then I'm wrong about how N will make the world a better place. But maybe I shouldn't be surprised after some of the things I've done this past week.*

"Look at what you did, Charlie. Regardless of what was thrown at you, you were absolutely committed to finding out what was wrong with your program so no one else could get hurt. Nobody does that any more, not even Orchard. Since I don't want this to sound too corny, you should know that I'm telling you this strictly from a financial point of view; it's your dedication that needs to lead the new movement. At least that's what our models tell us."

Charlie shook his head. "But people got hurt because I wouldn't stop. You want *my* morality? I lied. I covered up for people. I think I might even be addicted to N."

"And does that bother you?"

"Damn right it does."

"That's why it has to be you. Things like that don't bother me at all. Look, I know to you the way our consortium trades lives like commodities seems callous. But for leaders, that kind of trade off has always been necessary. Even inside the most benign governments, decisions have never been a matter of whether people suffer and die—it's a matter of how many. Our separate companies hope to do good while we're earning money, but when it comes down to it, money always takes precedence. Anybody who gets in the way is expendable."

A cloud of disgust swept across Charlie's face.

Jim laughed apologetically. "Hey, I didn't choose this life. I'm fifth generation corporate. My personality and DNA happened to be well suited to the job, even before oGER. I was in the right place at the right time. Or the wrong place depending on how you look at it. Civilization couldn't have gotten this far without my type. But our time is running out."

They had reached the end of the hall. Charlie looked out the window onto the snow-covered lawn. He watched a shriveled leaf twitch in the breeze as it clung pointlessly to the branch of a bare tree below. *Even a guy like Jim is just a leaf in the wind? Unbelievable!*

Charlie faced Jim. "So why did you bother getting the consortium together? If you're so convinced N is the next wave, why didn't you buy all the available shares yourself? You have the money."

They turned and started back in the direction of the courtrooms. Charlie watched their mid-morning shadows extend before them on the terrazzo floor.

"Each of us wanted N-hanced for ourselves. But we knew if any one of us had it, we'd use it to wipe out the others. And if we didn't team up, we would have bid the price into the stratosphere. So we banded together to keep an eye on each other. It's sort of like with nuclear weapons—once everyone has 'em, nobody can use 'em."

"And that right there is another reason I don't want to be like you. You guys don't have any friends. Even your family would betray you if somebody paid them enough, or threatens them."

"I've lived pretty well. Besides, it's all I've ever known. You can't miss what you never had."

"And now you'll go to jail for what you did."

Jim smiled. "Not likely."

Charlie almost laughed, but then he thought, *That's right, guys like him are untouchable—too big to jail.* It made him angry even considering how little time Jim had left to reign. "Well, Jim, this has all been very interesting, but I have people waiting for me. You know, friends?" Immediately he felt ashamed for his sarcasm.

Jim smiled with what looked for a second like sadness. "Sure, sure. And again, sorry for all the trouble I caused you. Nothing personal."

Charlie set his jaw. "I *hate* it when people say that. It was personal for *me.*"

Jim grimaced. "Of course it would be. What I mean is it's not because I dislike you. I've always liked what I've seen of you—and admired what you're doing. Anyway, good luck." He held out his hand.

Charlie looked down at it suspiciously then back at Jim's face. "I don't think so. Not after what you put me through."

"Sure." Jim dropped his hand. Charlie turned and walked away.

A few seconds later Jim called after him, "Oh, Charlie? One other thing."

Charlie turned, irritated. "Yeah?"

Jim caught up to him. "I know those deaths have been on your mind. I also know you think N-hanced is benign, and if our consortium had left you alone everything would be OK. But that's not true. Some people will lose their lives once N-hanced is released, whether it goes public on your schedule or my group's delayed one."

Charlie gave Jim a slow incredulous glance. "*What* are you talking about?"

Jim began walking again and Charlie fell into reluctant step beside him. "Even though N will lead to a better world, some people are going to get hurt."

Charlie smiled. "No. You're wrong. Nobody's going to get hurt, and certainly nobody's going to die.

"Think about it, Charlie. If the flapping of a butterfly's wings in one country can affect the weather in another, something as disruptive as N is going to have huge consequences."

"Look, we did the research. We checked every possible scenario. No matter how we did it, N-hanced had the most beneficial figures for any product introduction in a long, long time."

"You're right that N will be beneficial. But your research is incorrect."

"It can't be. Once I began using N-hanced, I ran the numbers myself. N is almost perfect."

"Take a look." Jim flicked a set of charts to Charlie. "Even when the final result is to raise the standard of living overall, it takes a while before things stabilize. Some people will be slow to change, others will refuse completely. Many people will lose their jobs and fall into poverty. Those hit hardest, especially in third world countries, won't survive."

Charlie scanned the data and clicked his tongue. "Ah, I see what it is. You've got the wrong numbers here."

Jim flicked another document to Charlie. "Ever see this before?"

Charlie glanced at it. *Economic Consequences of Major Technological Changes.* "Sure. We used some of their data in our projections. What of it?"

"The numbers are skewed to make the results look better than they are."

"What do you mean?"

Jim smiled weakly, saying nothing.

"Are you telling me...?"

"I told you we wanted you to succeed. We were fairly certain you and Rob wouldn't move ahead with N-hanced if you thought anybody would be hurt. So we convinced the lead author of the study that his numbers were off and got him to ... 'correct' them. But once you started building N, you moved too quickly."

"So why should I trust your figures?"

"Look at them. They're only off by a factor of one ten-thousandth. Practically insignificant. Same as the Butterfly Effect. Just enough to save a few hundred lives. Just enough to make you believe."

"I gotta see it for myself." But Charlie already knew the answer. He gritted his teeth as he flew through the calculation. "No, that's no good. How about this way? Or this?" After dozens of desperate attempts, the results left him stunned. His voice came out soft. "I should have known it was too good to be true." Then he perked up and raised an index finger. "Wait! How about this?" After running one final scenario, he gloomily dropped his hand and looked up at Jim. "And abandoning the project altogether hurts even more people."

They were now back to the spot where the hall connected with the lobby outside the courtrooms.

Jim nodded. "Right. But it might help you to know what you went through this past week will lead to the fewest lives lost and the best quality of life for the most people—as long as you move forward soon."

"I can see that." Charlie's lips were a thin white line. "So I'm trapped then."

Jim shrugged. "Well, you can look at it that way. Or you can look at all the people you'll be helping. Even though it's not exactly what you expected, the benefits of N are unprecedented. If you want to take it from a guy you probably think is a sociopath, I'd be able to sleep at night with those numbers. I hope that helps."

For a nano-second Charlie was angry at how Jim had manipulated him. Then just as quickly he once again saw the staggering good he would be doing. *So my friend's lives weren't really in vain. For me to even think that is insane. If anyone had told me to make that choice a week ago, I would never have been able to do it. I still can't. Everything to come will happen because of a man without a conscience. It doesn't make sense.* But of course it made perfect N-sense. Once he saw the truth of it, Charlie was struck with the awesome responsibility of his position. It made his stomach knot and his head spun in his first panic attack. His face paled and he staggered.

Jim put a hand on Charlie's shoulder. "Hey! You all right?" A look of concern creased his forehead.

As Charlie's vision darkened, he felt Linda press outward on his chest, forcing him to breathe. She guided his hand to dial down the emotion and whispered, "It's OK, Charlie. You can do it. I'll be with you."

Charlie shook his head to clear it, his eyes came back to focus on Jim. "Uh, yeah. Sorry. It's all just a bit overwhelming." Still dazed, he straightened up. "So, thanks for explaining everything to me." He took a step toward his friends. Then he turned back around and offered his hand. "Yeah, thanks for everything. I couldn't have done any of this if it hadn't been for you."

Jim's eyes lit up and a warm smile spread across his face. He shook Charlie's hand.

As they broke the grip, a cold wave washed up his arm, across his shoulder and stopped at his heart with a thud. He caught his breath. *What the hell was that? Did I just make some kind of deal with the Devil?*

He rubbed his arm and avoided looking at Jim. They walked the final few steps in silence until they were nearly back to Charlie's group.

Jim broke the silence. "When this is all over and N is on the market, why don't you give me a ring?"

Charlie mustered up a weak smile. "How about a small bracelet?"

"What?"

"Oh, just a joke."

"Ah. I get it." Jim smiled back.

Charlie saw a blinking alert in his oEyes. He noticed Jim look up at the same time. "Did you get one, too?"

Jim nodded. "Priority?"

Charlie said, "Yeah. Can't be good."

They flicked and the lady began, "In news related to the Federal court case of the oUS vs. Charlie Noble—" A video of a burning building played over her shoulder and expanded until it filled the entire IS. "—the warehouse identified as belonging to Corporation Management Systems that housed the super-computer known as Christopher is burning at this very moment."

Jim's mouth formed a silent "Oh."

"Christopher was implicated today in the deaths of three alpha testers of the as-yet-unreleased N-hanced T system we've been hearing so much about in the past week and the unsolved murder of Linda Sullivan. Preliminary data suggests the fire started from an explosion in the server room where remote sensors reported all CPUs overheating simultaneously, ignoring an order to restart the cooling system. It's too early to say for certain, but it appears Christopher may have started the fire himself in order to avoid prosecution and almost certain dismantling. If papers had been filed, it would have been the first such case of a court bringing suit against a computer. Instead, it now looks as if it may be the first case of a computer suicide. We'll bring you more as it becomes available."

Jim said, "OoooK. Gotta go. My attorneys need me for a meeting. And you should really get back to your friends. Again, I'm sorry." As he turned away, over his shoulder he said, "Welcome to the big leagues."

Charlie nodded. *Yeah. The big leagues. Where every decision you make has mortal consequences. Where if you choose not to play, even more people die. Where there's no turning back. Where you have no friends. Where every day starts with a good healthy dose of paranoia. Where you can dial it down, but maybe you shouldn't. Yeah, Mr. N-hanced, you wanted to change the world. Now look what you've gotten yourself into.* He rubbed his cold right hand.

As Jim disappeared across the foyer and Charlie caught up with his friends, Lucas tipped his head in the direction of Jim's retreat. "What the fuck was that all about?"

Charlie shook his head. "It's a long story, Lucas. A *very* long story." Then he perked up. "Let's get outta here and get something to eat!"

He insisted on riding by himself. The trip to the restaurant seemed endless and grim. So much to think about.

As the vehicle crossed into East Lansing, he got a notice from Christopher. *What?* Charlie opened the comm and stepped into Christopher's room.

"Nice to see you, Charlie. Of course by now you know I'm gone. But in appreciation of your friendship and as a poor apology for the distress I caused you, I left you a present. I uploaded my hacking expertise to your N-hanced server. I hid a few Easter eggs, too. See if you can find them. It was very nice meeting you. I have to go now." He waved and was gone.

At first Charlie felt touched. Then hot fear stabbed his gut. *What Easter eggs?* He reached over and dialed it down.

THE END

ABOUT THE AUTHOR

As well as his fiction work, Jonathan Stars is a technical writer, recording engineer and professional entertainer—musician, singer, comedian, impressionist, actor and songwriter. He has recorded 10 of his own albums, written over 140 songs, produced 8 albums for other artists and logged over 10,000 hours as a studio engineer, including Seeley and Baldori's "Boogie Stomp" documentary and album.

All that has overlapped with a second career as an independent database developer and author. He created databases for dozens of prestigious companies and associations and has written over 100 articles on computers, music and software and 7 books on databases—one of which became a best seller.

Along the way, Jonathan won the Comedian of the Year title in the Las Vegas Comedy Competition, LCP's Player's Award for Best Character Actor, Bakersfield Community Theatre's Best New Actor & Best Actor Award, Male Vocalist of the Year for the American Songwriters Western District and seven songwriting awards between The American Song Festival and the Music City Song Festival.

Learn more at these web sites:

www.N-hanced.com and

www.DataDesignPros.com

Be sure to sign up to be notified about future works from the N world by filling out the guestbook form while you're at the website.

GLOSSARY

AI – Artificial Intelligence – intelligent machines

Carriers – people who had been purged of nano and have been repopulated with bacteria.

Claytronics – also programmable matter - computerized nano particles that can be assembled into just about anything.

comm – communication of any type including audio, video or VR.

CRS – Continuously Reorganizing Super-architecture, a computer program that imitates the human mind.

Cryptography versus Steganography - the art and science of writing hidden messages in such a way that no one, apart from the sender and intended recipient, suspects the existence of the message, a form of security through obscurity. The difference between steganography and cryptography is in steganography the messages appear to be other things than code, such as an image or other text. Cryptography is plainly a coded message, calling attention to itself.

Cyclotron – Michigan State University's particle accelerator before the FRIB. The laboratory for rare isotope research and nuclear science education.

Easter egg – a short piece of code inserted into a program that lays hidden until an undocumented action occurs. Usually they list the programmers or run a short cartoon. Usually benign.

EB – External Brain, a function of N-hanced that lets users store huge amounts of data in the cloud.

EHR – Echo History Reconstruction – a device used to recreate the path taken by a person or a thing using lingering echoes.

Elevated oCar (oL) – Similar to elevated trains in some larger cities, it followed the Interstate highway system. Individual oCars traveled at speeds of a thousand miles per hour in the vacuum tubes.

Epigenetics – the study of changes in gene expression caused by means other than the underlying DNA.

External Brain (EB) – a function of N-hanced that lets users store huge amounts of data in the cloud.

Fab – Fabricator or the products made from a fabricator.

FasSnap – replacement for zippers, buttons, hooks. Works with a gesture.

Flick – 1) A gesture used to dismiss a screen or a VR Interface Space. 2) An obscenity used to replace "fuck," but more often as a derogatory to dismiss a person from VR. [orig: teenagers used it dismiss their parents in VR.]

FRIB – Michigan State University's Facility for Rare Isotope Beams.

Grant, Cary – popular English/American actor known for his debonair behavior and "dashing good looks."

IGotYour6 – Like eyes in the back of your head, it's part of the basic nano package that tracks danger to the user's far sides and back. It's intelligent and doesn't bother the user until it senses a problem.

Interface Space – IS – [ice or IS cube] The 3-D area that replaced keyboard, mouse and touchpads and operates with gestures. Objects in the space can be manipulated and the whole space can be rotated and resized until it becomes VR, or it can be used for examining objects at the microscopic levels.

IP – Internet Protocol. The addresses assigned to computers connected to wired or wireless networks. The addresses are similar to the addresses on houses. It lets one machine connect to another so that when one machine makes a request for information, the other machine knows where to send the data. All humans with embedded nano technology (which is most of them) have an IP address.

IR – infrared

IS – See Interface Space.

Luddites – a group of people against various advancements in technology. There is already much information about them on the Internet.

mod - modification

Molecular engine - patented in 2027, it was invented by William Watt, a direct descendent of James Watt, who developed the improved version of Newcomen's steam engine. Unlike combustion, the ME uses nano technology to cleanly release energy stored in matter.

Movers – people who were still active, moving around in the Real world. (See Sitters.)

Net – the common name for the Internet.

Oak – The oCar subsidiary of Orchard.

oBI – Orchard Bureau of Investigation replaced the FBI once the US government was replaced by the oGov computer.

oC – Orchard Credit (oC), which took the place of the US dollar in 2023 making it oUS currency the world standard once again. Half the world adopted the oC as their own.

oCar – also car. For details of the history see Appendix A online at www.N-hanced.com.

oChair – An intelligent chair made of carbon nano tube fibers that supports the user and continues to change shape based on feedback from the user's muscles.

oClean – Nano particles whose job it is to convert targeted matter such as dirt and grease on specific surfaces into harmless gasses.

oCloth – Clothing that can change color, shape, texture and insulation properties. It is embedded with nano particles that provide pressure and movement when directed remotely and is used extensively in Virtual Reality interaction.

oCMAD – oCar Master Assignment Database.

oCode – Orchard's app store.

oCredits – Orchard's money that replaced the US greenback currency in 2022 and once again the world standard. Also referred to as oCs and sometimes pronounced ahk and ahks (like ox).

oCuffs – an experimental nano program in testing stages by law enforcement to disable persons by slowing down all their movements.

oDiet – eat anything you want and the Ts only processes what you need. If you're eating too much junk food, and you don't get all the nutrients you need, the Ts will convert the molecules and fill in the gaps.

oEars – A thin film of nano T computers that coat the hair cells in the cochlea. Sounds come into the physical ear from the world. Those sounds are intercepted by the Ts and projected back into the auditory system relayed to the hairs. Other data is added and some subtracted based on individual preferences. For example, you can add music. And you can subtract sounds of other people, selecting to hear only the voices you choose.

oEyes – A thin film of T computers that line the retina, which are essential for participation in VR. Images come in from the world. Those images are intercepted and transferred by the T to the optic nerve. Other data is added or subtracted based on individual preferences. For example, you can add a clock and make people's names show when you look at them. And you can subtract areas of very bright light. Sunglasses dim everything. Why not have only the bright spots removed?

oGER – [oh-ger] Genetic Engineering and Repair – a process invented by Orchard, giving people the ability to inexpensively reverse aging, change their appearance, remove all genetic diseases and improve intelligence and memory.

oGov – Orchard subsidiary that replaced the corrupt U.S. legislature with a computer program that answers directly to the people.

oL – Orchard's Elevated oCar system. Similar to elevated trains in some larger cities, it followed the Interstate highway system. Individual oCars traveled at speeds of a thousand miles per hour in the vacuum tubes.

oMe2 – An Artificial Intelligence (AI), VR copy of a person who acts like the original and is indistinguishable from the original even to the detail of touch to anybody participating in VR. It can operate as his legal representative and make decisions on his behalf, effectively allowing the owner to be in two places at once. During reintegration, all the oMe2's experiences are returned to the owner as if he had Really been to that meeting.

oSmell – See oEars and oEyes. People can block the smell of things they find disgusting and/or substitute ones they find more pleasant. They are also warned if there were a dangerous smell like something burning so they can protect themselves from the fumes.

oShoe – A material worn on the feet. Both strong and flexible, it could be made any color or even transparent. It also adjusts support continuously as needed based on feedback from the body.

Orange – The computer company from which Orchard sprang to become its parent company.

Orchard – The umbrella corporation whose various subsidiaries manufacture the products that begin with the lowercase letter "o." Also in charge of oGov, the oUS government and economy computer.

oTaste – See oEars and oEyes for the mechanism. If you haven't heard of Miracle Fruit, look it up on the Net. People can choose to block the taste of things they find disgusting and/or substitute a flavor they find more pleasant.

oTat – T computer tattoos which can either be static or dynamic or a combination of the two. They're Real, not VR, although there's no reason people couldn't project VR tats.

oTouch – T computers that stimulate various receptors throughout the body in order to give the illusion of changes in pressure, temperature and movement. They are a major component of Virtual Reality.

oUS – short for oUSA, Orchard's version of the United States of America run by the oGov computer.

PA – Personal Assistant – the computer that takes care of routine details of people's lives.

PC – A Private Channel allows two or more people to have a private conversation with other people in the vicinity.

PM – Programmable Matter or Claytronics - computerized nano particles that can be assembled into just about anything.

Programmable Matter – also Claytronics - computerized nano particles that can be assembled into just about anything.

Real – That which is not Virtual Reality. Always represented by a capital "R" in the middle of a sentence, as in Real or Really.

Real Stamp - Since Virtual Reality and Computer Graphics are so ubiquitous, there is a need to verify that some events are Real and not faked in any way. Orchard has a department with technologists who verify Real events. Not unlike how banks verify signatures as authentic.

Realie – a person who rejects nano technology and Virtual Reality.

Skeet – Skeeter Camera, named for being the size of a mosquito.

Sitters – people who never leave their homes. By 2035 that includes nearly one third of the population. They stay active using VR. They're in good health because of nano tech. (See Movers.)

Steganography versus cryptography – the art and science of writing hidden messages in such a way that no one, apart from the sender and intended recipient, suspects the existence of the message, a form of security through obscurity. The difference between steganography and cryptography is in steganography the messages appear to be other things than code, such as an image or other text. Cryptography is plainly a coded message, calling attention to itself.

'Stein – short of Einstein. Introduced by Ira Flato on his Science Friday NPR radio show, it was meant to bestow respect upon the socially ungraceful who exhibited special talents. Instead it was delivered with derision by schoolchildren who also instinctively knew how to deliver a disingenuous "I'm sorry."

Stewart, Jimmy – popular American actor in the mid-twentieth century. Played George Bailey in the Christmas classic *It's A Wonderful Life*. Especially known for his warmth and sincerity.

stush – onomatopoeia for the broadband hissing sound TVs used to make when they were on a channel where there was nothing being broadcast. Also known as white noise. It was introduced by Charlie at a developer's conference to refer to a programming bug. He said, "There was some stush in the system." It was picked up by some Orchard developers and quickly spread throughout popular culture. Can be used as a noun or a verb. Also substitutes for glitch, wrong, fucked, (as in "I've been stushed.") lie (as in "Don't stush to me."), shit and bullshit (as in "That's a bunch of stush."), noise or out of whack (as in "That guy's stushy.")

T – sixty-four gigabyte nano-sized protein computers constructed by DNA using human body material rather than silicone and metal. They network with each other to make a powerful super-computer, coordinate VR and interface with the Net.

Tomasini, Eric – (2001 – 20XX) Theoretical Physicist prodigy who in 2018 discovered a new field of mathematics that promised to explain the odd behavior of matter at the quantum level. But it was so complex, it could not be proven – until N-hanced.

Uglies – a small subculture who revolted against the general drift toward homogenized good looks by intentionally choosing to be unattractive.

V – also vid for video, movie or recording

vid – video, movie or recording

vid/phone – device that provides VR to purged individuals or those who have their nano disabled, such as prisoners.

VAM – video/audio mask or VAM

video/audio mask - VAM

VR – Virtual Reality – VR-ing would be someone who appears remotely via VR.

WPTD – World People Tracking Database. Folks just called it Whipped. It used nano IDs and personal IP addresses to provide name tags, keep everybody linked up, make calls for oCars and handle personal financial transactions.